<u>william boyd</u>
stars and bars

William Boyd's first novel, *A Good Man in Africa*, won the Whitbread Prize and Somerset Maugham Award; his second, *An Ice-Cream War*, was awarded the John Llewellyn Rhys Prize and was shortlisted for the Booker. *Brazzaville Beach* won the James Tait Black Memorial Prize and *The Blue Afternoon* won the Los Angeles Times Prize for fiction. Boyd lives in London.

INTERNATIONAL

Books by William Boyd

A Good Man in Africa

On the Yankee Station (short stories)

An Ice-Cream War

Stars and Bars

School Ties (screenplays)

The New Confessions

Brazzaville Beach

The Blue Afternoon

The Destiny of Nathalie X and Other Stories

Armadillo

william boyd
stars and bars

william boyd
stars and bars

Vintage International
Vintage Books
A Division of Random House, Inc.
New York

First Vintage International Edition, July 2001

Copyright © 1984 by William Boyd

Library of Congress Cataloging-in-Publication Data
Boyd, William, 1952–
Stars and bars / by William Boyd.
p. cm.
1. British—United States—Fiction.
2. Art—Collectors and Collecting—Fiction.
3. Eccentrics and eccentricities—Fiction.
4. Millionaires—Fiction.
I. Title.
PR6052.O9192 S7 2001
823'.914—dc21

Vintage ISBN: 0-375-70501-5

Author photograph © Jerry Bauer

www.vintagebooks.com

Printed in the United States of America
10 9 8 7 6 5 4 3 2 1

For Susan

contents

The 'Truly Strong Man,' calm, balanced, aware of his strength, sits drinking quietly in the bar; it is not necessary for him to try and prove to himself that he is not afraid. . . . In other words the Test exists only for the Truly Weak Man: no matter whether he passes it or whether he fails, he cannot alter his essential nature. The Truly Strong Man travels straight across the broad America of normal life taking always the direct and reasonable route. But 'America' is just what the Truly Weak Man, the neurotic hero, dreads.

CHRISTOPHER ISHERWOOD, *Lions and Shadows*

part one

TWENTY-FOUR HOURS IN NEW YORK

chapter one

LOOK at Henderson Dores walking up Park Avenue in New York City. I'm late, he is thinking; and he is, late for work. He is carrying his sabers in a thin bag over his right shoulder and trying to appear calm and at ease, but that permanently worried expression on his square open face gives him away rather. The crowds of Americans—neat, well dressed—stride past him purposefully, unheeding, confident.

Henderson walks on. He is nearly forty years old—birthday coming up fast—and just under six feet tall. His frame is sturdy and his face is kind and agreeably attractive. To his constant surprise, people are inclined to like him on first acquaintance. He is polite, quite smartly dressed and, apart from that slight frown buckling his forehead, he seems as composed and as unconcerned as, well, as you or me. But Henderson has a complaint, a grudge, a grumble of a deep and insidious kind. He doesn't like himself anymore; isn't happy with the personality he's been provided with, thank you very much. Something about him isn't up to scratch, won't do. He'll keep the flesh, but he'd like to do a deal on the spirit, if nobody minds. He wants to change—he wants to be different from what he is. And that, really, is why he is here.

He runs a hand through his thick fair hair, short, but cut long, as it were, in the English way. To the practiced observer, indeed, everything about him proclaims his Englishness. His haircut—already noted—his pale lashed eyes, the bloom on his unshaven cheekbones, his old blue suit with its double vents in the jacket, the dull worn gold signet ring on the little finger of his left hand, his navy-blue ankle-length socks (only butlers and chauffeurs wear black) and his shiny, well-creased, toe-capped black oxford shoes.

This knowledge—that he is so distinguishable—would distress him because, in fact, his grand and only dream is to fit in, to merge and blend with the identity of these earnest, enviable people on their way to work. Just another Manhattanite, he tells himself, as he transfers his sabers to his left shoulder, just like everybody else here. He frowns again slightly and slows down. This is his problem: he loves America, but will America love him back? Up ahead the lunatic is waiting.

"The furrier at midnight thinks his hands are full of clouds."

"Go away, please."

"The furrier at midnight thinks his hands are full of clouds."

Usually, Henderson Dores didn't speak to the madmen. He found that by pretending the person simply didn't exist—actually wasn't *there*—it was possible to ignore the most venomous rant. It was a trick he'd first seen perfected by timid dons at Oxford whenever they were accosted by importunate drunks in narrow lanes. The fixed smile, eyes straight ahead, and—abracadabra—there was no drunk. So, with a small effort of will he canceled the madman, set his features in the requisite mild false smile, took two paces to the left and set off again.

The lunatic loped along at his side.

Don't stop, that was the rule. He shouldn't have stopped, but what this one was saying made some sort of perverse sense.

He looked about him, trying to ignore the malign companion at his side. On this bright April morning New York seemed to expand and rejoice in the thin clean air. Above, the sky was an unobstructed blue. It was what he termed a meringue day: crisp, sharp, frangible . . .

A series of tugs at his elbow. You do not exist, Henderson said to himself, therefore you cannot be tugging at my elbow. His arm was gripped, uncompromisingly. He stopped. Vague fear stimulated his pulse rate. The undeodorized lunatic wore a beige overcoat (collar up), scarf, battered trilby and sunglasses, and held an opened black umbrella above his head. Henderson saw sweat slide from beneath the hat brim.

"Please. Leave me alone," Henderson said firmly.

The crowd swirled around this impediment.

"Charming people have something to hide." The lunatic spoke in a singsong woman's voice. His face was too close; his breath smelled curiously of old lemons.

"Leave me alone or I shall call the police."

"Ah, fuck you, asshole."

That was more like it. The lunatic stood back and leveled a finger at him, thumb cocked.

"Bam!"

Henderson flinched with genuine shock, turned and strode on. "Bam! Bam! Bam!" faded behind him. He shuddered. Good Lord, he thought, what a disturbing encounter. He eased the weight of his sabers and checked that the shoulder strap wasn't creasing his suit. *The furrier at mid-*

night thinks his hands are full of clouds. That wasn't too bad actually, he thought, calming down somewhat, for a crazy. It was like a coded spy-greeting, or a line from a better symbolist poem.

He trudged on up Park Avenue's gentle slope. Younger people overtook him. A pretty girl in an elegant, mushroom-colored silk suit walked strongly by, incongruous in her training shoes. Her breasts leaped beneath the sheen of her blouse. Her streaked blond hair was clamped with tiny headphones. She mimed to the song she alone was hearing. Henderson wondered whether he should wish her a "nice day." You could do that sort of thing here: confer cheery blessings on any passing stranger. *"Hey, enjoy your music!"* he could shout. Or *"Have a great lunch!"* or even *"Be well!"* He shook his head admiringly and said nothing.

He increased his speed. With the palp of a forefinger he squeezed moisture from his wiry blond eyebrows. He was getting a little concerned about his eyebrows. They had been unexceptionable, inconspicuous things until recently. Now they had thickened and coarsened; certain hairs had begun spontaneously to grow and curl: they were becoming a feature. Just like his nipples, he thought. . . . He checked himself: save the worries for the way home.

Home was a small apartment in a block on East Sixty-second between Lexington and Second avenues. Convenient enough for the office, if a somewhat uphill hike, but the evening downhill amble was a compensation for the early morning effort. He looked at his watch again. He *was* late. Astonishingly and gratifyingly he had fallen into a deep sleep sometime after five A.M. and had woken at eight, his head empty of dreams. He had felt a sob of relief in his throat: perhaps, finally, it was all going to change now; perhaps this was a sign—America really was going to work. . . .

He was keen on signs, these days; he analyzed them with the assiduity of an apprentice hierophant. And at first they all seemed to bode well.

He had arrived in America, at JFK Airport, some two months previously. It had been raining, heavy drops slanting yellow through the airport lights. He had half-planned to kiss the ground (given a discreet moment) pontifflike, but stepped straight from the plane into a mean corridor. He passed through surly immigration and taciturn customs in a benign trance: those drawls, those impossible names, the real gun on the real cop's hip.

Outside, the rain had worsened. A tall, very angry black man in a glossy oilskin controlled the queue for taxis with hoarse shouts and imperious gestures. The taxis and the queue formed an obedient line. The gleaming, battered yellow cabs . . .

Henderson stood beside the taxi marshal for a while, happy to wait. The man was muttering to himself under his breath. Askance, Henderson looked at his moustache, his thick curved lips, the way he seemed to keep moving even while standing still. Water dripped steadily from his cap's peak.

"It could be worse," friendly Henderson said. "It's snowing in England."

The taxi marshal looked around; the whites of his eyes were yellow like butter.

"Fuck England," he said.

Henderson nodded. "Fuck England," he agreed, nodding. "You bet."

It had been an epiphanic moment, he now thought, as he waited at a traffic light to cross to the west side of Park Avenue. An omen. The traffic stopped and he hurried to the island, paused and crossed again. He had pondered on it a long time and he had come to confer on his departure from England an importance that the ostensible and unremarkable business reasons wouldn't at first seem to warrant. He was going to a job in New York—granted—but he was also making an escape. An escape from the past and from himself.

He strode on more speedily, the aluminium guards on his sabers clinking dully together as the bag banged against his thigh.

He had quit Britain, he had decided, in a conscious and deliberate flight from shyness, in a determined escape from timidity. . . . A man on roller skates glided silently by him and leaned sinuously through the crowd. Henderson's admiration was immediate. *"Enjoy your skate!"* he wanted to shout after him, but he didn't. Why not? Because he was shy.

He was (he catergorized himself with no trace of self-pity) a shy man. Not chronically shy—he didn't stammer or spit or flinch or sweat in the manner of the worst afflicted—no, he was shy in the way most of his countrymen were shy. His flaw was a congenital one: latent, deep, ever present. It was like having a birthmark or a dormant illness; an ethnic trait, a racial configuration.

He stepped into shade cast by a tall building and gave a shiver from the sudden chill. Sunny start, rain later, the forecast had said. He had only his raincoat today, trusting the jovial forecaster. Perhaps that was a little foolhardy. He overtook two young men, strolling, talking loudly, one smoking a lime-green cigar. He screwed up his eyes as he walked through a slate-blue cloud of smoke, smelling the vomit smell of cigars, souring the crispness of the morning.

Shy.

True, his education and his upbringing provided him with a reasonably efficient kit of tools and methods to

overcome his disability. Observe him nattering at a cocktail party; see him engage his dull partner at a dinner table
with conversation and one would never guess the nature of
his disease. But it was there, and beneath this sociocultural
veneer he suffered from all the siblings of shyness too: the
feeble air of confidence, the formulaic self-possession, a
conditioned wariness of emotional display, a distrust of
spontaneity, a dread fear of attracting attention, an almost
irrepressible urge to conform . . .

He briskly turned the corner off Park, lurched and just
skittered around three raw, shiny steaming turds, freshly
deposited in the rough environs of a sapling root. He overtook the fur-clad crone and her nasty pooch. He shot her
a hostile, stern glance brimming with reproach. He longed
to demand where her poop-scoop was or at least make
some withering rejoinder. Only last week he'd heard of a
man in the city who, confronted with the sight of a splay-
legged Great Dane dumping its load in front of him, had
removed a gun from his jacket and shot the beast there and
then. A very, intrinsically *American* act that, he thought, as
he made his way down the street toward his office. A dis-
approving look, a tut-tut tightening of the lips, that was
the best he could manage. It was typical and it was what
was wrong. And that was why he'd had to leave, why he
had to come to America for the cure. Because, here,
shyness was banned; shyness was outlawed, prohibited.

That of course was nonsense, he realized, as he steered
around a postman pushing his trolley. There were plenty
of shy people in America, but they were shy in a different
way, it seemed; their insecurity had a different stamp to it.
And if he had to be shy all his life, then he wanted to be
shy like them.

He paused at the door of Mulholland, Melhuish, Fine
Art Auctioneers. Brave talk, he thought with heavy irony,

fine words. The only problem was he kept relapsing. He had been making real progress: look at Melissa, look at Irene. But he kept falling back. Consider the run-in with the madman a few minutes ago; he had handled that appallingly.

He stepped into the entrance hall, black-and-white marble squares, oak paneling.

"Good morning, Mr. Dores. How are you today?" the receptionist called from behind her desk.

Henderson, on his way past, smiled automatically, then stopped. That was not the way.

"I'm very well, thank you, Mary. Very well indeed. Thank you for asking."

"Oh . . . Oh. Good. You're welcome."

He entered the small lift. Elevator. He pressed CLOSE DOOR. They slid to, trapping someone's pale-blue arm.

"*Yawks!* Agh!"

He punched OPEN DOOR and Pruitt Halfacre stepped in.

"Didn't you see me, Henderson? Jesus."

"Sorry, Pruitt. Miles away."

"Jesus, God. That's *oil.*" Halfacre examined his crushed sleeve. "I'm going to have to charge you, Henderson."

Was he joking or was he being serious? Henderson could never tell with Americans. He smoothed his eyebrows. They ascended.

"Wonderful news, don't you think? At last, at last," Halfacre said.

"What?"

"You haven't heard? We think we may have an Impressionist sale. A chance at one, anyway."

"Good God!"

"Yeah. Tom has the details."

They stepped out of the lift onto the fourth floor. After

the plush of the lobby here was scarred paintwork, bright lights, worn linoleum.

"Morning, Ian," Halfacre said.

"Snap," said Toothe. He and Halfacre were both wearing bow ties.

"Great minds, Ian."

"Bit on the late side, Henderson?" Toothe said. "Naughty. You look very hot and bothered." Toothe was English, an English version of Halfacre. Two *sensitifs* of the worst kind. Henderson forgave Halfacre because he was American, but, to be honest, he disliked Toothe intensely.

"It's that haul up from the flat. Apartment," he said apologetically.

"Getting old."

"Death, where is thy sting," Halfacre said. Toothe laughed.

Henderson laughed too, waved gaily and left them in the corridor. He walked to his office, suddenly feeling angry. Getting old. Thirty-nine wasn't old. Impudent little sod. And who was he to clock-watch? Bastard. Forty on the horizon. Prime of life . . . But, then again, there were these disturbing things happening to his body. His eyebrows, his nipples, his shins, his arse. Ass.

As he approached his office door it opened.

"Oh."

"Hello." He greeted Kimberly, the immaculate Kimberly, his secretary. Eighteen going on thirty. The hair, the skin, the nails, the eyes, the clothes. Everything looked new, just on. Very spic, very span. In strong contrast to him.

"What are you doing here, sir?"

"Sorry?"

"The ten o'clock flight to Boston? The man with the Winslow Homers?"

"Oh, Jesus." Henderson remembered. "Oh, look, phone him up and postpone. Tell him I'm ill. I'll come tomorrow."

"Tomorrow's Saturday."

"Monday, then. God." He rubbed his eyes. "I overslept. Clean forgot. Sorry, Kimberly."

"There are messages."

"Already?" He looked at his watch. Nine forty-five.

"A Ms. Düsseldorf and Mrs. Wax."

"Fine."

Kimberly left. Henderson propped his sabers behind the door and sat down. He could see a section of Central Park through his window. The plane trees were just coming into leaf; the sun on the smooth hillocks made it look vernal and fresh.

Ms. Düsseldorf. That was Irene. It was a code he insisted on: she had to use a pseudonym—a city—whenever she phoned. The last time it had been Phnom Penh.

He wondered whom he should phone first. His mistress or his ex-wife. He should phone Melissa, he knew; she liked her calls returned. He phoned Irene.

"Hello, Irene. It's—"

"Tonight, don't forget, that's all."

"I'll see you there. I haven't forgotten. Christ, I asked *you*."

"Don't be late. I'll give you fifteen minutes, then I'm gone."

"I won't. Bye."

Henderson stood up and took off his jacket. He moved to the door to hang it up and paused there for a moment, his jacket in one hand, his square jaw in the other. He stroked his jawbone gently, like a man coming around after a novocaine jab. What on earth was he doing, he asked himself, getting more deeply involved with Irene when what he really wanted to do was remarry Melissa? He shook his head. This too was typical: a clear and pre-determined course of action had become complicated by his own maverick and wayward desires and his seeming inability ever to resist them. Now he was being driven to the brink of having to make a choice. The worst possible state of affairs.

As he fitted his jacket onto the coat hangar he saw the envelopes in the inside breast pocket, and among them the red and blue flashes of the airmails. Rushing out of the apartment that morning he'd snatched up his post without looking at it.

He laid the two airmail envelopes on his desk, feeling sensations of reverence and trepidation behind his rib cage. They were from Britain; his own handwriting was on the envelopes—he always sent stamped, addressed enve-lopes to ensure prompt replies. On one the postmark said NORTHAMPTON. With a blunt thumb he ripped it open.

Dear Mr. Dores,

Thanking you for your letter of 7 March. I re-member Captain Dores well. He was my company commander during the operations around Pinbon in '43. He was a fine and fair man and popular with the other lads.

I am sorry to say that I was taken ill with cere-bral malaria and sent back to India where I spent three months in hospital. By the time I rejoined the unit your father had died six weeks previous, and there was not much left of the company I'm sorry to say as we had seen a lot of action.

I suggest that you write to the following, who were in the company when your father was killed: Lance Corporal David Lee, Royal British Legion,

31 Hardboard Road, Chiswick, London, and Private Campbell Drew, Royal British Legion, Kelpie's Wynd, Innerliethen, Peeblesshire. I last saw these chaps at a regimental reunion in 1967 so cannot vouch as for their being still about.

As I said, Captain Dores was respected by all the chaps. It was a great sadness to us all to hear of his death at the time.

Trusting I have been of some assistance.

Yours sincerely,

Sergeant (ret.) Graham Bellows
2nd Battalion, Loyal West Kents.

Another blank, but at least he had another name to write to. He had already written to Drew. He looked at the postmark on the other letter—GALASHIELS—and this, doubtless, was his reply.

Drew's handwriting was large and jagged; he clearly pressed down very hard on his Biro.

Dear Sir,

With reference to your letter about your father. I was in the company near Pinbon when he died. It was a very difficult time for us all, operating as we were behind enemy lines. We had fatalities almost every day from disease, enemy action and even accidents. Your father was a good man and a good officer. It was a great blow to us all when he died.

Yours faithfully,

Campbell Drew

Henderson smoothed Drew's scored crisp page flat on

the desk. He sat back and exhaled. At last. Someone who had been there. But the letter was maddeningly obtuse and uncommunicative. What exactly had been going on that day—the twenty-first of March, 1943—in Burma? More precisely, what were the circumstances of Captain Dores' death? How, where, when and by whom? He felt a sudden envy for this heavy-handed Scot. Drew had known his, Henderson's, father; had served under him and conceivably joked and suffered with him; had shared a kind of intimacy, in short, that had been denied his son.

He stared at the reproduction of a Monet landscape that Mulholland, Melhuish had sold in London in 1963 for forty-five thousand pounds. The colors shifted. He let his eyes cross and attempted to go into a brief trance, hoping to expunge the sadness that seemed to brim in his body. It didn't work. Why didn't he feel more tired? he wondered. As a chronic insomniac surely he had a right to feel permanently exhausted.

Kimberly buzzed him.

"Mrs. Wax, sir. Line one."

With only the briefest pause, Henderson picked up the phone.

"Melissa," he said enthusiastically. "Just got your message."

"You haven't forgotten, have you?"

"Of course not." He wondered what he hadn't forgotten. Everyone reminding him today.

"See you later, then."

"Exactly." He fenced. "What time did you say again?"

"About seven. Bryant's looking forward to seeing you."

"Likewise. Seven it is."

Mrs. Wax hung up. He thought he heard a spat kiss come winging down the wire. That was something, he reflected, with dubious pleasure. He frowned. One of the most onerous of the multitude of conditions Melissa had laid down—before she would even consider the thought of their getting together again—was that the children of her second marriage should "learn to love Henderson as a father." Henderson, for his part, was so eager to please that he agreed to anything, including the rather staid ban on pre-remarital sex. Hence this meeting tonight. He remembered: it was Bryant's birthday, and Bryant was his step-daughter-to-be. He did some computing. Melissa's at seven. He was meeting Irene at nine, in the bar of a restaurant in SoHo. He should make it all right. Now all he had to do was buy the girl a present.

Henderson looked at his in-tray: three letters. With some guilt he realized it was only now that his mind was turning to his work and he had been in the building an hour. His own private concerns, as ever, took up an increasing portion of his day . . . He forced himself to concentrate.

Business couldn't be said to be booming at Mulholland, Melhuish. Which was precisely why he'd been brought out from England: to get things moving, whip up some trade, start making a name for the firm. He thought suddenly of Pruitt's news: prospects of an Impressionist sale. He winced; he should really be finding out more, exhibiting some curiosity, instead of reading letters and phoning girlfriends. After all, it was his area.

Mulholland, Melhuish had needed an "Impressionist man" and accordingly had sent for him. For some reason, the key factor in establishing an auction house in America was a large Impressionist sale. Only then did you seem bona fide; only then did you acquire a reputation. Or so the pattern had proved in the case of the New York offices of the other famous London auction houses. Little real, profitable business was attracted until there had been a significant Impressionist sale. It was a rite of passage. Why this should be so wasn't exactly clear; it was just one of the illogical rules of the game.

He drew concentric circles on his blotting pad. Mulholland, Melhuish had opened their New York office eighteen months ago. Since that day there had been no significant Impressionist sale. He had been brought over as a final gamble. As he was an authority on late-nineteenth-century French painting, his expertise, his academic contacts, his knowledge of the private collectors were meant to lure and instill confidence in potential clients.

At first—another sign, another omen—it had gone gratifyingly smoothly. In the first fortnight he had acquired for sale a large Berthe Morisot. Morale was raised; relief and hope became an almost palpable presence in the offices. But since then, nothing.

He drummed his fingers on the desk. This news of Pruitt's was a company triumph, but something of a personal failure for him. He just hadn't been working at it hard enough, he realized. His personal life and its problems were taking up too much time. If only Melissa had been more tractable. If only he hadn't met Irene . . .

He got up and looked at the crammed shelves of heavy art books, thumbed catalogs, sale room records. He wandered through into Kimberly's tiny office. She was typing, her gleaming nails snicking off the typewriter keys. Did they ever chip? he wondered. Did she ever get worried, break into a sweat? He ran his fingers through his thick hair and hitched up his trousers. He smiled aimlessly at Kimberly's curious glance. He really should go and find out about this sale, otherwise people would think he was sulking.

A head came around the door.

"Good Lord, I thought you were in Boston."

It was Thomas Beeby, his boss. Beeby was very tall and thin and would have looked like a classically distinguished English gentleman had it not been for his surprisingly plump, rosy cheeks, which gave him the disconcerting look of a superannuated cherub.

"Postponed, Tom," Henderson said. "Seems the man's sick." Kimberly's nails rattled on without a pause.

"But that's wonderful. You've heard the news?"

"About the sale? Yes, I was on my way—"

"Seems we may have the Gage collection."

"Oh?" Gage, Gage. The name rang no bells as a patron of the arts. "Gage."

"Come along, I'll tell you all about it. Thank God you're not in Boston."

He followed Beeby along the corridor to his office. From the floor below came the sound of the sale room filling up. Porcelain today. A deferential Toothe eased by to take it.

"It's all right, Ian," Beeby said. "Henderson's not in Boston. He can go now."

Go where? Henderson thought.

"Oh. Right you are," Toothe said, failing to keep the disappointment out of his voice. Henderson felt a brief elation. The little swine, he thought, never told me about this Gage collection, wanted to sneak off and keep it for himself.

Beeby put his hand on Henderson's shoulder.

"This is it, Henderson," he said. "This is what we've been waiting for."

They entered Beeby's office, slightly larger than Henderson's but no less functional. It had a better view of Central Park, however. The sun still shone on the trees; a distant honking rose up from Madison Avenue. Beeby lit a cigarette. Henderson could sense his excitement and he felt a sudden generous warmth toward the tall man. It was Beeby who had brought him to America, who had pulled the strings and created the job, and for that Henderson would be forever grateful.

"Loomis Gage," Beeby began. "Reclusive, southern millionaire. An old man with a small but very select collection. Some seventeenth-century Dutch—'school of' stuff—rather dull, nothing significant. But. But. Two fine Sisleys—'72, he says—two Van Dongens, a big Derain, a Utrillo, a small Braque and two Vuillards."

"Well!"

"I want you to get down there, Henderson. Check it out and then get it for us. Go straight for no seller's commission. Promise him a full-color catalog. Exhibition in London if he wants it. Anything."

"Right." Henderson began to share Beeby's excitement. He started adding up rough sums in his head, computing the 10 percent buyer's commission Mulholland, Melhuish would charge. They would do very nicely, thank you. More importantly it would signal their arrival in the New York auction-house world. . . . However, one aspect of this miraculous opportunity perplexed him.

"I hope you don't mind my asking, Tom, but—purely personal curiosity, this—what made him bring the paintings to us?"

"Sheer good fortune. He claims to have known old man Mulholland in the twenties. Asked to speak to him. When I told him he was dead he almost hung up. Then I said I was Archie Melhuish's son-in-law and he cheered up again. Stroke of luck, that's all," Beeby smiled joyfully. "Trumps came up."

Henderson smiled with him. Good old Tom, he thought, nice to see him looking happy for a change.

"I want you to get down there by Sunday."

"Sunday?"

"Yes."

"Of course." Henderson kept smiling. "Where is it? Exactly."

"He lives in a place called Luxora Beach."

"One of those purpose-built condominium things?"

"Actually I'm not all that sure." Beeby frowned. "It's in Georgia, I think. Or Alabama. Somewhere like that. All I know at the moment is you've got to be in Atlanta on Monday."

"Bit vague, isn't it?"

"Yes. But deliberately. He's concerned about his 'pryvacy.' Hasn't even given me his phone number yet. He's calling back this afternoon with the details. Anyway, sew it all up as quickly as possible."

"Right you are." He had an idea. "Wonderful news, Tom," he said to the beaming Beeby. "Very pleased. Congratulations." Impulsively—unusually—they shook hands.

Back in his office Henderson got Kimberly to phone Irene.

"Mrs. Düsseldorf?"

"OK, Henderson, what is it?"

"Do you fancy a few days' holiday? Starting tomorrow?"

"I don't know. Where are we going?"

"The South."

chapter two

HE was still feeling pleased with himself an hour later when Pruitt Halfacre came into his office.

"Free for lunch?" Halfacre asked. Today Henderson's benevolence knew no bounds.

"Grand news about this Gage collection," he said as they walked down Madison.

"Oh, yes. Yes," Halfacre agreed. He seemed a bit woebegone.

"Anything wrong?"

"We need to talk, Henderson."

"Well, sure. What about?"

"Can we save it till lunch? I'd like that."

They walked down some steps into a pale-honey and lime-green restaurant. The bar area at the front was full of brilliant women and tall, broad-shouldered men. Everyone spoke in loud firm voices and seemed laughingly at ease. Sadly, as he knew it would, Henderson felt his own confidence begin to ebb away. There must be some law of Newtonian physics to explain this phenomenon, he considered; something about the power of a superior force to sap and drain energy from an inferior one of the same type. He looked about him at the fabulous lunchers. Pruitt shouted clear strong welcomes to people he knew. I want to be like you lot, Henderson thought, as he felt his shoulders round and his chest concave; I want your confidence and purpose, I want your teeth and tans, he pleaded, stepping out of the way and apologizing to a waiter. It's not fair.

They shouldered their way to the bar, Henderson slipstreaming Halfacre. He caught gusts of a dozen different scents. Jasmine, rose, nectarine, musk, civet. Gems flashed demurely, expensively.

"Henderson, may I be totally honest with you?" Halfacre said in a deep voice at his ear.

Henderson looked around in astonishment. "Can't we get a drink first?"

A film-star barman approached.

"Morning, gentlemen. What is your need?"

"Dewar's on the rocks," Halfacre said. "With a twist. Henderson?"

"I'll have a Budweiser, please," Henderson said. "Straight up."

The barman was not amused. He dipped a glass in a crunching, glistening coffer of ice and filled it to the brim. He sloshed copious amounts of whiskey into it, cut a twist of lemon and dropped it in. How can they do that to perfectly good whiskey? Henderson thought. Ice in everything too. A profligacy of ice in this country. Immense wealth of ice. He drank some of his beer.

"You were saying"—he turned to Halfacre—"something about total honesty."

"Pruitt, your table's ready." It was the waiter.

"Thatcher, hi." Halfacre and Thatcher hugged manfully, with much clapping of hands on shoulders. "I heard you were here. How's it going?"

"Not so bad. I'm working on a novel."

"Great! . . . Hey, Jesus. Sorry about Muffy. I heard. I guess she couldn't hack it."

"You win some—"

"You lose some. Bastard, man." Halfacre spent a second deep in thought. "Thatcher, this is a colleague, Henderson. Thatcher and I were at school together."

"Good to know you, Henderson." Thatcher's grip was knuckle grinding.

"How do you do?" Henderson muttered, entirely unmanned by now. Thatcher led them through the shining throng to their table. Henderson felt as if his neck had disappeared and his shoulders were about to meet in front of his chin. He sat down with a sigh of relief. Halfacre seemed to have forgotten about their projected conversation so Henderson happily let it ride for a moment. He studied the menu and studied Halfacre above its uppermost edge. He looked at Halfacre's plain, lean face, his sharp jaw, his short hair, his—just donned—modish tortoiseshell spectacles. He considered his Harvard Ph.D., his "old" family, his modest but comfortable private income. Here was the paradigm, the Platonic ideal. American man, late-twentieth-century model. Look how easily he wore his clothes, how at home he was in this smart restaurant. Consider the masterful aplomb with which he could initiate and terminate casual conversations. Listen to the rigidity and reasonableness of his opinions. What was more, this man was engaged to an intelligent and beautiful girl. And what is even more, Henderson thought, this man is eleven years younger than me.

Thatcher reappeared to take their orders.

"Chicken omelette," Halfacre said. "Grilled plaice, side salad, no dressing. Sancerre OK for you, Henderson?"

"Lovely." Henderson's eyes skittered desperately over

the menu, searching first for something he liked, then for something he recognized. Halfacre's requests didn't even seem to be listed here. This sort of man ordered what he wanted, not what was offered.

"I'll, um, start with the, ah, *crevettes fumées aux framboises.* Followed by . . ." Jesus Christ. "Followed by . . . filet mignon with butterscotch sauce."

"Vegetables, sir?"

Henderson looked. Salsify, fenugreek, root ginger. What were these things? He saw one that was familiar. "Braised radishes."

The menus were removed.

"Sorry, Pruitt," he said, flapping out his napkin. "There was something you wanted to talk to me about."

Pruitt was drawing furrows on the thick white linen of the tablecloth with the tines of his fork.

"That's right." He paused. "How would you react, Henderson, if I said . . . if I said that the one word I associate with you is 'hostel'?"

"'Hostel'?" His mind raced. "As in 'youth hostel'?"

"No, for God's sake. As in 'hostel aircraft,' 'hostel country,' as in 'The Soviets are hostel to American policy.'"

"Oh. Got you. We say 'style.' 'Hostyle.'"

"Why"—Pruitt now held his fork with both hands as if he might bend it—"why do you hate me, Henderson? Why do I sense this incredible aggression coming from you?"

It took the whole of the unsatisfactory lunch (Henderson had been agog at his lurid shrimps and managed one mouthful of his candied steak) to convince Halfacre that, far from disliking him, Henderson on the contrary both admired and respected his colleague. That he was, moreover, an ideal confederate and a brilliant mind. Halfacre took twenty minutes to travel from skepticism through grudging apologies to overt gratitude. Henderson's quizzing established that the misconception had arisen a week before when Halfacre had called a greeting down a corridor and Henderson—so Halfacre had thought—had rather curtly returned it.

"And you thought it meant I disliked you?"

"God, Henderson, I just didn't know. It was so . . . you know, implicit with . . . with . . . What was I meant to think?"

"You said, 'Hi there, Henderson.' And I said 'Hello' back."

"But it was the *way* you said it."

"Hello. Hello. There is only one way."

"There you go again. *'Hler, hler.'*"

"But that's the way I *talk*, Pruitt."

"But I felt that you . . . Look, OK, so I'm a little paranoid. I know. I've got problems of self-alignment. I worry about these things. The aggression in this city, Henderson. The competitiveness . . . I mean, there are guys I was at school with, guys I grew up with—dentists, brokers—earning twelve times what I do. *Twelve.*" He went on listing his complaints and fears. Henderson watched him light a thick cigar to go with his "black tea," and wondered what Halfacre really had to worry about. If only *he* had Halfacre's problems . . . Then it struck him that perhaps all that was important to the Halfacres of this world was actually to be in a state of worry—about something, about anything. I worry, *ergo sum.*

"I think it's good for us to talk this way," Halfacre said around his cigar. "You know, if we—you and I—can get that sort of supportive holistic flow"—pushing motion with both hands—"God, could we generate and strengthen . . .

We internalize, Henderson. I internalize. All the time, I know. It's my fault. My *hamartia*, hah." He frowned. "And that can't be good, can it?"

"Well, no. I suppose. But on the other hand—"

"You're right. You're so right."

They walked slowly up Fifth Avenue, the huge park on their left, back toward the office.

"I'm very grateful, Henderson," Halfacre said.

"Don't mention it."

"I want you to know how I value our friendship. How much I admire your books, and your learning."

"Don't give it another thought." Henderson broke out in a sweat of embarrassment.

"No, I feel—"

"Let's go to the Frick," he said suddenly, inspired.

They paid their dollar each and entered the dim cool gallery. The plash of water from the courtyard, the solid gray stone and marble and the immaculate plants exuded a green tranquillity and worked their usual spell. Henderson relaxed. If only I could set my bed up here, he thought, I know I could sleep.

They moved slowly through a roomful of Goya, Lorrain and Van Dyck, then into another large room. Halfacre was silenced at last, looking at the paintings. Henderson's mind wandered, pondering the logistics of his trip south. He decided to drive, spend a couple of days on the road. See Kentucky, Virginia . . . one night in Washington, perhaps. Irene could give him a guided tour around the capital. He smiled at the prospect. Stay in really nice hotels. Find one somewhere near this Luxora Beach. Irene could swim and sunbathe while he worked at the Gage house during the day. Spend the evenings with Irene, just the two of them, Melissa and his conscience back in New York.

He paused. That was not exactly the sort of attitude one should develop toward one's future wife. He grimaced slightly. He wondered why he persisted in being so divided, so untrue to his best instincts, so wayward in regard to his duty. Perhaps Pruitt would say that was his tragic flaw. . . .

He looked around. Halfacre had gone on ahead. Henderson wheeled left and cut across the courtyard into another room. On the walls were Romneys, Gainsboroughs and Constables. For an instant he felt a tremor of homesickness for England. He thought dreamily of English landscapes, the reality behind the images hanging here. Now that it was April the leaves would be well advanced, and in the fields . . . The enormous, hedgerowless fields would be loud prairies of brutal shouting yellow, some European Community incentive having encouraged the farmers to sow every available acre with rape. And then in the autumn it was like driving through a war-torn country, vast columns of smoke from the burning stubble rising into the sky, the sky itself finely sedimented with flakes of ash. One weekend last summer, sitting outside a friend's cottage in the Cotswolds reading the Sunday papers, he had been driven indoors by a fragile rain of cinders that drifted softly but steadily down upon him from an apparently clear sky.

In this mood of harsh realism he turned to *Richard Paul Jodrell* by Gainsborough. There was the supercilious, self-satisfied face of England. And in *The Mall in St. James's Park* were the smug English belles, unchanged in two centuries. He could imagine the conversation, hear the very tones of their lazy voices. He peered closer. To his vague surprise one of the women looked remarkably like his mother.

He thought of her now, a sharp-nosed, well-preserved

sixty-five-year-old, living in her neat "villa" in Hove. Her over-made-up face, her gray hair cut in a youthful bob, her deep, unshakable and unreflecting conservatism. She spent a lot of time with her grown-up nieces and their young families, a rich and popular visitor to their green-belt homes. Henderson was her only child, and they gamely maintained an appearance of filial and maternal affection that on the whole effectively disguised mutual disapproval.

Henderson strode urgently out of the room. This was what he was escaping; that was his past, now behind him forever, he hoped. He slowed down and strolled through a roomful of frothing pastel Fragonards. No Halfacre. He retraced his steps.

Halfacre seemed hardly to have moved. He was standing in front of a Vermeer, *Mistress and Maid*. Henderson looked at him more closely. Tears ran down his face. His chest and shoulders twitched with little sobs.

"Pruitt," Henderson said with alarm. "What's wrong?" Had he somehow caused further offense?

Halfacre gestured at the painting.

"It's so true," he said. "It's so true."

Henderson suppressed his automatic sneer. That's the difference between us, he thought sadly. An immense unbridgeable gulf. We've both made art our career, but he can weep in galleries. I would rather die.

Henderson moved away, somewhat disturbed. He had no idea what to say and was suddenly uncomfortably aware of the progress he still had to make before he would feel at home in this country.

Look at the paintings, he told himself. He obeyed. *The Deposition*, by Gerard David. *The Painter*, by Frans Hals. *Judith and Holofernes*, by Jakob van Hoegh. He paused by this one, vaguely shocked by the relish of Judith's expression as she hacked her way crudely through Holofernes' neck. Judith had a pert, small-chinned face, heart shaped. Holofernes' tongue, livid purple and foam flecked, stuck out a good three inches.

"Pruitt, come and have a look at this," Henderson said. That should stop him crying.

Later that afternoon Beeby looked into the office with Gage's telephone number and the instructions about where and when to meet up. They were quite simple. When Henderson arrived in Atlanta he was to phone the given number between four and five P.M. He would then be told where to proceed.

"Is that all?"

"Afraid so."

"It's a bit cloak-and-dagger, isn't it? Is it all really necessary?"

"You know these types," Beeby said solemnly. "Insecure. Jealous of their solitude. He was absolutely adamant on proceeding this way. Adamant. We've got to respect it, Henderson. Can't afford to give offense."

"Softly, softly."

"Exactly." Beeby screwed up his eyes and waggled a hand. "He sounds a bit of a dodgy number. I think we'll have to go very carefully."

Henderson walked with him to the door. Beeby fiddled with his signet ring.

"Good luck," he said, and patted Henderson on the elbow. It was an expression of genuine affection and concern.

"Don't worry," Henderson said; his fingers brushed Beeby's sleeve, expressing his affection in return. Whole paragraphs of information and sentiment had been conveyed in the four words.

"I'll give you a phone once I've made contact. And Tom, it'll be fine."

"I know. See you next week."

Henderson watched Beeby's tall figure amble down the corridor. He felt his eyes moist. He's relying on me, he thought. Like a father. Almost.

chapter three

THE gym was down by the East River in the basement of an old building between the Queensboro Bridge and F.D.R. Drive. It was the only place in Manhattan where Henderson had been able to find a saber coach and so he charitably attempted to ignore its less salubrious qualities.

The basement windows were heavily barred and opaque with grime. The basement well was brightened by drifts of waxed-paper cartons and aluminum beer and soft-drink cans. The studded and battered double steel doors were luridly and professionally graffitied with futuristic names and numbers.

Henderson went in. An ancient man behind a grille scrutinized his Queensboro Health Club membership card.

"Is Mr. Teagarden here?" Henderson asked.

"Yep."

Henderson walked along a passageway and turned into the humid locker room. Thin avenues of gray lockers took up most of the space. Low benches ran between them. Three Puerto Rican kids in boxing gear smoked in a line near Henderson's locker.

He tried to undress with nonchalance. Then he pulled on his white socks and white polo-neck jumper and stepped into his white knickerbockers. He heard the chuckles and gibes break out behind him.

"Hey, what that shit you wearing?"

Henderson laced his gym shoes.

"Some kinda fairy, man?"

He slung his saber bag over his shoulder. Sticks and stones.

"Snow White. He Snow White!"

May break my bones. He picked up his mask, gloves and padded waistcoat. But names will never harm me.

"Spiderman! He Spiderman!"

He strode out of the locker room with as much dignity as he could muster.

The low-roofed gym area was surprisingly large. There was a boxing ring, a scrap yard of fitness machines—chain and pulley systems, canting seats and legrests, short conveyor belts with dials and handrails—and the usual barbells and weights for the glistening, walnut-brained beefcakes to toss around. There was a large padded mat area for the martial arts enthusiasts and, behind a door at the far end, a steam room and plunge pool.

In the far corner he could see Teagarden marking out the fencing *piste* with chalk.

"You're late," Teagarden said.

"Busy day," Henderson apologized. "And I've got to be out of here by half six."

"Ain't no reduction."

"Oh, no. I wasn't suggesting . . ."

Eugene Teagarden was black. The only black sabreur in America, he claimed, which was why he charged such high rates. He was slim and dapper, with a tidy wide moustache and a manner that vacillated erratically between hostility and scorn. He was, as far as Henderson could tell, a brilliant swordsman. He taught, moreover, not fencing but "zencing." The raw technique came with a heady garnish of philosophy and consciousness-expanding routines. Impelled by the continuous exhortation in America to exercise, Henderson had plumped for fencing, the only sport he had vaguely enjoyed while at school. It wasn't so much the exercise he was after as the topic of conversation it provided him with at dinners and parties. When the talk inevitably moved to working out, aerobics, discussions of the stride-length factor in jogging, Henderson could chip in with a fencing anecdote.

He took a saber out of his bag.

"Don't want to waste no time, then," Teagarden said. "Masks on. On guard."

Henderson slid on his mask, the big cyclopean fly-eye. He liked the mask; it made his head as featureless as a light bulb.

"Remember the drills," Teagarden said.

Controlled relaxation, Henderson intoned, controlled relaxation. This was the key to the Teagarden approach; this was the core of zencing. And this was why he persisted with Teagarden's abuse and truculence: it did him good, he hoped. He didn't need to exercise, he needed the therapy.

"On the toes."

Henderson rose on his toes, legs apart, left hand perched on his hip, the saber held angled in front of him.

"Feel that blade," Teagarden said, now masked and on guard opposite him. "You are that blade. There is only the blade. You do not exist. What are you?"

"I, um, am the blade."

"Controlled relaxation."

Henderson relaxed and tried to stay in control.

"Take your measure."

The sabers made contact. A tinny scratching sound.

"Feel it?"

"What?"

"The *sensation du fer.*"

"Oh, yes. I feel it."

"OK. *Flèche* attack any time you like."

The *flèche* attack was a sort of mad scampering charge that often took the attacker thundering past his opponent. At some point during the attack one was meant to deliver a cut to the cheek or the flank.

Henderson swayed. Teagarden was poised and immobile. Henderson thought he might fall over, he felt so relaxed.

He sang a song to himself, another of Teagarden's drills. For some reason he always sang "Nymphs and Shepherds."

Nymphs and shepherds, come away, come away. I am the blade, he reminded himself; I am the blade. *Come, come, come, come away.* He was going to make a *flèche* attack on Teagarden's left side—unorthodox—but administer a cut to the right side of the face—even more unorthodox. So fingernails of the sword hand down, sword arm straight behind the guard, breathe out, relax, a feint to the right and charge!

He felt Teagarden's stop cut jar on the inside of the right elbow and, almost simultaneously, the thwacking cuts to the head and left cheek as he galloped by, skewering air.

"What you doing, man?" Teagarden shouted, as Henderson caromed into a wall ladder. "You was wide open. You was fuckin' *slashin'*, too."

He wandered over, mask perched on the top of his head. "The cut is a twitch of your little finger." Ping, bock, rasp, scratch, ping. Teagarden's saber administered five cuts to Henderson's mask in as many milliseconds.

"You ain't Errol fuckin' Flynn. It's all wrist, man. You're like chopping meat." He swished madly in the air in illustration. "You ain't a butcher, you're a artist. You're a art man, it should come natural."

"Sorry," Henderson mumbled.

"OK. So just breathe."

They breathed for a couple of minutes.

"Controlled relaxation," Teagarden said.

Henderson relaxed.

"Let's do it this way," Teagarden said. "You're on top of a mountain, OK? In a white room. You was born there. You lived there all your life. Why? 'Cause you're the king of fencing. The lord of sabreurs. People come from all over to your mountain to watch you in your room. To watch your *flèche* attacks. Why? Because you *flèche* attack *purely*, man. Pure. Got that?"

"Mountain, white room, pure. Yes."

"Shut your eyes." His voice dropped a tone. "You are the lord of sabreurs in your white room on the mountain. Think about it. Imagine it. Be there. What are you?"

Henderson opened his eyes and looked about him edgily. Nobody appeared to be listening. He shut his eyes again.

"I'm, ah, the (little cough) lord of sabreurs."

"Louder."

"I am the lord of sabreurs."

"Louder."

"I am the lord of sabreurs!"

"Louder!"

"I am the lord of sabreurs!"

Henderson opened his eyes. People had stopped exercising; a small crowd had gathered. For some reason he felt curiously elated, almost light-headed with embarrassment. Only Teagarden could make him behave like this. Only in America would he have complied.

"OK. I'm going to feint at the head and you parry *quinte*. Got that?"

"Yes."

"Then parry at flank with *seconde* and riposte at right cheek."

"OK."

"Then I'll cut at flank, parry *tierce* on the lunge, make a counter-riposte to head and we'll take it from there."

"Fine."

"And do it purely, for God's sake. Pure."

In the locker room afterward Henderson and Teagarden toweled down after their shower. Henderson tried not to look at Teagarden's long thin cock and attempted as best he could to preserve his own modesty. Ever since leaving his boarding school he'd felt ill at ease being naked with other men. What made this occasion worse was that Teagarden was the first black man he had ever seen naked, outside of books and *National Geographic* magazines, and Henderson was concerned not to seem curious. He hummed "Nymphs and Shepherds" quietly and appeared unduly interested in a corner of the ceiling. Teagarden did a lot of unselfconscious walking around, his towel slung about his neck, but eventually put on his underpants.

Henderson told him he was going away for a few days and probably wouldn't make the Wednesday lesson.

"That's up to you," Teagarden said aggressively.

Henderson pulled on his shirt. Really, the man was impossible. The most neutral exchange of information denigrated into some sort of offense.

"Where you going?"

"The South. Georgia, I think. To start with. I've got to go to Atlanta first."

"Shit. What you want to go there for?"

"It's for work."

"Hell, you don't want to go down there."

"Why?"

"It's bad, man."

"Worse than here?"

Teagarden shrugged. "Maybe not. It's different, that's for sure."

"How? How do you mean?"

"Shit, I don't know . . . . Well, maybe everyone's the same everywhere. Dishin' out the same shit." Teagarden looked intensely at him. "Dishin' the shit. That's what it's all about, ain't it? Dishin' the shit?"

Henderson was perplexed. "Well, not all the time. Some of the time, but not *all* the time, surely."

Teagarden sat down to lace up his shoes. "That what you think?"

"I suppose I do."

Teagarden laughed. He seemed to find the notion genuinely amusing.

"Then good luck to you, Mr. Dores. You sure gonna need it."

A little unsettled, Henderson said goodbye and left.

Henderson picked up a cab on East Fifty-ninth Street and gave the driver Melissa's address. He sat back on the red Leatherette seat and tried to forget Teagarden's words and his laughter. He thought, with only second-order guilt, of going south with Irene. He felt at once tired and invigorated after his exercise with the sabers. Perhaps he would sleep tonight.

He banished all thoughts of Irene from his mind as he approached Melissa's apartment in the upper Eighties. Neither of the women in his life knew anything of the existence of the other. Accordingly certain levels of concentration had to be maintained to prevent a careless slip.

He paid off the cab and paused for a moment outside the doorway of the apartment block. It was cool and he stood beneath the firmament of shining windows collecting his thoughts. He adjusted his tie and cleared his throat. It was like paying court; then he remembered he *was* paying court. Last week Melissa had allowed that they were on the point of becoming "unofficially engaged" again. He was quite expecting her to demand a ring.

He had met Melissa at Oxford, in the mid-sixties, getting on for two decades ago now. He had been subsidizing his Ph.D. by teaching at a summer school that various American colleges held in Oxford. Melissa had been one of his tutees. Even then, with his love affair with America not fully developed, Melissa—fresh, her dark hair tied back, her impossible aura of cleanliness—had seemed overpoweringly alluring. She, as was confessed in the third tutorial, was recovering from the unhappy termination of a college love affair. Henderson's donnish affectations (French cigarettes, rumpled erudition), his utter dissimilarity to her previous lover (called, oddly, Jock, as far as he could make out) and the predictable student-teacher crush propelled them swiftly into as fervid a romance as he had ever known. It started with picnic lunches and progressed to half-pints in hot summer-evening pubs, then weekend trips to London. It moved quickly, with a strong momentum of emotion, because each saw in the other a timely and fortuitous answer to his or her particular requirements. They were married three months later in his college chapel (her daunting parents flew over for the wedding) and they rented a cold cottage in Islip. The momentum was still going a year later. Looking back on it now, it still seemed to Henderson to have been his life's only sustained experience of true happiness. That next summer they had gone to France and Italy. They were in the final planning stages of their next trip—to the States, Henderson agog with anticipation—when, one November afternoon, she came home early from her job to find him in bed with the woman next door.

This woman's name was Agnes Brown; its very drabness summed her up perfectly. It had been his sole occasion of marital infidelity and to this day he wondered how they had so fatefully contrived to find themselves in bed together.

Agnes was a faintly grubby woman who always seemed harassed and overburdened with chores and extra work. She was somewhat older than Henderson, a divorcée with three young, noisy and potentially neurotic children. Henderson and Melissa had come to know her quite well—as next-door neighbors will—but he had never entertained even a halfhearted sexual or erotic fantasy about her, for, in Agnes, Henderson recognized a fellow sufferer: Agnes Brown was shy. She confessed as much to Henderson and Melissa on numerous occasions, bemoaning her disability and the obstacle it posed to her ever finding a new husband.

For such people often the only means to physical contact is a collision, and one rainy afternoon she and Henderson collided. She had come to borrow one of Melissa's bright American magazines. Henderson picked it up, turned too quickly and bumped into her.

Why had he kissed her? In the intervening decade and a half that question had been asked hundreds of times, with no satisfactory answer. There was even less likelihood of explaining the fumbling embarrassed haste with which they had fallen on the sofa and the chilling, semiclothed shuffle into the bedroom some minutes later.

At first he told himself that he must have felt like a final dose of European grime before exposing himself to the gleaming hygiene of the New World, but as a motive it rang a little false. He knew that he had done it because he was shy too—though not as shy as she was. In the country of the blind, the one-eyed man is king. The same power equation applies to the parish of the mild, he now knew. There the modestly emboldened exercises real sway. Modestly emboldened, he had seized the opportunity: he simply didn't have the confidence to say no. The truth was, he thought, remembering the wet, rather sore clash of mouths, she was keen on me and I was flattered and weak. This was the fearful side effect of shyness. Because he lacked the confidence to disagree, to spurn, to go his own way, it was always easier to conform. He wasn't making love with Agnes that ghastly afternoon when Melissa breezed in to discover them, he was conforming.

And Melissa had gone by that evening. Infidelity was the one unforgivable crime. Henderson never got to the States that summer. Instead he received an alarming transatlantic battery of legal threats, injunctions and instructions. Somehow, somewhere (Reno? Mexico?) he and Melissa were swiftly divorced.

As inadvertent consolation and second-best course of action—something he and Agnes Brown were naturally inclined to accept as their lot in life—they joined forces for three years. But the hyperactive, squalling children and the doomed nature of their alliance (it got off to a bad start and seemed threatened thereafter) made a parting inevitable. It came—with sullen resignation, no tears—and Henderson moved to London to begin what he now termed the lost decade. He founded his "reputation" by writing his three books on the Impressionists, composed sundry articles, coedited an art magazine for four years, spent 1976 in France on a foundation grant, lectured on art history in art schools throughout the Southeast of England, edited a *Festschrift* for an old professor, wrote introductions to numerous catalogs. It was a flat, joyless and rather lonely time, of hard work and monotonous insolvency only periodically relieved by the odd financial windfall (two coffee-table books for a Swiss publisher, and the saving of half his foundation grant, which went toward the purchase of a small flat in Baron's Court). It ended—officially—in 1981 when Thomas Beeby—an old friend of his mother—offered him a job as a valuer at Mulholland, Melhuish.

He liked deliberately to think of the "lost decade" before he saw Melissa because it reaffirmed his new commitment to her and their eventual remarriage. Thus committed, he gave his name to the doorman, who phoned up, and looked suspiciously at him before allowing him to enter the lift. As it moved steadily up to the fifth floor, Henderson reflected that although his professional life (prior to Mulholland, Melhuish) had attained some sort of meager plateau, his emotional one had faltered and all but died after his divorce. Strangely, it was after Melissa's departure that his insomnia developed, the most persistent reminder of his foolishness that afternoon.

It seemed that there was no European equivalent of what Melissa had given him, or rather his maddened regret at his fall from grace punished him further by making all substitutes unsatisfactory. As time moved on from his divorce, his one year of marriage came to assume in his memory an almost legendary brightness and bliss, especially when compared to the few brief and sad affairs he experienced (with a brittle academic, a pretty but dull student and an ambitious subeditor at a magazine he wrote for). His fault, he admitted. He became, for steadily longer periods of his life, a sort of asexual. Sex played a minor, or solitary, role in his life: the eternal substitute at the football match, only rarely called from the benches and instructed to warm up beside the pitch. It took off its track suit, ran up and down the sidelines, but it wasn't really in the game anymore.

Melissa stood at the doorway to her apartment. At her ankles two Pekingese barked shrilly.

"Hello," he said, leaning forward to kiss an emerald earring.

"What have you got there?" Melissa asked.

"My sabers."

"How dashing," she laughed and pushed him in the chest. He rocked back on his heels. "My God, you're a funny man, Henderson."

He followed her into the Wax domain.

"Gervase, Candice, stop that!" she said to the dogs, still barking annoyingly. "It's Henderson. Say hello now." The dogs growled. "Say hello to them, Henderson. They've got to learn the sound of your voice."

"What? . . . You mean, say hello to those dogs?"

"Yes. Come on, just say hello."

"Hello, Gervase. Hello, Candice."

Melissa bent down and scratched their crowns with long nails. "Come on, babies, it's Henderson. Keep talking, Henderson."

Muttering greetings to the dogs he followed her through the hall.

Shortly before Beeby had offered him the New York job he had heard from Melissa. She wrote to tell him of her second divorce—from Mr. Wax—and obliquely to let him know that bygones were bygones. By the time of his third letter—a one-sided correspondence had begun—he was able to tell her of his impending arrival in New York—the "astonishing coincidence" that would bring them together again.

He had taken it, of course, as another sign, another portent and blessing on the enterprise. His memories revived and amplified themselves: a new print was made of his year of marriage. The reunion and the several dinners afterward had been warm, pleasingly coy, maturely reflective. Mentally, the way had already been prepared: it seemed entirely natural that they should seek to recapture their former happiness together. There had been no swooning revelation, no ardent campaign on either side. Their first kiss had a dreamy predictability about it to Henderson; he had been rehearsing it for weeks. The hints about consolidating their reconciliation had followed soon after.

The trouble was, Henderson now realized, that he had allowed himself to be driven on too easily by his own lonely aspirations rather than by any realistic assessment of what it involved or of life's many contingencies. . . . He frowned and looked at her neat legs. For example, he had never remotely taken into account the possibility of an Irene emerging. Or of the fact that both he and Melissa were now different people. And Melissa had changed radically too, in some ways. The dark glossy brown hair had gone, for a start. It was now blond, a streak job, shoulder length and held in place by fearsome mastic sprays. She was, if anything, slimmer, wore light expensive colors and was a little too heavily tanned. The moral imperatives remained implacable, however. She had married Irving Wax a year after leaving Henderson. Wax was very big in concrete and an exceedingly rich man. She had divorced him the year previous. "He was fucking his secretary, Henderson. What could I do? Really, you men are impossible."

He could recall her tone of voice exactly. No outrage, no indignation, just a calm logical assessment. Melissa's strength was that she was one of those women who know exactly what they want from life and set about methodically acquiring it. There was an unruffled placidity and certainty at the basis of their natures, as if life and the world were somehow in *their* debt. . . . When Henderson thought about his relationship with Melissa he sometimes asked himself if it had been not so much love and affection that had drawn him toward her, but envy. Envy's role in human emotional affairs was seriously undervalued, he considered. The people we fall in love with are very often people we envy. Marry them, become close to them, and that poisonous resentment becomes easier to live with, easier to handle. . . . How did that poem go? "Tight-fisted as a peasant, eating love." In that regard, he thought, enviously following Melissa into the drawing room, he hadn't changed that much at all, and Melissa too was as alluringly confident and sure of herself as ever—with the deep tranquillity of an abbess.

The drawing room was decorated in the same colors as Melissa's clothes: blond, beige and cream. She was completely camouflaged in it. Once, he looked around from pouring a drink and thought she had disappeared—but she had only moved in front of the curtains.

A twelve-year-old boy sat in front of a television set. He didn't acknowledge them as they came in. Irving Wax, Jr.

"Irving, it's Henderson. And switch that off."

"Hi." The boy glanced around. His mouth was a canteen of orthodontic braces; the first acne clusters were evident on his chin. In general the pubertal cocktail currently being shaken up inside him coarsened his features, making him look awkward, slightly subnormal.

"Hello, Irv," Henderson said jovially.

"Where's Bryant?" Melissa asked.

"I'm here."

Henderson looked around. Bryant was a tall, thin, pretty girl with short, wild, fair hair. Small breasts barely denting her baggy T-shirt, very old jeans, training shoes. He had never seen her looking anything but bored or sulky.

"Happy birthday," Henderson said and handed her the envelope that contained her present.

"What's this?"

"Open it, Bry," Melissa said.

She did. "Life membership," she read slowly. "Friend of the Frick? What am I supposed to do with this?"

"Aw, Henderson. How thoughtful."

"Yes. I thought—"

"Say thank you, little missy."

"Yeah, but what can I do with it?"

"Well. Ah . . ." Melissa looked at Henderson for help.

"You can go to the Frick free, for a start. For the rest of your life."

"What's the Frick?"

"For Frick's sake," snorted Irving Wax.

"I'll take you, baby," Melissa said. She mouthed "Thank you" at Henderson and pouted a kiss in his direction. Henderson stiffened. Despite the guilt he felt, he still wanted desperately to go to bed with Melissa. He called into mind memories of Oxford, all those years ago, and tried to ignore the ungrateful way Bryant tossed her membership card on the coffee table.

Henderson opened a bottle of champagne. They toasted Bryant's health and congratulated her on reaching the age of fourteen. She didn't really look fourteen, Henderson thought. If he hadn't known better he would have said twenty-two.

He sat beside Melissa on a long suede couch while a Philippine maid distributed birthday cake. Then they had coffee and Melissa lit a very long cigarette. Bryant's request for one was turned down. She was allowed two a day and had already exceeded her quota. Henderson was vaguely shocked at this. Eventually the kids wandered out.

Henderson kissed Melissa gently on the lips. He tasted lipstick and tobacco.

"Love you, darling," Melissa said absently.

"Me too . . . That is, I love you too."

Henderson put his hand on her thigh and kneaded it gently. Melissa combed the hair above his left ear with her long nails. Henderson realized he was smiling and frowning at the same time. No wonder: he felt at this moment greatly attracted to Melissa, and wanted keenly to remarry her, and yet simultaneously was planning a dirty weekend with Irene. Once again he was dismayed at the ease with which he fell into and coped with duplicity. Was this, he wondered, something that was basically—seriously— wrong with him, or did everybody behave the same? Perhaps it was the only response possible to the generosity of America: here you could have your cake and eat it too. . . . It was a very un-English notion, that, he reflected. We disapprove strongly of that sort of attitude.

"Melissa, darling," he said carefully. "I've got to go away tomorrow for a few days. Business."

"Oh? Where?"

Don't give away too many clues, he thought.

"Um, near Washington. Still waiting for details."

"Washington? But that's wonderful."

"It is?"

"Of course. You can go with Bryant. She's going to stay with Mom and Daddy Wax. Flying tomorrow."

"Ah. Shame. I'm driving, you see."

"Henderson! Take the train as a last resort. Nobody drives to Washington." Melissa laughed delightedly at this eccentricity.

"I do. I mean, you know how I hate flying." Something in his mind seemed to flail around, like a snake pinioned at the neck.

"Well, look, OK. So much the better then. You must drive down with Bryant." Melissa put her hand on Henderson's thigh. "Think how you'll be able to get to know each other." She prattled on. To Henderson's eyes the room seemed to darken with foreboding. His frail excuses and blocking tactics were swept aside as new plans were made and schedules altered. He began to feel sick and frightened.

"What time is it?" he asked eventually.

"Quarter of nine."

"Oh, God! I've got to go!"

chapter four

HENDERSON arrived gasping at The Blue Room just as Irene was leaving.

"Hey. You are one lucky guy," she said, pointing a finger at him.

They walked back inside. Henderson deposited his coat and sabers and followed her to the bar. Stark white, thin, naked trees had been planted here and there, and the tiny blue lights festooned in their boughs gave the place an odd doleful-yet-festive air. The bar was busy. People in New York, Henderson noted, seemed to consume alchohol in vast quantities.

"Good evening," another handsome barman said. Where do these guys come from? Henderson asked himself. Where are they made?

"Same again, please. And a large Scotch."

The glasses were plunged in the ice trough; the measures were poured from a height of three feet; a sliver of lemon peel was cut by clean powerful fingers.

"Oh and, um"—the lemon peel plopped into his whiskey—"no twist."

"Sorry, sir?"

"Cough." Henderson cleared his throat and thumped his chest. He coughed. "Nothing."

He turned to Irene and smiled at her.

"Here's how," he said in weak self-parody and sipped his drink. Then he leaned forward and kissed the muscle that ran from her neck to her shoulder. He noticed she was wearing high heels. It was a bad sign: she wasn't pleased with him. On high heels she was an inch taller than he. He told himself to relax. Controlled relaxation. He felt the whiskey sluice through his veins, geeing up the corpuscles. Irene looked at him and laughed.

"I don't know how you do it, Henderson," she said. "You make me so fucking mad. Then you show up with your golf clubs and I've got to laugh."

"My sabers," he explained. "How are you? Look nice."

"I've got a cold coming. I need some southern sun."

"Ah."

He had met Irene a month before at a private viewing in a Madison Avenue gallery. It had been raining and, like this evening, he had arrived late, damp and slightly out of breath. Standing at a wide white desk covered in catalogs and photocopied price sheets had been a dark, well-built girl. Absentmindedly, Henderson handed her his dripping umbrella and raincoat.

"I'm not the fucking hatcheck, numbnuts," she had said reasonably, and had turned on her heel, oblivious to his stream of aghast apologies. Later on during the dull party, while he was pouring himself a white wine at the makeshift bar, she approached with an empty glass and asked to be topped up.

"I'm not the bloody barman," he said, with a boldness that astonished him (he couldn't quite bring himself to say "fucking"). She found this very amusing. They started to talk and discovered that they disagreed violently about the paintings on show. Henderson thought they were puerile and derivative; Irene was a friend of the artist—hence her invitation—and greatly admired them.

Henderson had been initially and immediately attracted to Irene because she bore a considerable resemblance to a girl who worked in a butcher's shop in Spain, about and around whom he had spun a tingling sexual fantasy that had enlivened an otherwise banal and tedious holiday some years ago. He bought meat from this girl twice, sometimes three times a day, never saying anything more than *"jamón," "chuletas de cerdo," "es todo," "gracias."* The girl, unlike her tanned and rubescent clients, was pale, as if she never went out in the sun. She had broad shoulders and strong arms. She cut meat expertly and powerfully. Henderson stood across the bloodied marble from her, finding difficulty in breathing, while she handed him soggy, heavy plastic bags full of chops, steaks, liver, chicken breasts and any other cut of meat he could find in his dictionary. As he was staying in a hotel he had later to throw all this away. He spent a fortune on uneaten meat that holiday.

The girl came to recognize him, and they would make a long and direct eye contact throughout their transaction. Sometimes, counting out his change, her incarnadined fingernails would scratch his damp palm.

Irene, like this nameless she-butcher, was strong looking and pale. She had thick black hair that curled onto her neck. Her eyes were brown; her features were emphatic: prominent nose, distinct lips, unplucked eyebrows. And she was tall. That night at the gallery she had been taller than Henderson.

"You know," he had interrupted their futile disquisition on the paintings' merits, "you remind me of someone."

"Oh, yes? Who?"

"A girl who worked in a butcher's shop in Alicante."

Irene had looked around the room. "I suppose that's some kind of compliment."

"God. No, um, what I meant to say"—his left hand had clutched air, seeking straws—" to ask. Is . . . is if you had any Spanish blood in you. That's what I . . . yes."

"No. I'm Jewish."

"Oh." Nods. "Aha."

"You're not Jewish," she had said, a horror-struck expression on her face.

"Lord, no. I'm English."

Irene had laughed so hard, people had stopped talking and looked around.

Henderson considered her now, perched on a barstool. She was wearing a sleeveless dark-blue dress. Her skin looked almost pure white. White as a fridge. He put his hand on her knee.

"I can get away. No problem," she said. "When do we leave?"

"Ah, yes." Henderson swallowed hard and removed his hand.

"Mr. Dores? Your table is ready, sir."

By the time they sat down Henderson was covered in a fine sheen of sweat. How was he going to tell Irene that her place in the car had been usurped by Bryant?

"I've been to New Orleans," Irene said, "but never to the real South. Where exactly are we going?"

The waiter crept up behind Henderson.

"Hello there, people," he said cheerfully. "My name is James—"

Henderson looked around with a start. "Oh! Hello. My name's Dores. Henderson Dores." He rose to his feet. "This is Miss—Ms.—Stein." Unthinkingly, he held out his hand.

The waiter flashed a puzzled glance at Irene, before

shaking it. "Nice to meet you, sir." His discomfiture lasted a second only. "As I was saying, my name is James, I'm your waiter for this evening and I'll be looking after you." He handed over the menus. "Enjoy," he beamed, and left.

Henderson sat down. "Sorry," he said. "I thought . . ."

Irene stared irritatedly at him. "What do you think you're doing? Are you all right?"

"Yes, fine. Trying day, what with one thing and another."

She shook her head in mock despair. "Are you coming home with me tonight?" she asked, scrutinizing the menu.

Henderson did likewise, trying to ignore his popping cardiac valves. "Yes, please." He would have to tell her about the trip later. "Good God," he said, "what's happening to menus in this city?"

Henderson ate sparingly, his fillet of hake in lager and cranberry sauce failing to stimulate his appetite. Irene ate her two roast baby pigeons in fresh grapefruit nests with relish. Conscious of having to prepare the ground somewhat, he asked her if she was really sure it was all right for her to take a few days off work. Irene reassured him once more. She was a codirector—with her brother—of a firm that sold personal computers. She was her own boss, she reminded him; she could take a holiday when she wanted. Good, Henderson said, good.

When they left the restaurant it was after midnight and a light rain was falling.

"We'll get a cab on West Broadway," Henderson said. "This way."

Irene had a collapsible umbrella, which she erected. Henderson slung his saber case over his shoulder and linked arms with her. He smelled her hair, a vague fruit

fragrance—apples or sultanas—lingering from her shampoo. They made their way leisurely down the street, picking their way through the rubbish and the puddles, from
time to time pausing to look into the lighted windows of
the boutiques and small galleries that proliferated here. At
one of these windows, he kissed her. He shut his eyes and
gently fitted his lips to hers, her bottom lip snug in the
hollow between his two. He pressed his nose into her
cheek, felt his teeth bump and grate against hers as she
opened her mouth slightly. He felt suddenly helpless, vic-
tim of his rampaging desire.

They walked on, the rain a little heavier, the streets
almost deserted as people took shelter.

"I thought you said you knew your way," Irene said.

"I do. Along here."

They turned and walked down a shopless street. High
up he could see the lambent plant-filled windows of the
lofts. Rain runneled off the fire escapes.

"Next left, I think."

They turned. Someone jogged down the street in a
sodden track suit. These madmen really will jog at any
time of the day or night, Henderson thought with vague
admiration.

"I think we should go back," Irene said. "Call a taxi
from the restaurant."

"It's not far from here, I'm sure." Henderson stepped
out from the shelter of Irene's umbrella and looked up and
down the street. There was a junction at the top. He
looked for a street sign Nothing.

"Let's go back," he said suddenly. He had seen four
figures—strolling, unhurrying, masculine figures—turn the
far corner. He felt a spontaneous, improbable thirst. Irene
was rummaging in her handbag.

"I've got to blow my nose."

Henderson looked around again in what he hoped was an unconcerned, natural way. The figures—dark, lithe looking—had crossed to their side of the street with what seemed like more urgency. Henderson clenched a fist. He looked quickly right and left. They were alone. Irene still searched for a tissue.

Jesus Christ, Henderson thought, they say it happens to everybody sooner or later—like a car crash or a burglary. He felt a surging panic begin to overwhelm him. It's only when you haven't got any money that they kill you. Or pour petrol over you and set you alight. Or rape you. Gang-sodomize you. They were only ten yards away.

"Got it," said Irene, and honked noisily into a Kleenex.

"Run!" Henderson screamed, simultaneously flinging away the umbrella and giving Irene a mighty push. He hauled off his sabers and dropped them on the ground. His hand closed around his wallet, fat with credit cards and dollars.

"You can have it, you bastards!" he yelled at the muggers and with all his strength bowled his wallet in their direction. He saw it fly open and notes and cards shower out, then he turned and ran. At once he tripped over his sabers and barked his knee savagely on the road. Through tears of pain he saw no sign of Irene and assumed she had made her escape. He heard shouts close behind him. Without a rearward glance he got to his feet and started to sprint away up the street, making difficult progress as his belted and buttoned raincoat got in the way of his pounding knees—one of which felt as if it were on fire, the knee bone like some white-hot, abrasive nugget. He thrashed frantically on, though, skidding in a puddle, glancing off a dustbin. He was impelled to even greater efforts by another hoarse shout from behind and by the sound of running footsteps—light, energetic, athletic paces, slapping

on the wet tarmac. Oh, God, just don't let them pour petrol on me, he prayed. Just don't let them kick all my teeth out. He thought he was going to vomit with the effort. He felt a hand clutch at his elbow. He screamed and thrashed out wildly behind him, somehow forcing himself to keep running. A hand caught his flying coattail.

"OK," he bellowed in mingled rage and terror as he was hauled to a stop, "Kill me, kill me! I don't *care!*"

He collapsed gasping against a wall, the end of the street and safety still a dark twenty yards away. Would anyone hear his screams?

Both his arms were firmly gripped. "Sir," a quiet voice came. "Relax, please, sir. We have your wallet and your money here."

Henderson lay in his bed in his apartment. Alone. He felt like a man awakening from a deep coma, or like an airliner emerging from a dense cloud bank into clearer air. The white clouds were his shame and embarrassment. Occasionally they swirled around to reengulf him, but now, several hours later, they appeared finally to be on the wane.

The mighty push that he had given Irene, and that was meant to propel her up the street, had in fact been badly askew. She had thudded heavily into a wall and collapsed, wordless and winded, to observe her frenzied screaming lover hurl his wallet at four returning moviegoers and then run frantically away, raincoat cracking, tumbling and falling in desperate panic-stricken flight. Two of the young men had helped her to her feet and pumped air into her lungs while the other two had overtaken the bawling fearful Henderson. He had reconstructed this version of events later. Shame rendered him a docile automaton. Irene had been bundled into a passing taxi (*now*, they passed) while he, with the assistance of the four young men (they were so helpful) had scrabbled about in search of his scattered damp money and credit cards.

He looked at his watch. Half past three. The last time he had looked at his watch it had been twenty-seven minutes past three. This was, he reckoned, insomnia's cruelest curse. Time dawdled. Time loitered. Time forgot what it was meant to be doing. Henderson could lie awake and review his entire autobiography in merciless detail—all the false starts, the self-delusions, the errors, the if-onlys—in the time it took for the minute hand on his watch to advance one tiny calibrated square. He turned over. He turned over again. He got hot and thrust a leg out from beneath the quilt. It got cold. He drew it back in. He looked at his watch. Twenty-six minutes to four.

By rights he should have been in bed with Irene. Those round, flat breasts with their curiously small dark nipples. Her unshaven armpits. Her smells. . . They had slept together twice before. The first time, as he had hovered uncertainly above her (his first sex in eight months, all technique forgotten, trusting hopefully to instinct), she had reached down, grabbed his cock at the root and virtually—there was no other adequate verb—plugged him in. The second time, as he had humped away with damp-browed, slack-jawed abandon in the dark, she had said in his ear, "Shall we stop, Henderson? Do you really think it's worth it tonight?" He had stopped at once, his shock at the matter-of-fact reasonableness of her tone detumescing him rapidly. She had said that it all seemed a bit pointless that night—if he'd forgive the expression. She wasn't in the right mood for all that shoving and pounding. Nothing to do with him, she had added, it was just that at certain times she found the sex act, well, ludicrous and absurd. He had found himself agreeing, to his surprise, but there was a quality about Irene's scornful logic that, once engaged, brooked no argument. It was like the laser eye of a guided missile: once locked on it couldn't be evaded, no matter how one jinked, sidetracked or doubled back.

Tonight, though, until the disastrous arrival of the four "muggers," had been different, and would have been different, he felt sure. He sank his teeth into his pillow. He enjoyed being with Irene: she could be so odd, so strange. The first time he had gone back to her apartment with her, she had invited him in, then picked up a block of wood and a hammer lying in the hallway, placed the wood against a wall and hammered at it for a couple of minutes—an act she repeated every quarter of an hour. She explained to her baffled guest that her neighbors had been redecorating their apartment for the last month at all hours and, now that they were finished, she was letting them have a taste of their own medicine. The last Sunday, she confessed, she had drilled and hammered for a good two hours. "I give," she said, with a tough smile and looking at him directly, "as good as I get."

That was true, Henderson had come to realize. And there also, he admitted, was the source of Irene's potent allure. She was the very antithesis of him. Rather as cannibals are renowned to eat the brains of their enemies to acquire extra intelligence and cunning, so Henderson fancied his association with Irene might allow some of her forthright vigor to strengthen his soul. . . .

He sat up and replumped his pillows. Over the years, as he had first located, analyzed and tried to face up to his problem, the suspicion had grown that it in some way wasn't his own fault, that in some way his country was to blame. Perhaps.

With a great thrashing heave he turned over.

He slid his hand into the cool crevice between sheet

and pillow. That was what he needed. He thought of his lamentable day. He needed some of that strength. He itched with residual shame. There was no hope in ringing her up, asking if he could come around. No hope. . . Besides, he didn't know if he was up to it himself. When he had fallen over his saber bag he had cut and grazed his right knee rather badly, and ruined his suit.

He looked at his watch. A quarter to four.

He turned on his side, hunched into his pillow and closed his eyes. But his brain's life bubbled on, like an indefatigable partygoer. It was something about bed, something about his body's being in repose that seemed to trigger it into hyperactive motion. He ran through his favorite sexual fantasies, duly got an erection, but then found he was thinking about the problems of replacing his American Express card, which had not been uncovered by the diligent search he and his four new friends had carried out.

He wondered if he should take a sleeping pill, but decided not to. They left him more tired the following day than his usual undrugged night on the rack. Once, in a fit of frustration, he had taken three of the particular brand he was prescribed. They made him go to sleep, after a fashion, but what was worse was that he stumbled around like a moron for the next day—heavy-lidded, rubber-lipped, senses all but shut down, barely able to string three words together. At times in any given night he did drift off but never, it seemed, for more than half an hour. It was a source of constant wonder to him how his body survived on such meager rations. He had read somewhere that eight hours of sleep per day was a mythical requirement. He was living proof of the fallacy—if such a concept was possible. For a while he played around with the words: can you prove a fallacy, disprove a fallacy . . . ?

He woke up to a horrible grinding noise punctuated by shouts and clangs. He rubbed his eyes. Wearily, he went to the window and looked out. The back of his apartment block overlooked the rear of a large hotel. In the courtyard behind it, two huge green garbage trucks were being filled with rubbish. Eight-foot dustbins—the size of a steamer's smokestacks—were rumbled out from the kitchen by gangs of men, attached to a hydraulic arm, and automatically tipped into the truck. Throughout this, the men engaged in constant shouted conversation, competing valiantly with the whining hydraulics, the rumbling cast-iron wheels of the dustbins and the surging, churning noise that emanated from the viscera of the garbage trucks.

For the first week that he had lived in the apartment block, Henderson had hung out of his sixth-floor window and had vainly issued requests for a little less noise. "Excuse me," he would call, "is there any chance of you men keeping the noise down?" The men seemed to hear him and shouted back but he couldn't make out their replies. It had no effect, in any event. The noise lasted for fifteen to twenty minutes and took place between four and five in the morning, every morning. When, outraged, he had raised the matter with other residents of the block they assured him he would get used to it very soon. To a man and a woman, it seemed, they now slept tranquilly through the infernal din.

But they weren't insomniacs. Henderson turned away from his bedroom window, went through to his modern kitchenette and made himself a cup of tea. He took a sip and thought about his drive south with the charming Bryant. At least it would please Melissa. He thought fondly of her for a moment. She might not be as exciting as Irene but, under the current circumstances, that seemed like a huge asset. Perhaps, he thought, he should wind up the Irene affair. But that idea saddened him. But then perhaps it was already wound up. You could never tell with Irene.

To distract himself he went back into his sitting room and took out pen and paper. He had decided to write to Lance Corporal Drew and urge him to reply promptly with all the information he possessed about Captain Dores' death.

"Please do not worry about sparing my feelings," Henderson wrote. "I never knew my father and am consequently deeply concerned to learn as much as I can about him. I know the place and time of his death, but not the manner of it. If you can tell me anything—or provide me with the name and address of anyone who can—I will be eternally grateful."

He wrote out an envelope addressed to himself and rummaged in the desk drawer for his supply of British stamps. As he did so, he uncovered an unmarked, age-yellowed envelope. He felt his face spontaneously screw up with disappointment and regret. It was a letter from his father, written on his last leave home, before he departed to the Far East, to his unborn child.

Henderson had learned of its existence only a year and a half previously and it had been responsible for initiating this quest to discover the details of his father's death in action.

One afternoon, in the middle of a desultory conversation, his mother had referred casually to "that old letter of your father's." After the incredulous and heated recriminations had died down ("It's taken forty years for you to deliver it!") his mother had hurtfully handed it over.

"Read it," she had said, a hint of tears in her voice. "You'll understand why I never gave it to you."

He unfolded it now, a curious taut expression on his face, and spread it carefully on the tabletop.

My Darling Girl,
In case anything should happen to me I want you to keep and treasure this. All I have is at your disposal. My faith in you is as my affection for you and knows no bounds.

With all my love,
Your Old Dad

Henderson had tears in his eyes as he read this, tears of frustration. Every time he read this letter he had to suppress a monstrous urge to tear it up.

"He was absolutely convinced you were going to be a girl," his mother had said. "Utterly convinced. Nothing I said would change his mind. 'Look after my little girl' were his last words to me. I thought it would only upset you. It *bas* upset you."

Henderson sat back in his chair. There was a vague tremble running haphazardly through his body. He put the letter away and sat for a while tracing the contours of his nose with thumb and middle finger. The knowledge that letter contained represented his life's greatest disappointment, all the more bitter because there was nothing he could do about it—could ever have done about it. It seemed absurd to worry about a father's speculations on the sex of an unborn child in 1943. . . . But if *you* were that unborn child . . . ? Somehow by being born male he had let his father down, even though the man had never known.

He stood up. "This is ridiculous," he said out loud. He

must be cracking up. He forced himself to think of something else. Irene. There must be some way of getting Irene south. Perhaps a quick, contrite visit tomorrow. Work out some sort of compromise? He paused. Contrition, apologies, compromise, backslide.

He watched his tea cool, its taste metallic in his mouth. He felt an old, familiar anger at his indecisiveness. What did he really want from his life? Melissa or Irene? Always assuming they'd have *him*. . . . He was tired of his own company, he realized; he wanted to inflict it on somebody else, before he got too old and it all got too late.

chapter five

HENDERSON walked into the diner around the corner from his apartment. It was long and thin and tastelessly decorated in colors of maroon and brown. In a corner near the door, two or three hatstands crowded in on a blond Latin American woman who kept the till. Along one wall ranked booths filed back into the gloom. Opposite them was a high Formica bar, with fixed barstools. Behind the bar in the middle was the stainless-steel kitchen.

The diner was staffed with the friendliest middle-aged ladies Henderson had ever met. By his third breakfast there he was thinking of them as favorite aunts, so overwhelming was their celebration of his arrival each morning. The women all had the same hard-curled perm in varying shades of gray. Their voices were harsh—cigarette harsh—but kind. When they weren't telling Henderson how wonderful it was to see him again, they joked and grumbled loudly to each other, shouting unconcernedly the length of the diner or joshing with Ike. Ike was the short-order cook and enjoyed teasing the waitresses and laughing at them. He did this constantly ("Martha, is that new shoes? What yo' old man do to you this weekend?") regardless of the fact that the "girls" never ceased bellowing their orders at him.

While he talked and traded insults he shimmied and swerved above the grills and toasters. He could crack three eggs in one hand, butter five muffins, scramble, poach, fry and slice without breaking into a sweat. At busy times the orders were coming in every three seconds. Henderson never saw him write anything down. And all the while he kept up the banter. "Hey, Joy, what you settin' yo' hair in now? Ceement?" He found his own jokes intensely diverting; his face would screw up as if in pain, his knee would bang the door of a fridge, he'd buckle slightly to one side.

This morning, being a Saturday, the diner was less busy. Henderson still felt irritated and let down by his wasted night. His eyes were hot, his nasal passages dry and prickly. He nodded to the olive-skinned blonde at the till and allowed Martha to hang up his coat.

"How are you today, Mr. Dores? Feelin' fine today?"

"Not so good, I'm afraid, Martha."

"Mr. Dores ain't feelin' so good, Joy!"

"Did you sleep last night, Mr. Dores?"

Henderson had confessed his insomnia in week one.

"No, not very well."

"Mr. Dores din't sleep last night, Joy!"

"That's too bad. Sorry to hear that, Mr. Dores!"

"Looks like Joy din't get too much sleepin' done neither." Ike's left leg gave way and he dug his elbow into his hip.

"Two eggs over, bacon, toast a bagel," Joy bellowed from the recesses.

Two eggs hit the griddle as she spoke; a bagel slammed into a toaster; rashers fizzed under a grill.

"Martha wisht she could be kep awake nights. Right, Martha?"

"Not by you, that's for sure."

76

High-pitched wheezing from Ike.

"What's it gonna be this mornin', Mr. Dores?"

Henderson thought. "Poach one, scramble one on lightly toasted rye. Three rashers of bacon—burned—um, cottage fries. Orange juice and a toasted English, one side only."

"Poach one, scramble one on pale rye. Cremate the bacon, three. Fries. Toast an English, one side only."

"Actually, could you make that poach two, no toast, hold the fries, same bacon and a bagel and lox?"

"Ike, make that last one poach two, no toast, hold the fries, bagel and lox."

Henderson smiled with guilty satisfaction. He had been trying for days to concoct an order that would thwart Ike's astonishing memory and coordination. This was a new and unfair ploy, changing the order after it had been delivered.

"You comin' out wit me tonight, Martha?" Ike asked over his shoulder.

"Not if you was the last man in the world!"

Ike ran on the spot for five seconds.

"Scramble one on a muffin, to go. Two eggs up, cremate the bacon!" Joy boomed.

Henderson tensed. Three orders at once; Ike and Martha were still shouting at each other. The juice came. About—it seemed—thirty seconds later his eggs were in front of him. Two poached, three perfect crisp rashers, a bagel and lox. He sighed and looked up. Ike was drinking icewater.

"Don't get a breakfast like that in England, do you, Mr. Dores?" Martha asked.

Henderson had to concede the rightness of this remark. The last time he'd ordered a cooked breakfast in

England, the egg yolk had nestled in a halo of transparent albumen, the grease in the fried bread had furred up his palate for several hours and he had been unable to remove the barklike rind from the floppy bacon.

The thought of England subdued him. He ate his breakfast quickly, silently resolving to make his peace with Irene before he picked up his hired car. Perhaps she could fly down and meet him later? He'd suggest it to her, make up some story about a colleague coming in the car at the last moment.

Outside, he stood for a while on the pavement. The sun shone, but it was cooler today after the rain. He breathed deeply, flexed his shoulders and summoned a cab from the slow-moving stream of traffic. He got in and sat back on the wide seat. He was beginning to feel slightly better. The city in the morning always had that effect on him. The cab took him smoothly across town to Irene's apartment on the upper West Side.

Once there, he paced up and down for a moment or two rehearsing his apology before attempting to step into the lobby. Irene's apartment was in an old brownstone that had been extensively renovated inside. There were heavy plate-glass doors at the entrance, through which he could see an expanse of tiled flooring leading to a stainless-steel lift. A small man sat at a kind of lectern to one side.

The heavy glass doors would not open. Henderson pressed the buzzer beneath a loudspeaker built into the wall.

"Yeah?" The little man spoke into a microphone at the side of the lectern.

"I've come to see Ms. Irene Stein."

"She expecting you?"

"Well, not exactly . . ."

"Name?"

"Dores."

The man pressed some buttons on the console in front of him and spoke—inaudibly to Henderson—into the microphone.

"She's not in."

Henderson pressed the entryphone button again. He detested these machines.

"Could I speak to her, please?"

The little man ignored him. Henderson rapped loudly on the thick glass, hurting his knuckles. Wearily, the man got off his stool and approached the doors. Henderson recognized him. A small Slavonic-looking fellow with a waxy, heavily pored skin. He had one of the most negligible foreheads Henderson had ever seen: his hairline began an inch above his eyebrows. On his nylon blazer was pinned a badge. A. BRA. This was Adolf Bra, Irene's doorman.

By leaning his weight against one door, a half-inch gap could be created. Bra approached.

"Could I speak with Ms. Stein?" Henderson repeated firmly. Speak "with," he thought. Good God.

"Ms. Stein is not within her domicile."

For some reason this pedantry made Henderson even angrier.

"Did you learn that at doorman school? Look, you know me. And I saw you speaking to her, for Christ's sake. I just want a word."

Bra looked at his fingers. With the edge of one thumbnail he slid something from beneath the other.

"I told you. Ms. Stein is not within—"

"Her domicile. I know." Henderson forced a smile. "I don't believe you. I'm a friend of Ms. Stein. If you can't let me speak to her I shall report you to—" He couldn't think to whom. "I shall report you."

Bra waggled his forefinger and leaned toward the gap. Reflexively, Henderson did the same.

"Go suck your cock," Bra breathed. His breath had a pungent, pickled odor, as if he lived exclusively on a diet of capers.

Henderson recoiled, too surprised and nauseated to retort. If he had had his saber he would have driven it through the gap in the door and skewered Bra's narrow body.

"You'll regret this!" he shouted. He should have sworn as colorfully back at Bra, he realized seconds later, but he felt he had already made something of a fool of himself, a capital crime in the Englishman's book. Reverting to type, he gathered what he could of his dignity around him and smiled pityingly at Bra, now back behind his lectern. Common little man, he said to himself. Serf. Nation of peasants, what do you expect? Diet of turnips and liverwurst. Vitamin deficiency, rickets, inbreeding. Subnormal, subhuman . . . He checked himself, feeling suddenly ashamed. He'd have him in the gas chambers next. The man was only doing his job—albeit uncourteously; there was no need for such poisonous hatred.

He walked up the street until he found a phone, inserted a dime and prodded out Irene's number.

"Hi there, this is Irene. I'm really sorry I'm not in right now—"

Answering machine. It was like trying to see the President.

"—promise I'll get back to you. *Beeee.*"

Henderson wanted to say he was sorry, explain everything, categorize his emotions.

"Irene. This is Henderson. . . . I'll phone tomorrow."
He hung up. His voice had sounded stilted, pompous.
She'd never phone back someone who spoke like that. . . .
He stood alone on the street, balked, frustrated, all his
good intentions stymied and snookered. What more could
he do? There was nothing for it but to hire the car, collect
Bryant and head south.

part two

THE SOUTH

chapter one

HENDERSON hired his car. He had asked for a medium-sized model, yet what he got was bigger than anything on the roads in Britain. The girl at the rental agency assured him that this was the standard size. They had larger cars if he wanted one. He said no.

In the car the hood seemed to stretch ahead like the flight deck of an aircraft carrier. He slotted the gear into drive, touched the accelerator and felt the car pull strongly away. He couldn't hear the noise of the engine. The power steering, he discovered, allowed him to maneuver with two fingers. The thought of barreling down the freeways in this behemoth suddenly sent a tremor of boyish excitement through his body, displacing his gloom and disappointment. God, this is *fun*, he thought as he surged up the ramp from the underground car park; it's like some sort of massive toy.

By the time he had driven home, collected his suitcase and then driven uptown to Melissa's apartment, the steely-blue car had lost the glass from a taillight, acquired a scratch running the length of one side and received a dent in the left-hand front fender. Furthermore, on the course of his journey he had been described as a cunt, a fuckhead, a jiveass honkie, a sackashit and a muthafuckah by the other snarling drivers he had fouled up or interfered with in some way or other. Pedestrians—meek, timid creatures in Britain—had kicked his tires and thumped the bodywork with their fists. One particularly irate jaywalker went so far as to gob—greenly and with astonishing volume—on his windscreen. He managed to park not too far from Melissa's door but sat still in his car for five minutes or so (windscreen wipers going) trying to regain his composure.

Melissa welcomed him at the door, Candice yapping in her armpit.

"Hello, darling." Their cheeks touched; he felt her hair sharp on his face.

"Candice, don't shout at Henderson."

They went through into the main room. Gervase joined in the shrill noise. He thought: If we ever get married again, those dogs are out—pronto.

"She's just packing her things. Won't be a second." Melissa sat down beside him on the enormous sofa and took his hand.

"Are you OK, baby? You look tired."

Henderson told her of his troubled night—postmugging—of the garbage men and their matutinal seminar group. Melissa looked genuinely sympathetic. She put her hand on the back of his neck and scratched his nape gently. It was an automatic gesture; Henderson recalled it from their early days; it brought him out in a warm rush of affectionate goose pimples.

"The sooner we get you installed here the better," she said.

He felt grateful and secure. Melissa had things under control. He was suddenly certain he would be happy with her. He put his hand on her shoulder: so thin, so neat. The silk of the *eau de Nil* blouse was cool under his palm. He felt the thin strap of her bra. It would be silk too, he knew: crisp and clean on that day, with a discreet and pretty edging of lace.

"I can't wait," he said, with a slight tremble of sincerity in his voice, and touched her neck with his lips. This was a mistake, he realized at once, remembering how she sprayed her neck liberally with perfume. He sat up, his mouth full of a sour foreign taste.

"Could I have a drink of something?" he asked, swallowing acrid saliva. "Coke? Seven-Up?"

"Bryant, honey, can you get Henderson a Coke?"

"Why can't he get it himself?"

"Bryant!"

"It's all right," Henderson said. "No problem. I'll go."

He drank some water in the brilliant kitchen. When he came back, Melissa had gone somewhere, and Bryant was standing alone in the room.

"Well," he said. "Yes, whew . . . well."

Bryant looked at him as if he were slightly mad. She was wearing blue striped trousers that stopped at midcalf, a very old, faded gray T-shirt and an expensive-looking leather jacket, all pockets, flaps and buckles. Her hair was tousled and uncombed.

Spoiled brat, he thought. Those dogs wouldn't be the only inhabitants of the Wax household to get a rude awakening when he moved in. He put his hands in his pockets and looked around the room as if he were seeing it for the first time. This is absurd, he thought. She is a fourteen-year-old girl and I am a thirty-nine-year-old man. So why do I feel nervous? He stopped himself just in time from whistling "Nymphs and Shepherds." Bryant looked at him, apparently quite relaxed. It's true, he reflected; she *is* very cool and mature for a teenager. He thought of himself at her age: his awkward, boiling adolescence. His freezing fearful schooldays, the chasms of timidity, the deserts of anguish he had daily to traverse. No points of comparison there. What had been wrong with his education, his environment, his family? Think what torments he would have avoided if he had been like Bryant.

"Where's Irving?" he asked, with a gasp of relief, finally thinking of something to say.

"Don't know."

"Ah." Henderson nodded vigorously, spun around on his heel, slapped his pockets as if searching for a missing wallet. This was some traveling companion Melissa had foisted on him: he'd have more fun with a Trappist monk. He resolved to drive south with the greatest possible urgency.

Melissa came in with the two dogs and they prepared to leave. Bryant crouched down and embraced the animals.

"Bye, Candice. Bye, Gervase. Be good, I'll see you soon," she said in a fake-sad voice. For an instant Henderson saw the young girl in her.

"Phone me," Melissa said, hugging her daughter. "Lots. And you too," she whispered in Henderson's ear as she kissed his cheek. She glanced down. "Gervase, *stop it!*"

Henderson had imagined that the pressure on his lower leg had been caused by contact with the sofa edge, but looking down saw Gervase trying to fuck his ankle with slant-eyed, panting ferocity.

"Agh! Get off!" He sprang to one side, stamping the animal free from his leg. For the second time that day he wished he had his saber. *Flèche* attack: Pekingese kebab.

"I'll be back next week," Henderson said, turning back to Melissa. "I'll see you the—*Jesus Christ!*" The mutt had somehow gained the arm of the sofa and was trying to bury its head in Henderson's groin.

"What's wrong with that dog?" he demanded. "Shouldn't you have it seen to? Spayed or whatever?"

"Come on, Gervase. Don't be a naughty boy."

Bloody dogs! he swore to himself, picking up Bryant's case and backing out of the door.

"Bye, Gervase! Bye, Candice! Bye, Mom!"

"Say goodbye, Gervase, Candice. Say goodbye to Bryant and Henderson."

The most sensible women could be reduced to idiots when it came to animals, Henderson thought, contenting himself with a brief wave. There was not the slightest possibility of his actually vocalizing a farewell to those dogs, he vowed. He'd never be able to meet his eyes in the mirror again.

They hummed down in the lift, the faint barking soon lost to earshot, and with little fuss installed themselves in the car.

"Well," Henderson said, hands on the wheel. "Here we are. Go south, young lady." He looked around to see if she had caught the allusion, but Bryant was too preoccupied searching her multitude of pockets for something. She found it, and turned to face him, blowing hair out of her eyes.

"Smoke?" she asked, offering him a squashed soft-pack of cigarettes.

The Lincoln Tunnel plunged them beneath the Hudson River. They emerged on the far bank to drive through Union City to the mighty overlapping cloverleafs of Interchange 17 of the New Jersey Turnpike. Bryant was on to her third cigarette and Henderson saw the road ahead through a thin gray mist. His eyes smarted and his nose itched with incipient sneezes. Bryant sat with her legs folded beneath her, her head propped on a fist, looking emptily at the shabby cityscape passing by.

They motored south among a surge of large, surprisingly dusty and battered cars and truly enormous lorries, all changing lanes and shifting about the road—as fidgety and illogical as a school of fish. As Henderson became used to the eccentric driving conditions (so different from the impeccable lane adherence on British motorways) his initial tension was slowly replaced by irritation. Why hadn't he simply refused to take Bryant? Said it was impossible? It was typical, he saw, of his own particular weakness. He was too easily manipulated and put upon, too decent and obliging for his own good. He did everything Melissa asked of him and here was his reward: a rude, taciturn, chain-smoking ingrate as his traveling companion for the next two days. He was tempted to drive through the night to Richmond (home of the Wax grandparents) just to get rid of her. He felt a tear crawl from his left eye and squinted around to see Bryant lighting her fourth cigarette from the dashboard lighter. She lit the cigarette with the unreflecting professional ease of the habitual smoker, applying the little, glowing hotplate to the end with barely a glance, inhaling and puffing smoke from the corner of her mouth until the tobacco caught.

"You can get lung cancer from cigarettes, you know," he said.

"Sure. And emphysema and cardiac arrest and they kill cowboys. I know all that." She sat back and smiled for the first time. "It's a calculated risk. Don't you ever take risks, Henderson?"

"Not if I can help it," he said.
She looked at him. "No, I guess not."

They drove on through New Jersey. Sometimes the turnpike was raised high on stilts over a baleful marshy landscape, studded with small brown lakes and acres of tall
reeds. Here and there a huge concrete-and-glass power
station would rear up like an island, its cooling towers dis-
gorging steam, humming wires looping out from its hot
dynamos to feed the sprawling suburbs and distant cities—
Edison, Metuchen, Plainfield, Sayreville. Powerlines, he
saw, were everywhere. Electric cables had a prominence
and visibility in America that was wholly unlike the neater,
tidier Europe. Now he thought of the power stations as
vast mills, churning out their miles of cable to enmesh the
entire country with its warp and weft, cables that festooned every townscape and streetview, a great tangled
net of fallen rigging over the land, holding it together.
The effect was, he thought, to make everything appear
messier and half finished, ramshackle and run down. American streets and roads looked, to his eyes, unnecessarily
fussy, with wire and cable stretched all over the place.

There was generally, he saw, as he looked at the scene on
either side of the turnpike, more ironwork of all kinds in
evidence: from the gawky, teetering TV aerials to the criss-
cross cantilevers of the road signs, most of which looked in
need of a paint. In Britain, he thought, we maintain our street
furniture to an extraordinarily high degree; everything looks
new and neat on the roads. Gangs of men roamed the country
furiously repainting the white dashes of the lane dividers. He
thought of some of London's streets with their multitude of
lines and zigzags: double yellow or single, the various flashes

on the curbs, the grids and arrows. You needed a dictionary to park your car these days.

But here everything looked well used. The verges were dusty and ragged; where road ended and verge began was a matter of real ambiguity. In England edges were distinct. Curbstone production had never seen such boom years. Verges were sharp, and well defined: finished off, beaded, seamed. Sometimes in America you saw the same rectitude, but usually edges were frayed and worn. There was no manic energy expended in maintaining them.

So what? he thought later, suddenly bitter. Here energies were directed to making the important things work—like telephones, food production, heating and cooling—not dissipated in buffing up road signs or polishing cats' eyes. By their verges and street furniture shall ye know them. . . .

His somber mood continued to darken as they bypassed Philadelphia. He was getting thoroughly disenchanted with the belching smokestack in the front seat beside him. For the most part he drove in tight-lipped silence. He could be as sulky and withdrawn as any spoiled teenager, he told himself with quiet satisfaction: no trouble in descending to that level at all. He contented himself with looking at the scenery and pondering on its strangeness: all the houses made of wood; the astonishing number of playgrounds, tennis courts and baseball diamonds scattered generously about.

Unfortunately his ill humor seemed to make Bryant relax, as if it had been the very self-consciousness of the adult-child relationship that irked her. Now that he was being selfish too, she seemed to unwind. She switched on the radio for a while and sang quietly along to some of the pop songs. She proffered the odd remark: "Hey, look at that neat car!" or "I spent a weekend in Philadelphia one night."

Henderson confined his replies to monosyllables. Then she said: "Do you know that you have really quite a lot of hair growing out of your ears?"

Henderson did indeed know. It was one of the catalog of alarming body changes he'd been registering recently. He had rather too much hair growing out of his nostrils too, if it came to that, for his liking. He certainly didn't care to be reminded of it.

"These things happen, you know," he said. "As you grow older your body changes. It'll happen to you too," he observed with some relish. "Things will happen to your body when you're a mature woman that you won't be too pleased about."

"I'll have plastic surgery."

"Don't make me laugh."

She shrugged. "So how old are you, then?"

"Thirty-nine."

"Is that all?"

"What do you mean, 'Is that all?'"

"I don't know. I guess I thought you were older." She scratched at something on the dashboard. "I mean, Grandpa Wax has got hair in his ears too. You've almost got as much as him. I just figured you were, you know, older."

Henderson felt himself coloring. The nerve, he thought. The little bitch. He tried desperately to think of some way of getting his own back.

"We're staying at the Jefferson-Burr tonight, aren't we?" Bryant asked.

The Jefferson-Burr was one of Washington's grander hotels. If you hung out of certain bathroom windows you could glimpse the White House lawn. Melissa had booked two rooms.

"No," Henderson lied, revenge inspiring him. "It was full up."

"Oh. Where are we staying, then? The Hilton?"

"No, no. It's a little way off yet. I'll tell you when we get there."

chapter two

SKAGGSVILLE MOTOR HOTEL, a tatty billboard proclaimed at the side of Interstate 95, along which they now drove, NEXT EXIT.

"Here we are," Henderson said.

"You're kidding!"

"Best I could do at short notice."

The motor hotel stood in an expanse of crowded car park. It was long, three stories high and as functional as a toolbox. Henderson ordered Bryant to stay in the car while he "checked" their reservation.

The lobby was carpeted in a worn orange sunburst pattern, with matching curtains. Underfoot it felt vaguely adhesive. It was ideal. By the reception desk was a little notice board.

THE SKAGGSVILLE MOTO   HOT

WELCOMES

THE DELAWARE FIBERGLASS CURTAIN WALLI G CONVENTIO

"Welcome to the Scaggsville Motor Hotel," echoed a small plump receptionist. "Are you with the convention, sir?"

"Me?" Did he look like a fiberglass curtain-walling contractor? he wondered. "No, no. I just want a room for the night." He put down his credit card on the desk. "Two rooms."

She looked at a chart. "We don't have two rooms left, sir. The convention."

"Oh."

"I have a junior suite."

"What's that?"

"It's like an extra-large room with two double beds, some armchairs. Sorta like a suite but in one room."

He thought. What should he do? Press on?

"Your name, sir?"

"Dores. Look, I'll be back in a second."

He dashed outside to the car

"They've only got one room. A junior suite."

"What's wrong with that?"

He realized he was getting in a bit of a flap. Calm down, he told himself. He went back in. Bryant followed at her own pace. Henderson signed his name on a card, was given his key and told where he could find the room.

"Great," he said, a little worried. This wasn't quite how the revenge was meant to function. He turned. Bryant was looking at a mildewed picture of the Capitol hung on the plastic pine paneling.

"Enjoy your stay, Mr. and Mrs. Dores," caroled the friendly receptionist. Henderson whirled around in horrified protest, but the girl was on the phone. Good God, he thought, this is probably some sort of federal offense—crossing state lines with a minor masquerading as a wife.

Bryant looked at him through thin eyes.

The room was at the very end of a very long corridor. Outside the door was a mumbling drinks dispenser and an ice machine. They had a good view of the car park. The same orange sunburst pattern encountered in the lobby prevailed here too.

"This is it," he said. "Not too bad."

It looked lived in, certainly. By keeping his eyes restlessly on the move and never allowing them to settle for a second, he found it was just about possible to avoid noticing the many little rents and stains and cigarette burns, legacy of a thousand previous occupants.

There were, as promised, two double beds, and a pale-green, three-piece plastic suite with the bonus of a baby's cot in one corner. Henderson looked in vain for a shred of natural fiber or piece of wood. Perhaps that was why the curtain-wallers had their convention here—they felt at home.

"I've seen worse," Bryant said, not nearly as put out as she should be. She turned and looked at him.

"Let me get one thing straight," she said. "This 'Mr. and Mrs.' business. You're not going to try and fuck me, are you?"

"Good God, *no*! I wouldn't dream . . . How dare you . . . A simple error on the part of—"

"Relax," she said. She was beginning to sound like Teagarden. Henderson mopped his burning face, aghast at the obscenity of the notion.

Bryant threw her jacket on the bed. "Just checking."

They ate in the hotel dining room at half past seven. It was full of large men rather uncomfortably and self-consciously dressed for "business" in suits and ties. Henderson ordered a steak, which overlapped his plate by a good inch on either side. Bryant had a vegetarian salad and three cigarettes.

Henderson managed about eight square inches of his steak and pushed it aside. He felt strangely depressed, which he put down to having been in Bryant's company for most of a day. This didn't bode well for the marriage. He sighed, and thought about tomorrow. He wondered when they would get to Atlanta. Beeby had phoned Gage to let him know Henderson was on his way. They would make an early start in the morning, get Bryant dropped off as soon as possible . . . He looked around the dismal dining room, suddenly missing New York. He wished he were staying at the Jefferson-Burr, instead of this anonymous hotel. Too clever by half, he considered ruefully. This was what happened when he tried to be malicious or cunning: he ended up inconveniencing himself. He was condemned to remain ineffectual, tolerant and nice.

Bryant tipped saccharin into her Sanka.

"What exactly are you supposed to be doing on this trip?" she asked.

Henderson told her about the Gage collection, its significance, what he had to do when he saw the paintings.

"Where does he live, this old guy?"

"Somewhere called Luxora Beach."

"Are you going there?"

"Later. I'll get directions in Atlanta."

"Are you staying with him?"

"No. I'll probably stay in a local hotel."

"Could I come?"

"*What!?*"

"Can't I come with you? I've never been to the real South."

"Absolutely out of the question."

"Come *on*, Henderson, I won't get in your way."

"Completely impossible."

"I just can't stand the thought of a week with Grandma and Grandpa. You don't know what they're like."

"Too bad."

"Plee-*ease*."

"No. No. *N, o.*"

"God!" She looked genuinely irritated. Touché, at last, he thought triumphantly, smiling to himself. She couldn't take being denied.

After dinner Bryant went back to the junior suite complaining of a headache. Henderson walked down another quarter-of-a-mile corridor to the bar. It was called The Barbary Coast but for the life of him he could see no thematic reflection of this motif in the place's wholly unremarkable decor. It was filled with grim curtain-wallers who were being entertained by a haggard country-and-western chanteuse seated at an electric organ on a small dais at the end of the room. Two bored waitresses in very short, beige, satin dresses ferried drinks to and fro.

Henderson sat at the bar, sipped at a large Scotch and thought about phoning Irene in an attempt to rebuild a few of the burned bridges. Unaccountably, as he sat and drank, he found himself getting more and more dejected and heavyhearted. He looked suspiciously at his whiskey. He felt an immense weariness of spirit descend on him, as if some deity had personally and unequivocally confirmed that all the follies and inexplicable cruelties of the world were man's lot, and that attempts to ameliorate them were utterly vain and futile.

He looked around him. The curtain-wallers' faces were slumped with a similar bitter wisdom. Was it something to do with the Scaggsville Motor Hotel itself? he asked himself. Some curse on the hapless building? Some maverick charge in its static electricity? He wondered if he had been drugged. . . . Then he realized what the source of the universal *tristesse* was.

The haggard chantense had a repertoire consisting solely of the most morose country-and-western numbers in the songbook. She set her Japanese electric organ (thin as an ironing board) to "plangent," and sang heartrendingly of suicide, abortion, adultery, desertion, mental and physical cruelty, alchoholism and terminal illness. Her own face, pale and scored beneath dyed blue-black hair, seemed to testify to firsthand experience of these various afflictions— but perhaps that was merely the side effect of singing that type of song each evening.

The tune she was currently playing seemed vaguely familiar; a recent or current hit, Henderson thought. He listened to a verse.

> *Each gnat she cooked me a fan dinner,*
> *Each gnat I throwed it on the floor,*
> *Then I took mysailf to town,*
> *Till the mornin' come aroun',*
> *Drinkin', gamblin' 'n' sleepin' with some whore.*

She switched to her machine to "soughing violins" for the chorus ("I was the happiest, meanest, full-time, signed-up sinner") but Henderson decided that he'd had as much as he could take.

He walked down the endless corridors feeling markedly more happy with every step he took away from the mournful saloon. Some convention, he thought. He had heard they were usually an excuse for a riotous booze-up. The curtain-wallers would return home to their wives shriven and repentant.

He let himself quietly into his room. The lights were out; Bryant seemed to be asleep. He went softly into the bathroom. The basin area was scattered with pots and tubes, grips and makeup. Long fair hairs clung tenaciously to the wet enamel.

He confirmed that the door was locked and took off his clothes. His body had a yellowish whiteness under the lights. He swiftly checked out the crisis areas. His nipples, once neat buttons beneath a shading of chest hair, had grown into wide, pink, coarse teats. Always rather hefty, he had never worried unduly about putting on weight: he ate and drank as he wished and carried the usual penalty padding as a result. But now he had critical weight loss: his buttocks were disappearing. They were shrinking. His trouser seats, usually stretched and shiny, were now loose and flapping. He turned sideways and looked in the mirror. A good kilt-wearing arse, a Scottish girlfriend had once complimented him. If he wore a kilt now its rear hem would hang inches lower than its front—be brushing the backs of his calves. And, talking about legs, his legs were going *bald*. Normally covered in a springy furze, his legs, from the knee down, had gone smooth and shiny. And yet all this extra hair was sprouting from his ears and nostrils. . . . He wondered if some back-street trichologist would transplant his nasal and aural growth, resow it on the desert slopes of his shins.

He stepped into the shower. For getting on for thirty years he'd never considered his body. It did its job; it looked fair enough; its distribution of muscle and hair was unexceptionable. But now it was saying, "Hold on a moment," "Hang about, friend." It was getting tired of staying in shape; it was getting clapped out; the first signs of four decades of wear and tear were manifesting themselves. It was getting old.

He plunged his head beneath the powerful jet of the shower, trying to forget. Even in the crummiest motel you got a decent shower. He remembered the shower he had had installed in his London flat. It had a weak, two-inch spread. It pattered feebly on one shoulder when you stood beneath it; it took five minutes to dampen your hair. Getting the temperature right required meticulous hair-fine adjustments of the taps—you needed the touch of a safecracker.

After he had dried himself he wondered what to do about getting into bed. He normally slept naked but realized that, tonight, probity demanded he make a change. He pulled on his underpants and stepped quietly into the bedroom.

Bryant sat up in bed smoking, her bedside lamp on. She was wearing pale-blue cotton pajamas, monogrammed B.W. Henderson stood there, suddenly conscious of the crammed codpiece of his Y-fronts, his hairless legs, his fat nipples. He slid into his bed between the crackling nylon sheets.

"You shouldn't smoke in bed, you know," he grumbled. "With the static in this place we could be vaporized in a white flash."

Bryant ignored him.

"And you left the bathroom in a mess."

"Mom wants you to call her. I phoned while you were out."

"Oh. Right." He felt pleased. He prodded New York. As he was waiting for Melissa to answer, Bryant leaned forward to stub out her cigarette. As she stretched for the ashtray he got a clear view down the front of her pajama top. Her small firm breasts with small, odd, domed nipples. He felt embarrassment and shock clog his throat.

Melissa answered.

"Melissa? It's Henderson." His mind skittered about. My God, he thought, my hands are shaking.

"Henderson, darling, thank you. It's so kind of you. I really want you to know that I appreciate it, darling. I really do."

"Don't mention it." So American: all this sincere gratitude for a returned call.

"Are you sure it's not inconvenient?"

"No, no. Not at all. Quite the opposite."

"God, you are wonderful. I'd forgotten. You lovely man, you. There aren't many men who'd do this, I know. I want you back here quickly."

Doubt began to seep through his body.

"Well, it's not much—"

"Modesty. Come *on*, Mr. Englishman. I love it! No, darling, I just wanted to tell you myself that I think it's so kind of you to ask her. And you know it'll be interesting for her too: see you at work, learn about—"

His scalp crawled with a horrible sick alarm as he suddenly realized what she was talking about. Melissa nattered on about how she'd phoned Grandma Wax and explained the new plans. Henderson turned and looked at Bryant. She had snuggled down in her bed and was smiling innocently at him. He felt a rush of loathing for this premature adult as he muttered assurances into the phone. He said goodbye.

"That is one of the most scheming, most disgraceful acts of . . . *lying* I have ever witnessed," he began, his voice shaking with rage.

"God, Henderson, I won't get in the way."

"I don't care. It's pure bloody selfishness."

"What's so selfish? Why can't I come? I won't get in the way. You're the selfish one. You don't want me to come. Why not? What's so wrong with me being there?" Her tone was injured, a wronged child's voice full of that hectoring self-righteousness that appears when children know they've got an adult on the run.

He ranted on for a while, but he knew it was too late now. What was worse, he knew *she* knew.

"I can't understand why you're so fired up," she said with arch, false innocence. "Look how pleased Mom was. Don't you think that's nice?"

She was right, but he didn't admit it. Perhaps it was a sign: that he should concentrate on Melissa, forget Irene . . .

He lay awake for hours, itchy between the nylon sheets of the Scaggsville Motor Hotel. He ran through the burgeoning options that had suddenly appeared in his life. The road ahead had seemed so straight and sure; now he faced a fan of avenues. He fretfully pondered the alternatives as the cold-drinks dispenser shuddered dismally outside his door and the ice machine's thin lonely rattle punctuated the very slow progress of the night.

chapter three

INTERSTATE 85 carried them safely through the Carolinas. The weather had grown steadily warmer as they drove south. Now, in Georgia, the late-afternoon sun burned down from a clear blue sky and Henderson switched on the air conditioning in the car. They motored along, windows up, in a chill cell. Outside the country was—to his eyes—surprisingly, but monotonously, wooded, with a tough-looking breed of average-sized pine predominant. The highway cut straight through this consistent greenery, the only variation coming with the thin towering signs of the gas stations, roadside motels and supermarkets at intersections. HOLIDAY INN, OMELETTE SHOPPE, COWBOY BARBECUE, BI-LO, STARVIN' MARVIN, FOOD GIANT, STEAK & ALE, WIFE SAVER. These signs, a hundred feet high, like enormous swizzle sticks, loomed over the forest.

On the drive south from Skaggsville, Henderson had remained terse, resolutely maintaining his anger. But Bryant seemed not to care: indeed, she was almost cheerful, singing along or beating out a rhythm to the songs—now exclusively country and western—that came over the radio. Henderson had traversed every wave band in fruitless search for music that wasn't gravid with sentiment, but in vain. The only alternatives were religious stations offering prayer-ins, waterproof Bibles ("for poolside reading") or ghastly homilies.

"Don't you like country and western?" Bryant asked.

"I *loathe* it."

"I like it. It's sort of . . true."

"My God," Henderson said, "if that's your version of 'true' then I feel sorry for you."

"OK. So what's not true about them?" Bryant persisted.

"Look, I don't want to talk about it," Henderson said. "It's bad enough having to listen to that . . . that *pap*, without having to indulge in close reading of the lyrics."

Bryant shrugged, and found a new station. Henderson looked at her thin arm with its shine of blond hairs as she twiddled the dial. He felt edgy and uncomfortable beside her now. He was almost sure, moreover, that she wasn't wearing a bra. He wished devoutly that he hadn't caught a glimpse of her breasts last night. It was curious the changes it had wrought in his view of her: no longer a petulant minx whom, for the sake of her mother, he had to tolerate; the "glimpse" had introduced new ingredients into her personality—femininity, nubility . . . sex.

They saw Atlanta from a long way off, the towers of its downtown district silhouetted against the sinking sun, a few small, bruise-colored clouds dawdling above the city.

"We'd better phone now, I suppose," Henderson said.

"Do you think it's far away?"

"What?"

"Luxora Beach."

"Well, it's one hell of a drive to a coast, that's for sure." The same thought had occurred to him earlier.

"Maybe it's on a lake." She was looking at a road map. "There are a lot of lakes around here."

"Maybe."

They pulled off the freeway at the next junction. Henderson found a phone booth while Bryant went in search of a "comfort station," whatever that was.

He tapped out the number Beeby had given him. It rang for a very long time and he was just about to hang up when a woman answered.

"Yeah?"

"May I speak to—with—Mr. Loomis Gage."

"What?"

"Loomis Gage. May I speak—"

"What?"

Jesus Christ. "Loo-mis. Gage."

He heard her shout someone's name. Through the phone came a faint noise of a television set, then a man's voice.

"Yeah? Who is it?"

"Mr. Gage? Mr. Loomis Gage?"

"No. Who are you?"

"My name is Dores. From Mulholland, Melhuish—New York. I'd like to speak to Mr. Loomis Gage."

He had to repeat this three times; the man seemed to be some sort of imbecile.

"Oh, yeah." Then suspiciously, "Oh, *yeah*. . . . Don't hang up."

Henderson fed more money into the phone. The man came back.

"You was expected this morning."

"There must be some mistake."

"Beckman's been waiting in Atlanta all day."

"I couldn't have got here any sooner, I'm sorry."

"Well, he'll be at the corner of Peachtree Street and Edgewood on the hour. Can you make it for six?"

"I think so."

"He'll look after you."

This is preposterous, Henderson thought. "What does he look like?"

"Thin, kinda long fair hair."

The man hung up.

Henderson realized his palms were sweating. He suddenly felt a bit fearful. The setup was so weird; mad, even. He thought of his usual valuation trips: a pleasant weekend in some sumptuous house; civilized, cultured talk about art. Christ only knew what Beeby had landed him in. He began to wish that he'd let Ian Toothe come in his place; it certainly would have saved him a lot of problems.

Bryant returned from her comfort station.

"So what happens?" she asked.

"We've got to meet a man called Beckman at a street corner in Atlanta."

"Sounds good." Her eyes widened. "What then?"

"I'm not absolutely sure."

They drove down the extreme length of Peachtree Street. Atlanta seemed halfway through some sort of massive redevelopment program: crumbling facades on old buildings gave way to empty brick-strewn lots, then some spanking new skyscraper surged up from a multilevel piazza with thickets of trees and gurgling fountains and fishponds. As they got near the city center the buildings grew higher and more impressive: vast circular hotels, mirror-glass cliffs dominating small landscaped parks and squares.

The streets seemed oddly quiet, in strong contrast to New York at this hour. They were a little early for their rendezvous—only three blacks lounged at the corner of Peachtree and Edgewood—so they parked the car and wandered around for a while. They went into a concrete cave and took an escalator deep down into the earth. At the bottom they emerged into the immaculate concourse of a vast subway station, clean, shiny and vacant. A couple of ticket collectors looked curiously at them.

"Where is everybody?" Bryant whispered. "It's like being in the future."

They went back up. A very thin white man with straggling long blond hair twitched and shimmied on the corner, looking edgily at the blacks.

"Mr. Beckman?" Henderson said.

The man whirled around in alarm, arm raised as if to ward off a blow. Henderson leaped back.

"At fuckin' last," the man said. "I've been waiting here six fuckin' hours."

"I explained—"

"You got a car?" He had a thin, lined face. A narrow palate with soft overcrowded teeth.

"Yes."

"I'm in that pickup." He pointed to a blue pickup with large fat wheels and gleaming chrome. "Follow me."

Henderson followed the pickup through Atlanta's suburbs. Soon they were on another freeway. He saw signs for Anniston and Birmingham. They were driving west. He wondered if they were going to Alabama. He suddenly wished he were back in his apartment in New York, or strolling down to the Queensboro gym for a saber bout with Teagarden. Bryant stared fixedly at the pickup ahead.

"Wow, is that guy weird. Did you see his eyes?"

"I wasn't looking at his eyes. Did you see his teeth?"

"He kept blinking all the time, like he had grit in them."

They drove west for an hour or so, then turned off at a town called Villa Rica. From there they followed a succession of two-lane country roads. It grew darker. Henderson switched on his headlights. They drove through tiny townships—Draketown, Felton. Bryant pored over the map.

"Any idea where we are?" Henderson asked.

"No. I'm kinda lost."

"Are we in Alabama or Georgia?"

"What difference does it make?"

"I don't know."

They drove on. Bryant switched on the radio.

". . .terminally ill. And he said to me, 'Father, what will heaven be like?'" The voice was deep and mellifluous.

"Oh, *no*," Bryant said disgustedly, reaching out.

"Leave it on a second," Henderson said, horrified.

"And I could not answer the man, dear friends, that . . . terminally ill man. What is heaven like? I had no reply in his hour of need. Just then my dog, Patch, who I had left in the car outside, somehow managed to get out and came running into this man's house to look for me. I heard him scratch on the door. I opened it and let him in. And then, friends, I knew. So I said to this . . . terminally ill man, 'Sir,' I said, 'heaven is like this room. Patch has never been in this house before but he entered this room with absolute trust and confidence and without fear. Why? Because he knew that I, his master, was inside. So you too may go to the Lord and scratch on the door of heaven with trust and confidence and no fear. We do not know what is in the "room" of heaven, but we know that God is there and we need have no fear of joining Him inside.' Good night, everybody. Tune in next week on WNBK in Tallapoosa for the *Sunday Sermonette*. This is the Reverend T. J. Cardew. God bless you all. Amen."

"Good grief," Henderson said.

"Can we find some music? This is boring."

Eventually, after another half hour's driving they saw a sign: WELCOME TO LUXORA BEACH. Then another: LIONS CLUB OF LUXORA BEACH WELCOMES YOU. Finally: LUXORA BEACH CITY LIMIT. POP. 1,079.

By now it was quite dark. They drove by single-story wooden houses on either side of the road, then into an area of street lighting. It revealed a narrow main street flanked on one side by a railway line. Beyond the railway line was a wide tarmacked area fronting a shabby row of flat-fronted, flat-roofed stores. Henderson read LUXORA BEACH DRUGS above a dark window. All the windows were dark except for one bar. The red neon bow tie of a Budweiser sign and the blue rosette of the Pabst logo set pretty highlights on the mat dusty cars parked outside.

Beckman's pickup turned and bumped across the railway line. Henderson followed suit.

"Wrong side of the tracks," he said with a nervous chuckle.

They left the paved road and drove along a winding dirt lane with—from what he could see through the dust Beckman's wheels drew up—scrubby undergrowth on either side.

Presently they passed through rickety wooden gates and beneath a wrought-iron arch with THE GAGE MANSION written on it in dirty white scrollwork. In front of them in the faint moonlight, Henderson could make out the bulk of a rather large house ahead. The drive swept them around in a generous semicircle. The headlights picked out small groups of tall trees, which seemed strategically placed to aid some landscaped composition. Lights shone from a few windows.

The pickup stopped. Henderson stopped. He looked

at Bryant, who returned his nonplussed stare. For the briefest of moments they seemed allies. He stepped out of the car. In front of the house was an immense double-wide mobile home made of ribbed aluminum and some sort of plastic wood veneer. Power lines hung between it and the house. Looking back Henderson saw that the drive formed a perfect circle. He moved away from the car in an effort to gain some better conception of the architecture, but it was too dark. It was, he thought, of little consequence anyway. Even the finest building would have been vitiated by the hideous adjacency of the mobile home. He wondered why it was there.

"He's inside," Beckman shouted from the pickup and drove off around the drive and back out of the gates again.

Inside the house or the trailer? Henderson asked himself. He removed their cases from the car.

Bryant was peering in a curtained porthole punched through the ribbed aluminum.

"There's people inside," she said.

There was a call from the house. "Mr. Melhuish, is that you?"

"Oh, God," Henderson said weakly. "Let's go."

He and Bryant climbed up a dozen or so steps to a wide wooden veranda that appeared to circle the house. A small man stood outside double front doors.

"Mr. Melhuish," he said, and shook Henderson's hand vigorously. "A pleasure to meet you, a real pleasure. I'm Loomis Gage."

"My name is Dores," Henderson said apologetically. "Didn't Mr. Beeby explain I was to come?"

The small man laughed cheerfully.

"Dores, Melhuish. Who gives a rat's rump? It's all the same to me. Come on in."

They stepped through the doors into the hall to be

112

greeted by a considerable blare of noise. From somewhere above them came the thump and twang of rock music, and from a room on the right a television boomed.

"This is my stepdaughter!" Henderson said, obliged to raise his voice. "Bryant Wax! Stepdaughter-to-be, that is!"

Bryant looked around her with mild curiosity. "Hi," she said.

"You do business with your family?" Gage shouted back.

"Well . . !"

"I like that!"

"What?!"

"I said, I like that!"

"Rarely!"

"Excuse me one moment!" Gage took some steps up the stairs.

"Turn that damn music down!" he roared. He paused, ear cocked. The volume was reduced. He descended and opened the door of the room that contained the TV. It was quite dark, apart from the bright colors on the screen. Gage turned the noise off but left the picture flickering. He switched some lights on.

"That's better," he said. Loomis Gage was small and plump, and clearly very old, though he seemed sprightly enough. His face had its full quota of tucks and dewlaps and his eyes were watery. Yet he had a shock of pure white hair, as dense and springy as a teenager's, which seemed at odds with his advancing years. His nose was noticeably snub too, Henderson saw, and thought it a curiously indecent feature on a man as venerable as this. Gage wore a short-sleeved yellow sport shirt and khaki trousers. His neat potbelly pushed against an engraved silver buckle the size of a side plate.

"Please sit down," he said. "You too, Brian."

"T," said Bryant. "Bryantuh."

"You're a girl, aren't you?"

"Of course."

"I knew it." He glanced proudly at Henderson. "I may be an old man but I can still recognize a female—even if they've got men's names."

Henderson looked around. No pictures on the walls. The room was large and wood paneled. Twin ceiling fans stirred the warm night air. The furniture was old, worn but comfortable looking. Nowhere was there any sign of ostentatious wealth. He felt a brief twinge of unease.

Bryant was engrossed in the silent TV.

"Can I offer you a drink, Mr. Dores? Bourbon, martini?"

"A beer would be very welcome."

"'A beer would be very welcome,'" Gage chuckled to himself. "I like that." He pressed a bell push on the wall.

"So you're the man who thinks he can sell my paintings for me." He looked Henderson up and down. "How old are you?"

Why was there so much speculation about his age these days? "Thirty-nine," he said. He heard a car pull up outside.

"Thirty-nine," Gage repeated. "How old do you think I am?"

"Sixty-five?" Henderson guessed, and was rewarded with a bleat of sardonic laughter.

"I'm as old as the century, my boy. But I'm as healthy as my sons. Hell, I'm healthier."

Henderson didn't know what to say.

The door opened and a dark, big man came in. He wore a tight, embroidered denim suit and had a scalloped warlock's beard.

"Sorry, Dad. Didn't know you had company."

"Come on in. This is Mr. Dores. His daughter, Bryant. This is my son, Freeborn."

"Very pleased to know you, sir," he said sincerely to Henderson, shaking him vehemently by the hand. "And you, Miss Dores." He took some paces backward. "If you-all will just excuse me I won't derange you further."

He had glossy, springy hair like his father, Henderson saw, except it was black. He looked like a professional wrestler or an amusement arcade proprietor: someone on the very fringes of the entertainment business. He had heavy gold-colored rings on several fingers. He smiled at everybody and left.

A dull-looking middle-aged woman came in. She looked tired and hostile.

"Alma-May," Gage said, "will you make up Cora's old room for Mr. Dores' daughter? We have an extra guest."

"What?" The outrage was genuine. "No way!"

"Alma . . ."

"God sakes." Muttering, she left.

"Don't go to any trouble," Henderson said quickly. "We were planning to stay in a hotel."

"Well, abandon your plans, Mr. Dores. I won't hear of it. Damn. Forgot to ask her to bring your beer. I'd better get it myself." He went out through a door at the far end of the room. Outside, Henderson heard Alma-May's voice raised in passionate argument.

"Now see what you've done," he said accusingly at Bryant, but she ignored him.

"Mr. Dores?"

He looked around. Freeborn's bearded face smiled at him from the doorway.

"May I have a word, sir? If it's not too much trouble. In private."

"Of course."

Henderson followed him out through the front door onto the porch. Freeborn, he noted, was not only large and tall but also very fat. But it was all held roughly in place by the strength and tightness of his shirt and trousers.

Freeborn smiled and scratched his beard. At last, Henderson thought, somebody sane.

"Excuse me asking, sir, but am I right in thinking you are the man from the New York auctioneers which wants to sell my daddy's paintings?"

So there *were* paintings. "Yes, that's right," Henderson said amiably. "We have the privilege to—"

"I think, to be fair, that I should inform you of a certain fact which has a bearing on your business."

"What's that?"

"That if you don't get your fuckin' ass out of this house by noon tomorrow I'm gonna bust your fuckin' head with it." His voice was still reasonable, the smile still in place.

Henderson felt something slip and slide in his intestines.

"Look here—"

"You gonna be one sorry fucker if you ain't gone. Know what I mean? Sorry."

Henderson nodded. Freeborn patted his shoulder.

"You got the idea. Nice meeting you, Mr. Dores."

Henderson stood alone for a couple minutes breathing very shallowly in an attempt to restrain the trembling that suffused his body. The last time anyone had threatened him such a direct, virulent and intimate way had been at prep school. Nothing in his experience as an adult had prepared him for such seemingly disinterested aggression.

He walked carefully back inside. Gage and Bryant sat side by side on a couch watching TV.

"There's your beer," Gage said, unconcerned by his absence. "Relax. We'll talk business in the morning."

Henderson sat down docilely and sipped his beer. His head seemed to be full of clamoring voices all shouting competing instructions and plans of action. This must be what it's like for Ike on a busy morning in the diner, he thought aimlessly, feeling a new admiration for the man's expertise. . . . He concentrated. Should he tell Gage of his son's unprovoked menace and threat? But how could he? He'd barely been in the Gage Mansion for five minutes. "Excuse me, Mr. Gage, but your son says he's going to bust my head with my ass." No, it wasn't on. He had to speak to Beeby, that was what, and at once.

"Mr. Gage? Could I make a phone call?"

"I'm afraid I won't have a telephone in my house. But Freeborn has one in his trailer. He won't mind."

"It's quite all right," Henderson said. "Hate to disturb him. Not important."

He sat on wordlessly with Gage and Bryant, trying to concentrate on the television. Within minutes he was totally lost, as the program—a love story, he surmised—elided confusingly with the commercials every two minutes, it seemed. More confusingly, the same people—or astonishing lookalikes—appeared to be acting in both. Soap flakes, shampoo, dog food, then the young couple were meeting in a bar; they seemed happy. They were joined by young happy friends . . . but that turned out to be an extended beer advertisement. He wondered distractedly if the young woman and the dog had been part of a commercial after all. He tried to recollect the upshot of the scene he had witnessed: was she happy or sad as she walked through the woods with her canine friend? Suddenly a fat man was sitting on the hood of a car and making fantastical guarantees. Henderson's brain reeled. He thought he glimpsed the young lovers again but they were still selling beer. Eventually he saw the credits roll and he knew that it was over, whatever it had been. He hoped they were happy. He sat back exhausted, his brow aching dully from the constant frown he had been wearing.

A woman of incandescent beauty announced that she would read the *World and National News*.

"Mrs. Nazarine Kilgus, Furse County assessor, announced today that the annual How's Your Health Fair will be held next month at the Olar National Guard Armory in Olar. Mrs. Kilgus said that everything would be free, except for an optional blood test, which will cost eight dollars."

An hour later, halfway into a movie—this, Henderson had managed to follow—Gage stood up and switched off the TV.

"Shuteye at the Ranchero Gage," he announced and rang the bell for Alma-May. She didn't appear, so Gage himself led them upstairs. He ran briskly up to the top landing and stood there waiting for them.

"Not even out of breath."

"Most impressive," Henderson said.

They walked along a passageway toward the rear of the house. As they passed one door they heard rock music thumping away. Gage beat fiercely on this and shouted, "Shut that noise up now!" It died away to a muffled throb, like the distant pulse of a generator.

"I loathe and despise that modern music," Gage said. "Which is why I have the television on so loud. I'd rather hear mindless babble than that garbage he listens to."

Gage opened a door. "Bathroom. He, by the way, is Duane, Alma-May's boy. Beckman sleeps up at the front.

Cora and I are opposite you on the other side. Freeborn and Shanda have their trailer. Alma-May has her annex behind the kitchen." He paused. "One other thing I should tell you. We're vegetarians here. So no meat or fish in our diet."

"Fine," Henderson nodded.

"Good," Bryant said.

Bryant was shown to her room and was bidden good night.

"Everything OK?" Henderson asked her.

"What do you mean?"

"Nothing, nothing." He hurried on to his own room. At the door Gage shook his hand solemnly.

"Breakfast is very informal, Mr. Dores. Show up when you've a mind and help yourself. We'll talk in the morning."

Henderson watched him go, wondering if he'd missed his best opportunity to inform on the alarming Freeborn. He felt strange and frightened, suddenly out of his depth. He went into his room and sat down on the bed.

Once, on holiday in the Mediterranean, he'd been sailing alone in a dinghy a mile or so away from the beach. Beneath him had been bright, clear, turquoise water, with the odd dark patch of rock or weed sometimes visible on the sand floor a few fathoms below the keel. And then he'd sailed over the edge of the continental shelf, or some great chasm in the sea bed, and the sparkling turquoise had given way to a dense, cold, inky blue. The little boat sailed on as before, the sun's heat on his shoulders was unfaltering, but at that instant he felt like screaming. All those black miles of water beneath him, pale things swimming there. He turned back at once. He had a horrible fear of depths. . . .

He pulled back the coverlet on his bed and noticed

with a spasm of irritation that it was unmade. He saw the folded sheets resting on a chair in the corner. This Alma-May person, he reasoned, was clearly some kind of housekeeper, so why didn't she keep house? Angrily he made up the bed. Even without Freeborn's unprovoked venom he would have needed no encouragement to leave this bizarre household at the earliest opportunity. Tomorrow he and Bryant would check into the nearest hotel—nearest decent hotel—Gage's objections notwithstanding, and take things from there. At least, also, he'd be obeying the letter of Freeborn's injunction if not the spirit.

Somewhat composed, he opened the long floor-to-ceiling windows at one end of the room and saw that a smaller balcony ringed the house on this upper level too. He stepped out, leaned against a pillar and gazed at the dark countryside. He could hear Duane's rock music faintly, carried to him on a gentle breeze, then it stopped suddenly. In the darkness beyond, crickets kept up their monotonous creaking. A big moth fluttered heavily past him and into his lighted bedroom. He leaned out and looked up at the sky. The stars were there, reassuringly occupying their ordained places. A line of some half-forgotten poem came into his head. "The lines are straight and swift between the stars" or something. He felt slightly calmer out there in the open beneath their neutral light. He rested his hands on the balcony's balustrade and breathed deeply, wondering first how soon he could leave the house and second when he could encourage Bryant to return to the Wax grandparents.

He massaged his face. Perhaps the paintings would make the difference. He longed suddenly for the Mulholland, Melhuish office, the comforting bulwarks of his job, his routine, his colleagues. Out here he felt weak and unprotected, alien and unfamiliar. Freeborn had threatened to "bust his ass." Why, for God's sweet sake? What was he to Freeborn or Freeborn to him?

Panic and fear assailed him once again and he knew too—with a profound weariness—that sleep was out of the question this evening. The long march of the night lay ahead, the tossing and turning, the pillow punching and posture changing. He sighed, feeling a deep sympathy for himself, and turned back to his room.

The large moth—the size of a wren, it seemed to him—that had fluttered past him on the balcony was now clumsily attacking the ceiling light, casting a leaping giant shadow over the walls and bed. Henderson wondered what to do: whether to try fashioning a weapon big enough to deal it a mortal blow or pray it would fly away of its own accord. He was reluctant simply to swat this large and rather magnificent creature. He felt protective about but terflies and moths: they formed a select subclass of insects that he charitably spared from the normal ruthless pogroms he visited on the other members of their kind.

As he stood there impotently the moth settled obligingly on the wall near the ceiling. He stepped on the bed and cautiously pinched its clasped wings between thumb and forefinger. The moth's legs bicycled vainly in the air as he carried it gingerly to the window giving on to the balcony. But then, somehow, a wing came off and the moth dropped to the floor with a soft thud, its loose wing fluttering down like a leaf to join it moments later.

Henderson felt shocked. The moth flapped and scrabbled uselessly on the wooden floor, turning in tight circles. Henderson imagined a thin moth-scream of horror and pain. Spontaneously, he stood on the damaged insect, hearing a faint crunch—like standing on a cookie—before kicking the lifeless body out onto the balcony. He felt exhausted. The simplest acts—the most banal necessities and plans—seemed to bring in their train only absurd and trying consequences.

He undressed wearily, switched out the light and got into bed. He felt wide awake, his mind as active as a candidate's, sitting a crucial exam. He heard the dull bass of rock music start up again. Duane, Alma-May's son. How and why was his aural tyranny over the household tolerated? And who was Cora? What was he going to do with Bryant? Would Freeborn really bust his ass at noon tomorrow? Would the Gage collection solve Mulholland, Melhuish's problems? Was it likely that Irene would forgive him? And Melissa? These and other thoughts jostled and elbowed their way through his mind as he turned on the left, then on the right, lay supine, then prone, discarded his pillow, retrieved it, doubled it, weighted the bedclothes with dressing gown and quilt, kicked them off and somehow, at some time, found some minutes of repose.

chapter four

CAUTIOUSLY, Henderson entered the Gage kitchen the next morning. He felt bad: tired and irritated, but not so irritated as to welcome a confrontation with Freeborn. But there was no sign of him, or anyone else for that matter. This was a little surprising, as he had assumed that Bryant at least would be present as her room had been empty.

He poured himself a cup of coffee from a jug stewing on the cooker. Alma-May came in and nodded curtly in response to his "Good morning."

"Is Mr. Gage about?"

Alma-May indicated a letter propped on the breakfast table. It was addressed to Henderson, was from Loomis Gage and informed him that he could view the paintings that afternoon when he, Gage, returned from unspecified business matters.

Henderson realized that this delay would of course violate Freeborn's noon deadline; but surely, he reasoned, he could count on the protection of Gage senior? One thing was clear: he couldn't move to a hotel until he'd seen the paintings.

"Have you seen Bryant—Miss Wax—by any chance?"

"She done gone off with Beckman, early this morning."

"Good Lord. Where?" he asked with alarm. Melissa

would never forgive him if . . . He stopped. Alma-May's head had jerked around sharply at this invocation of the Good Lord's name.

"To Hamburg."

He felt suddenly weak, then realized this must be Hamburg, Georgia, or Hamburg, Alabama, or wherever.

"Why, may I ask?"

"To the labrotory. Beckman's lab."

This was getting out of hand.

"His labrotory—laboratory—in Hamburg?"

"You got it."

"I see. . . . And Mr. Freeborn? Is he . . .?"

"On the road."

And what does that mean? he thought.

"What does he do, on the road?"

"He sails."

"?"

"Sails things. Co-mercial traveler. Sails medical supplies. You know: lint, bandages, restraining straps. Got a line in mouthwashes, suppositories. That kind of thing."

"So it's just us alone in the house," he said with a fatuous little laugh that he instantly regretted. No rock music emanated from Duane's room so he assumed the boy was away.

"There's Miss Cora," Alma-May reminded him with heavy suspicion. "And Shanda."

"Oh, yes."

After breakfast—eggplant hash and some pale-gray, tasteless sago/porridge-like substance—Henderson decided that the first priority was to phone Beeby. Encouraged by Freeborn's absence he approached the double-wide mobile home outside the front steps and knocked on the door.

It was opened by a young, quite pretty girl in an advanced stage of pregnancy. She wore a grubby white smock with blue piping, and incongruous high-heeled strappy shoes. Her copious blond-streaked hair had been badly permed into what was meant to look like a mane of cascading curls, and two brittle wings were flicked back at each temple. A gold chain with an *S* on it hung around her neck, which was disfigured with a raw-looking love-bite.

"Are you the man from New York?"

Henderson confessed he was, after getting her to repeat the question a couple of times. This was no doubt the person who had answered the phone yesterday. She had a powerfully glottal, twanging accent.

"Oh." She stood in the doorway at the top of three steps twiddling a cigarette lighter in her hands, apparently content to stare.

"I wonder if it might be possible for me to make a telephone call?"

"A half-owned car?"

"A telephone call."

"A left front hall?"

He picked up an invisible receiver and dialed the air.

"*Oh.* You want to phone. C'mon in."

Henderson climbed the steps. The trailer was surprisingly capacious, or rather would have been if the vast amount of junk inside had been removed. The room was dark, the curtains being drawn, and only one table lamp was lit. There were many anonymous-looking white parcels and packages stacked against the walls, which he took to be supplies of medical wadding.

"I'm Shanda Gage."

"Henderson Dores."

"Pleased to meet you."

She showed him to a glass and wrought-iron chair beside a small table, upon which stood a telephone. He sat down and smiled, not trusting the simplest words. Shanda moved listlessly about the room shifting packages with a knee, going through the motions of tidying up.

Henderson called Beeby, collect.

"How's it going?" Beeby asked. "Gage called briefly this morning, said you'd arrived. Everything seems OK, looking good. What's the place like?"

"It's a madhouse," he said softly glancing at Shanda.

"What? Speak up."

"Fine. Lovely old place." If Beeby thought things were going well there was no point in relaying Freeborn's threat.

"What about the paintings?"

"Seeing them this afternoon."

"Wonderful, wonderful. Keep in touch."

"Bye, Thomas."

Henderson hung up. Shanda came out of a doorway with a tray holding two coffee cups. Henderson braced himself.

"Thanks," he said, smiling and nodding.

Shanda sat down opposite him. She pressed the top of a black-lacquered toy roundabout-thing beside her and it began to rotate slowly, a music box somewhere in its innards playing "The Blue Danube." After a second or two various little doors in its side sprang open to reveal niches filled with cigarettes. Shanda helped herself to one.

"Smoke?"

Henderson shook his head and held up a hand. He took a sip of his coffee and concentrated on what Shanda was saying. She had paused in the act of putting the cigarette in her mouth. She held it inches away from her lips, the lighter flaring in her other hand. She looked at the ceiling. Henderson noticed it was spattered with stains.

"Freeborn's in Montgomery," she said, with all the deliberation of an aphorist.

"I see."

"He's a good husband." She stuck the cigarette between her pink lips and lit it, dragging avidly on the smoke. Henderson's eyes smarted in sympathy for the infant in her womb. She sat back in her chair and scratched an ankle. She had thickened with pregnancy; her shoulders and upper arms were creamy and soft with excess fat. He suddenly thought of the loathsome Freeborn paying his vampiric attentions to her neck, which was also soft and creamy, he noticed, with three well-defined creases in it. Shanda blew smoke at the ceiling.

"Freeborn's a salesman."

"Mm-hmm?!"

"Yeah. I don't care for that Cora, do you?"

"Who?"

"Cora Gage. Freeborn's sister."

"I've yet to meet her."

"No, Cora. Freeborn's sister."

"I. Don't. Know. Her."

"You will." She rolled her eyes and scratched the underside of one heavy breast. She stubbed out her cigarette. Henderson and Freeborn Gage, Jr., breathed a sigh of relief.

"Where you from?"

"England."

She gave a little shy chuckle. "You know, I'm trying, but I just can't make out what you say. You know, it just sorta sounds like mn, aw, tks, ee, cd, ah, euh, to me. Sorry." She shrugged.

"Can I?" He did his telephone mime.

"Oh, sure. Go ahead."

He called Irene, collect.

"Will you accept a collect call from Henderson Dores, Luxora Beach—"

"No, I will not." The phone went down.

"Not at home?" Shanda asked.

"No."

"Did Freeborn ever tell you that I was fourth alternate in the Miss Teenage South Carolina pageant?"

"No."

"Well, I was. It was last year. We were married then but he told me to enter for it all the same, you know, under my own name? I'll be twenty next month so I guess it was my last shot. And, well . . ." She patted her belly.

She pointed to a large silver column on top of the television set. It looked like a scale model of an elaborate cenotaph. Politely, he inspected it. SHANDA MC NAB, it said, FOURTH ALTERNATE. Once on his feet he considered he could decently leave. Shanda brushed past him to open the door. She already smelled sweet and farinaceous—of milk and talcum powder—he thought.

"Use the phone anytime," she said. "It's nice to talk. I don't get many visitors coming by. And that Cora, well, you can't talk with her."

"Thank you," Henderson said. "Bye for now."

He noticed the increasing heat of the day and the undisturbed blueness of the sky as he crossed the drive to get a better view of the house. But then as he walked by his car he saw to his astonishment that one of its front wheels was missing, the axle resting on a pile of bricks. He felt a sudden shock and outrage, followed by disquiet—like a householder opening his front door to discover his home burgled and vandalized. Who? How? Why? Questions yammered again in his brain. Of the three cars and a pickup that had been parked outside the house the night before, only one—a particularly large, dusty green monster, the color and patina of a battle-scarred tin helmet—remained. He told himself to calm down. There was doubtless some perfectly innocent explanation. He probably had a puncture and one of the household had thoughtfully removed the tire to get it repaired. It couldn't be any plot to immobilize him. . . . He laughed scornfully—out loud—at the suggestion. The noise of his laugh sounded pretentious and hollow. There was, he realized, one sure way to find out. He opened the boot. His spare tire was there. He could change it anytime he wanted. He felt relief slither down his spine to weaken his knees.

However, he couldn't be bothered changing his tire now. Too hot. He walked out into the middle of the grass circle ringed by the drive and looked back at the Gage Mansion.

It was an old, solid-looking wood-and-brick plantation house, with none of the pseudo-Grecian elegance of those usually featured in tourist brochures or films about the Civil War. The ground floor was set on a semiraised basement and was reached by wide steps that gave on to the two-tiered encircling porch, supported, on the ground floor, by double stuccoed-brick columns. The split-shingled pavilion roof, with a steep hip, formed a cover for the upper gallery, the roof slope supported here by unembellished wooden colonnettes. Four small brick chimneys were grouped at the center. It was a fine, nicely proportioned house, derived in the main from the French Colonial style, he saw. At some stage its woodwork had been painted green but wind, rain and time had rendered this down to a flaky lichenous mixture of sludge-grays and browns. It was in need of some care and attention, but had it been in the most gleaming, pristine condition it could have done nothing to counteract the awful proximity of Freeborn's mobile home, parked a mere six or seven yards from the front steps. The large number of dirty motor vehicles usually nosing at its sides didn't help either. It was like some old broken-down sow giving suck to an assorted metallic farrow. Neglect and indifference were all it seemed to evoke; few traces of its romantic past lingered in the air.

The small park it was set in was better tended. The coarse tough grass had been cut back to ankle height. The scattered trees were tall and in fine leaf. From his bedroom window that morning he had looked out onto a garden at the back of the house, wild and overgrown and in riotous flower, the graveled paths and their low box hedges almost obscured by the profusion and fecundity.

He walked around the side of the house. From here he could see the clapboard extension built onto the back that, he imagined, composed Alma-May's annex. He pushed open an askew wicker gate in the tangled hedge that marked the garden boundary and made his way with difficulty along a path to emerge at a small square of lawn. Here the grass was knee high and alive with butterflies. He picked a flower from a nearby shrub and smelled it. Sweet and musky: redolent of Shanda.

He looked up at the rear elevation of the house. A smaller set of steps led down from the porch to the garden. Because of the wide porch and gallery and the overhang of the roof, it was hard to gain an accurate idea of the house's size: just how many rooms it had and how they were laid out within the basic rectangle of the design. He started counting windows on the upper story. Eight. He thought he saw someone move behind one of them but then he couldn't be sure. A minute later he heard the sound of a car starting and then driving away. Shanda? Alma-May? Cora?

He went up the back steps and tried the back door. Locked. He followed the porch around to the front door. Some of the windows he passed were firmly shuttered and he wondered if the rooms behind them held the Gage collection.

He walked into the hall. The house was quiet and felt empty. He wandered around the ground floor, peering into rooms he hadn't visited. There was a large dining room, a den with a dust-mantled Ping-Pong table, another reception room with all the furniture shrouded in sheets, with the exception of a large grand piano. Such paintings as were on the walls were framed prints, family portraits or watercolors by patent amateurs.

He went quietly upstairs. He paused at the top, checking for noise. Nothing. He put his hands in his pockets and hummed tunelessly to himself, wondering if he really should be prowling around in this way. To his right ran a corridor off which were Duane's, Bryant's and his rooms. He turned left. He opened a door and looked in. An utterly characterless bedroom with scattered clothes and an unmade bed. On a chest of drawers stood a sizable component from an internal combustion engine. Beckman's room? Other doors revealed a large walk-in closet heaped with folded sheets and towels, a bathroom and another room, entirely empty. The corridor led him around a corner. Two doors were set on either side of the passage, which came to an end at a casement window overlooking the back garden.

He tried one door. It was locked. So too was the one adjacent. He tried a door on the other side. It swung open. The room was dark, the curtains were drawn and no lights were on. He stood poised in the doorway for a moment, listening. Not a sound. He saw a small sitting room with some old leather armchairs. There was a strong smell of stale cigarette smoke. Were these Gage's rooms? Or Beckman's? Through ajar double doors in one wall he could make out a single bed. There was a dull metal stereo set placed on some shelves amid a rubble of LP's, magazines, newspapers and stacks of books. Some pictures hung on the wall behind them but the gloom was too intense to make them out. He walked carefully over to them, stepping around the piles of reading matter and scattered records.

He stopped suddenly. A small light glowed on the stereo's console. The turntable was revolving. A record was playing soundlessly. He could feel the echo of his heartbeat rebound from the roof of his mouth. His startled eyes followed a wire that led from the stereo set across the littered carpet and onto a divan tucked into a far corner of the room. Someone was lying on it.

"Who's that?" a woman's voice asked. "Duane? Keep your fucking hands off of my records."

Thick-throated and trembling, Henderson stood to attention.

"Ah, no," he said. The person lay on her back, as far as he could see, and had made no move to turn round.

Henderson began to talk. "Terribly sorry to wander in, name's Dores, actually looking for Mr. Gage's paintings, um . . ." He took a pace or two forward. He started explaining again. Now he could see that the person lying on the divan was a very small young woman—Cora Gage, doubtless. Henderson stopped talking because he realized she couldn't hear him. She wore headphones and very dark round sunglasses. She sat up, removed her headphones and turned her sightless eyes in his direction.

"If you're not Duane, who the hell are you?" Her voice had the faintest of southern accents. She expressed no surprise at a stranger walking, uninvited, into her room; her tone was weary and dry.

"The name's Dores." Henderson explained again who

he was and why he'd made the mistake of coming in. He held out his hand then snatched it back, realizing she couldn't see the proffered gesture. He could hardly say "Shake" like some cowboy in a saloon.

"He hangs his paintings in his own rooms," she explained. "Across the corridor. But he keeps them locked up. So Freeborn and Beckman can't get at them."

"Ah." This made no sense, but, then again, that was hardly surprising.

"*Awe*." She imitated him. Henderson charitably ignored this. Blind people were preternaturally sensitive to noise, he knew; she was probably savoring the timbre of his voice, as if making some sort of a sonic filing card for her memory, as sighted people might make a note of a face or a view. She was wearing jeans and a man's shirt. She swung her legs off the divan and sat on the edge. She was very small and thin, not much more than five feet, he guessed. She had a pale, sallow face and wispy, untidy brown hair scraped into crude bangs on either side of her head. In the blurry light, with her round opaque lenses, she looked like some mutant night creature, some lemur or kinkajou.

"I assume you're English," she said, looking straight in front of her. Her hand groped along the coverlet and came in contact with a pack of cigarettes and a lighter. She lit one with only the briefest of hesitations.

"That's right, yes," he said, in the eager respectful tones he used to all crippled, deformed or socially disadvantaged people he met. His voice said, "You have been born with a handicap but I am not shocked or repelled. On the contrary, I respect and admire you for your efforts in overcoming it and will treat you exactly as if you were normal and entire."

"I have an illogical but profound dislike of the English," she said.

Henderson laughed. A come-on-you're-joking chuckle.

"What's so funny?"

"Nothing. I—"

"Why did you laugh, then?"

Henderson looked about him as if calling on an invisible audience for support.

"Well, because I assumed you were joking, I suppose."

"Why?"

"Well . . ." Good God! "I suppose because one just doesn't say that sort of thing in all seriousness to someone one's just met moments before."

"Oh, doesn't one? But I do. I hate the English."

"I'm sorry to hear it." He sensed a hot pelt of embarrassment cover his entire body. He backed off a couple of steps and waved his hands about.

"Perhaps if I, if we were to get to know each other I might, um, be able to—ha, ha—persuade you to, to, reconsider. Or at least exclude me from the general slur." Somehow he had reached the door. He wished he hadn't given that little laugh.

She puffed on her cigarette and made no reply.

"Well, I won't disturb you further. Sorry to have—"

"Goodbye, Mr. Dores."

"Bye."

He shut the door and walked slowly down the corridor. He understood what Shanda meant. What an astonishing woman, he thought. What a . . . bitch, there was no other word for it, blind or no. He shook his head in sagacious sorrow. He wondered what had brought it on. Had her blindness been caused by a crash in an English make of car, a Jaguar or Aston Martin, say? Or had she been a forceps delivery handled by a clumsy and strong-fingered English gynecologist? He turned the corner realizing with some distaste that his armpits were moist and squelching. No, there was something deeper there: that sort of aberrant hate—if he was any judge of human nature—was to do with affairs of the heart turned sour. Unrequited love. Probably ditched by an Englishman for a girl who could see. Some right-thinking, sensible, sane, pragmatic Englishman. Turned her into a bitter, chain-smoking, reclusive Anglophobe. He trotted down the stairs, feeling marginally reassured by his armchair psychology, and saw Freeborn come in the front door. He resisted the temptation to check his watch.

"You still fuckin' here?" Freeborn said, pointing at him. "You got about a hour and a half."

Henderson slowly arrived at the foot of the stairs.

"Look, I might as well tell you," he said nervously, "that I'm not leaving here until I have completed my business with your father."

Freeborn, who had been heading across the hall in the direction of the kitchen, abruptly changed course and strode powerfully over. Henderson raised his hands to chest level, then tugged at the loose skin on his neck.

Freeborn put his huge face with its dense, neatly clipped beard very close to Henderson's.

"Listen, you English fuck. You ain't gonna do *no* business with my father. It's been done, see? Those pictures are sold already. He's a old man. He don't know what he's been talking about, so get yo' shit out of here."

"Your father has asked my company to do a valuation on his paintings and I don't intend to leave until *he* tells me to."

Freeborn looked at him. "You been warned, man." He spread his hands reasonably. "I can't say fairer than that. Just don't fuck with me."

"The last thing on earth I want to do is 'fuck' with you," Henderson replied bravely. "I suggest you take the matter up with your father if you're unhappy about my being here. I'm simply doing my job."

"Yeah, and look, keep away from Shanda, heah? I catch you messin' with her, boy, and you—"

"I was only making a telephone call, for God's sake."

"That's my fuckin' phone, man. You keep yo' chickenshit hands off of it, no-good English mofo." With that he turned and marched off into the kitchen.

Henderson went slowly back upstairs to his room. This sudden hostility from all quarters left him feeling weak and thoughtful. He wondered, once again, if Beeby knew what he was talking about. . . . And what, moreover, had Freeborn meant by the statement that the pictures had been sold already? Or was that all his clenched fist of a brain could come up with as a ruse? Like a lot of people, Freeborn could at times give the impression of being astonishingly stupid, but it was too risky an assumption to elevate into a truth. He resolved, for what seemed like the hundredth time, to quit the Gage Mansion the minute his evaluation was done.

Feeling sorry for himself in this way made him think of Irene, his comforter. Perhaps he might just still manage to entice her south after all if he wrote to her. She might not answer the phone but surely she'd open a letter. After he had finished here—if all went well—he could justifiably claim a couple of days off. Irene might relent at the prospect of a weekend in Charleston or Savannah. . . .

He took a writing pad and envelope from his case and sat down and wrote her a letter to this effect, well larded with apologies and excuses for his craven behavior on the night of the "mugging," and concluding with as overt a declaration of love and affection as he had yet allowed himself ("with absolutely *all* of my love, H"). He was wary of sentiment. Or rather he was all in favor of sentiment but uncertain, not to say ignorant, of how best to express it.

As he sealed the envelope it prompted thoughts of the last letter he had written. He wondered vaguely whether Lance Corporal Drew would be able to enlighten him about his father's death. . . . And what would his father have made of his son's current predicament? he asked himself. Perhaps the saddest and most lasting consequence of Captain Arnold Dores' death in the Burmese jungles in 1943, Henderson thought, was that he, his son, had no vision of the man, no personal private image to cherish or be consoled by aside from purely fanciful or wishful ones. Such photographs that the family possessed were almost counterproductive. In blurry black and white they showed a neat, thin man in baggy flannels with a small moustache and very short hair. Even the more professional shots were undermined by a forced and unnatural smile that exposed the rather wide—and to his son's eyes, unsightly—gap between his father's front teeth. These secondhand images were further disappointing in that they confirmed the distressing fact that Henderson drew most of his features—his square face, his rather small nose—from his mother. He didn't look like his father at all.

If the only sort of immortality we were guaranteed, he thought, going to the window and looking out at the wilderness of the back garden, was the image of ourselves that lived on in the minds of those who survived us, then his father had been singularly unfortunate. He tapped the edge of the envelope against his thumbnail. Even his widow's reminiscences were commonplace and uninspiring. "A charming, sweet man" was the last verdict his mother had passed, when questioned by her son; but she said that about everyone she didn't actively dislike. Perhaps she'd forgotten, he thought. But that made him angry: people had a duty to remember. Friends and family ought to talk and gossip about the dead as if they were alive. . . .

He turned away from the view and paced unhappily about the room. Maybe he should get Melissa to summon Bryant home. Tell her that this mad southern scientist was experimenting on her daughter in his "labrotory" . . . He sighed with exasperation. Then he realized he'd forgotten about Freeborn's latest threat. He'd have to work on the amenable Shanda, make sure that he could phone whenever Freeborn was out of the way and perhaps get her to relay any messages secretly to him. How typical of Loomis Gage not to allow a phone in his house! he thought angrily. It was precisely the sort of selfish affectation millionaires went in for. . . . He told himself to calm down. He found he was still irritated by his encounter with the blind and mysterious Cora. It was lucky he was so pro-American, he reasoned, otherwise the Gage family would have given him serious grounds for a bit of Yank bashing himself. But they weren't Yanks, he realized, they were "Rebs" or "Confeds" or whatever they called themselves.

His complaints were interrupted by the sound of a car arriving. He wondered if it was Gage. But the blast of rock music that ensued some minutes later informed him that the driver had been Duane.

The noise forced him downstairs to the kitchen, where Alma-May made him a processed-cheese and gherkin sandwich for lunch. She professed ignorance to the two questions he asked of her, namely, where was Gage and when was he due back?

"Duane said your car had a flat this morning," she said.

"I thought it was something like that."

"Mr. Gage tol' him to get it fixed."

"Oh. I'm very grateful. Do you think he could put on the spare, if it's not too much trouble?"

"I'll tell him."

138

chapter five

AFTER lunch, Henderson realized there was nothing for it but to walk into Luxora Beach and post his letter. At least it was something to do.

At the front door he saw Shanda teetering around outside her mobile home on her high heels.

"Shanda," he called softly, and went over.

"Hi. How're you doin'?" She had both her hands pressed into the small of her back, her belly straining fiercely against the material of her smock. Henderson felt a little uncomfortable talking to someone who was so ostentatiously pregnant, but he persevered.

"Um, look, Shanda, I was going to ask, that's to say I was wondering if you might just possibly see your way to doing me a little favor," he began confidentially, but then stopped as he saw her eyes cloud with incomprehension.

"It's my back," she said slowly. "It's killing me."

Henderson pinched his nose. There was no alternative; he'd have to speak American, otherwise they would be here for hours.

"Well, shucks," he began again, trying to recall his Huckleberry Finn and Ring Lardner. "I reckon I jist plumb done gone and forgit to ask you to do me a service, like, goshdarn it." It was a little overdone, he admitted, but, like an orchestra tuning up, he had to get in key.

"Oh, yeah?" Shanda's look was uneasy and relieved at the same time, like a monoglot UN delegate whose malfunctioning translation machine has just been restored, only to hear news of a military coup back home.

"If'n you-all done git some calls," Henderson persevered, "could you-all tell me? On the sly like?"

"Well . . ."

"I'd sure be mighty grateful."

"OK. I guess." She looked around. "I don't know if Freeborn . . ." She frowned, then smiled. "What the hell, he ain't around much. He don't tell me nothing, neither. I'll tell you when he's away, so you can use the phone too." She smiled again—conspiratorially—and rubbed the back of her neck with a hand.

"Thank you, ma'am," Henderson said. "Our li'l ol' secret. Have a good day now."

He walked off, rather impressed with his grasp of vernacular. Now at least the outside world would be able to make contact. One step in the right direction.

It seemed surprisingly hot for April, and during the trudge into town along the featureless lane he was obliged to remove first his tie and then his jacket. A mile or so up the road, Freeborn roared dustily past him in his big car, one hand high out of the window, his middle finger spearing the air. Henderson, checking instinctively that there were no witnesses, gave him a V-sign back. It all seemed a bit feeble and adolescent, but, as with Bryant, he found it no problem descending to Freeborn's level.

Sweaty and not a little footsore he arrived some fifteen minutes later at the main street of Luxora Beach. In front of him was the railway line and beyond that the road. To his left was the shopping area. The neon of the bar signs still burned palely in the afternoon air. The town was very quiet—in fact he could see no one on the streets at all. Above the main street, strung on a wire cable, a set of traffic lights blinked redundantly. There were no cars to stop.

He crossed the railway and headed toward the wooden spire of the Baptist church. Down these side roads were small businesses and stores: LUXORA BEACH AUTO AC-CESSORY; LUXORA BEACH AGRICULTURAL WHOLESALERS; ELECTRICAL GOODS; DR. TIRE; LUXORA BEACH FERTILIZERS, HEBERT HACKETT RAFT, JR., PROP.—"REAL MANURE"; LUX-ORA BEACH GRAIN AND SEED MERCHANTS.

At the post office—not far from the church—a wooden building flying the Stars and Stripes, and below it the Stars and Bars, he posted his letter (express) to Irene. He noted the glass-boothed public telephone outside it and wondered if he should try and call her again, but on reflection decided to let the letter do its work first.

He walked back to Main Street, business over. What an effort, he thought, just to post a letter. The afternoon sun was still beating down fiercely and there was still little sign of life. He stood in some shade on the raised wooden sidewalk and looked up and down the dusty road. Where am I? he thought. What am I doing in this place? He longed for a car or a lorry to drive through town. On the door of the shop next to him was a notice: CLOSED SUN-DAY. SEE YOU IN CHURCH.

He thought suddenly—illogically—of his father. Per-haps it was because he felt as strange and out of place here as his father must have at times in the fetid jungles of Burma. From placid drizzling Hove to hot dangerous Burma . . . Henderson looked about him. He tried to imagine Arnold Dores standing beside him now. The thin man in his baggy trousers, his short oiled hair, his neat moustache. What would he say? What advice would he offer? Would he smile, and expose the unfortunate gap between his front teeth? "Now look, son, if I were you, I'd—" What? He exhaled. The fragile chimera of Arnold Dores disappeared.

A large maroon car started up in the parking lot in front of the shops. It drove slowly along before turning to bump across the railway tracks and wheel onto the main road. He saw that there were two girls in the front seat with blond hair like Shanda's and a lot of makeup. They cruised leisurely past him, staring at him with candid curiosity. They wore scant T-shirt tops, tight across their breasts. The car was battered and filthy. Old cigarette packs, magazines and handbooks were piled in a loose drift between the dashboard top and the windscreen. The car moved on slowly down the road; it seemed to trail a frisson of sexuality, like smoke—of the most tawdry and flashy sort, he conceded, but impressively potent for all that. Somewhere there was a life in Luxora Beach.

Intrigued, and smiling to himself, he crossed the road. There was a look, he thought, watching the car disappear from sight, that was common to a huge proportion of American girls. It ran the gamut from Shanda to millionaires' daughters. First there was the mane of hair or an attempt at a mane—blond preferably, but not essential. Then there was a *lot* of mascara and all the rest: blusher, eye shadow and lipstick (usually pink). And then something must glint or glisten on the head—earrings most commonly, but a necklace or hairslide would do. He added some more details to the archetype—pushed-up breasts, white strappy high-heeled shoes—as he headed for the Gage Mansion road. Then he saw Beckman's pickup parked in front of the bar with Bryant sitting alone in the front seat. He changed course.

"Have a nice day?" he asked caustically.

"Oh, hi. Yeah, it wasn't bad. He's not so weird as I thought. He's weird, but not that weird."

"In future do you think you could possibly let me know when you're going on an outing?"

"I was just keeping out of your way. I thought you'd be pleased." She picked at the material on her trousers. "Seen the paintings?"

"No. Gage has been away "

"Beckman says they're already sold."

"Well he's wrong," he said impatiently. "Where is he, anyway?"

"In the bar."

"Right. I'll ask him."

Henderson paused at the door of the bar, second thoughts crowding in on him. Then he pushed through the door.

For four o'clock in the afternoon the bar was astonishingly busy (so this was where everybody was)—and very dark. There must have been two dozen men in the long, thin room. As his eyes grew accustomed to the murky atmosphere he saw that they were all white, all wearing work clothes, and all more or less drunk. Tentatively, he approached the bar. In addition to purveying alchohol it also sold, he noticed, handkerchiefs, a range of pens and combs. All the fitments and plastic advertisements for beer were decades old.

"What'll it be?" the pasty-faced, oily-haired barman asked him. No southern courtesies here.

"I'm looking for Beckman Gage."

"*Beckman!*" the barman shouted down to the end of the

room. There, Henderson saw an ancient mechanical skittle machine and Beckman bent over it.

Beckman gave up his game and wandered over, beer bottle in hand. He wore similar clothes to the men in the bar—denim and a checked cotton shirt. Odd garb for a laboratory, Henderson thought, but then again, he probably swabbed the floors.

"Hi," Beckman said. "Beer?"

"Please."

Beckman's longish, straw-colored hair gave him an initial appearance of youthfulness, but when his face was scrutinized its lines and wrinkles were more apparent. Henderson guessed he was in his mid-thirties—far too old for Bryant, he reassured himself.

A long-necked beer bottle was banged down on the bar and its top flipped off with an opener.

"Could I have a glass, please?" Henderson asked without thinking. The barman looked at him with heavy suspicion—as if he'd just asked for the ladies' room—before raking around on some shelves beneath the bar and presenting him with a thick, finely scratched and semi-transparent glass.

"Cheers," Henderson said. Beckman smiled, his eyelids fluttering like an ingenue's. He seemed to blink about two times a second, Henderson calculated: it must be like seeing the world lit by a stroboscopic sun. To his alarm he sensed his own blink rate going up in sympathy.

"Thanks for taking Bryant to your, ah, lab."

"Hey, a pleasure. Nice kid. Sure talks a lot." Blink-blink-blink-blink.

Pause.

"She's my stepdaughter. Or soon will be."

"I know. Congratulations." Bat-bat-bat-bat.

Henderson turned away and forcibly held his own fluttering eyelids steady with thumb and forefinger. Making eye contact with Beckman was instant conjunctivitis. He addressed the beer in his glass.

"What is it exactly that you do at your lab?"

"Well, I'm what's known as an elementary-particle physicist. You know, quarks, neutrinos, antimatter—that sort of thing."

"An elementary-particle physicist?" Henderson strained to keep the laughing incredulity out of his voice. The poor guy. "Fascinating."

"I think so."

There was another pause. Then Beckman said, "Listen, please don't worry about my blinking. It happened in Nam. I nearly got blown away."

"Really? I hadn't actually noticed. . . . I thought . . ." Henderson changed the subject. "Bryant said something about the paintings—your father's paintings—already being sold."

"Yeah, that's right. Some months ago. Freeborn sold them."

Henderson felt a twinge of alarm. "Are you sure?"

"I guess so."

"There must be some mistake."

"You tell me."

"Who did he sell them to?"

"Some guy called Sereno. I don't know. Maybe you'd better ask Freeborn."

I'd better ask old man Gage, Henderson thought; I'm sure he'll be fascinated.

"Can I hitch a ride back to the house?"

"Surely. Let's go."

They went outside and got into the pickup, Bryant sitting between them. She had put on sunglasses—maybe to hide her blinks, Henderson thought. She seemed very at ease and unconcerned.

They bumped off down the track.

"When I was in Nam," Beckman began, unprompted, "'68, Dac Tro province. No, it was Quang Tri. They called in an air strike on this hostile ville. 'Cept the fuckin' air force dropped the bombs right on our fuckin' platoon. Three dead, six injured. I woke up two days later in a hospital, not a scratch, but just blinking like shit. Haven't stopped since."

"God," Bryant said in awe. "You've been blinking like this all these years?"

"You got it."

"Didn't you get any compensation? Some sort of pension?" Henderson asked politely.

"For what? I told you, I didn't have a scratch. I didn't even get a fuckin' purple heart. They sent me right back in."

"Good God," Henderson said, "that's barbaric."

"But at least you weren't dead," Bryant said. "Like the other guys."

"Yeah. That's something, I suppose."

They arrived at the house. Alma-May was sweeping the porch.

"Evening," Henderson said. "Mr. Gage back?"

"Yes."

"Oh, good."

"But he's gone away again. He was looking for you. For to show you the paintings, he said."

"Bloody *hell*. . . . Excuse me." Henderson looked around him exasperatedly. "Did he leave any message about the paintings?"

"No." Alma-May swept dust over his shoes. He moved aside.

"Do you know where he is?"

"No."

"Do you know when he'll be back?"

"No."

That evening, Henderson and Bryant watched TV after being served something called turnip cakes and a watery ratatouille. Beckman disappeared into his room. From upstairs came the remorseless bass thump of Duane's rock music. Henderson got a bad headache at about half past nine. He went out into the warm night, stood on the porch and stared at the yellow windows of Freeborn's mobile home. He found no answer there and so went up to bed.

chapter six

"YEAH, we was on patrol near Loc Tri. No, no, it was Dhat Pho. Man, we was pissed. A real jerk-off patrol. Then we sees this like buffalo thing—kinda like a big cow? you know?—in a paddy field. That's where the gooks grow their rice."

"In a paddy field? I see."

"Yeah. Well, I guess it was about, oh, a hundred and fifty yards away. No, let's see, maybe a hundred and thirty." Beckman Gage, elementary-particle physicist, frowned as he tried to recall the exact distance. "Let's say one-forty. Anyway, so the sergeant says, 'The first guy to off that buffalo gets a six-pack on me.' Yeah. Well, I was like carrying the machine gun. The other guys start firing . . ."

Henderson felt himself nodding off. He'd had a good forty-five minutes of campaign anecdotes since lunchtime.

". . . and I laid ten rounds of tracer up its ass. It just sorta disintegrated. Like pink foam!" Beckman gave a dry chuckle and shook his head over the folly of his youthful days.

Henderson looked at his watch. He hadn't left the house all day in case he missed Gage, but the man hadn't returned. Bryant had gone shopping with Shanda in Hamburg, which turned out to be five or six miles away. He had been crunching his way through one of Alma-May's special salads—hard-boiled eggs, raw potatoes, squash and some tough purple leaf—when Beckman had arrived from his lab.

"It was kinda like the time we was doing hearts and minds in Tro Nang. No, Doc Tri—"

Freeborn came in. Henderson never thought he'd even be a tiny bit glad to see him, but he was. All the same he gripped the edge of the kitchen table defensively. However, Freeborn seemed to have forgotten about his deadline and ignored him.

"Beckman, can I have a word? Outside." He looked darkly at Henderson. He and Beckman went out into the hall.

Henderson heard Freeborn bellow *"Shut the fuck up!"* at Duane. Then about two minutes later he returned alone.

"Listen, you English dick, the only reason I ain't breaking your balls is that I love my father."

Henderson couldn't follow the logic of this argument.

"I give you one final warning," he went on. "If you so much as mention the name Sereno to my father you're a dead man."

"Look, I just want to do my job and get out of this . . . out of here," Henderson insisted. "You and your father can sort out your own problems. I've got no ax to grind."

Freeborn hitched his tight jeans up, and pointed at him.

"I'm going away for two days. If you're still here when I get back then you get your ass waxed. Got it?"

"Don't worry. I shall be long gone." Perhaps it was the anesthetic quality of Beckman's battlefield yarns but Freeborn's threats didn't seem to perturb him that much today.

They looked at each other for a while. Why does this

man dislike me so much? he wondered. What little scheme of his has my arrival foiled?

Alma-May interrupted their stare.

"Get out of my kitchen," she ordered grumpily. "I got to make you-all dinner, your daddy says."

"What dinner?" Freeborn asked.

"He's having a big dinner for Mr. Dose here. He's invited the preacher and his wife."

"T. J. Cardew? *Shit.* And Mrs. Cardew? Aw *no.*"

"That's the only preacher we got. And you-all got to be there, your daddy says."

Dinner was to be served at seven-thirty. Guests were to foregather in the sitting room downstairs from seven onward. Henderson bathed and put on his last clean shirt. He had only brought three, not anticipating his stay to be so protracted. He knotted his tie and combed his hair. As an afterthought he ran his comb through his densening eyebrows. He'd have to get them cut back soon, like a hedge. It had been one of the most boring days of his life, waiting vainly for Gage to show up. Bryant and Shanda had returned from Hamburg at four o'clock. When Henderson had asked her how she got along with Shanda, she had said it had been "fun."

He walked down the passage and knocked at her door. "You ready?" he called in a loud voice.

"I'm drying my hair!" she shouted. "Five minutes!"

They had to shout because Duane was playing his rock music at exceptionally high volume this evening. Henderson wondered if Duane would be honoring them with his presence that evening. He was curious to see what the youth looked like.

Gage himself was due to arrive later—so Henderson

had learned—with his two guests, T. J. and Mrs. Cardew. Cardew was the minister in Luxora Beach. Henderson recalled that someone named Cardew had been responsible for the sermonette he'd listened to the other night. He assumed they were one and the same. Were "T. J." simply his initials or were they some obscure Baptist rank? he asked himself as he walked down the stairs. He heard the clatter of plates from the kitchen and the distant clamor of a raging argument from Freeborn's mobile home. Good, he thought. With a smile on his face he sauntered into the sitting room.

"Oh," he said. "Hello again."

Cora Gage had been brought down and had been placed squarely in the middle of the largest sofa. She was wearing a plain black dress and some sort of effort had been made to get her hair in order. She even possessed— Henderson took the liberty of staring—a smear of pale-orange lipstick on her lips. She wore her dark glasses (like pennies on the eyes of a corpse, he suddenly thought) and, inevitably, she was smoking, her pack of cigarettes and lighter nestling in the sag of her lap.

"Help yourself to a jolly old drink," she said, looking straight in front of her.

"Thank you."

Set out on a table at one side were various types of whiskey and bourbon, some bottles of beer and what looked like a five-gallon flagon of wine—Californian, he read. With considerable effort he managed to upend this and splash some into a glass and reasonable amounts onto the table. He tried to mop this up with a paper napkin but only succeeded in making it fall apart and also getting his hands wet. With a little thrill of pleasure he wiped his hands dry on the cushions of a nearby armchair.

"Cheers," he said.

"Oh, jolly old cheers."

She really was an objectionable young woman, he thought. He stared at her thin body. The black dress was tight enough to reveal slightly out-of-proportion breasts— out of proportion in that someone her size, he felt, really should be flat-chested. He sat down opposite her.

"Pleasant evening," he said.

"Is it?"

"Well, yes. The weather—"

"Oh, it's the weather you're talking about. Of course, the *weather*. Very English of you."

"I just thought . . ."

He didn't finish. There was a pause.

"Do you know why I dislike the English so much?" she asked.

"I wasn't really prepared for sun. Funnily enough."

"I think, of all the reasons—spitefulness, condescension, pseudo-amateurishness—it's that air of superiority you affect whenever you open your mouths." She said all this very matter-of-factly, as if she were remarking that Alma-May had the afternoon off on Thursdays.

"It seems unusually warm for April," he persevered. "But then of course we're so much further south."

"It doesn't surprise me at all that you have this . . . this international reputation as hypocrites." She puffed at her cigarette. "The loud claim to be acting in the *public* interest which in reality disguises a ruthless *self*-interest."

"Quite overpoweringly hot yesterday, walking into Luxora. Do you have a rainy season here?"

"We call it winter, in our quaint way."

"Vague sort of tropical feel, if you know what I mean."

Ash dropped into her lap. Get your own ashtray, he said to himself cruelly, if you can.

"This sort of smugness, self-satisfaction . . ."

Henderson curled his upper lip in a smug, self-satisfied sneer.

". . . and yet you seem to be genuinely surprised when you're not treated as number one anymore. Genuinely."

"It's extremely kind of—Duane?—to fix my car." He was not going to be drawn by this girl, no matter how angry he got.

"And you still assume that the rest of the world wants to ape the British way; ape your manners, ape your style, ape your attitudes."

Something about the repeated use of the word "ape" made him bulge his lower lip with his tongue and allow his hands to dangle, knuckles inward, from his elbows. He crossed his eyes and mimed picking a nit from his hair and popping it in his mouth.

"Really, these are the wildest generalizations," he said, composing his features, and now rather enjoying himself. It was childish, he realized, like making faces at the teacher's back as she wrote on the blackboard, but rather wicked fun. He glanced over his shoulder to make sure they were still alone.

"Sad," she said. "Pathetic."

The finality in her voice made him suddenly irritated with her. He leaned forward and silently mouthed, "Oh, do fuck off, you stupid woman." He could see twin images of himself in her opaque lenses, bulging-faced, ex-ophthalmic.

"You too, asshole," she said, getting to her feet and strolling over to the drinks table, where she poured herself a shot of whiskey. "Still, I enjoyed the show. I liked the ape best."

Henderson's hand shook so much that Californian wine slopped over the rim onto his trousers. With a brief drum roll of glass on wood he set it down and dabbed at the stain with his handkerchief. He leaned back in his arm-chair as a shiver ran the length of his body. He opened his mouth to say something but all that emerged was a thin, reedy piping noise—like a sick or injured bird—but nothing else. His seized brain had gone out of control. No conceptual structures existed to cope with this sort of massive social shame, a gaffe of such epic proportions.

He felt a hand on his shoulder and leaped to his feet in alarm. It was Loomis Gage.

"Sorry to have missed you earlier, Mr. Dores." Gage seemed not to have noticed Henderson's starting eyes or oozing brow—he felt like a horse saved from a burning stable, almost whinnying in panic.

"Don't mention—" The words turned into a cough. He pounded his chest with a fist. "Not at all."

"I trust Cora's been looking after you."

"We've been having a most interesting conversation, Dad. Haven't we, Mr. Dores?"

"*Pweep.*"

"I want you to meet my other guests." Gage swept his arm around. "Our preacher from Luxora Beach, the Reverend T. J. Cardew, and his wife, Monika."

Henderson turned to greet the couple in the doorway. The Reverend T. J. Cardew was a dapper, fleshy, youngish man (mid-thirties, Henderson guessed) with curly black hair and long thin sideburns that terminated sharply at his jawbone. He wore a sober black suit, a red shirt with silver metal tabs on the collar and a loud checked tie. His wife sported a lime-green dress over which she'd thrown a white net shawl. She had square gold-framed glasses and reddish-brown hair, which was wound and back-combed into a beehive. She had a big frame and seemed larger all around than her husband. Her face was sullen, despite her bright-red lips and pale-blue eyelids. The primary colors did little to disguise the fact that she was deeply bored.

Henderson shook hands with them both. He tried not to look at Cora.

"How do you do? How do you do, Reverend?"

"Very nice to know you, Henderson. Just call me T. J."

Henderson doubted that he'd actually ever be able to do this, but smiled encouragingly.

"T. J. knows Europe well," Gage confided. "And Monika there is in fact of German origin. Mr. Dores is from England."

Monika Cardew looked marginally more interested.

"Where in Germany are you from?" Henderson asked dutifully.

"Berlin."

"We met," T. J. interjected, "when I was serving there. As chaplain to the Forty-third Airborne."

"An army bride," Monika said flatly. She had a noticeable German accent.

"What'll it be, T. J.?" Gage asked.

"Oh, I think a drop of the Goat, as usual, Loomis."

"You must try some of this, Mr. Dores," Gage said, holding up a squat brown bottle. Henderson took it from him and looked at the label. "Henry's Goat," he read. "Sour Mash Bourbon." On the label was a fine engraving of a tethered goat, and in the background a queue of people waiting outside a tumbledown wooden shack.

"Sippin' whiskey," Gage said. "The secret of my survival."

Gage poured him out a large measure in a small glass. Henderson, still shaky from the sudden revelation of Cora's normal vision, allowed himself a sizable gulp. The liquid had a thick smooth quality and slid down his gullet as easily as an oyster.

"Very pleasant," he said, before what seemed like a small fragmentation grenade exploded in his stomach. A column of flame rose up his esophagus. He shuffled his feet and breathed thin streams of hot vibrating air out through his nose. Some sort of dazed smile, he hoped, registered on his features.

"Goodness," he said.

"Sort of creeps up on you," Cardew laughed unattractively.

Gage administered more drinks and regularly pressed the bell to summon Alma-May.

"That boy sure loves his modern music," Cardew said, acknowledging the bass rhythms vibrating from Duane's room.

"Do you like rock music, Mr. Dores?" Cora asked him innocently, lenses unsparingly focused on his face.

"No, I don't, as a matter of fact. I prefer classical music."

"You and Cora have something in common, then, Mr. Dores," Gage said, putting his arm around his daughter. "She is a wonderful pianist. Will you play something tonight for us, honey? After dinner?"

"No."

"No persuading our Cora." Cardew beamed. Gage seemed unperturbed by the abrupt refusal. Alma-May came in with a tray of canapés, followed by Freeborn and Shanda. Shanda's eyes were bloodshot and she looked sulky. Henderson stood up and offered her his seat but Freeborn steered her away to a sofa.

"I understand your daughter is with you, Henderson," Cardew said. "That's nice."

"Well, actually," Henderson began, then decided that

it might be as well to leave the reverend in his ignorance. Cardew leaned over.

"I understand too that she's a very attractive teenager."

Henderson didn't know how to respond. "Takes after her mother," he commented edgily.

"Oh, yes?"

"How is Patch?" Henderson asked.

"Who?"

"Patch. Your dog. Scratching on heaven's door, with no fear."

"I'm sorry?"

"In your sermon. On the radio. I listened to it."

"I don't own a dog, Henderson. I'm allergic to fur."

"But you—"

"What you might call poetic license."

"Some more Goat?" It was Gage dispensing bourbon.

"Please." Henderson offered his empty glass. He was getting used to its virulence.

Gage seemed in a good mood. His plump face was flushed, his dense hair a little tousled.

"The man who made this stuff in the old days was called Henry Stewart. A Scotchman. He had his own still in back of his house and he also had a prize billy goat. And the good ol' boys, when they wanted a refill, would take their nanny goats along to be sired. If they were asked where they were going they would say they were going around for Henry's goat. And the name stuck."

"Fascinating story."

Gage sat down on the arm of Henderson's chair.

"In fact that's how I met Hem and Scott in Paris. In the twenties. I was in the American bar at the Ritz and these two guys came in. They'd already had one too many, I could see. Then this one guy—Hem—says, 'You got any Henry's Goat?' I couldn't believe it. I went right on over and introduced myself. Seems Hem got a taste for it when he was working on the *Texas Star Bugle*."

"You mean the *Kansas City Star*," Henderson said politely.

"No, no. It was the *Texas Star Bugle*."

"And you got to know them?"

"Sure. I knew them all—Hem, Scott, Gertie, Alice, Pablo. Hell, I was rich in those days. I don't pretend it wasn't me picking up the tabs that they liked, but"—he paused—"it was good, as Hem used to say. And I wanted to buy some paintings and they told me what to buy. Good paintings."

"Ah, yes, the paintings."

"I'll show you after dinner." Gage squeezed his shoulder affectionately. Henderson felt a sensation of calm spread through his body for the first time since he had arrived in Luxora Beach. He felt suddenly fond of Loomis Gage and his patchwork memories. Or maybe it was simply the Goat going to work.

"Let me freshen that for you."

Cora came around with a silver casket filled with cigarettes. Henderson noticed that Beckman and Bryant had arrived. Bryant and Shanda were engaged in a serious intimate conversation.

"Cigarette, Mr. Dores?" Cora asked.

"No, thanks." He kept his eyes on her right shoulder.

"Are you enjoying your visit to the South?"

"Very much."

"You don't mean that, do you? You can't wait to leave."

"Hardly. Well—"

"But you've got perfect manners."

He was beginning to find her constant irony intensely wearying.

"It so happens that one of the things I happen to believe in very strongly," he said, in a low voice, a little more forcefully then he had intended, "is that there are certain decencies, certain social routines that we should observe whatever the cost. Otherwise it . . ." He shrugged, he hadn't really considered the consequences. "It all falls apart."

"And you wouldn't see that as typical British hypocrisy? Say one thing when you mean the other?"

"Not at all. We all have duties and obligations that bore us. Total honesty doesn't work in society." He was encouraged by his fluency. "The alternative to that is a sort of, a sort of ghastly Californian candor where everything in the garden is lovely no matter what the evidence to the contrary is. No, that is, disrespect intended," he added, his confusion returning.

"Mmm" was all the reply she made, as if she had just had some thesis confirmed. "Excuse me."

Henderson felt himself panting slightly as if he'd just run upstairs.

"I find Cora a fascinating girl, Henderson, don't you?" Cardew whispered into his ear. "Very intellectual. She was a very promising student in medical school. Dropped out, just like that. No reason. No one knew why. But that . . . impulsiveness adds to her attraction." They both looked at her, then she turned around and looked at them. Cardew raised his glass.

"Why does she wear those sunglasses all the time?"

"I really don't know, Henderson," Cardew said. "As far as I'm aware there's nothing wrong with her eyes. She rarely removes them. They give her a—heh!—mysterious allure, don't you think?"

Henderson sipped his Goat.

"Will we be seeing you and your lovely daughter in our church this Sunday, Henderson?"

"Well, Reverend—" He blinked fiercely. The Goat had brought on a sudden attack of double vision.

"T. J., please."

"I'm afraid we will be gone by then."

"Oh." He frowned. "Loomis told me you'd be here at least two weeks."

Henderson almost dropped his glass. "There must be some misunderstanding."

"No doubt, no doubt. We have a strong and loyal congregation here in Luxora Beach, Henderson. I think you would enjoy our service."

"Alas, Reverend." Henderson spread his hands apologetically, observing a social routine.

"T. J., please. All my flock know me as T. J. I don't stand on ceremony. Would you pass me a cigarette, Henderson?"

Alma-May came in. "It's ready," she said, and left.

Henderson drained his glass with relief and stood up, only to find the room had acquired a gradient that he hadn't noticed before. He adjusted his stance to compensate. Three glasses of Goat were clearly enough.

The guests filed across the loud hall into the dining room. Henderson heard Beckman telling Monika about a fire fight in Duc Pho province. Shanda waded over toward Henderson.

"Evening, Mr. Dores."

"Howdy," Henderson said. "You-all doin' fine?"

"Oh, yeah. I guess."

Cora's head snapped around at his words. Everyone had to raise his voice over the rumble of Duane's music.

"Can't you hush that moron up for an hour or two?" Freeborn demanded angrily of his father.

"It's the boy's only pleasure," Gage called back amicably. "We won't hear it in the dining room."

"I'll get that baboon," Freeborn muttered and set off up the stairs.

"That's why we moved into the trailer," Shanda said. "Freeborn and Duane kept beatin' up on each other. They just don't get along."

They went into the dining room. Henderson had glanced into it briefly on his furtive patrol of the house the day before. A dull crystal chandelier hung above a long polished table. The room was paneled and the panels had been painted a creamy pale green. On the walls were family portraits, done by local artists, he assumed. He recognized the Gage children: slim beardless Freeborn, Beckman and Cora, as a young girl of about twelve, minus her sunglasses. On an end wall was an older Victorian oil of a plump bearded man in a navy-blue military uniform.

"My father," Gage said, noticing him looking at it. "It's not for sale," he added with a smile. "He died when I was two. In the Philippines. The gugus—"

"Daddy," Cora said, "I don't think we want that story before dinner."

They all sat down under Gage's direction. He placed himself at the head of the table, Henderson on his right, Monika Cardew on his left. Beside Henderson was Shanda and beyond, Cardew and Cora. Across the table were Beckman, Bryant and an empty seat for Freeborn, who, Henderson assumed, must still have been remonstrating with Duane.

A confused shouting came from behind the door. Then Alma-May burst in with a tureen of soup in her hands, followed by an oddly cowed-looking Freeborn.

"You tell him to leave Duane alone, Mr. Gage," she said, crashing the tureen down on the table angrily.

"I just ast him to turn the goddamn noise down, is all," Freeborn grumbled petulantly, sitting down.

"It's all right, Alma-May," Gage soothed. "We won't bother him again."

Alma-May sullenly served up the soup, which was solid with vegetables. Then she effortfully dispensed wine from another five-gallon carafe. Henderson drank his wine, chewed the soup and listened to Shanda, who, he discerned after a minute or so, was telling him about her day with Bryant in Hamburg. Beyond her he could see Cardew leaning too far across the table, talking energetically, and with wide gummy smiles, to Bryant, who looked back at the reverend with overt suspicion.

"How are you liking Luxora Beach?" Monika Cardew asked.

"Um. Very . . . Yes, liking it a lot. Yes. What I've seen."

"There's not much to see," she said.

"Why is it called Luxora Beach?" Henderson asked in mild desperation. "Is there a lake nearby, or a river?"

"Good question," Gage said. "We've got the Ockmulgokee River flows by the town, but there's no beach that I know of. Ask T. J." He distracted the reverend's attention from Bryant's breasts.

"T. J., Henderson has a question for you."

"Yes, Henderson."

"I was wondering how you explain the 'Beach' in Luxora Beach?"

"Well, goshdarn. Do you know, Henderson, I've never thought to ask."

"Just curious."

"Good golly, it only goes to show what a stranger's eyes can illuminate for you." For some reason he whipped out a little notebook from his breast pocket and wrote something down. "How long have we lived here, Monika dear?"

"Eleven years," Monika said with feeling.

"And I never thought to ask. Thank you, Henderson, thank you sincerely. I shall endeavor to find out the answer."

"Just idle curiosity." He emptied his glass.

"Freeborn, will you offer our guests more wine?" Gage asked.

Alma-May cleared the soup plates and returned with more dishes. She set down crammed bowls on the table: great mounds of various beans, corn on the cob, some sort of sopping green vegetable, curious knobbled dumplings.

"Down-home cooking for our English guest." Gage raised his glass.

A heaped plate was set in front of Henderson.

"What are these things?" he asked weakly, playing for time. He didn't feel the least bit hungry. What was more, Henry's Goat was having a curious effect on his body. Bits of him seemed to go numb while others prickled with an urgent rash.

Beckman pointed to the green stuff. "That's turnip greens," he said. "And that—the rice and beans—is hoppin' john. That's black-eyed bean stew. And those are corn dogs."

"Hoppin' john?" Henderson said. "Why that name?"

"Because," Freeborn said at his shoulder, sloshing wine into his glass, "once you've ate it, it sends you hoppin' to the john."

Henderson laughed nervously; he thought it safer. Though no one else did.

"And that bean stew?" Freeborn continued. "It's been stew once but I don't know what it is now. Hyar-har."

Henderson filled his mouth with hoppin' john. Inoffensive stuff. He drank some more wine, then wondered if that was wise. Perhaps it was the mix of Californian plonk with Henry's Goat that was making him feel so odd. Now, light-headedness was alternating with nausea. He looked down the table. Bryant's eyes and expression seemed to be communicating a message of some sort but he couldn't decipher it. Cora sat behind a plate that contained a solitary pile of beans. There was a babble of conversation as everyone tucked into the main course.

"Why are you a vegetarian, Mr. Gage?" Henderson asked. "Religious reasons or just taste?"

"Oh, no, I'm not a vegetarian."

"But why—?"

"Not me personally. Alma-May is. She turned vegetarian two years ago. Won't have meat or fish in the house. Point-blank refuses. What else could we do?"

"Oh. I see. . . ."

"Are you familiar, Henderson . . .? Henderson? I was saying, are you familiar with Upper Heyford, England?" It was Cardew, shouting across Shanda's back.

"It's near Oxford, Reverend. An air base, I think. Yes, I know it vaguely."

"Henderson, please call me T. J."

"Right."

"You see, I was stationed there for a while. I don't suppose you know a Mr. John Fairchild of Upper Heyford?"

"No. I'm afraid—"

Freeborn interrupted. "That's where we got our bombs and missiles, ain't it? And, yeah, can you tell me," he went on, warming, "what you Britishers have got against our bombs and missiles?"

Henderson chewed manfully on his beans, wondering how he could get off this topic.

"I think, um, the main objection is that we, that is, Britain, don't have any control over the—"

"Of course not. They're our bombs. We made 'em. You

got your own, don't you?" Freeborn's expression seemed to say QED.

"Tell me, Henderson, is there a reason for the name of every English village?" Gage asked, frowning thoughtfully.

"Well, yes, often. 'Chipping,' as in Chipping Sodbury, means there was a quarry there. 'Hurst,' as in—"

"Henderson?"

"Yes, Shanda."

"My maiden name was McNab. That's a Scotch name, right?"

"Yes, indeed."

"I thought so."

"We are allies," Cardew said, intensely. "What I personally can't understand is this hostility between allies. I mean we are there—our weapons, our young men—to defend the West."

"Luxora Beach . . ." Gage said, obliviously. "You know, I think I like the fact, you know, that there isn't a logical reason. There's too much logic in the world. I like it sorta . . . arbitrary like that."

"There is a Luxor on the Nile," Cora said. "Perhaps it was an Egyptian who settled here first."

"But that's logic again, Cora. You're looking for logic."

Freeborn leaned across the table and pointed his fork at Henderson. "I mean we had to win World War I and II for you guys, and we'll probably have to do it for World War III and IV.'

"I think the argument," Henderson said, "is that you're fighting your wars in Europe, as it were. That if Europe is the battleground, then it suits . . . I mean, not that I . . ." He felt his head spinning.

"Actually I believe there were no Egyptian immigrants to this country in the eighteenth century," Cora said with mock solemnity.

"Come to think of it, when was the town founded?" Gage asked. "T. J.?"

"Excuse me, Loomis, I have to deal here with something Henderson said. Now, Henderson—"

"Could you pass me the turnip greens, Henderson?" It was Beckman. "Just sorta shove them down thisaway."

"That statement of yours, Henderson."

"What statement?"

"It whitewashes the American blood spilled in Europe."

"Actually, I wasn't quite saying that, um, J. P." Henderson felt the controls slip from his hand.

"Look, there's an easy answer," Gage said cheerfully. "If you don't want us there, say the word and we'll haul ass. Save us a slew of dollars, that's for sure."

"I find your remarks, Henderson, deeply disquieting. Do our own allies in Europe really—"

"With respect, T. V., that's not the point at issue."

"Henderson, say, can you reach over that wine?"

"OK, OK, so the Reds take over England," Freeborn said. "So who gives a sick dog's dump?"

"Freeborn, *please!*"

"Is England the same place as Scotland or what?" Shanda asked. "That's what I want to know."

"Why, Henderson, why does antinuclear always equal anti–Uncle Sam?"

"To be honest, E. T., I think you've lost the gist—" He had to strain to hear now, above the crescendo of noise. Everybody was talking.

"Hell, man, we're all ant-eye war, aren't we? I tell you, in Nam—"

"Henderson, I would say this to you. To your people, Henderson. Tell them, Henderson, tell them we are your friends. Do not turn us away, for God's sweet sake!"

"Look, M. G., or whatever your blasted name is—"

"Man, when you got incoming, hell, are you ant-eye war!"

"*Why*, Henderson, *why*?"

"Why what? You stupid bloody—"

"—leave you alone, then see what happens—"

"—you got Scotland, OK? You got England—"

"—wasting slopes in Dac Tro—"

"—God's abiding love—"

"—someone who'd been to Egypt?—"

"*WAAAAARGH!!*"

Everyone stopped talking at once. The scream had issued from the lips of the Reverend T. J. Cardew. He had leaped wildly to his feet, knocking over his chair, and was now white with pain and clutching his right knee with both hands. In the subsequent alarm and fuss, amid the shouted questions and commiserations, Henderson saw Bryant surreptitiously bring her hand up from beneath the table and replace a fork.

Henderson stood up and felt the room wheel and bank. He heard the black-eyed beans, hoppin' john, corn dogs and turnip greens in his stomach clamoring for the open air. "Excuse me," he mumbled, and left the room. He ran to the front door, sprang down the front steps and vomited into an azalea bush.

He leaned weakly against the wall, the world still tilting and reeling. He hawked and spat and kicked loose earth over such bits of his regurgitated meal as he could see. He moaned quietly to himself. He felt terrible. Rough careless hands were clenching his intestines, tugging and squeezing. He breathed deeply, recalling a Teagarden drill. Controlled relaxation. Inhale, exhale. Controlled relaxation.

There was a breeze outside. It blew across the moonlit grass, bringing with it a scent of pines. He looked up at the constant, uncomplaining stars. He heard the distant rush of a freight train on the Luxora Beach line, and the human cry of its call. If he hadn't felt so ill and drunk he might have been overcome with melancholia.

He wandered about in a rough figure-of-eight pattern, had a final spit and was about to go back inside when he heard the sound of a telephone from Freeborn's mobile home. He stumbled across. Yes, definitely ringing. He swithered for a moment. Should he go and get Freeborn? Something about the tone of the ring, he thought wildly and fancifully, made him convinced it was a call from New York. He tried the door. Locked. The phone continued ringing. He ran to the front steps, ran back to the door and tugged vainly at it. The ringing stopped. In his anger and frustration he punched the door and bruised his knuckles.

"*Ouch!* Bastard!" he swore.

He turned around and saw the orange glow of a cigarette on the porch.

"Having fun?" Cora said.

"The phone," he said. "It was ringing. Then it stopped." Strange displacements and shiftings were still going on in his abdominal region. The last thing he required was a conversation with Cora.

"So I heard. How are you feeling?" She looked oddly malignant in her black dress and black glasses in the darkness of the porch.

"Not so good. I think I'd better make my excuses."

"Daddy wants to show you his paintings."

"Oh, yes, of course. Gladly." He climbed the front steps. The smell of her cigarette smoke mingled with that of the pines and the lingering acidity of his vomit. It was not a pleasant conjunction.

"Everything has sort of calmed down in there," she

said. "T. J. explained that the pain was an old football injury. It sometimes gets him like that. Out of the blue."

"Ah."

"Your daughter looked a little skeptical."

"Yes. She would."

There was a pause.

"Look," Henderson began. "I want to apologize about my behavior earlier. It was unforgivable. I don't know what possessed me. I mean, even if you *had* been blind . . . that's to say, well, really, it's hardly the sort of thing one should do—especially at my age." He looked out at the night. "Appalling."

"Don't worry about it. And, remember, I did rather lead you on."

The porch light was switched on. It was Gage.

"Feeling better, Mr. Dores? The Goat can get you that way."

"I needed a breath of fresh air."

"A breath of fresh air. I like that. Ready to do business?"

Henderson said good night to Cora and wearily followed Gage back inside and upstairs.

He felt a new wave of nausea hit him as Gage unlocked his door and switched on the light. Henderson saw a generous sitting room with a bedroom off it, a replica of Cora's suite across the passage. There was an old leather chesterfield, an antique escritoire and a large glass-fronted, largely empty bookcase against one wall between two windows. The other three walls were covered in paintings and photographs, most of the larger canvasses with brass picture lights over them. On one wall in pride of place was a large amateurish oil of a woman, idealized and prettified, and surrounding this were numerous black-framed photographs.

"Mrs. Gage," Henderson was informed. "God rest her soul. Died fifteen years ago."

Henderson wandered over. The photographs were an odd mixture. Gage shaking hands with various dignitaries—Henderson recognized two American Presidents, a toupeed crooner and Ernest Hemingway—and a large photo of a café scene that bore the heading PARIS, 1922. There were various studio portraits of the Gage offspring, charting the usual transformation from smiling child through shifty adolescent to banal adult.

Suppressing a belch, and making a mighty effort to clear his head, he turned to the paintings. If he hadn't felt so drunk and under the weather he would have been elated, the object of his visit having finally been achieved. In the event, it was as much as he could do to keep them in focus.

Beeby's summary had been accurate. On the first wall were four not very remarkable, school of so-and-so, muddy Dutch landscapes of the late seventeenth century, he guessed. There was also, with this group, a portrait of a bearded man and a small allegorical work.

The other wall was devoted to the twentieth century. Henderson noted the two large Sisley landscapes—a river lined with poplars, an orchard screening red-roofed barns—a Derain—a green barge on a red river—two bold still lifes, a rather run-of-the-mill Braque Cubist interior, a Utrillo street scene under snow and two shimmering, translucent Vuillard interiors.

"That's where I was staying," Gage said, pointing to the Utrillo. "Max painted it for me."

Henderson knew he should be computing value and expressing huge enthusiasm but a fair portion of his mind's attention was still claimed by the structural redevelopment going on in his torso. It sounded like men moving furniture from room to room.

"A remarkable collection, Mr. Gage. I like them very much."

"I bought them all in one year," Gage said nostalgically, "1922. I had more money than I knew what to do with." He laid a hand on Henderson's shoulder. "Tell the truth, I went to Europe for a good time, no intention of buying paintings. But there you are. I met Hem and Scott. They said a man like me ought to collect some art, so I did. Bought direct off of some artists, off their friends, one or two dealers, and shipped them home. I thought about buying some more over the years, but there didn't seem much point. I had my paintings. I liked them. I didn't need any more."

"I can see exactly what you mean," Henderson said, diplomatically. "There's no point in accumulation for accumulation's sake."

He moved back to the Dutch paintings.

"I bought those because I was homesick," Gage said. "They reminded me of around here."

Henderson couldn't spot any similarity between the wet somber landscapes and the countryside near Luxora Beach.

"And that feller there reminded me of my father. And the other one"—he indicated the allegory—"hell, it's just a dirty painting." He caught hold of Henderson's elbow and whispered in his ear. "Tell you a secret. It gave me a hard-on when I saw it in the gallery. Still does, sixty years later."

To avoid having to reply, Henderson peered closer. The painting was small, twenty by fourteen inches approximately. In a rather badly painted allegorical landscape—

crags, woods, cataracts, stormy mouse-gray clouds, a distant view of sea and luxuriant islands—was a simple columned temple or shrine. Within this, glimpsed between the widely spaced columns, were two women. One woman was in the traditional sackcloth and ashes of mourning. She knelt, hands clasped, but her head was turned away toward the other. Even though she was in an attitude of prayer her face wore a broad smile. The other woman—dark, slim, younger—was laughing too. She was holding up the skirt of her robe to reveal her pudenda. She had plump creamy thighs, slightly parted. Her vaginal crease was clearly visible and some tiny single-haired brush had been used to touch in a near-transparent smoke of pubic curls. By her feet was a jug. The smiles on the women's faces were wide—almost crude grins—wide enough to reveal their teeth.

He looked at the young girl again. To his shame he felt a stirring in his trousers. He turned quickly to the portrait. Some hefty Dutch burgher with a dense beard. There was a slight resemblance to the portrait in the dining room. He remarked on this to Gage. He had to say something.

"And you say your father died when you were two?"

"That's right," Gage said.

"My father died before I was born."

"I'm sorry," Gage apologized, as if he were in some way responsible.

"He was killed in Burma, in the war. The Second World War."

"Now, there *is* a coincidence," Gage said. "My father died in a war too. In the Philippines."

"What war was that?"

"Our war against the Philippines"—this was news to Henderson—"1899–1902."

"What on earth was the United States doing fighting a war against the Philippines?"

"I don't rightly know," Gage said thoughtfully. "We killed three million of them too."

"You're joking."

"No, sir. But the gugus got my daddy. When they killed him they cut off his pecker and stuck it in his mouth."

"Good God! How appalling!" Henderson touched his mouth and his groin reflexively.

"Nasty little war, that one," Gage said. "Seems that's what the gugus did to their victims."

"The 'gugus' are the Filipinos?"

"That's right. But I don't think there's any call for that kind of mutilation."

"Lord, no," said Henderson, unsettled. "Absolutely not."

Then, to his astonishment, Gage dropped into a boxer's crouch and fired a volley of jabs at the air in front of his face. Henderson was almost sick on the carpet, so taken aback was he. He reeled away.

"You a boxer, Mr. Dores?" Gage asked, still darting lefts and rights.

"No. I . . . no, I'm not."

"That's a fair fight. Whew." Gage stopped and patted his chest. "But there's no such thing as a fair fight outside of a sporting arena, wouldn't you agree?"

"It's a point, I suppose. I don't really know."

"Five'll get you ten your father didn't die in a fair fight. Just like mine."

"I've no idea." He ran his fingers through his hair. "Funnily enough I've been trying to discover for the last year how in fact he did die. Been writing to men who served with him, that sort of thing."

"No such thing as a fair fight. Remember that." Gage paced up and down his room. He seemed strangely flushed and excited. "You a sportsman?"

"Not really. I do a bit of fencing from time to time."

"Fencing? You mean . . . ?" He did a hand-twirling flourish and lunged with an imaginary sword.

"Yes."

Gage laughed. "Are you putting me on?"

"No, no, I assure you. I enjoy it."

"The word 'foible' comes from fencing, am I right?"

"Yes. The foible is the weak part of the blade."

"Foible . . ." Gage paused. His exertions had tousled his thick white hair. Henderson noticed how it seemed to spring straight up out of his skull for an inch before its weight caused it to fall over. A remarkable head of hair, he thought. Gage was looking at the carpet and tugging at the loose skin beneath his jaw.

"Know what unites us, Mr. Dores? Every swinging dick, as we used to say in the army?"

"Well, it depends . . ."

"We all want to be happy, and we're all going to die."

"Yes, that's true."

"You might say those are the only two unchallengeably true facts that apply to every human being on this planet."

"Indeed." Henderson's eye shifted nervously about the room, glancing at the paintings. "Beauty is truth, truth beauty, etc. . . . That sort of thing seems a little rarified sometimes in this day and age."

"I couldn't have put it better myself. Tell me something, Mr. Dores." Gage wandered over to the Vuillards. "We all want to be happy and we're all going to die. Wouldn't you think that if everybody knew that, acknowledged that, things would be different?"

"I don't know."

"Yeah . . ." Gage frowned. There was a pause.

"I think these are my favorites." Henderson indicated the Vuillards. "Magnificent." He was disturbed and unsettled by the little old man. Vaguely shocked too by the news of Gage senior's hideous mutilation. He wondered if his own researches into his father's death would turn up something as distressing. Better perplexed ignorance, perhaps, than that sort of knowledge. . . . He grimaced. Some blend of complicated writhing and uncoiling was going on in the depths of his abdominal cavity. He forced himself to concentrate.

"With paintings of this quality we would be happy to waive our seller's commission. Naturally, there will be a full-color catalog and—"

"Let's talk about the details tomorrow, Mr. Dores. It's getting late." He opened the door; he looked a little troubled. "And I must get back to my guests."

Henderson said he thought he would go straight on to bed as he was still feeling the worse for wear. Gage left him at the top of the stairs and he walked slowly along the corridor to his room. As he passed Bryant's room she came out.

"Hi," she said. "How are you feeling?"

"Where are you off to?"

"Duane asked if I wanted to listen to some of his records."

"Well, try to keep the noise down, OK?"

"Sure. And listen, Duane said he's sorry but he'll try to get your tire back tomorrow."

"Good. Look, what, um, happened with Cardew?"

"Oh, God. He kept sorta trying to twine his legs around mine, so I let him have it in the knee with a fork."

"Oh."

"Dirty old men. I hate them."
"See you tomorrow. Good night."

As he undressed, Henderson felt overwhelmed with tiredness. He climbed wearily between the sheets and laid his head with a sigh of relief on his cool pillow. Within seconds it became uncomfortably warm. He turned over. His ears were like hot plates. He lay on his back, breathing steadily, trying to summon up a mood of controlled relaxation. He was still awake an hour later when he heard the Cardews' car drive away.

At least and at last he had seen the paintings, he told himself. He farted noisily. What had he eaten? Was it the corn dogs, the hoppin' john or the turnip greens? Or was it all down to Henry's Goat? . . . He'd phone Beeby with the good news tomorrow. He couldn't see any major problem with Gage; they got on fine and he seemed happy enough to sell. He pondered vaguely on Beckman's notion of Freeborn's premature sale. They were so obviously Gage's *personal* possessions it seemed inconceivable that his son would have any independent claim on them himself.

But why was Gage selling? It was a question he rarely asked of his clients—it was none of the auction house's business. Often, though, some reason was voluntarily given: security concerns, death duties, a move—but seldom, however, the most common: poverty. He strongly suspected this was what applied here. Gage was broke. Clearly he had been rich once, but everything about the household spoke of galloping penury.

He wondered how he would get through to Beeby the next day. Freeborn had said he was going away so perhaps he could prevail on Shanda without fear. He didn't fancy having to walk into Luxora Beach every time he wanted to make a phone call. . . . And when was that cretin Duane going to fix his car? He was paying good money for it precisely to afford him the mobility he now required, and yet it stood uselessly outside on three wheels, gathering dust.

Thinking about phoning Beeby reminded him of the call that had come through to Freeborn's trailer. He felt sure it had been for him, but who? Beeby? Melissa checking on Bryant? Irene? The mild sensual stimulus provided by Gage's sixteenth-century bit of erotica set up aches of longing for Irene. She should get his letter by tomorrow. . . . He had to get her down here, to patch things up. He couldn't let one disastrous night ruin everything. He would send her a first-class return ticket to Atlanta, book them both into the plushest hotel they could find and have three or four undisturbed days together after this whole business was over. He ran through half a dozen scenarios of their reunion. Sleep had left him far behind now, he realized. He should get up and read, make notes on the paintings. He compiled a swift catalog in his head, estimating possible prices. The Dutch paintings were curiosities and worth nothing significant. But the Sisleys and the Vuillards were important, and the Braque . . . He thought suddenly of Gage's father and his father. They had both died in the East in a war and had never known their sons. A strange coincidence. It made him warm to the little man. . . . Still gets a hard-on from his dirty painting. . .

He found himself thinking again of Gage's father's horrible death. Surely nothing so dreadful would have befallen Arnold Dores in Burma. To his surprise he found himself worrying for his father's safety, as if he were still alive and still involved in his perilous mission. Take care, Dad, he said to himself—and then rebuked himself for his absurd sentiment. It had been an odd moment, though, a kind of eerie time shift. He felt suffused by a low, steady sadness, which gradually gave way to unease. He hoped he wouldn't hear of anything too awful. . . .

chapter seven

THE next morning Henderson got out of bed and fell over. He sat on the floor for a few seconds and watched his hands shake. A largish prism seemed to be wedged between his spine and his rib cage. The internal triangle. His viscera felt stuffed to capacity with gravel. His eyes throbbed painfully, as if they had been removed from their sockets, bounced up and down on the floor and reinserted. He crawled back between the sheets.

Bryant looked in later to inform him she was going to Atlanta with Duane to buy some records. Henderson waved her on her way. At lunchtime Alma-May brought him a pickled-cucumber and chopped-onion sandwich. He crawled out onto the balcony and threw it into the garden.

In midafternoon he received a visit from Cora.

"How are you feeling?" she asked. She stood in the center of his room, cigarette burning in one hand. She seemed quite friendly now.

"Not so good," he replied. "Very weak. Chronic indigestion. Intermittent nausea. It must be that sipping whiskey."

"You got a phone call, Shanda says. A Miss Irene Dubrovnik? You've to phone back."

"Oh! Oh, right. Good. Thanks very much."

She left and Henderson shakily got dressed. His back was aching, as if his spine couldn't take the strain of keeping his body erect. He went to the lavatory and sat there for five minutes, teeth gritted and eyes watering with the pressure, but nothing shifted.

He tottered carefully down the stairs and shuffled over to Shanda's trailer. Out in the park an old black man drove about on a miniature tractor cutting the grass.

Henderson knocked at the door and Shanda let him in.

"Can I use the phone?"

"The phone? Sure."

He sat down warily on the glass and wrought-iron seat. He wondered what Shanda did with herself all day. She settled down on a sofa and leafed through a magazine. He punched out Irene's number. He felt excited but a little inhibited by Shanda's presence and subdued somewhat by his weakened state.

"Hello, Irene. It's Henderson."

"Hi. I got your letter."

"Look, I'm really sorry about all the—"

"Forget it. How are you?"

"Actually, I've got the most appalling indigestion. I drank something called Henry's Goat and ate something called hoppin' john."

"Red-neck food, Henderson. You've got to be reared on that stuff. Have you had grits yet?"

"It feels like it." Perhaps that caused the stuffed-gravel sensation. He shifted slightly in his seat, turning his back toward Shanda, who was listening with candid curiosity. He felt huge relief and gratitude at this restoration of feeling between him and Irene.

"Listen," he said, "can you get down here?"

"I don't know. When?"

"This weekend. We can stay in a hotel. Then we'll take

a few days and drive around. Charleston, Savannah, somewhere like that "

There was a pause.

"OK, maybe I can get down on Friday night."

"I'll meet you at the airport. Atlanta."

"No. I don't know which plane I'll get. I'll come straight to the hotel."

"Great. Hang on a sec." He turned to Shanda. "Shanda, what's the very best hotel in Atlanta?"

"Excuse me?"

"Hotel. The very best. In Atlanta."

"Well . . . I guess Monopark 5000. But it's real expensive."

It sounded more like a brand of hair conditioner than a hotel, but he would have to take her word for it. He relayed its name to Irene, who said she'd heard of it and the massive complex of shops, plazas, banks and adventure playgrounds out of which the enormous hotel soared.

"See you there," he said. "Friday night." His voice went hoarse. "Bye." He put the phone down.

"Was that your wife?" Shanda asked. "I mean your fiancée. Bryant's mommy?"

"No." He thought quickly. "A business associate." No word of Irene's trip must reach Bryant's ears. He asked if he could make some more calls ("seein' as how Ah'm darned well a-sittin' by the phone") and received Shanda's permission. She went off into the kitchenette to make him some coffee. He called Beeby and told him the good news, gave him a description of the paintings and approximate market prices and said that Gage seemed entirely happy and prepared to sell through Mulholland, Melhuish.

Beeby's joy was profound. "We are all in your debt, Henderson. Great news. When are you coming home?"

Henderson told him of his plans to drive around for a few days, explore the South a little further.

"Take as long as you like, my dear boy, as long as you like. What about the Dutch paintings?"

"Very average, as you thought. There is one curiosity." He described Gage's dirty picture. "I can't place the myth. I thought Pruitt might know."

"I'll ask him. Enjoy yourself."

Henderson put the phone down. Shanda came back with a cup of coffee. Her love-bite had faded to a brown smudge. Her distended breasts swung unrestrained, it seemed to Henderson, beneath a bright floral-patterned maternity dress. They sat and chatted as best they could for a few minutes. He thought she asked him if he and "Bryant's mommy" were going to get married in a church. He told her no, and sketched out the arguments in favor of a registry office wedding.

"I'm sorry?"

"Registry office."

"Red just offed his what? His wife?"

Did they have registry offices in America? "No. A registry office."

"Air defense officer? Who? Red?"

"Fiss. Fiss. Aw-fiss."

Shanda lit a cigarette and smiled worriedly at him.

"You know, it's still not working," she said. "Sometimes it's fine an' I hear you OK. But other times it just goes. I'm lost."

Ten minutes later, Henderson stepped exhausted from the trailer. He walked around the side of the house, belching quietly to himself in an attempt to dislodge the ball of warm air trapped behind his rib cage. He wandered down the cool overgrown alleyways of the back garden feeling slightly more at ease. Apart from his clogged and costive body, his life was beginning to pick up again. He was finally getting on with his job and was reconciled with Irene. The last few days had been an absurd and regrettable hiccup. It was as if in driving south he'd passed into some anarchic and frustrating time zone—like Alice falling down the rabbit hole—but now things were returning to normal.

He pushed through a screen of laurels to find himself on the banks of a large brackish stream. On the far bank was a dense pine wood. Over to his right was a stone bench, upon which sat Cora.

"Mr. Dores," she called. "Come and admire the view."

He joined her on the bench. She wore black cotton trousers and a white blouse, and with her short hair looked obscurely Chinese.

"The view?"

"My mother planned to construct a vista here. But it never got made."

"I see. Shame." They sat and looked at the pine trees some thirty or forty feet away across the stream.

"I suppose you think," she said, "that it's a rather pretentious idea. A southern lady playing at being a landscape gardener."

"Not at all," he said defensively. He changed the subject. "I was very impressed by your father's collection."

She turned her sunglasses on him. "Is he going to let you sell them?"

"I hope so."

"Do you like *Demeter and Iambe?*"

"That's the one where. . . ."

"The girl is holding up her dress. Yes."

"What did you call it?"

"*Demeter and Iambe*. It's written on the back of the canvas. I don't know who the hell they are, though."

"I can fill you in on Demeter, I think. Goddess of the harvest. Her daughter, Persephone, was kidnapped by Hades, god of the underworld, one day while she was gathering flowers. Demeter goes wild with grief, permits no harvest for a year. Mankind about to perish, Zeus persuades Hades to release Persephone. Harvests restored. I don't know where Iambe fits in. One of the rarer Greek myths, I suppose."

"I sup*poase sowe*," she imitated his accent. Henderson smiled. He could take a joke.

"Are you married, Mr. Dores?"

He explained—roughly—the position in regard to Melissa.

"You divorced her and now you want to remarry? Why?"

"Well . . . I think because I now realize that the only time I was truly happy was when I was married to her and, well, I think I can be happy again." He was a little astounded at his honesty. Having uttered the sentiment he reassessed it in the light of his recent phone call to Irene. Was it true? Yes, he told himself and remarked again on the boundless capacity for self-deception that resides in every human being.

"So I take it Miss Dubrovnik isn't your intended."

"Who? Oh, no. Why would . . . what would make you think that she might have been?"

"I don't know. It's just that when I told you she'd phoned you looked so pleased."

"She's a colleague. She, ah, had some important news for me about the paintings. Actually I'm meeting her in Atlanta on Friday. Some problems of dating, provenance, that sort of thing. Seventeenth-century Dutch is not really my area."

"What is?"

"Late nineteenth. I'm what's known as an Impressionist man."

"The Impressionist man," she said grandly.

"Yes." He couldn't tell why he felt uneasy.

"I see."

"May I ask you something?" he said, emboldened by the friendly turn the conversation had taken.

"You may."

"Why do you wear your sunglasses all the time?"

She looked at him. "Because I'm an impressionist man as well, you might say. An impressionist woman."

"I don't follow."

"Because everything looks nicer. The country, the weather, the people. They all look more as they should."

Henderson wasn't quite sure if she were being serious. "You mean as you somehow imagined they would? Ideally speaking."

"Let's say, as I *think* they should. Without my glasses the world doesn't look as bright or as richly colored. The people look nastier too." She puffed at her cigarette, sending small clouds up into the branches of the tree that overhung the bench.

"Stands to reason," Henderson said without much conviction.

"Do you want me to take them off?"

"Well, I . . . I mean only if—"

She took her sunglasses off and turned her face toward him. It seemed an almost profane and indecent gesture, as if she'd suddenly exposed her breasts or, like the girl in the painting, raised her dress. Her eyes seemed small and were brown like beer. English bitter, he thought, how apt. Her

face seemed bland and empty. It was impossible to as-
sess—with the removal of such a dominant feature—
whether she was pretty or plain. It was like a good friend
shaving off a beard he's worn for ten years. Someone entirely different—unknown—is exposed beneath.

Henderson felt uncomfortable. A fly buzzed around
her face and she flapped it away. The removal of her sunglasses seemed to imply an intimacy between them, as if
she were doing something specially for him. He hadn't
asked her to oblige, he reminded himself.

"I think," he said with insincere gallantry, "you look
much nicer with them off."

"Remember I'm seeing you differently too," she said,
scrutinizing him. "I've torn away a veil."

He smiled edgily. The fly buzzed back, around his
head this time. Just then the distant sound of rock music
came from the house.

"You're not quite so hostile to us Brits, today," he said.

She laughed. "Life can get a little boring around here.
Don't blame me if I try to liven it up a little. Create some
tension. I like to draw people out, you know. Force them
to be themselves."

"Well, your blindness was very convincing. Your contempt for the English too."

"What about your contempt for us Americans, then?"

"What contempt? We don't have any contempt for
you. *I* don't, certainly."

She looked hard at him. "Well, we don't care, anyway.
We know it's all brought on by envy."

He decided not to be drawn out any further.

"Why are you living here, if you don't mind my asking?
I heard you dropped out of medical school."

She replaced her sunglasses. "I was going to be married," she said in a quiet, solemn voice. "Three days before

the ceremony my fiancé was killed in a car crash. I came back home. That was six months ago."

"Oh. I'm really sorry." He felt very sad, all of a sudden. "I didn't realize . . ."

"Actually, that's not true."

"Really." He felt angry, all of a sudden. What *was* true in this family?

"I was at medical school. After a while I just couldn't see the point. All those illnesses, you know. Not just the big heavy ones; it was the horrible little ones: the 'syndromes,' the 'diseases,' the ones named after people. Too many of those to cope with."

There was a pause.

"Duane seems to be back," Henderson said. "Will he have fixed my car or is that too much to hope for?"

"See you later, Mr. Dores."

That afternoon Henderson took Polaroid snapshots of all the paintings. Going around clockwise from the door, he measured each painting, took it off the wall to check the back, made a brief description and noted the title, the signature—if there was one—and the date. Back in New York he would consult the *catalogue raisonné* of each artist but he felt instinctively that all the paintings were "right."

He broke off for dinner. His saliva glands squirted into action when Alma-May entered with a large steaming casserole dish containing what she described as spaghetti bongaleeze. It turned out to be a vegetarian version, however, with various types of nut substituted for the meat. It was reasonably tasty, though, and Henderson ate his modest portion with some enthusiasm—mixed with vague qualms about whether one could actually overdose on vegetable fiber. His bowels seemed to have shut down entirely: the drains were well and truly blocked.

Pudding turned out to be apple pie, cooked in a roasting tin with inch-thick whole wheat pastry. Alma-May had halved the apples but this was the only concession she had made to fruit preparation. In his portion Henderson found a twig with a few leaves on it. Perhaps Alma-May simply lined her roasting tin with pastry, set it on the ground in the orchard and shook the trees till the fruit fell in. . . .

Bryant seemed quite content and after dinner went back upstairs to rejoin Duane and his music. Henderson caught her alone for a moment and asked her if she was enjoying herself.

"Sure. It's OK."

"You're absolutely positive you don't want to go home?"

"Yes. I'll stay."

"Did you have a good day in Atlanta?"

"It was all right."

"Tell me, what's Duane like?"

"He's OK."

He sat and watched television with Gage and Beckman until about eleven o'clock and then went to bed. He undressed and looked at his naked body in the mirror. His belly was as hard and distended as a gourd. He looked at his hairless shanks and collapsing buttocks and was not well pleased with what he saw. He made a half-hearted resolve to exercise. Perhaps he should take up jogging? But then he remembered he *did* exercise: he zenced. He did a few zencing drills, up on his toes and lunging until his calves ached. Then he climbed into bed.

He thought for a while about his coming reunion with

Irene. It was, he thought, a little uncharacteristic of her to relent so quickly. Perhaps she had missed him? Perhaps, he speculated, she had fallen in love with him? This, however, proved beyond the powers of his imagination.

He settled down on his rack waiting for the night to pass. From time to time there were ominous rumblings and pingings from his hard bloated stomach. What he needed was some stodge: some cholesterol, carcinogens and red meat. Alma-May's regime was too harsh: more suited to an animal, some robust herbivore, a camel or a giraffe; some beast with a mouth full of flat grinding molars, and whose idea of a delicacy was to strip the bark from a sapling. His model of late-twentieth-century man just wasn't designed for such rigors. If he didn't have some monosodium glutamate within the next twenty-four hours he'd start getting the shakes.

He heard Duane's music stop and the night noises were left to themselves. He worried vaguely for a while about the population explosion, the disappearing rain forests and the destruction of the ionosphere by aerosol sprays, and at some point in the small hours consciousness left him.

chapter eight

THE next morning Henderson completed his rough catalog and showed it to Gage.

"All that remains to be settled now, Mr. Gage, are the prices and the date of the auction." He handed over his estimate of the paintings' value.

	Reserve	Estimate
Sisley, *Le Verger à*		
Voisins	$500,000	$550,000–$650,000
Les Toits de		
Marly	500,000	600,000–700,000
Derain, *La*		
Bélandre Verte	300,000	400,000–500,000
Von Dongen,		
still life	100,000	100,000–150,000
still life	100,000	125,000–200,000
Braque, *L'Atelier*	280,000	350,000–500,000
Utrillo,		
Montmagny en		
Hiver	200,000	250,000–300,000

Vuillard, *Petit*

Déjeuner	200,000	225,000–300,000
Intérieur Bleu	150,000	200,000–250,000

"You'll see that the reserve column totals two million three hundred and thirty thousand dollars," he said. "That's the minimum for which we will allow them to be sold. Needless to say, that price is kept strictly confidential. I've based it on current sale-room performance, but, for example, I think Vuillard is grossly undervalued at the moment, but there you are. Anyway, absolutely no problem about meeting the reserve, I'm sure. Lots of them will go much higher as well. The Braque, the Sisleys . . ."

"Two million three," Gage pondered. "Where do you guys make your money?"

"We charge the buyers a ten percent commission on top of the sale price. We normally charge the seller a rate too, but in this case we are happy to waive it."

"Nice business. What about the landscapes?"

"I don't think we're likely to clear more than another, oh, hundred thousand, if we're lucky."

"I see."

"Well, it's been a pleasure—"

"You mean you're finished?"

"Well, me personally. There's the insurance, packing, transportation, catalogs, exhibition and advertising to be taken care of, but that will be in the hands of our very capable staff. If you're happy with these reserve figures, then there's nothing more for you to worry about."

"Oh." Gage seemed disgruntled.

"Is there anything wrong?"

"I guess I didn't figure you'd be through so fast."

"I am just the valuer and assessor," Henderson explained. "My job is really quite straightforward. And I have," he added gently, "been here since Sunday—four days. I'm usually no longer than an afternoon."

Gage appeared to be deep in perplexed thought. "I see. I suppose you'll be going soon."

"I thought tomorrow."

"Mmm."

Henderson left him and went to check on his car. He wondered what was bothering the old man. He had put up with the bizarre household purely because of the importance and magnitude of the sale. Us valuers, he told himself a little smugly, don't like to linger. Pruitt Halfacre rarely took more than an hour.

He walked down the front steps. It was another clear hot day. His car had already acquired its coating of dust and its metal sides were hot to the touch. He walked around it and saw with irritation that the wheel still had not been replaced. Bloody Duane, he thought. There was nothing for it. He took off his jacket and rolled up his shirt sleeves. He had last changed the wheel on a car sometime in the 1960's on a motoring tour of the Loire Valley, but all he could remember of the exercise was some hideous complication with the jack and subsequent acrimonious row with his then girlfriend.

He walked around to the back to open the boot and noticed that the small flap over the petrol cap was ajar. He looked closer. The cap was loose. He strongly doubted whether any petrol remained in the tank. He opened the boot. The spare tire had gone.

He made a couple of circuits of the car muttering and nodding to himself with an expression of sardonic wisdom on his face, like a man whose worst suspicions about humankind have just been unequivocally confirmed.

"Everything OK?" It was Shanda standing at the doorway of her mobile home fanning herself with a magazine.

She came carefully down the steps and teetered over in her high heels, like a soft-soled bather on a cruel shingle beach. Henderson pointed to the petrol tank.

"No pet . . . No gas," he said.

"I know. Duane siphoned it out this morning. He said to tell you."

"Why? Good God. What's he playing at?"

"He din't have no gas in his car."

Henderson put his hands on his hips and looked around at the scenery.

"He took your spare too. He said you'd got all different types of French tires on your car. He's trying to get them matched."

Henderson rubbed his eyes. "I'm leaving tomorrow," he said.

"Look, your jacket's fallen on the ground." Shanda bent down to pick it up, but, for some reason—her high heels and the disequilibrium of Freeborn Gage, Jr.—she fell over, giving a little squeal of alarm. Henderson helped her up. Shanda was giggling, and he wondered suddenly if she was a little drunk. Her pregnant belly bulged against his hipbone. It was soft and springy, in strong contrast to his own cast-iron gut. She put an arm on one of his shoulders while, wobbling on one leg, she attempted to adjust the strap of a high heel. Henderson stood there patiently, a reliable leaning post. He heard a car and looked around. Duane, he earnestly hoped, with two wheels and some fuel. But no: it was Freeborn.

The car thumped to a halt and Freeborn bounded out, not bothering to shut the door behind him. Shanda gave a low groan—she was still struggling with her shoe.

"Hi, darlin'," she called. "Get your friends?"

Henderson saw two suited, smart-looking men get out of the car behind her advancing husband. Shanda became bipedal. Freeborn's ten spread fingers pronged fiercely into Henderson's soft chest, bruising, and propelling him with disturbing ease back against his car.

"*Ouch!* Steady on!"

Freeborn now had a forefinger practically up Henderson's left nostril. His large face loomed three inches away. Henderson had a close-up view of the fjordlike contours of his carved and clipped facial hair. What painstaking efforts it must require, the thought entered his mind, unbidden, to shave around those gulfs and promontories, those peninsulas and bays each morning—surely defeating the ostensible purpose of growing a beard in the first place, namely to rid one of the necessity of that tedious chore.

"I fuckin' warned you, scumbag!" Freeborn's breath had a curious antiseptic tang. Perhaps the result of a judicious swilling of the mouthwash he peddled along with his medical wadding.

"Come *on*," Henderson said, hurt. "She fell over. I helped her up."

"You don't touch her, heah?"

"What was I meant to do? She couldn't get up; she was like a turtle on its back or something. Helpless."

"You calling Shanda a turtle? Bastard!"

Freeborn hit him in the stomach, and something terrible happened to his jammed intestines. He fell to his knees. Everything went red and fizzing for an instant. He heard Shanda scream. His vision cleared and he blinked away his tears. It hadn't really hurt. How remarkable! He stood up unsteadily. He backed off. Pingings and rumbling were coming from his gut, like a dam about to break. He farted uncontrollably. Freeborn advanced on him rubbing his sore fist. There was only one thing for it now, Henderson calculated. Total panic. He turned and ran.

Too late he realized he should have run down the road

to Luxora Beach. He sprinted up to the trees at the park's edge and looked back. Ungainly Freeborn lumbered after him yelling imprecations. More gainly Henderson dodged his swinging punches easily and ran back toward the house.

"Stop him, stop him!" Shanda beseeched. Freeborn's two guests looked on in open-mouthed astonishment.

"Who?" Henderson shouted.

"You, you!"

Did she want *him* to stop, or stop Freeborn?

Freeborn pounded up, his face florid, his breath coming in hoarse, phlegm-rattling gasps. Henderson looked quickly about him, then snatched a bamboo-cane prop from a flower bed. The large sunflower it supported keeled gently over as if in slow motion.

Henderson held the cane in front of him. Left elbow on hip. Controlled relaxation: *flèche* attack, cuts to the head. Freeborn stopped abruptly, a look of puzzlement on his face. Shanda's whimpering died away as they all contemplated Henderson on guard.

Henderson flourished his cane, wiggling the tip at Freeborn's face. Nobody moved. Then Henderson suddenly felt tired and foolish. He sensed the beginnings of a blush through his sweat.

Freeborn turned away.

"Get me a beer, honey," he said and spat two or three times on the ground. He turned to his guests. "Gentlemen, let's go inside." With uneasy smiles the two men skirted Henderson and went into the trailer. Freeborn followed, and Henderson was left alone.

He stuck the cane back in the border and attempted to right the fallen sunflower. As he picked it up, the great nodding head, the size of his own face, came away in his hand.

*　　*　　*

That afternoon, after a lunch of panfried nut rissoles and
turnip slaw, Henderson went in search of Duane. Mobility
was his chief concern now: he had to be in Atlanta in
twenty-four hours for Irene.

"He ain't here," said Alma-May. She didn't know nothing about "no tires."

On the way back into the hall from the kitchen he met
Freeborn and his two guests. There were no introductions.
Freeborn ignored him as he ushered the two men up the
stairs. Henderson assumed they were going to see Gage.
He wondered what for.

He went outside and made his way to a ramshackle
collection of old sheds some distance away from the main
house. Here he found the old black gardener who kept the
grounds in order. Henderson asked him if he knew where
he might lay his hands on a spare tire and a gallon of
petrol.

"Luxora," the old man said. "Dr. Tire. They's a gas station there too. You can get gas there."

"Thank you," Henderson said, smiling politely.

Returning to the house, he quickened his pace when he
heard the dull throb of music emanating from Duane's bedroom.

He knocked on the door, failed to make out any reply
and pushed the door open. The walls were covered with
shiny posters of rock stars and sportsmen. There was a
lingering fetid smell of unwashed, overused sheets garnished with a hint of ashtrays long unemptied. The noise
of the music was immense and palpable. It seemed to stir
strands of his hair. Four speakers the size of traveling
trunks stood in the corners of the room. Bryant sat alone

on the bed, cross-legged, smoking, bobbing her head to the rhythms of the drums.

"Bryant!" he shouted.

She looked around, got up and turned the music down.

"What do you want?" she said.

"I'm looking for Duane."

"He's not here."

"I can see that. What are you doing here?"

"He said I could listen to his records anytime I want."

"Well, he's got two of my tires and a tankful of petrol and I'd like them back."

"I know. God, he's only trying to help," she said disgustedly.

"It's a funny way to render assistance. Why did he have to siphon my petrol?"

"He'd run out of gas. He had to have gas to take your tires to try and match them. I said he could."

"Very decent of you. . . . Tell him to get it all back together by tomorrow morning. We're leaving."

"What?"

"Well, *you're* leaving. I've got a business appointment in Atlanta. Make up your mind whether you're going back to New York or Richmond."

Bryant said nothing. She took a trembling drag on her cigarette. Henderson noticed it was hand rolled.

"I say, that's not dope, is it?"

To his utter consternation Bryant started to cry. She began to sob and sniffle. She sat down on the bed. After some thought, Henderson sat down beside her. He felt a disquieting dampness beneath his thighs; it was rather like sitting on a riverbank. He stood up.

"Look, I'm sorry. I didn't mean to accuse you of smoking grass, or whatever." Now she was pushing all her fingers repeatedly through her hair.

"Ah, just go away and leave me alone, you . . ." She leaned over the amplifier and turned the music up again.

With a sigh, and overlooking the implicit oath, he left the room. On the landing at the head of the stairs he encountered the sauntering figure of Cora.

"Hi," she said. "I hear that you and Freeborn nearly came to blows over Shanda. Very chivalric."

"We did come to blows. Or rather blow. There was only one actually delivered—American, too."

"But then you were going to play swordfighting, I hear."

"Self-defense," he said, a little frostily. "Anyway, I'm off tomorrow. All done. All 'through,' as you say."

"That was quick."

Henderson explained that in fact it was slow. He then told her of the mysterious offense he had caused Bryant.

Cora shrugged. "What do you expect? She's probably finding it hard to come to terms with you as a father."

Henderson considered there was some rightness in that observation. He realized he treated Bryant as if she were a slovenly waitress in a restaurant, with hectoring aggression, rather than in any spirit of paternalistic goodwill. He had never felt at ease with her, and after that night in Skaggsville their relationship had acquired even less welcome contours. . . .

He felt suddenly depressed at the thought of his impending marriage to Melissa. It wasn't so much Melissa that he was reluctant to take on; it was the prospect of a lifetime's tense and problematic contact with Bryant and metal-mouthed Irv that got him down. He pursed his lips. Then he realized that by some association of ideas—prompted no doubt by recollections of the view down Bryant's pajama top—he was staring vacantly at Cora's chest. She crossed her arms.

"How old is Duane?" he asked. "As a matter of interest."

"Oh, I don't know, really. Thirty-three, thirty-four, I guess."

"Thirty-three? Thirty-four?"

"Didn't you know?"

"Good God." He felt an obscure but powerful sense of worry. "I'd somehow got the notion he was seventeen or eighteen. Thirty-three . . ."

Cora laughed unrestrainedly. It was the first time he'd heard her laugh, he reflected.

"Are you going straight back?" she asked.

"Not directly. I've got this business meeting in Atlanta first." He wasn't really concentrating; he was busy reconstructing his Identikit of Duane.

"With Miss Dubrovnik?"

"Who? Oh, yes. Yes." He thought wildly. "I told you about it. It's a problem of dating one of the paintings. I've taken Polaroids, close-ups . . . technical matter I'm not really equipped to deal with."

"So she's some sort of genuine expert. Unlike you."

"Mmm."

"Is she Yugoslavian? That name—"

"Yes. Yes, I think so. Originally, you know." They stood and looked at each other for a beat or two. She doesn't believe me, he thought. I wouldn't believe me either.

"You don't happen to know," he asked, "who those two men were with Freeborn, do you?"

"Don't you know them? They come from your hometown."

"What? Hove? Surely not."

"No, stupid. Roach City. They own a gallery in New York."

chapter nine

HENDERSON clattered down the front steps and set off at a brisk walk for Luxora Beach. Although riven with worries at this new problem, he could still muster an intense frustration at having to walk miles to get to a telephone. It was like living in the Wild West, some frontier town in the 1890's. The next thing they'd be telling him that the Indians had cut down the wires to make ornaments. . . .

He glowered at Freeborn's trailer and paused. Was it worth risking it? Would Shanda let him in if Freeborn wasn't there? But what if he was? He kept on walking.

He was drawn up again by faint cries behind him. He looked back, saw it was Alma-May and retraced his steps.

"Mr. Dose! Mr. Dose!"

"Yes, yes. Here I am."

"Got a message from Duane. He called Shanda 'bout ten minutes ago. He says he can get the tires for your car."

"Excellent. When?"

"Saturday."

"But that's *useless*." He actually stamped his foot in the dirt of the drive. "I'm going away tomorrow."

"It's them French tires, he says."

Henderson stroked his forehead with the fingers of both hands. He had strong doubts about this "French tires" excuse. Duane had probably pawned them to buy records. "This is madness," he said rhetorically. "I arrived here on Sunday. My car has a puncture. Some ghostly figure volunteers to fix it. A week later it's still out of action. Madness."

"What's a 'puncture'?"

The walk into Luxora Beach took place beneath the full glare of the late-afternoon sun. Henderson arrived at Main Street in his now-familiar state of perspiration and irritation. In a petulant assertion of his own rights as an individual he decided to visit a gas station at one end of the street that—he had noticed previously—bore the sign DRIVE-THRU BURGERS. He crossed the railway tracks and the main road and made his way down the raised sidewalk to the gas station. A pickup and a car were parked outside the flimsy cage. A girl—blond like Shanda, bold makeup, gleaming earrings—leaned out of the window, talking to two other girls in a maroon car. They looked vaguely familiar: he had seen them—laughing—on his last visit to town. They all stopped talking as he approached. A straining extractor fan hauled thick air from the kitchen. There was a powerful smell of fried onions and cooking oil.

He examined the menu.

"A burger, please."

"Onions? Mustard? Pickle? Ketchup?"

Affirmative on all four counts. He paid and the burger duly arrived: a gray ice-hockey puck in a mean bun, a brown ruff of onions and the sectioned knob of a gherkin poking out beneath it. He took a huge jaw-cracking bite. Oil dripped down his chin onto his tie. He snorted astringency from his nostrils. His eyes watered. Mustard and ketchup squelched between his teeth. Still chewing, he took a long draft of Coke. The girls in the car watched him in horror-struck curiosity. He might have been Neanderthal man wolfing the steaming flesh of a mammoth. Bliss.

He heard the rap of knuckles on glass and looked up. Beckman sat behind the wheel of the pickup beaming hugely. I can't escape this bloody family, Henderson thought, and wandered over.

"Hi there, Henderson. Like our squirrelburgers?"

Henderson managed a smile. "Just felt like some meat. I'm not really used to a vegetarian diet, you see."

"That ain't *meat*, man." Beckman gave a high, delighted laugh. "Or, anyways, surer 'n shit it don't come from no steer."

There was, Henderson had to confess, a faint aftertaste now, the like of which he'd never previously encountered. A sort of renal gaminess, but somehow artificial tasting— as saccharin is to sugar—chemically engendered. He sent his tongue into the crevices and corners of his mouth. He pumped his saliva glands. He could not only taste it, it also filled his nasal passages, seeped along his sinus, like gas in a mine shaft.

"It's not squirrel really, is it?" he asked, in the sort of weak voice that pleads to have confirmed that a leg is being pulled.

"Minkburgers," Beckman grinned. "Weaselburgers." He gave a hoot of laughter. "Stoatburgers."

Henderson dropped his cooling rodentburger in a trash can and gulped down his Coke.

"Come and have a beer," Beckman invited.

Henderson said he had to make a phone call first but would see him in the bar in a minute or two. Slowly he made his way toward the post office. He now felt distinctly queasy. What with the current marmoreal state of his bowels it would probably be with him for weeks.

He slumped into the phone booth and requested directory inquiries to provide him with the number of Monopark 5000. Then he dialed the hotel. A series of cheerful girl-voices booked him a suite for the following night. Would he like a suite with a whirlpool bath? Why not. This brought to mind images of mixed bathing with Irene and he began to feel slightly better.

He gulped air. The prism wedged between spine and sternum had had its corners worn down like a pebble on a beach, and had shrunk to the size of a large cooking apple. He badly needed a drink to wash away, or at least mask, the taste of the burger, which seemed if anything to be getting stronger. He headed for the bar.

There were about ten pickups and cars parked outside the bar. Inside there was a lot of raucous laughter of Cardew's "heh-heh-heh" variety and much upending of beer bottles. He saw Beckman at the skittle machine and nervously made his way through the denimed throng, muttering apologies and bestowing edgy smiles. The machine was simplicity itself. A wooden ball was rolled down a chute—the direction and gradient of which one could alter—in an attempt to knock down the skittles. Those bowled over were rerighted by means of string attached to their crowns. The only mechanical device in the game twitched this taut whenever a skittle was floored.

Beckman crouched intensely over the chute, emitting a holler of glee every time he knocked any skittles over. It seemed a strangely banal pastime for an elementary-particle physicist, Henderson thought, but maybe this was simply his way of unwinding after a trying session with the quarks and neutrinos darting quantumly around his lab.

"Let me buy you a drink," Beckman offered, after a few more games.

They approached the bar. Two beers were produced, plus a glass (unrequested) for Henderson, accompanied by a look of condescending pity from the etiolated barkeep and curious glances from the relentlessly joshing good ol' boys.

"Don't worry about it," Beckman said comfortingly. "They think all you English are fags anyway." He pulled at his own bottle. "So, how's it going anyway?"

"Just about finished," Henderson said. "We'll be off tomorrow."

"Hell, I thought you were going to be here for weeks."

Henderson explained in broad outline what his job entailed. He also mentioned his immobile car and Duane's worthless promises. He wondered if there was anything Beckman could do to speed up Duane's repair work.

"Look, no problem, I'll drive you to Atlanta," Beckman volunteered. Henderson told him of his business meeting at Monopark 5000 (greeted by a whistle of admiration from Beckman's lips) and his wish to spend a few days touring the more scenic regions of the South.

"No sweat," Beckman continued. "You take my pickup. Come Saturday, when Duane's fixed your car I'll drive it into Atlanta and we can trade. I'll meet you Saturday, say four o'clock, corner of Peachtree and Edgewood, same as before."

"Great," Henderson said. "Saturday at four, then. Turned out to be a lucky day after all. It started badly," he explained.

"Hell, I knew it would be a good day for me. Been feelin' good since this morning."

"Oh, yes? Why's that?"

"Simple. Had me a five-turd crap before breakfast. Can't beat it for settin' you up."

"Really?" He paused; there really was nothing one could say in response. He tried not to imagine this source of contentment. "I'm very grateful, Beckman. This meeting, it's very important."

"No problem. What are friends for?" His fluttering lids made the remark seen incongruously coy. Henderson felt another twinge of alarm at this announcement of his new status, but he decided not to challenge it. Instead he asked another question.

"Do you happen to know who those two men are who arrived today with Freeborn?"

"You mean Ben and Peter? Nice guys."

"Who are they? If you don't mind my asking."

"They're friends of Freeborn. Some kind of business partners? They had a big deal going or something. They were down here about a year ago. They're the guys he sold the paintings to."

Henderson screwed up his face. "Are you sure?"

"Well, something like that." He looked at his watch. "Shit. I gotta get back."

Henderson sat silently on the drive back to the house pondering the news. What had Freeborn done? Sold the paintings—his legacy, no doubt—to finance some nefarious deal? Mortgaged them in some sort of way? Then his father goes and ruins everything by deciding to sell them himself. H. Dores, Esq., turns up, and sets off a panic. It certainly explained Freeborn's hostility.

He was still pondering the ramifications of this plot when he stepped into the hall. Gage, Freeborn and the two men were standing at the foot of the stairs chatting amicably.

"Henderson," Gage called. "Come and meet our two friends." Gage seemed almost unnaturally cheerful, Henderson thought. He was introduced to the two men: one, Benjamin Sereno; the other, Peter D. Gint. Sereno was small and dark. He had an enormous moustache that seemed constructed on a different scale from his body, but that, Henderson swiftly realized, was deliberately intended to obscure or draw attention from his lips. He had lips like Toulouse-Lautrec: thick, claret colored and wet. They made Henderson (still queasy from his rodentburger) even more nauseous: they reminded him of thin fillets of liver, or, due to the hirsute proximity of the moustache, a wound in the flank of an animal. He swallowed a mouthful of saliva. They shook hands. He noticed an ostentatious carbuncled ring set with a red stone. A lot of American males sported these, Henderson had observed, only Sereno's stone was held in an inch-high plinth and must have weighed a pound.

Gint was burly with receding blond hair. His short collar was prominently monogrammed P.D.G. At some point in his youth his entire face had been ravaged with acne, leaving him with skin pitted like a peach stone. The scourge was still not past: an angry wen pushed his collar askew, a mini-Krakatoa about to blow. Whatever they looked like, Henderson thought with mingled worry and relief, it certainly wasn't New York gallery owners.

"You're with Mulholland, Melhuish, right?" Sereno asked amicably.

"Yes. Yes, I am."

"Fine firm." He nodded. "Congratulations."

"Good firm," Gint agreed. He had a soft voice that didn't match his face.

"What's the name of your gallery?" Henderson asked, disingenuously.

They looked at each other. "Well, Sereno and Gint," Sereno said. "You mean you haven't heard of us?"

"I'm afraid not. I've only been in New York a couple of months. Whereabouts is it?"

"It's in back of Canal," Gint said. "Between Eldridge Street and Allen Street."

"Is that the Lower East Side?"

"You got it."

"Ah." Henderson suppressed his shout of laughter. He looked at Gage. The man seemed unperturbed by this information. They might as well have said their "gallery" was in Harlem or the South Bronx. But the smiles were all polite, waiting for the conversation to continue.

Cora came down the stairs. To Henderson's surprise Sereno went to meet her.

"Cora," he said. "Good to see you again." He kissed her on the cheek. To Henderson this came as a shock, almost an affront. Those fat wet lips on Cora's small face.

"You remember Peter?" Sereno asked.

Gint raised a hand. "Hi. We met last time."

"Are you guys staying with us?" Cora asked, in familiar tones.

"No. In Atlanta." Sereno offered Cora a cigarette and lit it for her. "Monopark 5000. Quite a place."

Henderson tasted voleburger in his mouth.

"Isn't that where you and your colleague are staying tomorrow?" Cora asked. How did she know? Shanda.

"Hey, that's wonderful," Sereno observed. "Let's all have dinner. Freeborn, Cora, Shanda, you and your colleague."

"Alas, I'm fully occupied that night. Very sorry."

"Carbon dating," Cora said.

"Dating who?" Gint asked, then laughed. Sereno joined in with enthusiasm.

"That wit," Sereno said. "I love his wit."

"Could I have a word?" Gage asked softly, touching Henderson's arm. "In my room." He trotted off up the stairs. Henderson made his goodbyes to the gallery owners and followed obediently.

Gage stood in his room at the escritoire studying some documents. He waved Henderson to a chair and handed him a piece of paper. It was a list of his paintings with prices beside them.

"I'll come right out, Henderson. Sereno and Gint have made me an offer for the paintings."

Henderson saw that the figures approximated closely to his own, except in one crucial degree: Sereno and Gint were offering $100,000 each for the four Dutch landscapes, the portrait and the allegory.

"But this is absurd," Henderson said in desperation. "Have you seen what they're offering for the landscapes? They must be mad."

"It's up to them. Their estimation of the value."

"But nobody would *ever* pay this amount. It's preposterous."

"One man's opinion, Henderson." He moved away to look at the Dutch paintings. "I must confess"—he kept his back to him—"that I feel you have been a little—what shall we say?—hasty in pricing the landscapes. I ask myself . . . I wonder if your urge to leave us has influenced your evaluation."

Henderson protested loudly. Gage turned.

"Look, I want to sell through Mulholland, Melhuish," he said benignly. "For the sake of my friendship with Eddie

Mulholland and, if I may say so, with you. But I can't afford to take a half-million loss." He came over and patted Henderson's shoulder. "I'd like for you to stay on a few more days. Consider the Dutch paintings some more."

"But I'm going to Atlanta tomorrow. Then, um, other business demands—"

"I'm really sorry to hear that. But I appreciate your time. Thanks for coming down."

Henderson felt faint. He improvised. "Actually, this meeting in Atlanta is with a . . . an art historian and expert, precisely to do with, er, some ambiguities in my dating of the Dutch paintings. It may, in fact I'm sure, it'll cause me to reconsider."

"Great. So, have your meeting and return here. Let me know the result."

"Yes." Henderson shut his eyes.

"I'm in no hurry. My decision can wait a few days."

Henderson stood up. "May I ask how you got to Sereno and Gint?"

"They're business associates of Freeborn. Freeborn suggested I get a second bid on the paintings. It makes sense. He called them up and they came on down."

"I think I should tell you that I think they know as much about art as I do about suppositories."

"Can I be honest? I don't really care, Henderson. I'm not giving the paintings to a museum. They are offering me cash now. I don't have to wait for an auction."

"I'd be very suspicious—"

"I think that's my business, Henderson. Freeborn has told me that they are new to the art world. They're starting out. But so what? They've got money." He punched Henderson lightly on the shoulder. "Healthy competition, Henderson. A fair fight. Stay on a few days. Think, relax, enjoy yourself. I'm sure we'll work everything out."

*　　*　　*

Henderson walked slowly down the stairs. This was disaster from a quarter he'd never anticipated. Nightmarish possibilities and problems presented themselves to him. What would Beeby do if they lost the sale? What would Irene say about another cancellation? That was the first priority: he had to phone Irene, put her off for a few days. Then warn Beeby of the new developments.

He walked outside and listened for noises from Freeborn's trailer. It seemed quiet. Perhaps he had gone off somewhere with Sereno and Gint. He could hear the faint sound of a television. Shanda watching a soap. He knocked. Let it be Shanda, let it be Shanda, he prayed.

Freeborn opened the door. Behind him Henderson saw Sereno, Gint and Shanda watching TV.

"What the fuck do you want?"

"Is there any chance . . . ? I'd be most grateful if I could . . . Could I make a phone call?"

"No."

The door was slammed shut. Henderson thought he heard him say, "It was that English asshole," followed by loud laughter, but perhaps it was just the television. He suddenly didn't feel like telephoning anybody. He would just have to take his chances and endeavor to make the best of it.

chapter ten

HENDERSON packed glumly the next morning. His fear and concern over the arrival of Sereno and Gint had grown. What was going on? Could they really buy the Gage collection for four million? Or was it all part of some monumental bluff? . . .

Another portion of his brain writhed with apprehension at having to tell Irene of the radical truncation of their little holiday together. He was hoping now that his one night with her would be a sufficiently lyrical experience for her to forgive him. He would have to choose his moment with care. . .

Also, in Atlanta with its functioning telephones, he would call Beeby and tell him of this new development and work out some sort of a counterattack. Perhaps they could guarantee the reserve prices; work up the Dutch pictures' value somewhat; suggest to Gage that—given enough publicity—the sale price might go even higher on the Sisleys or the Braque? That might work.

As he closed his case he felt thankful that in one area at least—his nether regions—everything was functioning normally at last. The squirrelburger, like some potent catalyst, had shifted the blockage in the small hours of the morning. It had proved to be the most efficient laxative he

had ever encountered. He felt altogether fitter, younger—
lighter than he had done since arriving in Luxora Beach.
And despite his looming crises he experienced too a re-
peating tremor of excitement at the prospect of seeing
Irene. It seemed like years since he had spent some time in
the company of a human being with whom there were re-
ciprocal feelings of affection. Here there was only strangeness, cynicism and malevolent dislike.

He walked down the passage to Bryant's room. He had
told her last night that she too was leaving and had given
her a choice of destination. She had opted sullenly for
New York with no trace of her earlier protests. Perhaps
she was, after all, keen to get away as well.

He knocked on her door. No answer. Duane's room
was quiet. Henderson knocked again and pushed the door
open. The room was empty. Propped on the pillow was an
envelope addressed to him. He tore it open.

Dear Henderson,

I have decided not to go back home. Duane
and I are going to be married. Don't worry. We
love each other. I will tell Mom.

I thought it would be best if I wasn't here when
you left. See you tomorrow. Have a nice time in
Atlanta.

Bryant

P.S. Duane says he is going to get you a complete
new set of tires.

Henderson watched his hand shake, the paper cracking
in his fingers. He felt a sudden terrible fear at the wrath of
Melissa, like some wretched vassal's of a warlord. He

tugged at his lower lip, tested some teeth for looseness. He swallowed. Calm down, he told himself, this is a fantasy, pure fantasy, it can't happen. She's a minor, she's only *fourteen*. She can't marry a man old enough to be her father. Who was this invisible Duane? What sort of evil perverted slob was he? And what a fool *he* had been to allow them so much time in each other's company. Two teenagers listening to records . . . He put his hand on his heart. It was beating ferociously. He turned the letter over and wrote, "I will talk to you when I get back. On *no* account tell your mother anything. H."

This new problem added itself to the others jostling for prominence in his brain, loud hooligans looking for trouble, trying to make life hell. They were penned up at the moment—just—but they could break out at any time, storm the streets.

In a perplexed trance, with a dumb, cretinous look on his face, he walked down the stairs and outside. His car stood on four piles of bricks, tireless. The bonnet was open. He looked in. Nothing obvious seemed to be missing, but his ignorance of the internal combustion engine was total. Solenoids, carburetors, magnetos could have been sequestered for all he knew.

He felt an immense futility descend upon him and he bowed his head impotently under the strain.

"Hi there." He looked up. It was Shanda. Did she keep watch on him? he wondered, irritated. She was like some omnipresent guardian of the front steps.

"Hello."

"What happened to your car?"

"Duane."

"That boy. I guess he means well, but . . ." She left her reservations unspoken. Boy? Henderson thought. Why do they refer to a thirty-four-year-old man as a boy? There was the source of his misconceptions.

"You wanna use the phone? Freeborn's away."

"No, thanks." He paused. "What's Duane like?" he asked slowly.

"Duane? Well . . ." Shanda came closer. Henderson thought he smelled alchohol on her breath. "Myself, I think he's a little bit, you know, *weird*."

"Oh, God." Henderson felt his weakness return, a sort of mild ache in his spine and knees. If a member of the Gage family pronounced someone "weird" then the reality must be truly alarming. But no, he told himself firmly, that problem was shelved until tomorrow; more pressing disasters awaited his attention. He climbed into Beckman's pickup.

"You are coming back, aren't you?" Shanda asked with a note of alarm.

"Yes," he said. "Tomorrow and tomorrow and tomorrow."

"Oh, good. You have a good time now, hear?"

From this side of the country too, Atlanta was visible from many miles off. Like Gothic cathedrals in medieval times, a reassuring prominence always on the horizon. The skyscrapers of the downtown district were hazy and indistinct against the soft lucency of the midafternoon sky. The more miles he put between himself and Luxora Beach the better he felt. He had even quite enjoyed roaring along the highway in Beckman's pickup.

When he reached Atlanta he had some problems locating the hotel in the city's daunting system of one-way streets. He could see it, three or four blocks away, an impressive slab of steel and reflecting glass, but he seemed able only to circle it: no street led directly there—it hovered out of reach, a massive illusion. Eventually he parked the pickup and attempted to make his way there on foot. He saw signs for the MONOPARK COMPLEX, then MONOPARK 5000 HOTEL. He went through an arch beneath a shopping mall, up a dark ramp of a corridor, and pushed through swing doors at the far end.

He found himself in a tall brilliant lobby. Thick wands of sunlight shone through vast overhead windows onto a marble floor. There appeared to be numerous entrances. The one through which he had emerged was clearly not the most significant. Various doormen and bellhops stood around in stylized cavalry uniforms: boots, hats, gold epaulets, even dinky sabers at their belts. At the rear of the lobby was what appeared to be a dense wood of twenty-foot-high trees. In front of this forest was a long reception desk. This Henderson approached with due reverence and awe. The experience was, he thought, akin to appearing at heaven's gate with the sin-virtue equation still in balance.

"Dores," he said to the tanned cavalryman. "D, o, r, e, s. I have a reservation."

"Good afternoon, sir," he said. "Welcome to Monopark 5000." He tapped out the name on a computer keyboard. There was a whirring and clicking and the machine fed out a piece of plastic with holes punched in it.

"What's this?" Henderson asked. "A credit card?"

"Your key, sir. Need some help with your case?" The smile never budged.

"No, thanks. I can manage."

"You are in Suite 35J. Follow this path"—he gestured at an opening in the forest wall—"go through the atrium and take one of the scenic elevators to the thirty-fifth floor. Enjoy your stay at Monopark 5000."

"Right." Henderson picked up his bag and looked dubiously at the path, which was signposted TO THE ATRIUM. He felt like an explorer leaving base camp. "Goodbye," he said to the man and set off.

He had imagined that the trees were merely a decorative screen but he was wrong. He found himself in a copse, a grove, a veritable spinney of weeping figs, silver birches and stands of bamboo. A soft greenish light filtered down from above; xylophonic music burbled from hidden speakers. Other paths bifurcated from his. CONVENTION RESERVATION he saw, TO THE INDIAN VILLAGE and SWIMMING CREEK. These signs were deliberately "Old West": chunks of varnished wood with the message burned on with a branding iron. The frontier theme was enhanced by the sudden appearance from behind a tree of a waitress in fringed buckskin waistcoat and miniskirt. Henderson gave a shrug of alarm. There were stripes of war paint on her cheeks and forehead.

"Cocktails, sir?" she asked. "At the Indian village."

"What? Oh, no. I'm looking for the atrium."

"Keep right on to the end of this path." She slipped away into the trees.

He followed her instructions and broke out into a towering atrium some twelve or fourteen stories high. Before him stretched a lake, blocking his way, some thirty yards across, dotted with islands furnished with seats and sprouting plants. Over on the left of the far bank was a cluster of wigwams, which on closer inspection turned out to be a large restaurant and bar area. On the balconied far wall, a dozen scenic elevators rose up and down, some of them disappearing into holes in the roof like silent glass scarabs.

Henderson let out a spontaneous gasp of surprise. He had heard of this new breed of American hotel—the hotel as wonderland, as secular cathedral, as theme park—but his imagination had been deficient. Plants grew every-where; fountains splashed; the light was pale, neutral and shadow free.

A cowboy wandered over and handed him a wooden paddle.

"Good God, what's this for?"

"For the canoe, sir."

Henderson looked to his right. Sure enough, a dozen canoes were tethered to the concrete bank.

"Do you mean I've got to paddle myself across to the elevators?"

"I can do it for you, sir, but a lot of our guests like to make their own way."

He saw an intrepid aged couple set off, little shrieks of delight coming from the wife.

"Oh. Right."

The cowboy led him down to a canoe, deposited his bag in the bow and helped him in. Henderson settled down.

"Listen, are you sure these things are stable? Perhaps you'd better—"

The cowboy pushed him off. "Enjoy your stay at Monopark 5000, sir."

Henderson found himself drifting into the middle of the lake. He looked about him. The various islands were linked to the far bank by large round stepping-stones. Indian maidens tripped across these carrying drinks from the huge gloomy bar area. Hesitantly, Henderson dipped his paddle in the water and performed a couple of gentle strokes. The canoe, thin aluminum painted to look like birch bark, skidded easily across the surface and clanged into the side of another canoe traversing the water. This was occupied by a high-ranking military man—a general, judging from the stars that flashed on his shoulders—in a smoky-green uniform.

"Sorry!" Henderson laughed. "Haven't quite got the hang of this. Ha, ha."

"Remember to paddle on both sides," said the general, with a false grin, and pushed him away—a little more forcibly than need be, Henderson thought, as his canoe turned through 180 degrees and he found himself facing the forest grove again.

He dug his paddle in and the canoe moved off in a smooth arc. He cut across the bows of some more-competent guests.

"Hey, watch out for the rapids!" one of them called—or at least that's what Henderson thought he said.

"What?" he shouted back over his shoulder, a little alarmed. It seemed to him not inconceivable that in Monopark 5000's fanatical pursuit of verisimilitude they should have installed genuine wilderness hazards: rapids, submerged rocks, alligators . . . However, his call went unheeded and, his attention distracted from his course, he soon had another collision, this time with a cocktail island.

"Pow! Pow! Pow!"

Henderson looked up. A little boy shot at him with leveled fingers from behind the cover of the circular banquette seating.

"Waylon, stop that," his father commanded. "Having trouble?" he called to Henderson. "Can I throw you a rope?" Other people on the island stood up, smiling at Henderson's seaborne invasion of their territory.

"Hit the beach!" called one, to tumultuous laughter.

"Pow! Pow!"

"I'm fine," good sport Henderson called out with artificial gaiety. "Lost my compass." More laughs.

"Pow! I got him, Dad. *Pow!* I shot him, I shot him!"

"Waylon, stop it, I told you."

Cursing under his breath, Henderson leaned forward and pushed off. He would have liked to connect the flat of his paddle with the little brat's head. The canoe shot backward in a tight spiral.

"Watch out!" someone screamed from behind.

Panicked, Henderson thrust his paddle into the water too forcefully. His arm plunged under the surface up to the elbow. Furious, he threw his paddle down and tried to wring his sodden sleeve dry.

"Watch where you're going!" shouted two angry guests avoiding his drifting canoe.

"Sorry!" Henderson called merrily, though his throat was thick with anger and frustration. "Lost control."

"You're not supposed to fool around like this, you know," a heavy-jowled, blue-rinsed matron admonished from the prow of a canoe being maneuvered by a grinning cowboy.

"I know," Henderson replied, then forced his "jolly" voice out between gritted teeth. "Sorry!"

After a couple more minutes and half a dozen more cheery cries of "Sorry!" he finally gained the opposite bank. Utterly exhausted, he was helped ashore by two vastly amused cowboys who assured him they'd never seen anyone have such difficulty before. Henderson felt as if he'd just completed a two-week Outward Bound course. His arm dripped water, the muscles in his neck were in spasm and his shirt was transparent with sweat. What sort of demented, perverse architect had designed this hotel? he wondered. He was going to write to the owner, insist that some sort of causeway or bridge be provided for those not aquatically inclined.

He held his damp sleeve away from his side as he ascended in a scenic elevator. The splendor of the panorama below—grove, lake, islands, scudding canoes—was entirely lost on him.

He walked down the corridor on the thirty-fifth floor, past Suites G, H and I, toward Suite J, which lay at its end. As he fiddled with his piece of card, inserting it in a slot at the side of the doorframe, the general with whom he'd collided on the lake stepped out of Suite K opposite. The smile on his face dissolved.

"Oh," he said, badly concealing his disappointment at the sight of Henderson. "Finally made it."

"Yes," Henderson said. "Great fun."

The general looked up the corridor, grunted and disappeared back inside. He was obviously expecting someone, Henderson thought, as, with a buzz, his door swung open.

Suite J was plushly and lavishly appointed, right down to a scattering of little china ornaments on various surfaces. There was a small sitting room, and off this was a bedroom with a canary-yellow, king-size bed. In the bathroom the large triangular bath was canary yellow too. Moreover, it was oddly ribbed, and provided with several curious movable chrome nozzles and handgrips. This was the whirlpool he'd so blithely requested, he realized. He looked at the luxury of the room and hoped the expense would be worth it. He thought Irene might be taken by the whirlpool bath.

He took off his wet jacket and pungent shirt and decided to try the bath out. A hot bubbling soak was just what he required. For ten minutes he studied the instruction manual on how to operate the whirlpool mechanism, then set various dials and switches on the wall and ran the water. When it was full he stripped off and climbed in. The hot water was ideally soothing. For a moment he wondered if he should even bother with the whirlpool option, but decided that he might as well get his money's worth. He reached up and flipped the switch. At first nothing happened apart from a humming and grinding noise. Then suddenly the bath erupted in foam, as if he'd been attacked by a shoal of piranhas, and heavy fists thudded simultaneously into his body.

He screamed with shock and pain—one thundering misdirected jet had pulverized his groin—and leaped out of the bath. His body was red and throbbing. He felt like a huge bruise. The tub frothed and gurgled like an acid vat in a horror film. He switched it off and within seconds it became an ordinary hot bath again. He decided not to get back in: the pleasure had been spoiled, somehow.

Wearily he got dressed and checked the time: four-thirty. He wondered when Irene would arrive. The evening, she had said. He sat down and phoned Beeby. He told him only that Gage was unhappy with his valuation of the Dutch paintings and was stalling on fixing a date for the auction. Beeby couldn't understand. Was Henderson absolutely sure they were insignificant pictures? Yes, Henderson said, no doubt, very run of the mill. However, he was checking out the portrait—which was why he was in Atlanta, needed a reference library, he lied fluently. Beeby sounded worried and impressed on him the need to bring matters to a speedy conclusion. Henderson told him the results of his valuation and said he thought Gage was looking for another half million for the Dutch paintings. Out of the question, Beeby said, they'd make a huge loss, especially if they underwrote the reserve. They batted ideas back and forth for a while to no great effect. Eventually Beeby exhorted him to do his utmost and told him he had Pruitt Halfacre on another line.

"Henderson. How's it going?"

"Well, up and down, Pruitt."

"You know that painting, the allegory? I've been doing some work on it; it could be Demeter and Iambe."

"Good God, you're right." Henderson was very impressed.

"But it's not."

"No?"

"It's Demeter and Baubo. Very unusual."

Pruitt told him it was a variant myth. After Persephone had been stolen by Hades, Demeter had wandered the world, crushed by her grief over the loss of her daughter. However, in Eleusis she had been jolted out of her sorrow, and had broken her fast, by a serving maid, either called Iambe, who in one version told her dirty jokes, or, in another, called Baubo, who made Demeter laugh by raising her skirts and exposing her genitalia. After that Demeter ceased to mourn for Persephone and the world got its harvests back.

"The fascinating thing is you only find that myth in the *Songs of Orpheus* and *Protrepticus* by Clement of Alexandria."

Henderson wrote it all down. "Pruitt," he said, "I'm phenomenally impressed. Great help."

"Who's the painting by?"

"I don't know. But it's no good. It was just the myth that floored me."

"It is a little arcane, for sure."

"Absolutely. Listen, Pruitt, do you know a New York gallery by the name of Sereno and Gint?"

"Never heard of them."

"I thought so." He said goodbye and put down the phone. He took out his Polaroids and looked at the painting again through his magnifying glass. He put the magnifying glass down and thought about what Pruitt had told him. Odd myth. It made no sense. He phoned Melissa.

"Henderson! At last. When are you coming home?"

"Very soon, I hope," he said with feeling.

"How's Bryant? She sent me a postcard. She seems to be having a good time."

"She is." He swallowed. "She's made friends with a . . . a very nice girl called Shanda."

"Oh, good. Darling, I'm so grateful to you, honestly. You're sure she's no trouble."

"Not. Not at all."

"Baby, I've got to run. Dying to see you. Irving sends his love."

She hung up before Henderson could send his love back to Irving. He felt suddenly uneasy about the barriers of deceit he was erecting. To Beeby about Sereno and Gint; to Melissa about Duane; to Irene about their planned holiday . . .

Beeby phoned back. How much did Gage want for the Dutch paintings? Henderson repeated the Sereno-Gint estimates.

"Good Lord," Beeby said. "But if they're so mediocre how can he ask so much for them?"

"He's a shrewd old devil. He knows we want the others."

"All right. Go to fifty thousand dollars each. But he must pay for insurance, printing the catalog and advertising. We might just break even. Let's pray one of the others comes good. The Sisleys are fine, you say?"

"Yes. I'll do my best, Tom."

"I've never done this before, Henderson. It goes against the grain. We must have a date for the auction soonest too. When will you be back?"

"Monday or Tuesday," he said without much confidence.

He hung up. He passed both hands over his face, tugging at his features, pulling his eyelids down, flattening his

cheeks. He felt disturbed and unsettled but not just because of the farcial events on the atrium lake. They were
deeper qualms he was suffering: more spiritual and meta-
physical. His self-doubt, his lack of faith in his own capac-
ities, always considerable, had grown these last few days
like a tumor. He was beginning to feel unable to cope.
The struggle to fit his personality to his new environment,
to emulsify with his chosen culture like oil and vinegar,
just wasn't happening. It was too unyielding; he and America just weren't creating the harmony he had expected. It
simply wasn't enough, clearly, to be keen, to wish earnestly for something to happen. Perhaps all marriages were
made in heaven, he thought glumly. He had an awful foreboding nothing was going to work out.

And what then? Back to England? But he had been mis-
erable there. All his hopes resided here. To fail to find
himself in the U.S.A. didn't bear contemplation. He felt,
for the first time in his life, slivers of black despair begin to
insert themselves into his spirit. Like the first pins in a
voodoo doll. What was it Gage had said? "We all want to
be happy and we're all going to die." It didn't leave you
much.

He heard the sound of footsteps in the corridor and
immediately recognized their weight and cadence as
Irene's. He ran joyfully to the door and threw it open.
Across the corridor the general did the same. They both
looked at the astonished face of a black maid.

"Mo' towels, sir?"

Henderson and the general sheepishly accepted a towel
each. Henderson noted that the general was in mufti.

"I thought—" Henderson began, smiling.

"I'm expecting someone," the general said. He was
wearing loud checked trousers of the sort favored by
champion golfers, a short-sleeved shirt and a silk scarf tied

at his throat. It looked incongruous beneath his hard taut face and cropped gray hair. Out of uniform he had lost all his confident authority. Just another man. He raised a palm and stepped back inside.

Henderson called the front desk and asked where the best reference library in Atlanta was and, after a brief pause, he was given the relevant information. He heard more footsteps in corridor—not Irene's, he was sure—followed by a knock on the door. He got up and opened it.

"Room service, sir." A white-jacketed waiter carried a tray holding champagne in an ice bucket and a large plate of smoked salmon and brown bread.

"There must be some mistake."

"This is 35J?"

"Yes."

"And you are General Dunklebanger?"

"No. I think you'll find him in there. In 35K. K, not J."

By this time the general had come to his door.

"General, I think this is for you." Henderson was amused to see the embarrassment on the general's face.

"Oh, yeah. Yeah, I guess. . . . Just take it right on in. Sorry to bother you," he said to Henderson.

Henderson shut the door, and smiled. He doubted somehow that the champagne was for Mrs. Dunklebanger. Mind you, he thought, it's not such a bad idea. He phoned room service and ordered the same for him and Irene. The episode—a glimpse of the human face behind the military machine—had cheered him up somewhat. He went back into the bathroom and ran his electric razor over his chin once more, concentrating on the skin around the lips, until it was completely smooth. Irene often refused to kiss him if there was a hint of bristle. "What do you think it's like for me?" she would say. "You try rubbing your face with sandpaper, see how sexy it is."

The phone rang.

"Henderson?" It was Irene. "I'm at the airport. I'll be there in twenty minutes."

"I'll see you downst—" But she had hung up.

He felt hollow-chested with pleasant anticipation. He shut his eyes and tried to conjure up Irene naked. The broad shoulders, the low flat breasts with their tiny nipples, her unshaven armpits, the black dense hair on her cunt, her strong legs . . . He took a deep breath. God, how he had missed her.

On the way down in a scenic elevator he scanned the canoes plying back and forth but none of them contained Irene. He debated whether he should meet her at the front desk but decided not to deny her the pleasure of seeing and experiencing the atrium and its marvels herself. It was certainly busier than when he had arrived. The cocktail archipelago were fully populated and noisy. All the canoes seemed to be in demand.

He went into the bar area. The wigwams were in fact canopies over private booths. Vegetation grew lushly everywhere. The tables and chairs had a roughhewn makeshift aspect and the long bar looked like a reconstituted corral. He wouldn't have been surprised to see a few ponies tethered here and there. At the bar the barman sported a feather headdress, wampum beads and buckskin. He raised his hand and said, "How."

Hang about, Henderson thought, this is taking the leitmotiv a little far, isn't it? He checked that no one was looking then raised his own palm—swiftly turning it into a neck scratch.

"How. A bloody mary, please."

"Right away, sir."

The drink arrived in a glass the size and shape of a storm lantern. A whole hand of celery sprouted from the top. Henderson picked it up and sucked self-consciously on a straw. Everything in this "hotel," he thought, conspired to make him ill at ease. He put his glass down and went in search of the gents' toilet.

Here at least some sort of orthodoxy and normal scale prevailed: white tiles and chrome. He had half expected to be issued with a spade and instructed to go and dig a hole. He took his place at the urinal trough, unzipped and let fly. His gaze rested blankly on the white tiles in front of him.

"Hi there," came a voice from his left. He ignored it. People just didn't talk to each other while they urinated—it wasn't done.

"Mr. Dores."

He looked around with genuine irritation. It was Sereno, in the next but one stall. To Henderson's astonishment Sereno leaned sideways and extended a hand over the vacant space. Good Christ! Henderson gasped inwardly, he surely doesn't expect me to shake hands while I'm peeing. This was intolerable. But Sereno's hand remained. Henderson, swapping hands, shook Sereno's briskly and briefly.

"Hello," he said stiffly, and returned his gaze to the tiles.

"You remember my partner, Peter Gint?"

Henderson looked around. Beyond Sereno was the pebble beach of Gint's face. Why were they peeing together? Like girls at a discotheque?

"Hi there," Gint said softly, reaching around Sereno's back. After a horrified pause, Henderson leaned over and shook his hand. I don't believe I'm doing this, Henderson thought. Why don't we hold each other's tinkles?

"Good to see you again," Gint said.

"Mng."

"Some hotel," Sereno opined. "Eighth wonder of the world."

They all finished simultaneously. Henderson washed his hands with untypical thoroughness, lots of soap and hot water. Sereno combed his hair and moustache.

"Please join us," he said as they walked out. He indicated one of the nearer cocktail islands. Henderson saw Freeborn, Shanda and—to his surprise—Cora.

"Really, thank you, but I'm meeting—"

"*Hey, Hendursin!*" Shanda waved and called. He saw Cora's shades snap around.

"Come on," said Sereno. He seemed annoyingly confident. Shouldn't they, as rivals for the Gage collection, be warily circling each other?

They made their way to the island, Henderson being extra careful with the stepping-stones.

"Well, hello there," Cora said. "Is your 'colleague' here yet?"

"Expecting her any moment."

"Sit here," Shanda ordered. She was clearly drunk. In front of her was an enormous beaker full of blue liquid and chunks of fruit. She dragged him down.

Sereno spoke. "Would you and your colleague—what did you say her name was?"

"Dr. Dubrovnik. Dr. Irene Dubrovnik."

"She's Czechoslovakian," Cora said.

"—like to have dinner with us?"

"I'm afraid duty calls. But thanks all the same."

"Did you say Czechoslovakian?" Shanda asked.

"How's her English?" Cora asked.

"Excellent." Henderson desperately scanned the open surface of the lake. He saw Irene being paddled across by a cowboy. She was looking about her with an expression of aghast incredulity. Henderson rose to his feet.

"Well, good to see you," he said. "Enjoy your dinner."

"Do bring your colleague over, we'd love to meet her," Cora said disingenuously.

"Oh. Right." He picked his way back across the stepping-stones and strode around to the place the canoes berthed. Irene was being helped ashore.

"My God, Henderson," she said in a loud voice. "This hotel. I can't believe it." She leaned forward to kiss him.

"No kissing!" Henderson said, trying not to move his lips. "Don't kiss me!" He shook her formally by the hand.

"What?"

"We're being watched."

"By who?"

"The Gage family." He took her elbow in one hand and her small case in the other and began to walk her around toward the cocktail island.

"But so what? For Christ's sake."

"Listen. You're called Dr. Dubrovnik; you're an art historian from Czechoslovakia."

Irene stopped. "Henderson, I'm warning you." Her voice was stern. "I'm not playing any of your stupid games."

"Please, it's vital. Just for a minute or two. I'll explain later." He felt a light sweat moist on his face. They made their way across the stepping-stones. He glanced at Irene. Her eyes were narrow.

"Dr. Irene Dubrovnik," Henderson announced, and introduced her to the other members of the family.

"A pleasure to meet you at last," Sereno said. "I'm familiar with your work."

"How. Do. You. Do?" Cora said slowly, as if talking to a peasant or simpleton. "Welcome. To. Our. Country."

"D'you miss Czecho, Czechlso, Miss Dubronick. Nick?" Shanda burped.

"May we offer you a drink?" Sereno asked, all oleaginous charm, signaling an Indian maiden.

"Yeah. I'll have a large Scotch, straight up with a twist," Irene said, looking at Henderson.

They sat themselves down. More drinks were ordered. Some sort of tremor had established itself in Henderson's left thigh and, mysteriously, his indigestion had returned. He felt a fire in his throat. To his alarm and dismay he found himself sitting between Sereno and Freeborn. Cora lit a cigarette and exhaled. Irene vigorously fanned the air.

The drinks arrived. Henderson buried his head in the cool clump of celery frothing from the top of a new bloody mary. Please, God, he prayed into the leaves, let her play the game.

"Dr. Dubrovnik," Cora said. "Excuse me, Dr. Dubrovnik?"

Irene refused to acknowledge the pseudonym.

"Isn't this hotel quite astonishing?" Henderson piped up. "I had quite a problem with my canoe, I must say."

"What'd he say?" Shanda asked Gint.

"His canoe," Gint said.

"Mr. Dores," Sereno breathed in his ear. His large moustache and glossy purple lips were close to his face. "We may be rivals, but I'm glad that we can behave in a civilized way."

Henderson stood up. "No rest for the wicked," he said cheerfully. "We must leave you good people to your dinner."

"Wha's he say?"

"Thanks for the drink." Irene drained hers in a gulp.

"Goodbye, Dr. Dubrovnik," Cora said.

Irene ignored her.

"Dr. Dubrovnik?"

"Goodbye," Henderson said, hauling Irene away by the arm.

They walked off. Henderson waved farewell. Just made it, he thought, as nausea joined forces once more with indigestion.

"Don't ever land me in that kind of shit again," Irene said coldly. "I don't want to play in your fantasies."

"I'm sorry," he said. "It was necessary. Things aren't going so well . . ." He sensed this wasn't the moment to tell her of the canceled trip. "That chap Sereno's trying to buy the paintings too."

"Who's that weird girl in the shades?"

"Gage's daughter, Cora."

"God, spooky."

They were in a scenic elevator. Irene looked out at the vista and laughed. "Jesus Christ, Henderson, only you would choose a place like this." She leaned against him. He took in her appearance for the first time. She wore a dark-green jersey dress with buttons down the front, and flat-soled beige shoes. He ran his hand down the warm furrow of her spine. No bra.

In the suite the champagne and sandwiches had been delivered. They had a glass of champagne. They kissed. He pulled her through into the bedroom and they fell onto the bed. Irene propped her head on a hand and looked down into his face.

"Has it been a bad week? Really that bad?"

"The worst ever."

"Poor Henderson."

"Let's not talk about it."

"But I want to hear everything."

"Later."

"Well at least it's all over now."

Henderson swallowed. Was this the moment to tell

her? But Irene ducked forward and kissed his forehead. He shut his eyes. Then he felt her lips on his left eyelid. Her dark mouth closed hot over the socket. The tense tip of her tongue massaged the eyeball through the lid. Technicolor photomatic explosions seemed to brighten the inside of his skull. His left side erupted in goose pimples.

"Stop it, please," he said weakly. She pulled back and he opened his eyes. Her face was blurry through warm pink tears.

"What's that?" he said. "Where did you learn that? It's appalling."

"I like to feel your eyeball squirm beneath my tongue. It sort of throbs."

"But I can't see anymore. It hurts."

"It's designed to stimulate *me*, dummy."

He unbuttoned her dress at the neck and pushed it back to reveal one breast, pale and flat with its small immaculate nipple, milk-chocolate brown. He pressed his weeping eye against it. He felt his nausea and indigestion dissolve into relief. At last, he thought, at last.

He got up and took off his tie and shirt. He kicked off his shoes with pantomimic abandon, removed his socks and trousers. Irene lay on the bed and watched him with a smile. He eased off his increasingly taut underpants.

"Well, hello there," Irene said.

He slid onto the bed to join her. He found it pleasantly erotic to be naked while she was clothed. Methodically he undid more buttons to expose both breasts. He bent his head.

"Let's stay here tomorrow," Irene murmured. "This hotel is fun." She kissed his crown.

Henderson sat up. "Ah," he said slowly. "I was going to tell you. There's been a hitch. I've got to go back."

Blankly, he watched himself detumesce—the organ showed uncanny prescience, he thought.

"What? To New York?"

"No. Luxora Beach."

"Bastard," she said with chilling matter-of-factness, doing up her buttons. "But you needed a quick fuck, just the same."

"Listen, it wasn't like that, honestly," he pleaded. "I've only just found out. Everything has suddenly gone horribly wrong. Nothing but disasters." He launched into a garbled desperate narrative about Gage, the picture, Beeby. The arrival of Sereno and Gint, Freeborn's maneuverings, Gage's second thoughts, Bryant's shocking betrothal to Duane . . ."

"And who the hell is Bryant?"

"*Oh, Christ.* . . . Ah, she's a girl. . . ."

"You can't help it, can you? You sad fuck."

"She's only fourteen. She's not a friend. Jesus." He shut his eyes and pulled the coverlet around him.

"So what are you doing with a fourteen-year-old girl?"

"She's the daughter of . . . Thomas Beeby. I promised him I'd—"

"Bullshit, Henderson. You prick. You English prick."

Why, he thought wildly, should the adjective make the noun more pejorative?

There was a knock at the door.

"Bloody hell!" Henderson swore. He jumped off the bed and grabbed his dressing gown. But Irene had already gone to the door. He heard a voice. A woman's voice.

"Oh. I'm sorry. Is this . . . is this 35J?"

Henderson fought furiously with an inside-out sleeve.

"That's what it says on the door." Irene replied coldly.

Then he heard a wail, a keening, distressed cry. Christ, who can it be? he thought. Bryant? Cora? Melissa?

Shanda? Fearfully, he peered through the crack at the doorjamb. He saw Irene, her arms folded sternly across her chest, confronting a young blond woman in military uniform with corporal's stripes on her sleeves. She was sobbing fiercely into her cupped hands. A WAF or WAC, he thought; what ghastly new nemesis is this? Then the woman looked up and screamed in his direction.

"Alvin, you bastard! I never want to see you again!" She turned and ran down the corridor.

Alvin? Just a moment. His spearing hand finally engaged the stubborn sleeve. He sprang to the door.

"What fucking game is this, Alvin?" Irene demanded.

Just at that moment the door opposite was thrown open and a harassed General Dunklebanger appeared, zipping up his fly. He looked disbelievingly down the long corridor at the fleeing WAC.

"Mary?" he said looking piteously back at Henderson and Irene. "Was that Mary?"

"I think there's been—" Henderson began, but he was interrupted by a bellow of primeval grief from the general, who set off thundering down the passageway after his beloved. Henderson took a few futile paces after him. He saw the general arrive at the lift doors just as they closed in his face. He darted to and fro—there were three lifts serving the thirty-fifth floor—pressing buttons frantically. Eventually another lift arrived and he leaped in. Henderson shook his head in astonishment. A few other guests had emerged from their rooms to see what the fuss was. Henderson realized he was in his dressing gown. He returned to his own door. It was locked. Oh, Christ, no. He tapped softly on it with his fingertips.

"Irene," he whispered. "Open up. I can explain everything." He looked over his shoulder and smiled reassuringly at the curious guests.

"Irene," he hissed. *"For God's sake open up!"* He rapped again.

He had to wait a full ten minutes. He passed the time whistling quietly to himself, pacing unconcernedly to and fro in a tight oval, affecting profound interest in the pattern and texture of the corridor carpet for minutes at a time. Finally the door opened and Irene stepped out. She had her case in her hand.

"I'm getting out," she said. "You stay in the madhouse with the crazies. Goodbye."

She walked purposefully away. Henderson dithered for a moment.

"Irene, wait," he called.

Farther down the passage a man's head popped out of a doorway.

"For God's sake, will you people please party in your rooms?" he demanded of Irene.

She said something to him in reply that caused him to start back in shock.

Henderson ran back inside and started to pull on his clothes. There was nothing to be gained by pursuing her in his dressing gown. He felt an ascending panic stirring within him. Irene's tone had been so uncompromisingly final. She *couldn't* leave, he told himself: she had to hear him out. Given his predicament, anyone would understand. She couldn't abandon him like this. He clawed on his jacket and trousers. He pulled on his left sock and found his left shoe in a corner. He looked around the room for his other shoe and sock. He found the sock, but not the shoe, such had been the frivolity with which he had disrobed.

"Oh, *God*, please," he prayed out loud, peering under the bed. He saw it: at the back in the middle, flush against the skirting board. He tried to reach it but his fingers were inches short. He struggled mightily to shift the bed but, for some unknown reason, it appeared to be bolted in place. In his mind's eye, he saw Irene being paddled across the atrium lake. There was nothing for it. He ran awkwardly out of the room and sprinted like a clubfooted athlete down the passage to the lifts. He pressed the descend button. Obligingly, one lift was already ascending rapidly to his floor. Thirty-three, thirty-four, thirty-five, *bing!*

The door opened. For an instant he saw General Dunklebanger leaning despairingly against the lift side. Then, with a cry of pure rage, the general surged out, fingers closing around Henderson's throat, and they fell grappling to the floor. The man was wiry and tough, but Henderson—strengthened by his own urgent needs and panic, and his body brimming with adrenaline—struggled free.

The general was on his knees, panting hoarsely.

"Leave me alone, you mad bugger!" Henderson shrieked. The lift doors were still open. The general got to his feet, adopting a shaky wrestler's stance, and began to advance on him again.

"She got the wrong room number, you bloody cretin!" Henderson yelled in frustration. "It's not my fault!"

The general paused, then folded to the floor in a heap, making childlike crying noises. Henderson jumped over him and into the lift. The doors slid to. Henderson punched button number one.

As he emerged high in the bright space of the atrium, he peered out hopefully at the scene below. There was Irene! Just getting into a canoe. The lift came to a halt and Henderson ran out. "Irene!" he called. "Wait!"

The atrium floor was busy with people. Henderson dodged his way through the crowd to the canoe-embarking point. Some child shouted, "Look, Mom, that man's only got one shoe!"

A small queue had formed at the lakeside, all the canoes were in commission. Henderson pushed his way to the front.

"Excuse me, sir, but would you wait in line? It'll only be a couple of minutes."

Henderson saw Irene approaching the far bank.

"Irene! Wait!" he bellowed plaintively across the water. Everybody looked around. Except Irene.

"Give me a canoe!" he begged.

"Sir, please! Two minutes." The cowboy's strong arms held him back.

Henderson looked at the lake. He could see the bottom clearly through the dancing water. Eighteen inches down, two feet at the most, he calculated.

He jumped in.

He went in up to his waist, gasping at the shock of the cold water. *Waist deep!* he exclaimed with mad outrage. That's dangerous. What about safety regulations? . . .

He began to slosh his way heavily across to the far shore, arms above his head, a creaming bow wave at his waist, like a determined marine invading some Pacific island. There were shouts, laughs and a few screams from onlookers and hotel staff, but he was possessed with unfamiliar single-mindedness. He forged on through the water. Canoes took avoiding action. "Irene, wait!" he cried again. To his dismay he saw her get out of her canoe and march into the forest.

"Stop that woman!" he bellowed hoarsely. "She's sick. She's forgotten her medicine."

Willing hands reached out to help him as he reached the far bank.

"Life and death," he gasped. "Matter of." And stumbled into the trees.

He broke out into the lobby and limped-ran—clunk-splat, clunk-splat—across to the main doors, leaving a trail of wetness like a slug. A taxi pulled away into the main street. Another rolled up promptly to take its place at the foot of the steps. The driver leaped out at the sight of the distraught and dripping Henderson.

"Follow that cab," Henderson croaked.

"Hey, man, no way." The taxi driver was fat and needed a shave. He blocked Henderson's access to the car, short stubby fingertips laid gently on Henderson's heaving chest.

"Look, it's a matter of life and death, for God's sake!"

"Sure it is. That's what they all say, bub. But no way you gettin' in my cab like that, man. Soakin' wet, only one shoe. No way."

"I'll give you a hundred dollars!"

"Let's see your money."

Henderson wrestled with his sopping hip pocket and produced his wallet. He opened it up: an anthology of credit cards, two tens and three singles.

"You don't got no hundred bucks, man. You just better go on back inside, dry yourself off." The taxi driver considerately helped him back up the steps to the lobby, Henderson suddenly as quiescent as a chronic invalid being ushered back to bed. "Go on now, man. You go on change your clothes. Then I'll give you a ride."

A dark listless resignation had settled on Henderson as he was paddled back across the atrium lake. A large and curious crowd watched him disembark, Sereno and Cora among their number.

"Is Dr. Dubrovnik all right?" Sereno asked.

"That was some display, Mr. Dores. Most impressive," Cora said. Her lips weren't smiling, but her dark lenses obscured eyes bright with amusement, he felt sure. But he was too weak and overcome to make any riposte. He limped off toward the scenic elevators and his lonely room.

chapter eleven

PREDICTABLY, Henderson slept briefly and uneasily, troubled by violent dreams, that night. But in the morning found, to his surprise, that his mortification and embarrassment did not reach the zenith he might have suspected. Too many potential disasters lay ahead, with hectoring claims on his attention. And besides, there was nothing he could do about Irene now, he realized. It would have been utterly pointless to follow her to Atlanta airport and attempt to engineer a reconciliation in the departure lounge. That would have to await his return to New York, whenever that might be.

As he lay alone in the big bed, he thought back over his manic wade through the atrium lake more with astonishment than shame or self-rebuke. He tried to recreate the thought processes that had led him to behave in such a rash and widly conspicuous manner, but in vain. It was as if the semishod, disappointed lover bellowing his anguished pleas across the crowded pond had been another person, such was the uniquely strange nature of the act. He had, he realized, for the first time in his life, given absolutely no thought to the reactions of others. He hadn't cared; he had been totally indifferent to opinion. He frowned.

The one meager consolation of the whole saddening business was that he was now freed to concentrate on securing the pictures for Mulholland, Melhuish. Beeby's new offer on the Dutch pictures, some judicious hope raising on the prospective auction prices of the Sisleys . . . Gage needed money; money would have to be the spur. Publicity, prestige exhibitions in London—they carried no weight.

He got out of bed. Then there was the problem of Bryant and Duane. He got dressed. He hoped desperately that a firm talking-to and reminders of Melissa's monstrous displeasure might make the girl see sense. He couldn't imagine what had got into her head. Duane, a thirty-four-year-old layabout with a liking for loud music and a chronic incapacity to fix cars . . . what could a pretty, privileged girl like Bryant see in an almost mythically disfavored human being like that?

He ordered breakfast from room service. He felt also, if he was honest with himself, a certain amount of jealousy. If she could want to marry a lout like Duane, why was she so hostile to *him?* Good Lord, he thought, I'm beginning to sound like Pruitt Halfacre. But this morning, awash with self-pity and hurt, he needed to be liked by someone.

His breakfast was wheeled in. Coffee and orange juice in a sunny chair. He was still unsettled, he realized by one of his dreams that had been unusually virulent and detailed. It was about Irene, and in the dream she had cut his head off with a small, not very sharp knife. He had felt no pain and managed to protest throughout his decapitation, seeking some explanation for this hostility. Irene—her breasts bare, as they had been the night before—had said only one thing: "Because you're weak, weak, weak," and then renewed her efforts with the knife to the rhythm of her words.

As he sipped at his orange juice he squirmed anew at the phantasms of his unconscious mind. Irene's erotic violence, her breasts swaying and bobbling as she sawed, gouts of his own blood fountaining up from his torn throat and severed windpipe. It was lucky, he thought, that he was no Freudian, otherwise he'd be in a bad way: rather a lot of guilt and self-contempt swilling around. Just as well, he reflected, that his art-historian training provided him with the reference and he didn't need to go poking around in his id. . . . It was all clearly derived from *Judith and Holofernes* by Artemisia Gentileschi . . . or by Jakob van Hoegh.

He wondered vaguely what to do for the rest of the day. Thinking of Jakob van Hoegh reminded him of his ostensible purpose in visiting Atlanta. He might as well spend some time in the library, going through the motions, see if there was anything that would conceivably justify revaluing the landscapes.

The William Russell Pullen library of Georgia State University proved happily to be not far from the Monopark 5000 complex. Henderson paid off the taxi driver and wandered through a modern plaza with scattered fir trees and curious-looking lights. He entered through wide glass doors set in the blank brick facade. Nobody noticed him; nobody demanded credentials. He consulted a bright wall map, hummed up a few floors in a lift, asked a pretty coed where Fine Arts was and duly discovered the relevant well-crammed rows of bookshelves.

After some time spent browsing through books on seventeenth-century Dutch painting, he further confirmed his belief that Gage's dank mundane landscapes were nothing more than that. He flicked through his notes on the paintings. "Demeter and Baubo" caught his eye. *"Protrepticus—* Clement of Alexandria."

He sought out a reference librarian, a cheerful girl called, so the identity card of her lapel informed him, Ora Lee Emmet. Ora Lee, after some punching of keys on a VDU and a search through hefty catalogs, said that the only copy of Clement of Alexandria's *Protrepticus* that they possessed was an inferior French translation on microfilm.

Half an hour later, Henderson sat before a blue screen and twiddled up the glowing text. Old Clement, as far as Henderson could make out, was ranting on at all the base and obscene rites and rituals associated with classical mythology.

"How can we be astonished at Barbarians," Henderson translated slowly, "when the Athenians and the rest of Greece—I blush to talk of it!—possess in the figure of Demeter a religion which is absolutely shameful?"

Henderson turned the wheel. Clement recounted the story. Demeter wanders around Greece searching for Persephone. In Eleusis, exhausted and *toute désolée,* she sits down by a well. Eleusis is inhabited by shepherds and swineherds. And Baubo. He translated on: "Baubo, having received Demeter, offers her a drink (a mixture of *farine, d'eau et d'une espèce de menthe.*) But Demeter refuses it because she is in mourning. Baubo, *très chagrinée* and deeply offended, uncovers her private parts and exhibits them to the Goddess. At this sight Demeter accepts the drink—delighted at the spectacle!"

Outraged of Alexandria railed on at the Athenians and quoted some lines from the *Songs of Orpheus:* "Baubo drew aside her robes to show all that was obscene The Goddess smiled, smiled in her heart, and drank the draught from out the glancing cup."

Henderson switched off the machine.

What did it all mean? A good laugh is the best medicine? Keep your sunny side up? There's nothing worth getting *that* depressed about? Everything's pointless?

He moved floor to find the classical dictionaries. There was, predictably, vast material on Demeter, of her grief and fasting after the loss of Persephone, the breaking of her fast and the ending of her mourning at Eleusis. In every version, however, that had been achieved by Iambe and her dirty jokes. So who was Baubo.

Half interested, he began to leaf through other books on classical mythology looking for references on Demeter and Baubo. He found only one, in *Myth, Ritual and the Primitive Mind* by Max Kramer.

"Vulgar comedy and lewdness" he read, "was common ritual practice. Its purpose seems originally to have been for the promotion of fertility, but it came later to be associated more generally with the dispelling of evil spirits and as a favoured antidote of gloom and despair. Thus Hercules released the hapless Cercopes—whom he was on the point of killing—when they had caused him to laugh over their jokes about his astonishingly hairy buttocks (*Melanpygos*); and the same ritual significance is found in the story of Demeter and Baubo, when Baubo made Demeter laugh by raising her skirts and exposing herself to the Goddess when Demeter was in mourning for Persephone."

He sat slumped at his desk. It was late afternoon. He hadn't worked so hard in years, and although he was exhausted he felt a vague exhilaration. He chewed on the end of his pen, suddenly remembering Irene back in New York; Bryant and Duane's impending marriage; Sereno, Gint and Freeborn. He looked around the tranquil library, the ranked booths, the earnest students—all dressed for the athletic field, it seemed—hunched over their books. He contemplated the stacks of learned volumes piled in front of him, the dull gloss of the illustrations, the crammed rows of type . . . He turned his head and gazed out of a window at the sunlit towers of downtown Atlanta. What shambles waited for him out there?

He yearned suddenly for the warm security of study and research, the ostrich calm of the library, the utter pointlessness of some scholarly avenue up which he could pedantically stroll for the next decade or two. Out there, in the hot streets, in Luxora Beach, in the Gage Mansion, life lounged like a gunslinger, waiting for him—nothing but hurt, dissatisfaction and baffling twists and turns ahead.

He remembered when, in his childhood, two brothers who lived along the road had briefly taken him up as a friend. They were slightly older than he—robust, dirty-kneed, wild little beggars, he recalled—who came around to his mother's house on any pretext.

"It's Phillip and Colin," his mother would tell him. "They want you to come out to play."

"But I don't want to go out and play," he would wail. "I want to stay inside."

He sympathized strongly with his younger self. That was exactly how he felt at the moment. He longed to stay indoors, he didn't want to go out and play.

Thinking of his home and his childhood in this way reminded him of his quest for news of his father. He thought for a moment of telephoning New York, of asking the doorman to go through his mail to see if Drew had replied. But what if there was a letter? He couldn't have it sent down here, and he certainly didn't want its contents read down the phone.

He ran his fingers through his hair. Wearily he closed his books and assembled his notes and photographs. Beckman would be waiting. The time had come.

chapter twelve

IT was remarkable, Henderson thought, how swiftly anger and frustration could dispel calm and serenity no matter how assiduously these last two emotions were cultivated. He looked at his watch. Six o'clock. He had been waiting two hours at the corner of Peachtree and Edgewood for Beckman and his car. Two empty hours. Enough was enough.

He walked back to Monopark 5000 to collect his case. He had managed to secure a place in the hotel car park for Beckman's pickup, and had left his overnight bag with a receptionist in the lobby. He would simply return to Luxora with the pickup. Too bad if that idiot was waiting at another street corner.

In the lobby he picked up his bag.

"Hope you enjoyed your stay at Monopark 5000," the receptionist said.

"Well . . . I certainly won't forget it."

"We won't forget you either, sir. Come back and see us again."

"We'll see."

"Excuse me?"

Henderson turned. It was General Dunklebanger,

checking out. He looked terrible—worn and harrowed—despite his smart uniform.

Oh, Jesus, Henderson thought, this is all I need.

"Look, I'm really sorry about last night," Henderson began. "They'd already got our rooms confused; it was nothing to do with me. Just bad luck—rotten luck, that's all."

"Did she say anything?" The general's voice trembled; his dark eyes were bright with potential tears. "Anything at all? Anything she said. I've been looking all day. I can't find her, you see."

"Well . . . all she said was 'Alvin, you bastard, I never want to see you again,' and ran off."

"That's all?"

"Yes. Sorry."

"Just 'Alvin, you bastard'?"

"Yes. And 'I never want to see you again.' You're Alvin, I take it."

To Henderson's alarm he saw tears bulge at the lower lids of the general's eyes and glide their way down the seams and fissures of his weather-beaten face.

"I've got to find her," he repeated, and took his bottom lip between his teeth.

"All the best of luck." Henderson thought hard, trying to help. "She was in uniform. Won't she have to report back to base at some point?"

The general clutched Henderson's arm. "You've got to help me. You've got to help me find Mary."

"Look, I'm terribly sorry for you, I really am. But there's no way I—"

"*Please.* You're the only one." Now he held both of Henderson's shoulders. Henderson tried to ease himself free. Surely they wouldn't end up grappling on the floor again?

"What can I do?" he said. "If it's any consolation, my girlfriend ran out on me too about five minutes later."

"You see. Together we can find her!"

Gently Henderson prized off the general's fingers from his shoulders.

"Really, there's nothing I can do. I've got problems enough of my own. Massive problems. If only you knew—"

"You've got to help me," the general said in a loud, cracking voice, Heads turned.

"No," Henderson said. Poor guy, he thought. "I must go. I'm positive she'll be back any moment."

"Waaah!" bawled the general, standing in the middle of the lobby, as Henderson backed away.

"Mwah-waah-waah!" His hands hung limply at his sides, twitching as his shoulders heaved.

"What did you do to that man?" a shocked passerby demanded.

The general blubbered noisily on. Receptionists scurried anxiously out from behind the long desk to lead him gently away into the trees. People glared hostilely at Henderson. Astonishingly, a few women had begun crying too—in sympathy, Henderson supposed. He felt unmanned, full of worry. Everyone wore a preoccupied, troubled face. If a general in uniform can cry like a baby, they seemed to be thinking, where does that leave the rest of us?

His mind full of this baleful, admonitory image, Henderson drove back to Luxora Beach through the gathering dusk. He drove west, into the fire of the setting sun, which rinsed the few thin bars of cloud with a salmony golden light. He could feel a murky depression settling on his brain. He switched on the radio in search of distraction. Twanging guitars heralded a familiar tune.

> *She never said a single angry word to me,*
> *Though I cheated on her every gnat and day.*
> *She smiled when I come home,*
> *No, she never raised a moan,*
> *An' I laughed when I heard her 'n' the children pray.*

Henderson remembered the tune from the Skaggsville Motor Hotel. He listened on with horrible fascination.

> *Though he's the happiest meanest, full-time, signed-up sinner,*
> *Don' forget that he's your only paw.*
> *Lord, forgive him for his sins, an'—*

Henderson switched the radio off and drove to Luxora Beach in heavy doleful silence.

When he arrived in Luxora it was late. The main street, as ever, was devoid of traffic but there was the usual cluster of cars and pickups around the bar. The neon signs—the red bow, the blue rosette—shone cheerfully in the night. He stopped the pickup. Someone came out and he caught a glimpse of crowded figures, blurred by smoke, and the high excited voices of people having a good time. For a moment he felt like going in to join them, but he knew what a damper his presence would be to the locals, so he started up and drove on down the lane to the Gage Mansion.

The lights were on in Freeborn's trailer, but the main house was quite dark. Henderson parked the pickup, got out, stretched. He stopped stretching when he saw that his own car wasn't there anymore; just one brick—a crude rebus—stood in its place. He sighed. Did this mean that Beckman was still prowling the wrong junction in Atlanta waiting for him to appear? Or had Duane decided to change cars for him?

He clumped up the front steps and into the hall. No music, ergo, no Duane. And probably no Bryant. He felt an odd relief at having to postpone that confrontation. He switched on some lights, and the TV for company, before wandering through to the kitchen in search of some food. To his considerable disquiet he realized he was treating the Gage Mansion as though it were his home.

In the kitchen he found a barely warm loaf-thing, dark brown, as though made of meat. On closer inspection this turned out to be nuts, beans and pulses set in some sort of spongy dumpling. The fridge yielded a plastic box full of grated carrot. He cut a slice of nut loaf and added a spoonful or two of carrot. He was beginning to wish he'd stopped for a weaselburger in Luxora, but he was really too hungry to care.

He sat down at the frugal meal and started the long chew. He heard the sound of a car arriving, then Beckman sauntered in.

"Hi, Henderson. See you got back OK. Sorry to miss you, but I figured you were coming back anyways so it didn't matter none."

"You mean you didn't go into Atlanta at all."

"You got it."

Henderson thought of his two-hour wait at Peachtree and Edgewood. "Why not?"

"'Cause you didn't have no car, man. It wasn't there this morning."

"What do you mean it wasn't there?" He felt the sense of baffling weakness descend on him that he now associated with life in Luxora Beach.

"I got up this morning, no car. Simple as that."

"Duane?"

"Could be. I heard he was trying to get it fixed up and all."

"But there was nothing wrong with the bloody thing!" He drummed his fingers on the table. The crying general, the disappearing car . . . These were like portents in a Shakespearean play. Beckman was talking again.

"Some cars are real dogs. I remember back in Quang Tri we had an APC was a real mother. Always throwing tracks, breaking down. One day we woke up an' it wasn't there. Just like yours. Seems the sarge got stoned with some chopper pilots, drove it off to the airfield. They picked it up—used one of them big fuckers, a Chinook—flew out over a jungle and dropped it off. Figured if Charlie Cong picked it up it'd do the war effort more good fouling things up for the gooks." Beckman laughed at his anecdote, tucking his thin blond hair behind his ears, his eyelids fluttering like the wings of a hovering bird.

"Well, hello." Cora stood in the doorway, cigarette held beside her face. "My father would like to see you."

So there were people at home, Henderson thought.

"Catch you later," Beckman said. "Wait till you hear what happened next."

Cora and Henderson walked up the stairs together.

"How do you get on with Beckman?"

"Fine, fine. He tells me all about life during the Vietnam War."

"You do realize that he was never out there."

"Sorry?"

"He was 4F. Because of his eyes. Nervous complaint."

"No, I didn't know. I was sure—" He felt obscurely shocked at this news. He didn't know why. Nothing at the

Gage Mansion was what it appeared to be—he should have learned that by now.

"Dr. Dubrovnik get off OK? No ill effects from your stroll in the lake? Walking on water takes some practice, I hear."

"Oh, God. It was . . . Everything went wrong. It's difficult, um . . ."

"Don't worry." Cora laughed, but kindly. "But I was very impressed. Somehow it was the last thing I'd ever have expected you to do."

"Same here," he said thoughtfully. Then, "Look, I'd be terribly grateful if you didn't mention anything to Bryant. I wouldn't like her to get the, you know, wrong idea."

"Or Bryant's mother."

"Yes."

"Dr. Dubrovnik wasn't the most convincing art historian."

"Well . ." He made a wry face.

"Bit of a dark horse, Mr. Dores, aren't you? Lead a complicated sort of life."

"Not usually," he said candidly. "But since coming here everything has got rather out of control."

The were outside Gage's door. Cora looked quizzically at him for a moment.

"Go right on in. He's expecting you." She turned to her own door.

Henderson knocked and went into Gage's room. It was empty and the double doors to the bedroom were closed.

Gage's voice came from behind them. "Henderson. Give me two minutes."

"Fine."

Henderson took the opportunity of scrutinizing *Demeter and Baubo* again. There was the goddess in her tattered widow's weeds, laughing at the serving maid's outrageous display. The grin was crude, badly rendered, but was wide enough to reveal the goddess's teeth. Baubo was laughing too. They were having a good time, that was clear enough.

"Come on in," Gage called from his bedroom. Henderson walked through. Gage was shirtless and was patting his damp ruddy cheeks with a towel. His old chest and shoulders were covered in surprisingly dense gray hair.

"Having a shave," he said, and put on a clean shirt. "How are you, Henderson?"

"Oh. Fine."

"A successful consultation in Atlanta?"

"Yes and no."

"Freeborn tells me you created quite a stir. Something about shouting and wading across the atrium lake?"

Henderson colored. "Ah. Yes. I can—"

"Freeborn was insistent that anyone who behaved like that wasn't a man to do business with."

"There is an explanation. Of sorts."

"I listen to Freeborn but I rarely take his advice." He paused. "I guess you had your reasons."

Henderson scratched his cheek. "Yes. I think I did."

"Well, OK. Things I did when I was your age . . ." He came over and put his arm around Henderson's shoulders. "We got to sow our wild oats, don't we? Otherwise what the hell's the point? Know what I mean?"

"We all want to be happy and we're all going to die."

"You're learning, Henderson. You're learning."

Henderson smiled. Gage patted his shoulder.

"I like you, Henderson. Like you a lot. You're a bit quiet and withdrawn, but I've got to say I like you."

Henderson didn't know what to reply. He liked Gage too, he realized. He felt fond of the little old man. He wanted to tell him that, but something prevented him.

"Thanks very much," he mumbled.

Gage smiled and shook his head sadly.

"Now. What about our business?"

"I've spoke to Mr. Beeby and we've thought again about the Dutch paintings. We will raise the reserve to fifty thousand dollars each. I know that's not as much as Sereno and Gint, but if we get anywhere near our estimates on the others, you'll do much better."

Gage spread his hands. "There you are. A little extra consideration can work wonders."

"All the other conditions remain more or less the same, of course."

"Well, I think we've got a deal." Gage held out his hand. Henderson shook it. Gage's grasp was cool and dry.

"I'm delighted," Henderson said. He felt a thudding in his chest, a slackening. "Truly delighted."

"I don't think my son will be very pleased. Neither will Mr. Sereno or Mr. Gint. But they are *my* pictures, after all."

Henderson quickly ran through the next stages of the operation—packing, shipping, insuring.

"How soon can you sell them?"

"A month, perhaps slightly longer. We need to publicize, announce—"

"Good. Well, the sooner the better. I won't disguise from you, Henderson, my need for the money. The Gage Mansion, Beckman's lab, Freeborn's medical supplies venture, and various so-called sure things he's gotten me involved with, Cora's . . . well, these last few months Cora doesn't cost much—but she has to be looked after. It's all drained away over the years."

"I see," Henderson said, sympathetically.

"Know how I made my first million? Parking lots. Right after World War I. I saw all these new motorcars on the roads and I thought, guys will start driving them to work and are gonna need someplace to leave them. I had a little money saved up and I bought myself a vacant lot in downtown Atlanta. Leveled it out, painted some lines on the ground. The first real parking lot in Atlanta.

"You know, my parking lot was a kind of peculiar shape so I had to draw a plan of how to get the most number of cars into the place. Then I had my idea." Gage paused, adjusted his stance as he got caught up in his story.

"I took out a series of patents on parking-lot design. Filed them at the patent office. You look at any old parking lot today. What do you see? The basic grid, the parallelogram, the chevron, the interlocking chevron. I had patents on them all in the early twenties. Everyone who had a parking lot had to pay me to use the design. I had three lawyers touring the southern states serving writs. The money came flowing in. I bought more space for parking lots. Before I knew it I was the biggest parking-lot operator south of the Mason-Dixon Line. I made my first million, and then some more. But then in 1924 the Supreme Court declared my patents invalid and the bottom fell out of parking-lot design forever."

"Good Lord," Henderson said. "It seems such an obvious idea."

"All the best ones are, son. Every time I see a parking lot today I could weep. And those multistory garages . . . What the hell. It didn't bother me that much. I'd bought this place. I'd been to Europe and I had my art collection. In 1935 I got married." He paused.

"I only had that one good idea which made me all my money. I thought I had good ideas later but it turned out I was only going to be allowed the one." He laughed to himself. "Amazing how easy it goes, money. I've been poor and I've been rich, now I'm getting poor again and there's no doubt it's better being rich. Money can't buy you happiness, they say—and it's true, I guess—but it can buy you one hell of a lot of other things." He looked at Henderson. "You get me two or three million, Henderson, and I'll see the century out happy."

"I don't think you need worry. The Sisleys alone will—"

"You a happy man, Henderson?"

Henderson was a little taken aback. "Well, I wasn't. But then I thought I knew what would make me happy. But now I'm not so sure." He rubbed his hands together and put them in his pocket. "I'm afraid that doesn't make much sense."

There was the sound of someone coming into the next room.

"Loomis," came a voice. "It's me."

"Ah," Gage said, looking at his watch. "A little early, but never mind."

They both went through into the sitting room. Standing in the middle of the carpet was Monika Cardew, in a bright-orange dress, tight around the hips, and white high-heeled shoes. Her hair was still in its complicated beehive.

"You remember Henderson, Monika."

"Of course. How do you do?"

"Hello," Henderson said, trying to look insouciant.

"We won't be a second, Monika. Help yourself to a drink."

He followed Henderson to the door and opened it. He smiled.

"Fine woman, Henderson. See you in church."

Henderson shut the door. For a moment he stood incredulous. Then, remembering his good news, clapsed his hands together, looked heavenward and said, "Thank you, God."

"Everything go well?" It was Cora standing in her doorway.

"Yes. I think so. We got the pictures after a bit of renegotiation. I'm afraid your friend Mr Sereno has had a wasted journey."

"He's not my friend."

"I thought—"

"Wrong."

Henderson nodded. "That was, um, Monika Cardew."

"Yeah. She comes once a week. When T. J. goes to Tallapoosa to record his *Sunday Sermonette*."

"I see."

"It's been going on for years. Why else do you think Daddy spends so much time with T. J.?"

"Good point." He paused. "Well, I must get to a phone. It will have to be Luxora Beach. I can't quite see Freeborn allowing me to communicate my news over his line."

"Are you walking?"

"No choice. My car has disappeared into thin air."

"Feel like some company? I'd like a walk."

Henderson and Cora went down the front steps and out into the night. It was warm but from time to time a coolish breeze would blow. Cora wore an old blue cardigan over her baggy gray T-shirt and black cotton trousers. Soon they turned a bend in the road and the lights of the house were lost to sight. They walked along in silence for a while. All about them was the melancholy sound of crickets. It was, Henderson thought, one of the earth's most evocative of noises. Like an owl's hoot, or a gull's screech it summed up a whole cargo of emotions and moods. Now he felt sad and relieved, weary and grateful, strangely mature and wise. Up above him the stars shone in their confusing constellations.

Cora paced along beside him, a small intent figure, the top of her head bobbing at the level of his elbow. She lit a cigarette and he smelled the smoke. As soon as they had stepped outside she had removed her sunglasses. He looked sidelong at her now but it was too dark to make out her features. What a curious, complex person she was! he thought. He couldn't figure her out at all. Had she really abandoned a career in medicine? Or was that another Gage Mansion fantasy? What was she doing whiling away her life in her father's house? Smoking, reading? Listening to classical music? And what did she do for sex? he suddenly wondered crudely, and then felt embarrassed by his prurience. He found himself trying to imagine her naked: the slight girl's frame, with full breasts and a woman's hair . . . oddly stimulating.

"Lovely night," he said, derailing that train of thought. "You haven't, um, seen Duane and Bryant by any chance?"

"Bryant's in with Shanda watching TV, I think. I don't know where Duane is. There was some talk of him taking your car into Hamburg."

"Bryant told me that she and Duane wanted to get married."

"That's not funny, Henderson."

"It's not meant to be. It's true."

"You're kidding." She stopped.

"I wish I were." They started walking again.

"It sounds very unlikely to me. I mean, God, you know what Duane is like."

"Actually, as surprising as it may sound, I've yet to clap eyes on him. He's just some sort of malevolent spirit who's commandeered my car, as far as I'm concerned."

"Well, when you meet him you'll know what I'm talking about. God, marry Duane?"

They had reached Luxora Beach. Henderson didn't know whether to be comforted or alarmed by Cora's words. They crossed the mall and stepped over the railway tracks.

"Bar seems to be doing a roaring trade," he observed.

"Well, it's all we've got."

They walked down a dark side street to the lambent phone box outside the post office.

"Won't be a second," he said. As he put through his collect call to Beeby he looked at Cora's small neat figure pacing around outside. She paused to light a cigarette, looked up and caught his eye. She had an oval pleasant face, he could see, now that it wasn't disfigured by her dark lenses. She gave a mocking curtsy. He doffed an invisible cap.

Beeby answered.

"Thomas," Henderson said. "It's done. He agreed."

"You're sure?" Beeby gave a shout of exhilaration. "Henderson, you amazing man!"

"We shook hands on it ten minutes ago. I'll get everything tidied up tomorrow, be back in the office Monday."

"Fine. Superb. But I thought you were taking a holiday?"

"Slight change of plan, there."

"Have it another time."

"Right."

"You're a marvel."

After some more praise, he hung up.

He made one more call, To Melissa.

"Melissa, darling, it's—"

"Get her out of there, you bastard, or I call the cops!"

"What? Who?"

"*My baby*, you bastard, that's who! You're meant to be looking after her. She called me today, says she wants to marry someone called Duane. I mean, *Duane?* I ask you. Look, Henderson, I'm warning you—"

"Calm down, Melissa, Calm down, for God's sake. There's no need to worry." He felt his armpits moisten. "It's nothing, some girlish fantasy she has. A stupid crush. There's no problem—we'll be back on Monday."

There was a pause. Melissa started again, this time tearful.

"But I *am* worried, Henderson, I am. She said she wasn't coming home, that she was going to stay with this Duane person. She said she was very happy. It just didn't sound like her."

"Exactly," he soothed. "A passing infatuation. She doesn't know what she's saying, really. I've already spoken to her. Everything will be fine and we'll be back on Monday, I promise."

He uttered some more consoling platitudes and hung up. He wondered how he had managed to sound so confident and reassuring—he didn't feel it. He stepped outside the box, shaking his head.

"It's uncanny. One problem clears up, another steps into line."

"What is it?"

"Bloody Duane and Bryant. That was Bryant's mother, reaching hysteria point. The stupid girl phoned home."

"Take it easy," Cora touched his arm. "I'll get Daddy to talk to Duane—end of problem. He always does what Daddy tells him. Always."

"Would you? That'd be wonderful . I don't know what she's playing at. She's only fourteen, for Christ sake. At fourteen I still had two years to go to my first kiss."

Cora laughed disbelievingly.

"No, it's true. We tend to be late developers in England—if we develop at all. They lock you away, you see, for the duration of your adolescence with lots of other boys." He frowned. "It's a long haul," he added.

They set off back through the town to the Gage Mansion.

"You know that painting, the one you call *Demeter and Iambe*?"

"Yeah. What about it?"

"Well, I've discovered it's not Demeter and Iambe. it's Demeter and Baubo."

"So? It that important."

"Not really. Vaguely interesting." He explained what he had learned of the myth. "It seems that Demeter broke her fast and came out of mourning when Baubo flashed her . . . her privates at her."

"Her *privates*? You mean her cunt?"

"Well, yes."

"Say what you mean, Henderson, say what you mean."

"Sorry. I was just wondering what it could be all about. What it all signified."

"Demeter has had her daughter stolen, right? She goes into a kind of deep mourn. But she cheers up when Baubo shoots her a view of—"

"Precisely."

"Well it seems pretty obvious to me what it's all about."

"Does it?" He looked across at her. She looked back at him. He stumbled on a stone. Cora grabbed his arm.

"Christ!"

"You OK?"

They had stopped on a deserted stretch of the road. There was no moon yet, but a clear faint light from the stars. The crickets breeped steadily about them. Henderson knew, with sudden insight, both what he was about to do and all the good and strong reasons why he shouldn't. These crisis points had occurred before: he recognized the right path, recognized the wrong and chose the wrong. Sufficient to have stood but free to fall. It was, he felt, an understanding periodically offered him of a certain truth about the human condition. But perhaps, he thought, as he bent down to kiss Cora, that is a little grand. Not the human condition, then: the Dores condition.

His pouting lips met midair. Cora had stepped back. He clumsily reached out for her but she batted his arms away.

"What are you trying to *do*, Henderson? *God*. Get off, will you?"

"I thought—"

"I don't want to kiss you, Henderson. What makes you think I do? Why do you have to try and kiss me?"

He was glad the night hid his knotted, boiling face.

"Jesus," he began. "Misinterp. Look, I . . . Christ."

"I like you, Henderson. You're a nice guy. It's a big asset. But I don't want to make it with you."

He swallowed. "A ghastly misunderstanding. Misreading. I got carried away. I'm terribly, terribly—"

"Relax." Her voice was softer. "It's no big deal. Now we know where we stand."

He nodded wordlessly.

They set off again, walking up the road in silence. Cora gave a little chuckle and from time to time looked over at him. Fool, he said to himself, fool fool *fool* FOOL. They turned a corner and the house was in front of them. Lights shone from all the windows.

"Looks like everybody's home all of a sudden."

They walked across the park to the front steps.

"Listen, Cora," Henderson started, dry-throated, but was interrupted by the front door's being flung violently open. It was Alma-May, weeping piteously.

"Cora, baby! Cora, darlin'! Your daddy's dead, baby. Your daddy's dead!"

chapter thirteen

"YOUR father promised me—we shook hands on it, just minutes"—Henderson cleared his throat to rid his voice of the tremble—"just minutes before he . . . passed away, literally minutes—that Mulholland, Melhuish were to auction his pictures."

"Fuck you," Freeborn said. "You're lying, you bastard. Jesus, you don't expect me to believe this shit? You fuckin' English dork!"

"Mr. Dores," Sereno said, "we only have your side of the story. Well, it's not enough, I'm afraid."

"Look, I told Cora—"

"He did," Cora said. "That's true."

"So fuckin' what? It's just words. Ain't no proof. I say we take Ben Sereno and Peter Gint's offer now, 'stead of waiting for some pissant faggot auction in New York."

"These people," Henderson said, with genuine anger, indicating the two gallery owners, "are total frauds. I wouldn't trust them an inch."

"There's no call for such accusations," Sereno said, quite untroubled by the slander.

"Shut yo' fuckin' mouth," Freeborn said to Henderson, pointing a finger at him. "They're my pictures now an' I says they go to Sereno and Gint."

"One minute, Freeborn," Cora said. "There's Daddy's will. Beckman and me may have some say."

"I'll go along with Freeborn," Beckman mumbled. "Just as long as I've got my labrotory."

"Anyway, that will ain't read for two fuckin' weeks."

"Look, do you think we might conduct this discussion without constant profanities?" Henderson said.

"Fuck yo' ass, English shitbird!"

Freeborn, Beckman, Cora, Henderson, Sereno and Gint were in the sitting room. Across the hall in the dining room on the long table lay Loomis Gage, cold in his coffin.

Half an hour after Henderson had left him and Monika, Duane had returned to the house and had duly switched on his music. According to Beckman, who was passing through the hall, his father—wearing a dressing gown—had appeared at the top of the stairs and had bellowed furiously, *"Duane, turn that damn music down!"* Then he had shuddered, gone white, twitched and fallen over. Duane came running out of his room, picked Gage up and carried him back to bed. Beckman, with rare spirit of diplomacy, drove Monika Cardew home and collected the local doctor. By the time they got back, Gage was dead, and Duane—who was sitting impassively beside the body—said it had happened only moments before. Freeborn, Sereno and Gint had returned from whatever carousing or plotting they had been engaged in five minutes prior to Henderson and Cora's fateful arrival at the front steps.

All that night there had been a hectic traffic of doctors, undertakers and the—happily innocent—T. J. Cardew. Loomis Gage's instructions had been for a quiet family funeral. There seemed no purpose in delaying further and the service was scheduled for the next afternoon, 4:30 P.M.

And here they all were, Henderson thought, bickering about the spoils with typically wicked speed. Talk about funeral baked meats furnishing forth marriage tables. . . . He felt a shocked sadness at Gage's sudden demise. The family—with the exception of Alma-May—seemed to have accepted it with easy stoicism. He had liked the sprightly old man, more than he had realized. He remembered their last conversation with regret: Gage had offered him his affection but he had been too reserved or too trammeled up in securing the paintings to respond. What had he said? "Thanks very much." He was disgusted with himself, but then that was always the way, he reflected bitterly; you always leave things too late. As for old Gage, it might have been more apt if he had died some minutes earlier in the arms of Monika Cardew—*petit mort* suddenly *grand*—rather than through the effort of shouting at a parasitic lout to turn his rock music down. But the "grand design," he was aware, was very proficient when it came to faulty timing.

He felt too, along with his sadness, the bitter certainty of what he knew would be eventual defeat. Freeborn had assumed an air of swaggering authority, of the sort favored by junior officers who have just led a successful coup d'état. Cora alone could do nothing to counter her brother's new sway, and the full effect of Beckman's deluded craven apathy was more than apparent. He had been so close, he thought with a surge of harsh selfishness. If only Gage had died a few days later . . .

He slumped in his chair for a moment, the utter waste of all his efforts confronting him. He made one final desperate, futile try.

"Mr. Gage," he said seriously, mustering all his formality and *gravitas*. "Mr. Sereno, Mr. Gint. As far as I am concerned, Loomis Gage and I had made a binding agreement. If you proceed independently I have to warn you of potential legal—"

He leaped from his chair as Freeborn sprang across the room after him. Sereno, Gint and Beckman held him back.

"You *say* you had an agreement," Sereno said coolly, once Freeborn's lurid oaths had subdued.

"There must have been," Cora said. "He told me. He wouldn't have mentioned it otherwise, would he?"

"Did you witness any agreement?" Sereno asked Cora, as Freeborn was resettled in his chair.

"No." A glum, sidelong look at Henderson.

"Did anyone witness it?" Sereno asked.

"No. But—"

"You're welcome to take us to court, Mr. Dores," Sereno said. "But I don't think you'll get very far."

They all looked at Henderson. He stood up.

"You're making a terrible mistake" was all he could think of to say.

The afternoon sun warmed the pates of the large crowd of mourners in Luxora Beach's small, uncrowded cemetery. Henderson stood with the Gage family, who were ranked behind the Reverend T. J. Cardew. Across the grave on the other side was a group of some forty or fifty local people. The Stars and Stripes and the Stars and Bars on the post office flagpole flew at half-mast. The streets were empty, shops were closed, even the neon beer signs in the bar windows had been extinguished. Henderson looked around for Bryant, but she didn't appear to be present; neither was her beau or her future mother-in-law. Shanda had said she thought they were making their own way to the cemetery, but Alma-May had been so stricken with grief it wasn't clear if she would have been able to stand the strain.

Henderson hadn't felt like coming at all, but considered he owed it to old man Gage. He had been transported to the cemetery in a car containing Sereno, Gint, Cora and Shanda (Freeborn and Beckman were coming behind with the other pallbearers) and had had to maintain the control over his disappointment and bitterness for another hour or so. Sereno had offered him his hand and said, "No hard feelings." Against his better wishes, Henderson had shaken it.

All around him now was the sound of discreet muffled lamentation as Loomis Gage's body was strenuously lowered into the ground. Henderson looked dry-eyed at the cross atop the wooden spire of the Baptist church. Gall and wormwood, he thought, goats and monkeys. Someone up there is having fun at my expense. He tasted ashes in his mouth.

Then, as if in a dream, he heard his name being called. He looked around with alarm to discover he was the cynosure of all eyes. T. J. Cardew was pointing at him and talking in the loud overstressed voice preferred by preachers and soapbox orators.

". . . yes, Mr. Henderson Dores, of London, England, was an inspiration to me. It was his words that came instantly to mind when I heard of the death of my dear friend Loomis Gage. His innocent and yet profound words. Tell them what you said, Henderson; tell our good friends, the good people gathered here today."

Henderson took a frightened half-pace to the rear. What on earth is the man talking about? he asked himself in quickening panic. What was he meant to say? Should he fall on his knees perhaps? Dim memories of revivalist meet-

ings capered through his mind. Play for time: cry, "Halle-
lujah"?

"I'm sorry," he said, fingers on the knot of his tie. "I
don't, um . . ."

"Those simple words, Henderson, when we first met,"
Cardew prompted with a sad smile.

"Oh." He racked his brains.

"What you said to me—a question—at our first meeting. Remember? The question you asked me?"

"Oh, yes. . . . Got you."

"Go on, Henderson. Repeat your question."

"How is Patch?"

"I'm sorry?"

"How is Patch? That's what I said. When we met."

"No, sir." A slight tautening of irritation sent Cardew's
smile momentarily awry. A mutter of curiosity passed
through the crowd, like a cough in an auditorium.

"I refer," Cardew continued, "to that simple and touching inquiry you made of me. 'Tell me, T. J.,' you said, 'tell
me, T. J. How do you explain the "Beach" in Luxora
Beach?' Do you remember now, Henderson?"

"I'm afraid I don't actu—"

"And I said"—Cardew turned back to the crowd—"I
said to Henderson, 'Henderson,' I said, 'why, Henderson, I
do not know, Henderson.' And friends, I didn't know. And
yet I've lived among you now these last eleven years. And I
thought of Henderson's simple, childlike words—'How do
you explain the "Beach" in Luxora Beach?'—when I was
brought the news of my good and dear friend Loomis's
untimely sleep in the Lord. I thought, simple Henderson
here, a visitor to our town, asks an obvious, very simple
question, to which I cannot reply. And I bethought to myself, T. J., I said, T. J., how little we know of the Good

Lord's will, how much we take unthinkingly for granted when a simple almost foolish question can reveal—"

"Excuse me, T. J." A tall old cadaverous man held up his trembling hand. "But everybody knows why Luxora Beach is called Luxora Beach. It's because the early settlers done planted a grove of beech saplings they'd brung from Europe. 'Cept they all died the first summer—the saplings, that is. It should be Luxora Beeches—B, e, e, c, h, e, s."

"Well, thank you kindly, George, thank you. As I was saying, friends, Henderson's childish, ignorant question—"

"Hold on there one second, T. J.," a plump red-faced man interjected. "George is wrong. See, time was the Ockmulgokee River took a mighty swerve hereabouts and threw up a perfect crescent of white sand on the bank. When the first settlers arrived they found sand dollars on the beach. Now, Luxora was the name of the first mayor's wife. The town used to be called Luxora's Beach."

"Well, thank you, Willard Creed. Henderson's thoughtless, stupid question—"

"Willard Creed, that ain't true, an' you know it." A thin old lady with pale-blue spectacles stepped forward shakily. She addressed her remarks to Henderson. "You see, what happened was that the first trading posts here were set up by the Luxora Bleach Company of Montgomery, Alabama, in 1835. The store had a big sign up saying Luxora Bleach and folks kinda liked the sound of—"

"*Thank you, my friends!*" yelled Cardew over the hot debate that had sprung up. "Ashes to ashes, dust to dust. Amen."

Henderson walked listlessly back through the town with Cora.

"I think somehow Cardew blames me," Henderson

said. "He refused to shake my hand after the service. He seemed terribly upset."

"I think that's the kind of funeral my father would have enjoyed."

"Really?" He looked at her. He dropped his voice. "Listen, Cora, I haven't had a chance . . . I'm terribly sorry about last night. . . . I got carried away."

"Eoh, don't mention it," she said in her English accent.

"Pride comes before a fall," he said, as they walked past the post office. "Better get it over with, I suppose." He paused by the phone box. "I wonder what Beeby will say?"

"I want your resignation on my desk tomorrow morning," Beeby said in a tense furious voice. "How could you let me down in this way, Henderson? How could you?" He slammed down the phone. Henderson gently replaced the receiver and stepped numbly out of the box.

"How was it?"

He screwed up his eyes. "Pretty bad. He's just fired me."

"My God! But it's not your fault."

"Oh, he'll come around. I hope. Just a bit steamed up at the moment."

He was surprised at his comparative equanimity—until he realized it was false and that in reality he was in mild shock. Beeby had been beside himself, mad. Very badly let down, he had said, very, very, very disappointed. Henderson had never heard him speak with such icy purpose, not like his usual self at all.

They went over to the car. Sereno and Gint were in the front, Shanda crying softly in the back. Henderson slid in beside her. Cora liked to be next to a window so she could smoke.

"A very moving service," Gint said softly, craning around.

Henderson patted Shanda's shoulder and said, "There, there."

They drove back to the Gage Mansion in silence. Henderson suddenly felt oddly calm. Everything had gone so wrong that, for the first time in ages, he experienced some sort of certainty about the future. When all hopes are dashed, life becomes simply a matter of getting through the hours and days, he reasoned. With no ambitions or aspirations, a banal and docile survival is all that is required. Melissa outraged, Irene estranged, the pictures gone, jobless . . . all the various enterprises and schemes that had dominated his waking moments for the last few weeks were no more. Time stretched ahead for him, empty and unalluring.

He would have to start again, that was all, fill up the next three decades or so with new ploys and distractions. But he would lower his sights somewhat: no grandiose or pretentious notions about "change" or "finding himself." A return to England was the first priority: lowered sights were more at home there. he'd reclaim his Baron's Court flat from his niece and her friends and, as for work—his pulse didn't exactly quicken at the prospect—perhaps take up that promised commission on the Odilon Redon book. . . .

Back at the Gage Mansion he found Bryant packing her suitcases.

"Good girl," Henderson said. "We'll be off first thing tomorrow."

"You will. We won't."

"What do you mean?"

"I'm going away with Duane, to Kansas."

"Kansas? Why Kansas?"

"Girls can get married at twelve there."

"You're joking!"

"No."

"But that's disgusting. *Obscene.*"

Bryant explained that now that Loomis Gage was dead and Freeborn was the new head of the household, Duane didn't think he could stay around much longer, as he and Freeborn hated each other. So they were going to Kansas, where they could get married without delay.

Henderson took in this new setback with the phlegmatic patience of the consistently thwarted. He reminded Bryant of her age and Duane's, and the likely reaction of her mother.

"I'll take care of Mom," she said defiantly. "It's not your responsibility. If I want to do something you can't stop me and neither can she."

Henderson looked at her. She had changed in the brief time they had spent together. No longer a willful, spoiled adolescent, she had turned into a willful, spoiled adult. He was suddenly convinced too that she and Duane had slept together. He found this very depressing.

"Bryant, seriously . . . Duane?"

"Do you know him?"

"No."

"There you are."

In actual fact, he was on the point of giving them his blessing; he felt terminal exhaustion loud at his back, hurrying near. Bryant took a soft-pack from her jeans pocket and lit a cigarette.

"If you knew Duane you'd feel different," she said wistfully. "He's a sweet, lovely person. Very kind, very gentle." She exhaled and looked dreamily at the smoke billow and disperse.

"Where is he, by the way?"

"He's getting your car. And buying our tickets."

"At last."

He stood up. No, this was all wrong. This wasn't going to happen. He felt a sudden urge and strong determination to thwart Bryant's projected nuptials. Why? he wondered. . . . To curry favor with Melissa? Possibly, although that seemed something of a lost cause. To prevent a young girl ruining her life? That sounded altruistic and noble enough, but if he was honest he didn't care that much about what Bryant did with her life. No, he reflected, he had to stop the rot, that was all—and soon. The answer had something to do with not bending, not succumbing to the endless massive flow of events and phenomena. He'd been powerless to resist the current that swept *him* along, however fiercely he battled. Perhaps a passionless, disinterested attempt at deflecting someone else's might have more success.

"Well," he said, stirrings of an idea beginning to shift around in his brain. "It's your life, and you can do what you want, as they say."

chapter fourteen

HENDERSON packed his small case with his few possessions, then went in search of Cora to tell her he would be
leaving the next day. She was sitting in her room looking
out over the wild garden. There were no lights on but a
pink glow from the evening sun cast gauzy, kindly gleams
over her and the shabby furniture.

"I'm sorry," she said, "that it's been such a bad time for
you. I hope you get your job back."

"Who knows? Maybe it was the wrong job." He smiled
thinly. "I don't think I'm really suited to this place." He
gave her a brief résumé of his past fond ambitions, of his
conviction that everything was going to change for the
better once he arrived in America.

"How very sad for you," she said without a trace of
mockery. "Losing your hopes—that's much worse than losing the paintings."

He found her sincerity oddly disturbing. He didn't
know what to say. "What will you do?" he asked. "Go back
to medical school?"

"Don't worry about me. I've got plenty to do. But what
about you?"

He sketched out, with flimsy enthusiasm, his return to

275

London, the flat, the book on Odilon Redon, growing steadily more downcast as he did so.

"What about your Dr. Dubrovnik?"

"I think those hopes foundered in the atrium lake."

"Poor Henderson," she said. "We haven't treated you very kindly in this country, have we?"

"Could have gone better, I suppose."

She took off her dark glasses and smiled ruefully at him. "I *am* sorry about the pictures. Daddy left everything to Freeborn—the pictures, the house, what's left of the money—I don't need to see the will. He was a firm believer in primogeniture—very English of him."

Henderson shrugged. In the evening light her sallow skin had turned the color of a tea rose. He wondered if he should try to kiss her again. But then he further wondered why, given his past record, he should still wish to unleash more troubles upon himself. But his reluctance wasn't due to prudence, he realized: it was that famous reserve asserting itself again. Later, he'd regret not trying, he knew. That was the great feature about reserve: it walked hand in hand with regret; left you sadder but no wiser. You never knew what might have been.

He stood up. "I'll be making an early start. . . ." He held out his hand.

Cora shook it with facetious solemnity. "Jolly good luck and all that," she said.

He smiled foolishly, looking a fool again. Perhaps he should have kissed her, after all. . . . He felt a vast impotence, and tears of self-pity stung his eyeballs. He edged crablike to the door, gave a resigned but reassuring grin and left her room.

*   *   *

That evening Henderson and Bryant sat alone in the sitting room. Cora remained upstairs, Beckman was out somewhere and Duane had not returned. The absence of Duane—and necessarily the absence of his car—was something of a nuisance but otherwise the conditions suited his plan perfectly.

A red-eyed, sniffling Alma-May provided them with a supper of pulse stew and cinnamon pear bake and they watched an hour or two of TV.

"And where is Duane?" Henderson asked casually, about half past ten.

"He'll be back," Bryant said. "If not tonight, tomorrow morning. He said he had a few things to finish up before we left. Said they were important too—he might take some time."

For an instant Henderson wondered if Duane himself was having second thoughts about a lifetime with Bryant, but she seemed unperturbed by his not returning. Still, he had to press on with his own scheme. He couldn't assume Bryant would be conveniently abandoned.

Fifteen minutes later he announced he was going to make some coffee and would Bryant like some? A glass of milk, she said, and a cookie, not taking her eyes from the screen where angry hoodlums shot at each other from speeding cars.

In the kitchen, he prepared the drinks. From his pocket he removed his sleeping pills and poured the powder from three capsules into the milk.

"Henderson?"

He looked around with a guilty start. It was Shanda. She glanced over her shoulder and toppled into the center of the kitchen on her high heels. She leaned against the table and gave her belly a heave, like a man adjusting a heavy pack.

"Whatcha doin'?" she asked.

"Milk. For Bryant."

"Oh." She paused and flicked her wings of hair with the backs of her fingers. "You leaving tomorrow? Going to New York, Alma-May said."

"That's right." He stirred Bryant's milk as if that were what one always did with milk.

"Can I come with you?"

The clatter of the teaspoon against the glass rang like an alarm bell. Milk slopped onto the table.

"What?!"

"I have to get away, Henderson," she said in a rush. "I can't stand it here. I got to get far away. Someplace like New York. I want to go along with you." Shanda said this fast but tonelessly, staring at the savage points of her high-heeled shoes.

"Good God, Shanda," he blustered, appalled at this notion. "Don't be absurd. I, I, I . . . I mean, of course you can't come away with me."

"Of course I *kahn?*" Her eyes widened with hope.

"Can't. *Kahn't.* You *kahn't.*" Desperation. *"Kent.* You *kent* come with me. You *kent.*"

"Please, Henderson. I hate Freeborn. I hate the trailer. I hate the fuckin' medical supplies all over the place. I hate the smell of mouthwash. I hate the—"

"But—Jesus—what about the baby?"

"I don't care," she said darkly. "I'm not happy here. That's all that matters." She touched his arm. "Please!"

"No, Shanda. No, no, no." He shook his head. "I'm sorry. No way." He picked up his coffee and Bryant's spiked milk. The irony did not escape him: drugging a reluctant companion, spurning the eager.

"Just think about it, please? Think about it some more? I just have to get far away, that's all. You're the only per-

son I know who lives far away." She followed him to the
door. "Don't say anything now. I'll talk to you in the
morning." She clattered off back to her trailer.

Thank Christ, he thought, I'll be long gone. He felt a
thrill of excitement about his planned abduction. He went
through to the sitting room and told Bryant of Shanda's
request.

"She'll do anything to get away from Freeborn."

"Thanks a lot."

"God, does she hate that guy." She took a large gulp of
her milk. "Mng. Is this fresh?"

"From the carton."

"Probably yak milk or something." She drank the rest
and munched her biscuit. A few minutes later she looked
at her watch. "I guess Duane's not coming tonight. I was
hoping you and him could have a talk. So you could tell
Mom more about him."

"Shame. Perhaps I'll catch him in the morning."

"Yeah, well I'm sacking out." She got up. "See you."

"Sleep well."

After she had gone he sat on in front of the television. He
wrote a brief note to Cora explaining his hasty and unorthodox departure and giving her his New York address,
should she ever feel inclined to visit, while he was still in
the country.

After midnight, he switched out all the lights and went
softly upstairs. He slipped the note beneath Cora's door.
He paused outside Gage's rooms. One last look at the
paintings. He tested the door. Locked. Freeborn had se-
cured his property already.

He crept around the passageway. Beckman was away
too. He went into Bryant's room. She was snoring slightly,

her mouth slack, drool dampening the pillow.

In his own room he made sure everything was ready for a prompt departure and lay down fully clothed on his bed to wait. For once insomnia proved a blessing; there was no danger he would fall asleep.

He felt strangely calm. The act he was about to commit did not appear so outrageous in the setting of this bizarre household—*de rigueur* rather, almost run of the mill. Everything had gone wrong, but from somewhere he seemed to be deriving the capacity to *act*.

The hours moved by with their usual heel-dragging lethargy. He watched a wand of moonlight move across the wall and transform itself into the replica of a window, widening slowly, and then slowly begin to thin again. He got up for a drink of water and listened to the dark house, replete with night noises: clicks, creaks, the settings and stirrings of old timber. A platoon of burglars could have moved about without fear of detection.

He paced about his room in stockinged feet trying to imagine the future and confer on its prospects some dim allure. There was—surely, certainly, incontestably—room for another monograph on Odilon Redon. Time indeed for a reassessment of this exotic minor artist, with his fantasy and sentimentality. Sentiment was in vogue again, he thought he remembered someone saying, or about to be in vogue. If he could tap that vein. . . .?

When he got back to New York, he told himself, lying again on the bed, supine, head resting on the cradle of his interlocked fingers, he was going to be quiet and dignified. People—Beeby, Melissa, Irene—could rail at and abuse him as they saw fit (he checked his watch, just after three) and he would smile sadly and keep his own counsel. He would not be provoked, he would remain grave, sober, sagacious. . . . The star- and moonlit replica of the windowpane had acquired a faint peachy hue in the bottom two quadrants. A prefiguring of dawn. The light seemed to flicker and shift. He rubbed his eyes. A faint but sinuous ripple appeared, as if a muslin curtain had been stirred by a breeze.

Curious, he got up and went to the window. At the very foot of the silver garden a bonfire was burning. Quite a large fire too, he saw, gilding the trees and bushes with highlights of orange. He couldn't hear the noise of the fire and for a moment all he registered was the scene's strange and disturbing beauty.

Then he saw a broad-backed figure move in front of the flames: a thickset, masculine shape. Then, his eyes beginning to ache from the effort of focusing, it seemed to shimmer into a slim elfin one. He caught another glimpse of the wraith before it retired to the shadows. Henderson felt suddenly frightened. What the hell was going on? What was burning there?

He pulled on his shoes. He had to investigate, if only to see whether this worrying bonfire and its attendant might prove any obstacle to his own plans, due—he looked at his watch again—to be set in motion very shortly. He crept out of his room: all was dark, and, if not silent, as inactive as before.

He stepped carefully through the kitchen and out onto the back porch. Now he could hear the faint crackle of the flames. Allowing his eyes to become adjusted to the dark he waited some thirty seconds or so before advancing into the garden. The nail sickle of a new moon and the congregation of stars obligingly lit his way. He edged tentatively along an overgrown alley, pausing from time to time to listen to other noises, staring at the flickering flames to see if the mysterious stoker still tended his pyre. All he could hear apart from the electric trill of the crickets was the sound of his own breathing and the endless surge and flow of the blood in his ears.

He crept closer, moving from bush to shrub, from tree trunk to tree trunk. Then he saw a tall, oddly pear-shaped figure step in front of the fire. Henderson hid some twelve or fifteen feet away. The flames illuminated a heavy expressionless face. Henderson knew instantly who it was. He stepped casually out of the bushes.

"Hi there, Duane."

Duane turned around unconcernedly. "Yeah? Who is it?"

"What are you doing?"

Duane peered at him. "Mr. Dores, right? Hi." He had dark hair, parted in the middle and falling to his collar. His face had a stubborn, prognathous—but otherwise inoffensive—aspect. He was carrying a lot of extra weight, but his height and big frame compensated for the excess.

"Good to meet you, sir. An' hey, listen, I'll get your car tomorrow. I promise."

"Great." Henderson felt untypically calm. He looked at the fire. Its fuel seemed to gleam and glint strangely.

"What are you burning?"

"Oh. Mr. Gage's pictures."

Henderson felt his Adam's apple swell to block his throat. He knelt down. Testing first with licked fingertips, he slid a semicharred stick from the fire's edge. It had been a thin, finely worked section of frame; some of the dull-gold molding was still unburned. Using it as a poker he prodded at the contents of the fire. Frames, nothing but frames. Some intact, some broken. Empty frames with a few crisp, blackened shreds of canvas adhering to them.

"Why have you burned them?" he asked quietly, not wanting to provoke or cause offense.

"He told me to."

"Who?"

"Mr. Gage."

"When? Why?"

Duane put his hands in his pockets and gazed at the fire. "Well, you know, after he had his kind of attack . . . Beckman took Monika home and went for the doc. I picked Mr. Gage up and carried him back to his room. I felt kinda bad seein' as how he'd been shouting at me, and all. That it was sorta on account of me, like . . ." Duane paused.

"He was, ah, you know, breathin' all sorts of wheezes and gasps, and he says, 'Duane, you got to do one thing for me.' I says, 'Sure thing, Mr. Gage, what's that?' An' he says, 'You gotta take those paintings off of the walls and burn 'em. Burn 'em all. And don't let Freeborn or Cora or Beckman see you doing it. Don't let anybody know.' So I said, 'OK, good as done.' And then he said, 'Swear.' So I swore on the Bible and my mother's head. He told me to do it as soon as I could. . . ." Duane kicked aimlessly at a jutting frame.

"And then, I guess, he died. Though I couldn't be sure. Then Beckman and the doc came in."

Henderson picked up another section of frame. Holding it to the fire he could read the careful copperplate of its inscription. ÉDOUARD VUILLARD (1886–1940). He tossed it back on the fire. So much for the Gage collection. Smoke and cinders.

"But why did he ask you to burn them?"

"Hell, I don't know, Mr. Dores. Maybe he didn't have any more use for them seein' as he was dying. Maybe he didn't want for anybody else to have them. They were his own, sorta thing. Not anyone else's." Duane spread his hands. "Listen, I'm just doing what he told me, you know? I swore I would."

"I suppose so." Henderson rubbed his forehead.

"Mr. Dores?"

"Yes?"

"Did, uh, Bryant like kinda say anything to you? About us? . . . Not you an' me. Me an' Bryant. I'd sure like to talk with you—"

"Let's talk about it in the morning," Henderson said. He was suddenly reminded of his kidnapping plans. He had to keep Duane out of the way.

"I think I'll get back to bed," he said cautiously.

"I'll just stay on here. Make sure it all burns away. Check it don't spread, sorta thing."

"Good idea. In fact you'd better make absolutely sure. Be very careful."

"Don't worry, sir. I'll make sure."

"See you in the morning."

"Sure, and hey, I'll get your car back. Sure thing. Nice talkin' to you, Mr. Dores." Duane held out his big hand. Henderson shook it, smiled and walked quickly back into the house. In his room, when he bent down to pick up his bag, he thought he would faint. He paddled air onto his face with stiff hands. He felt as though some tiny but vicious fist were pounding him repeatedly in the chest. His legs trembled dramatically. Easy, boy. He summoned up one of Eugene Teagarden's breathing drills, flaring his nostrils, voiding his lungs. Nymphs and shepherds. In, out. Come away. Inhale. Exhale. Cough. Come come come co-ome away.

Then, marginally composed, he crept into Bryant's room.

Speed was crucial now. He switched on the light. Bryant slept on, mouth open, still snoring. Her clothes lay scattered all over the room. He thought of trying to gather them into her suitcase but decided there wasn't time. Anyway, the girl had enough clothes as it was. He picked up a pair of green jeans and a yellow sweat shirt. He would simply pull them on over her pajamas. . . .

He knew, or rather he thought he knew from their effect on him, what the consequences of taking three sleeping capsules were. One was not comatose and could be woken. And from there one could stay awake with some prompting, could walk, even talk a bit, just like someone who—logically enough—had been roused from deep sleep. The difference was that the sensation of bleary baffled consciousness never departed, as it did from a normal sleeper, normally roused; rather it prevailed for a further twenty-four hours. Or at least that had been his experience. He remembered his own stumbling, blunt day after he had taken the pills. His head turned quicker than his eyes. His hands were composed of ten calloused thumbs. His bottom lip grew oddly heavy, irresistably inclined to hang free from its partner. Saliva pooled in every oval cavity, causing embarrassing spillage, or else constant loud draining noises. After he had spent a couple of hours in the office like this, Beeby had ordered him home. Now Henderson was counting on Bryant's being similarly inconvenienced.

"*Bryant*," he hissed, and whipped the sheet back. He whipped it up again and turned away, one hand on his mouth, one across his forehead. The fist started punching again. He looked stupidly about the room. She was *naked*.

Bloody thoughtless bitch! he swore petulantly. He saw her pajamas crumpled by the bed. He rubbed his hands across his face as if he were washing it. His palms were warmed by the heat of his brow and glowing cheeks. There was nothing for it. He prayed Duane was still diligently supervising the fire. He pulled down the sheet again.

He felt guilt and shame swill through his body as—despite stringent moral injunctions to the contrary—he stared at Bryant's nude body in fascinated curiosity. The firm pointed breasts, the soft pale nipples, the skin stretched tight over the staves of her rib cage, the etiolated trace of a bikini bottom, the oddly touching, thin vertical stripe of pubic hair . . . He had to wake her up. He sat beside her. But first—evil Henderson—he covered a breast for a second with a hot shivering palm.

"Bryant. Wake up." He shook her, grabbed her wrists and hauled her into a sitting position.

"Wha . . .?"

He pulled the sweat shirt over her slubbed blinking face, tugged it down over those accusing breasts. Working like a harassed mother, he concertinaed the legs of the jeans and directed her boneless feet through the holes. Tug. Up to the knees. Keep the eyes on the toenails: chipped and scarred with aubergine varnish.

"Wha's happ." Swallow. "Ning. Hndrson?"

"We're going." Tug, heave. "Lie down. Make a bridge."

"Wha?"

"Make a bridge." He slid a hand, palm uppermost, between the warm sheet and her warm buttocks and lifted. She held it there. Mohican crest. He pulled.

"OK." There just remained the zip on the fly. He was disgusted to notice a straining behind his own.

"Hold it." Zip. Soft cilia brushed the knuckle of his forefinger. Then he pushed his hand down the left sleeve of her sweat shirt, located her left wrist and pulled it through. Right sleeve. She was dressed. He licked his lips and tasted salt. A palm wiped across face came away slick and shiny.

"Hennerson. I wanna go . . . sleep." Her eyeballs rolled, white in the sockets for a second.

He found some shoes, flat creased gold moccasins, and slipped them on her feet. Then he had a flash of inspiration. He tore a leaf out of his notebook and wrote in capital letters:

DEAR DUANE,

    IT'S NO GOOD. I DON'T LOVE YOU ENOUGH TO GO AWAY WITH YOU. I'VE GONE BACK TO NEW YORK WITH HENDERSON. IT'S ALL OVER. SORRY.

        BRYANT

He couldn't fret over composition or style. He just hoped Duane could read. He folded the note, wrote DUANE on the front and left it prominently on the pillow.

"Come on," he said to Bryant. "We're going to meet Duane. Don't make a sound."

He took her hand and led her out of the room. She came docilely. She lurched and staggered a bit and once said "Duane" in a loud clear voice, but they made their way down the stairs without being discovered and without too much difficulty. Henderson unbolted the front door and stepped outside onto the porch. There was a faint dawn-lightening in the sky by now; the stars were almost gone. His brick still stood in place of his car; even if the car had been there he realized he couldn't have used it. He had to leave with maximum stealth. And he was running a little late. He was counting on Duane's not visiting Bryant's room until after breakfast.

With his case in one hand and the other on her elbow he guided Bryant down the steps. The large bulk of Freeborn's trailer was completely dark. He felt the sweat cool on his face.

"See Duane?" Bryant mumbled.

"*Shh.* Yes." Goodbye, he breathed at the Gage Mansion, goodbye forever.

"Let's go."

"*Henderson?* Is that you?"

He whirled around, almost dropping his case with shock.

"Whatcha doin'?" Shanda stood at the foot of the trailer steps, wearing a pale-grey dressing gown.

"We're getting out of here," he whispered.

"I heard noises earlier. Were you moving' around?"

"No." It had probably been Duane. "Goodbye, Shanda."

"Hey, wait up a minute. I'm coming too."

"*No!*"

"Henderson, I can just go right on back in there and wake Freeborn. I'm sure he'd like for to know what you're all doin' out here."

"Oh, God, Jesus H. Christ. OK. Anything. But hurry, for God's sake."

"I'll be two minutes."

He felt his sinuses thicken and clog and his eyes screw up of their own accord. It could have been a sneeze but he knew it was tears of frustration. He shook his head angrily.

"Shanda?" muttered Bryant, lolling against him.

"Yes, she's coming too."

Subjective hours later, Shanda appeared. Henderson kept expecting the broad figure of Duane to amble around the corner of the house. Shanda wore a print dress beneath what looked like Freeborn's denim jacket. She carried a small nylon hold-all.

"Let's go," she said conspiratorially. "Hi, Bryant honey."

They set off down the road to Luxora Beach, Bryant's feet dragging rather at Henderson's brisk pace, Shanda making surprisingly good progress in spite of her high heels.

"What's wrong with her, Henderson?"

"She took a couple of sleeping pills."

"What?"

"Pills. Sleeping bloody pills."

"Oh. Got you."

"Are you sure you didn't wake Freeborn?"

"Sleepin' like a hog. Are you sure it wasn't you come by earlier? About three or four times?"

"No." Duane lugging pictures, no doubt.

They pressed on along the dark lane. The crickets were almost silent, only the odd solo voice joined by an early chirping bird. There was a refreshing moist coolness in the air. The dark had retreated; the light was gray and silver, the trees and bushes still and opaque. Glancing to his right he could see Shanda, taking giant unsteady strides in an effort to keep pace. Henderson slowed, out of respect for the jolting embryo.

Soon they arrived at Luxora Beach. A few lights were on; the solitary traffic light hanging above Main Street shone amber, amber, amber. The bar was dark and inert; no neon gleamed. They paused at the railway line. Shanda wiped some drool from Bryant's sweat shirt front. A distant rumble in the east turned into a monster truck that thundered heedlessly through the town.

"Are you sure she's OK?"

"Yes." Henderson looked around. "She's jist plumb tuckered out." Three cars stood in the otherwise deserted shopping area. What now?

"What now?" Shanda asked. She lit a cigarette and leaned against the stanchion of a railway warning sign.

"A bus, I thought. An early morning bus to Atlanta."

"A *bus?* Are you kidding? Ain't no bus in Luxora."

Henderson smiled stupidly. Of course not. He was thinking of tiny English villages, all with local bus routes. Stoppers. What a fool . . . . Just then he longed for an English bus, with its hard furry seats, its smell of wet coats, stale cigarette smoke and diesel. A surly fat yob of a driver with badges and a pencil behind his ear.

"OK, so we gotta hitch a ride," Shanda said.

They crossed tracks and waited. An odd forlorn threesome, Henderson thought. Shanda solicitously checked on Bryant, who was swaying about and mumbling that she was tired.

"You want a smoke, honey?"

"No. She can't smoke."

"OK." Shanda stretched back, both hands supporting her spine. "I'm glad I could come along, Henderson," she said sincerely. "I appreciate it."

"Mmm."

"No, I mean it. I couldn't have stood it there anymore, with Loomis gone and all. Loomis was the only person could keep Freeborn down." She shook her head. "You just get me to New York. Should be far enough away." She flicked her cigarette out into the road. It was getting distinctly lighter. Behind the church somewhere Henderson heard a car start up. Some upstairs windows shone yellow. A door slammed. A banal cock crowed. The flags on the post office flagpole still hung at half-mast for Loomis Gage.

Henderson stood on the dust verge and looked down the gray road. He felt his body was about to petrify from the tension. A smoky lemon stripe in the east heralded the approach of the sun. For an instant he had a sensation of the rushing massive rotation of the earth. It was ten o'clock in the morning in England; the sun was shining on the

Atlantic; it was the wee small hours in Los Angeles. A mile or so away the efforts and genius of some dead European artists had been reduced to ashes by a dim, innocent galoot, and their owner was starting the long process of decomposition in a box beneath the earth up on that hill. And meanwhile he, Henderson Dores, stood by the side of a side road in the hinterlands of America, with his enemy's pregnant wife and a drugged abducted girl, trying to hitch a ride to New York. What did it all add up to? he asked himself. Where was the sense?

He heard the sound of a car, then saw its headlights.

"A car," he said.

Shanda advanced two steps into the road. Henderson shook Bryant awake. She had been leaning against him, his elbow locked beneath her armpit. A looping filament of saliva glimmered between his jacket shoulder and her mouth, then she brushed it apart with a flopping wave of her hand.

Shanda stuck out her thumb and her pregnant belly. The car turned out to be a pickup. It stopped. The driver was a young man in a peaked cap.

"Mornin'," he said. "Where you-all goin'?"

Shanda explained. Henderson couldn't hear what she said but stood behind her with a friendly grin on his face. The door was opened and Shanda and Bryant got in.

"You get in back, darlin'," Shanda said. Darlin'? He obeyed. The back of the pickup was empty apart from a spade and two piles of sacks in the corners. Henderson sat down on one of them.

"You OK back there?"

"Yes," he said faintly, and the pickup moved off with a lurch. The other pile of sacks stirred, sat up and panted. A black dog, of indeterminate breed. A little unsteadily, like a man on a heaving deck, it advanced across the ribbed floor of the truck, its claws scratching on the pressed steel.

"Hello, boy," Henderson said wearily. A bit of rope led from the dog's collar to an attachment on the truck side. The dog sniffed at Henderson's knee and gave it a cursory lick. It took a step or two forward and nosed at his groin. What is it about me and dogs? he thought. The dog was intrigued and snuffled more enthusiastically, its tail beating gently against the tin cab back.

Henderson crossed his legs and turned away.

"Shoo," he said. "Clear off."

The dog sat down and looked patiently at him for the rest of the journey.

At Atlanta Airport, where the obliging driver had taken them, Henderson climbed stiffly out of the back and retrieved his suitcase. Bryant had been asleep the whole journey and had to be woken up again. The driver helped Shanda out and shook Henderson by the hand.

"Thank you very much," Henderson said.

"Good luck, sir," the driver said seriously. He was a young chap with, Henderson was surprised to notice, no incisors in his top row of teeth.

"God bless you, sir. God bless you."

"Thanks. Don't mention it."

When he'd gone Henderson asked Shanda what she had said to him.

"I said we was married, I was pregnant and Bryant was my little sister who was, you know, not quite right, you know, in the head? And that you had said she could come and live with us. He thought that was real kind. Then I said our car had broke down and we had to catch a plane."

Henderson looked suspiciously at Shanda. In the clarity of the early morning sunlight she seemed obnoxiously fresh. Her dyed blond hair gleamed and was quite fetchingly tousled if one ignored the inch of dark-brown root that was exposed here and there. Her large milky breasts and swollen belly strained at the pattern of her dress. She had rolled up the too-long sleeves of Freeborn's jacket and he noticed for the first time a little tattoo on her right forearm, but he couldn't make out what it was.

Bryant stood for a moment unsupported, blinking like an idiot, her head wobbling, as if unwilling to rest on the slim pedestal of her neck.

"Duane now," she said.

"Let's get inside," Henderson said. "I'll get the tickets."

He couldn't get on the first four flights out of Atlanta, but eventually found them three seats together on a plane leaving at half past ten. They left Bryant sleeping soundly on a velveteen bench and went in search of a coffee shop. There, Henderson drank some orange juice but pushed away his plate of fried eggs and bacon garnished with a scone and jam. Shanda tackled hers with speed and efficiency.

"What are you meant to do with that?" Henderson asked, pointing at the scone. "I've always wondered."

"The biscuit?"

"The scone."

"We call it a biscuit. Usually I just cut it in half and leave it."

He smiled encouragingly and watched her eat. Now that he thought about it he should in fact be very angry with Shanda for foisting herself on him in this way, but he was too tired to get indignant. There would be time enough to sort things out when he got to New York. He rubbed his eyes. He hadn't slept for twenty-four hours. So what else was new? He pressed hard, with all ten fingers, on his zygomatic arch, closing his eyes. They would have discovered his absence now at the Gage Mansion. Would Duane have realized his betrothed had been spirited away? And would Freeborn, Sereno and Gint have learned of the destruction of the paintings? He supposed he should have been experiencing some sense of outrage but nothing was forthcoming. The usual priorities seemed absurd today.

Shanda lit a cigarette.

"Y'all right?" she asked, blowing a gust of smoke into the air.

"I don't know," he said seriously. "I really don't know."

Henderson, Shanda and Bryant made their way through the fabulous modernism of Atlanta Airport. They boarded a driverless subterranean train in which a robotic disembodied voice told them where to stand and where to alight. At the robot's first words, Shanda gave a squeal of pleasure and Bryant said, "Duane?" They zipped along beneath the airport and disembarked at the correct place. Now the air was filled with a soft maternal voice breathing information about the various modes of transport available within terminal complex. Henderson felt suddenly safe and secure, until he realized that was precisely the effect aimed for and so became prickly and irritated.

They walked for—it seemed—a good mile down the plush spur of a terminal concourse until they found their departure lounge, full of immaculate businessmen.

Their tickets had been issued in the names of Mr., Mrs. and Miss Dores. Bryant fell asleep whenever she sat down and woke up obediently whenever they had to move. An attentive, concerned stewardess allowed the Dores family to board the plane first because of Shanda's condition. As she ushered a mumbling Bryant—"Duane,

Duane,"—down the aisle one of the cabin staff asked if she was all right.

"She's retarded," Henderson said with a sad smile. "She thinks she's in a train."

Sympathy and prompt service cocooned them from then on. Henderson asked Shanda to conceal her tattoo (an interwining of the letters *F, G* and *S, M* set in a garland of leaves and flowerlets) as he thought it didn't chime with the aura of sacrifice and endurance that enshrouded them. They sat down and then had to move when Shanda requested a seat in the smoking section (they lost some moral ground there), but eventually they were established.

The plane filled up with large clean businessmen, slinging briefcases into the overhead racks, breaking open newspapers, folding expensive trenchcoats with reverential care. Then two dozen enormous young men with very thick necks and wearing identical blazers swayed down the aisle to calls of welcome and good luck from many of the passengers. (A circus act? Henderson thought. A eugenics experiment?) Shanda excitedly told him who they were and what they were doing—the Ranchers gunning for the Cowpokes or something—but he assumed he had misheard.

And then the engines started and the plane moved away from its ramp and taxied out to the runway. Soft bells pinged, calm voices ran through crisis procedures and Shanda tried to order a screwdriver. As the engine noise increased and the plane began to rush down the runway, she reached across the dozing Bryant and took his hand.

"I hate flyin'," she said.

So did he, he suddenly realized, but hadn't got around to thinking about it.

Damp palm stuck to damp palm. Shanda shut her eyes and crossed herself. A bubble of saliva popped on Bryant's lips and Henderson looked past Shanda's contorted face out of the window. He saw the wonderful airport and the parked planes, then the nose lifted, the plane left the ground and angled up into the sky. In the glass oval he glimpsed spreading suburbs, a new factory, tall glass buildings and a lot of trees. And he left the South and his troubles behind.

part three

TWENTY-FOUR HOURS IN NEW YORK

chapter one

AT La Guardia Airport it was raining heavily. It seemed only right that the weather should have changed. The clouds were low and had that shade of uncompromising grayness that seems to promise their continued presence for a good while yet. But it was surprisingly warm and humid.

Henderson, Shanda and Bryant stood in line waiting for a taxi. He had given Shanda the keys to his apartment and a covering note for the doorman. He didn't want her around when Bryant was returned to her mother.

He felt some trepidation about this last course of action. He was well aware that in these circumstances relief could turn to anger with illogical speed. The mother hugs the scampering tot who has chased a ball into the road and just missed being squashed by the juggernaut. Then she delivers a stinging slap for ignoring curbside drill. Melissa would be overwhelmed with joy to see Bryant back, but Henderson expected he would receive the blow. He grimaced slightly. He was glad to be back in New York, glad to be free of the Gage family and Luxora Beach; but he was conscious that some of his failures dwelt here too: Mulholland, Melhuish; Melissa . . . and Irene. He felt a sudden whimpering need for Irene. Perhaps she would take him back, now that he had no job. . . . And that fact brought the future to mind and all its tedious humiliations: packing up, saying goodbye, returning to London, saying hello again.

Shanda's taxi arrived and she ducked in promptly, trying not to get wet. Henderson gave her his suitcase and the driver his address.

"I'll be along in an hour or so," he said to Shanda. "Or thereabouts," he added. He had a sudden mad impulse to try to see Irene. He stepped back beneath the eave. The rain was falling with steady purpose. Large puddles formed in the generous declivities of the road surface. Cars had their lights on, so intense was the murk. He felt clammy and uncomfortable—the pathetic fallacy working in his favor as usual. Bryant, who had slept through the entire flight from Atlanta, seemed to be coming around somewhat.

"Where are we?" she asked, looking about her with half-closed eyes. "Is Duane here?"

Henderson pushed her into their taxi without replying. She immediately fell asleep again, her head on his shoulder.

"Long trip?" asked the taxi driver. His identification card gave his name as Ezekiel Adekunle.

"Atlanta," Henderson said.

"*Ow!* Whatin you go dere for? Ah-ah." The taxi driver sucked in air through his teeth.

Good question, Henderson thought. "Been raining long?" he asked.

"You are Englishman?"

"Yes. Yes, I am."

"I am from Nigeria."

"Oh. I see. Been raining long?"

"Two days. We done get flash-flood warning."

300

With a wet sloshing of tires the taxi climbed a gentle
hill on the freeway. At its crest they were afforded a view
of the north end of Manhattan. The clouds hung low over
the city. The upper stories of even the more modest skyscrapers were engulfed by gray. His heart lifted at the
view, but only by an inch or so. They crossed the Tri-
borough Bridge and began the long drive south to Melissa's
apartment block. The low clouds, the relentless rain, the
teeming umbrellas on the sidewalk made the crowded
streets appear more fraught than ever. If your view up is
denied in Manhattan, Henderson thought, the place holds
about as much appeal as the Edgeware Road.

They arrived at Melissa's door. Henderson propelled
Bryant beneath the dripping awning.

"Welcome back, Miss Wax," said the doorman.

Bryant frowned, her brain trying to grasp this new information.

"Don't tell her mother we're here," Henderson said. "I
want it to be a surprise."

They ascended in the lift, stepped out and pressed the
buzzer on the thick door. He heard the harsh yelping of
Candice and Gervase. Henderson felt like leaving Bryant
on the threshold like a foundling, and tiptoeing away.

The door opened.

"*Baby!* Darling!" Hugs, tears, lavished kisses. Henderson followed mother and daughter into the sitting room.

"Is Duane here?"

"No, baby, he certainly is not." Aside, in a cold, dis-
tanced voice to Henderson. "What's wrong with her?"

"She's very tired. Early start. It was a difficult journey.
A cold coming we had of it."

"What are you talking about? Here, Albertine, take
Bryant to her room." Bryant was led away by the maid.
Melissa turned to face him.

"Now, my fine fellow, what are we going to do about you?"

Henderson listened, head down, as his character was put through the shredder. With the damp toe of his shoe he moved the pile of the carpet this way and that. He interjected the odd rejoinder to the effect that it had been—when all was said and done—Bryant's decision to come to Luxora and, indeed, come to think of it, Melissa's enthusiasm about the notion had been conspicuous. But these caveats went unheard in the acid rain of scorn that descended on him.

A natural release, he told himself, all that repressed fear and apprehension has to let itself go somehow. But by now anger had given way to irony. Melissa was wondering how Henderson had spent his "precious" time while her little baby was getting corrupted by some red-neck pervert. She had a certain amount to learn yet about her little baby, Henderson thought.

"I suppose you got your precious paintings and you'll go back to your precious office some kind of a hero. But what about Bryant? What kind of awful trauma—?"

"You might be interested to know, Melissa," he said, putting his hands in his pockets and taking them out again, "that the paintings have been destroyed and I've lost my job."

That silenced her for a while.

"What kind of man are you? You . . . you jerk-off. What sort of an excuse for a . . . You're pathetic. That's what you are, pah-thetic!"

"Goodbye, Melissa," Henderson said firmly, stepping abruptly to the door. He didn't need this. Gervase and Candice bounded from the sofa—where they'd idly been surveying the row—and came yapping and nipping around his ankles.

"Gervase! Candice!" Melissa screamed.

Henderson hornpiped out of her life.

He slammed the apartment door and leaned against it, a little breathless, like a heroine who has locked the inept lecher out in the passageway. He pressed the button for the lift, pursed his lips and shook his head sadly. Delete paintings, job and ex-wife. That only left Irene.

Going down in the lift he reflected with false calm that a lot of his sanity now rested on Irene's strong shoulders. He wondered if the present moment was the one in which to assail her. He looked at his watch. Nearly lunchtime. She would be at work with her bearded brother. She always ate in the same delicatessen . . . perhaps that would be the place. Just saunter in: "Hi, Irene, I'm back. Wow, what a time I've had. Busy tonight?" It sounded good, but he had grave doubts. Still, he was a desperate man now.

"Let me call you a cab, Mr. Dores," the obliging shiny-oilskinned doorman said, opening the glass panels of the doorway and blowing the whistle he wore around his neck on a lanyard.

Three mackintoshed men on the sidewalk turned around.

"Hey, Henderson," one of them called. "No problem. We got the car around the corner."

chapter two

PETER Gint, Henderson thought, had singularly bad taste in shoes. The model he was looking at, some two inches from his eyes, was a heavy brogue two-toned orange-and-brown number. That was the left shoe; the right rested on the back of his neck.

He was lying on the floor in the back of a car, heading, as far as he could determine, south through Manhattan. In the front were Freeborn and Sereno. Gint sat in the back guarding him.

When he had emerged from Melissa's apartment block the three men had surrounded him like old friends and had jovially led him away. Gint had showed him a gun, a black, clenched, snub-nosed-looking thing, and Henderson had decided swiftly to do everything they asked.

Once inside the car Gint had produced the gun again and asked him to lie facedown on the floor. No one had said anything, with the exception of Freeborn, who from time to time leaned over the front seat and said, "Bastard. We got you, you dipshit bastard."

Henderson stared at Gint's shoe. Some safety device in his body was preventing him from being sick all over it. He felt frightened, all right—but for some reason it wasn't overwhelming. Every time he tried to protest, Gint would increase the pressure on the back of his neck and say, "Shut up." Lying facedown he was, Henderson could see nothing of the city. He heard only the noise of the rain on the roof, the metronomic ticking of the windscreen wipers and the splash of the tires on the wet streets. How had they caught up with him so quickly? he wondered. But then on reflection he realized it wouldn't have taken brilliant sleuthing to have divined where he was heading—there were plenty of airports and plenty of planes to New York—and Bryant's presence would indicate a visit to Melissa at some early juncture. Bryant's address? . . . From her abandoned luggage, no doubt, or Duane.

He pillowed his head on his arms and waited for the journey to end. What would they do to him? he wondered. What did they want of him? The continued absurdity of his predicament had ceased to give offense. It seemed now, after everything that had gone before, an entirely apt and normal state of affairs.

Eventually, the car stopped. Henderson clambered out under the watchful eye of his captors. Glancing up and down the street he saw wet mean tenements, boarded shops, ribbed and battered garage fronts. He caught a glimpse of the twin thick legs of the World Trade Center descending from the low haze of the clouds. Above a door in front of him a fractured plastic sign read OK REFRIGERATION. The rain drenched his hair. The sidewalk gutters were overflowing; flotsam sped by, driven by strong currents. The raindrops rebounded six inches when they hit the stone and asphalt. Gint pushed him into the doorway, where Sereno fiddled with a clutch of fist-sized padlocks.

"What is this place?" Henderson asked. "Your gallery?"

"Shut the fuck up," Freeborn said.

Sereno opened the doors and Henderson was pushed through into a dark concrete lobby. A large industrial elevator faced him. The grille doors were slid open and they all got in. They went up two floors. When they emerged Henderson saw they were in a large white room, brilliantly lit and filled with the noise of light industry. In one corner sparks of molten metal flashed prettily around a man welding pipes together to form a knotted intestinal fist. Beside him another man filed down the edges of a sectioned girder, bright chrome and mounted on a three-foot-high marble plinth. From the far end came the hectic buzz of a high-powered spray gun as a man rendered a tall canvas dull maroon.

Sereno stood in the middle of the room and clapped his hands for silence.

"OK, boys, take a holiday. See you tomorrow."

The men stopped work. Henderson looked around him, astonishment momentarily displacing his fear. Large fresh abstract canvases were stacked in piles against a wall; a rubble of scrap metal filled a corner. Sereno talked to the men as they laid down their tools.

"I like it, José," Gint said to the man with the spray gun. "You're getting real good."

"What is this?" Henderson asked, looking at the painting. "What's going on here?"

"We call it color field painting," Gint said equably. "Sorta kinda like a big field, you know? Colored."

Sereno came over. "Corporate art," he said. "Know how many offices there are in this country? Know how many big empty lobbies they got? They need plants and they need art. Big good art, not too expensive."

"Big good art."

"That's what you got here."

A young Hispanic girl in a grubby jersey and a tight short skirt came out of a small office at the far end of the room.

"Hey, Caridad," Sereno said. "Take the day off. We need to use your office."

She had a piece of paper in her hand.

"Ben," she said. "I got a call. Two Rothko, one Kline—"

"Early or late?"

"Jus' black an' white, he say. Big one."

"Good."

"An' one Sam Francis."

"Who? Do we do Sam Francis? Is it in the catalog?"

"I got it," Gint said, emerging from the office with an art book. He held up the illustration.

"Can you do it, José?"

"Ow. Is difficul', this one." José scratched his head.

"Try it tomorrow. See you tomorrow, guys."

The men filed out. Caridad went back into the office for her raincoat. She came back and stood not far from Henderson, one arm sleeved, a small beaded bag between her teeth, as her other arm probed vainly for the empty sleeve. Henderson helped her on with her coat.

"These men are holding me against my will," he whispered. "Tell the police."

Caridad, coated, turned and belted him around the head with her beaded handbag, some rasping, spitting Spanish oath following swiftly.

Henderson rubbed his stinging hot ear.

Sereno looked pityingly at him as Caridad walked stiffly out.

"You're a cool one, Dores, I'll give you that. Always the ladies' man, eh?"

Henderson cupped his burning ear, his eyes screwed up, riven with a sudden deep hopelessness. Breakers crashed on a distant beach. He watched Freeborn and Gint shift the furniture—desk, plastic armchair, coatstand, telephone, small filing cabinet—from the office.

"OK, Dores, let's take a meeting."

Gently, Sereno propelled him toward the office. Inside Henderson saw that the one interior window was covered by an iron grille, diamond-patterned. The room was completely empty apart from one wooden chair. A small opaque window in the wall overlooked a filthy alleyway. The floor was wooden, heavily scored and badged with old dark stains. Ink, Henderson hoped. He couldn't hear any traffic noise and for the first time began to feel genuine alarm. These men, he was sure, acknowledged no civilized restraints to behavior.

"Now listen," he began. "I've been very patient, but I warn you—"

Freeborn pointed at him and he stopped talking at once. Henderson moved nervously to the window. Nothing out there. Freeborn had a swift whispered consultation with the other two, then took a few paces toward him.

"OK. Get the clothes off."

"Now just one minute—"

"We can tear 'em off, man, if you want."

Henderson shut his eyes. Slowly he undressed. He laid shirt, jacket, trousers and tie across the wooden chair. He stood in his underpants, socks and shoes.

"Everything off."

"Look, come *on*, chaps. Please."

Gint took out his gun and pointed it at him.

"We want nekkid, Dores," Freeborn said.

Henderson took off his shoes and socks. The floorboards were surprisingly cold; he worried vaguely about getting splinters in his soft pink soles. . . . The chill rose swiftly up through his body and reached the top of his skull in seconds. Goose pimples covered his body. He stripped off his underpants, threw them on the chair and held his trembling hands modestly in front of him.

"It's not that cold, is it?" Sereno laughed.

Henderson looked away.

Gint gathered up his clothes and took them out of the office, then came back, snapping a pair of pliers in his hands.

"What's that for?" Freeborn asked.

"You get a piece of skin in these, it's like tearing paper."

Henderson heard the blood leaving his head. He staggered a bit.

"Come on, Peter. Ben said I could go first," Freeborn complained.

"Aw, here, Ben, you always let me go first."

"Hold on there," Freeborn said. "I mean, whose house was he in? Mine."

"Yeah, but he's in our office now."

"But you wouldn't have got him if it hadn't been for me."

"Yeah, but I had to—"

"Boys, boys," Sereno said. "Relax. You got five minutes, Freeborn. Come on, Peter, give him the gun."

Sulkily Gint handed over his gun, then he and Sereno left. Henderson heard the noise of the lift.

Freeborn wandered over. He pressed the revolver barrel against Henderson's forehead.

"I ain't gonna kill you yet, fuck, but I am gonna shoot your fuckin' foot off of your leg in ten seconds if you don't tell me what you've done with the paintings." He pointed the gun at Henderson's white, twitching right foot. He looked down at his toes. The nails could do with a cut. He thought warmly of his foot's hundreds of tiny fragile bones, its calluses, its one dear persistent corn. Finally he could speak.

"You don't. You mean, you don't know that—"

"If I knew I wouldn't be here, mofo."

"—that Duane burned them all."

Freeborn grabbed Henderson's throat and tried to push the blunt barrel of the gun up his left nostril.

"*Lying.* Lying, you bastard!"

His big face and his glistening, cusped and trefoiled beard were very close.

"It's true," Henderson croaked. "Last night. I saw him. I caught him at it. He said your father ordered him. Before he died. Last words."

Freeborn stepped back, ran his fingers through his springy black hair. He looked over his shoulder, then aimed the gun at Henderson's groin.

"It's true," Henderson wept softly. "How could I have stolen the paintings? Think about it. Duane burned them. Ask anyone to check at the bottom of the back garden."

Freeborn was prodding and tugging at his plump cheeks, as if trying to force his features to change from increasingly troubled credulity.

"Say you're lying, Dores."

"It's the truth. I swear."

"Oh, Jesus, *no.* That dumb . . . that iron-brain, that fuckin' beam-head moron . . ." The gun dropped. Freeborn began visibly to tremble. "Oh, Jesus." He sank down on his haunches. Henderson told him the story again, in great and convincing detail, Freeborn's terror relaxing him somewhat.

"I gotta check it out." He stood up again. "You could be lying, Dores. Shittin' me." Doubt registered in his voice and eyes. "I gotta be careful. Very careful."

He approached Henderson again. "I don't know if

you're telling the truth, but whatever you do, don't tell Sereno or Gint, man, or we're dead. Both dead. *D, e, d*, you know?"

"I don't see why I—"

"They'll kill me, boy. They'll kill you too, sure as shit."

Freeborn paced around the room. "I'm gonna check this out. If you're right, *if* you're right, then I've got to fix up some way . . ." He paused. "I need some time." He ran his fingers through his hair. "Time," he repeated. "Look, I know, we'll say you hid them in Luxora someplace. Yeah. Let's say, uh, you rented a garage off of . . . of, um, Ed Beak, yeah. And—"

"Just a second. Why the hell should I go along with you, for God's sake?"

"'Cause those mean mothers'll blow us both away for sure, numbnuts!" he shouted in shrill panic. "I'm tryin' to save your ass as well as my own!" He paced around some more.

Henderson kept quiet, though he felt profound unease at being inveigled into this alliance.

"OK," Freeborn said. "We go back to Luxora. That'll take time. Good, good." He stopped. He seemed suddenly on the verge of tears. He clenched his fist, and pounded it on his hip. "That pea-brain! That asshole! Why did he do that? I'm gonna kill him! I'm gonna roast his *balls*!" Henderson assumed Duane was the object of his venom. "Stay cool," Freeborn advised himself. "Stay calm. Take it easy."

"Listen, you're not going to leave me here like this?" Henderson spread his arms.

"Got to, man. No other way. It's got to look right. Can't you see? If they suspect . . ." He focused blankly on the middle distance, rubbing his beard. Henderson sensed his terror, like a gas; blood turned to soda in his veins.

"What have those two guys got on you?" Henderson asked.

"I owe them, man," Freeborn said in a small voice. "*Owe*. You know? I owe them all kinds of shit. From way back, for a long time." His face slumped. "It would've been all right. 'Cept you came along." He paused, then his voice became a harsh whisper. "They got me by the balls. One in each hand." He held his hands out in illustration. He came over. "Play along with me, Henderson. We'll get out of this. But don't say nothing about that fuckwit Duane. That's all."

Henderson smelled his antiseptic breath.

"Yeah, and where's Shanda?" Freeborn asked. "She's with you, right?"

"At my apartment. Look, she asked. I didn't—"

"Hey, that's cool. No sweat. Done me a favor there, boy." He raised his eyebrows. "Sorry. But I gotta do this."

Freeborn punched Henderson in the nose, quite hard. Henderson heard a noise in his head like a walnut being crushed and everything went white and calm for a moment. When he opened his eyes it was as though he were swimming underwater. He was on his knees. Blood surged steadily from his nose, splashing over his chest and belly.

"Sorry, Henderson. Had to do it. Wow, it looks bad."

Henderson spat gouts of salty blood out of his mouth.

"Ben! Peter!" Freeborn called.

"Clodes," Henderson said, a knuckle up each oozing nostril.

"Sorry." Freeborn went out, returned with Henderson's shoes. "Best I can do."

Sereno and Gint came in.

"What you do?" Sereno said, wrinkling his nose at the blood-boltered sight.

"Says they're in a garage in Luxora. I'll check it out."

"We'll check it out," Sereno said.

Gint still had the pliers in his hand. "Shit. I was going to tear his nipples off. Always works."

Henderson, who was getting up, slumped back at this. His nipples throbbed spontaneously.

"Let him sweat it out," Freeborn said. "Case he ain't telling the truth."

"I'll be back," Gint said, clicking his pliers.

They left. Henderson heard the bolt being slid to.

He sat on the chair while the last drops of blood plopped from his nose. Judging from the puddle on the floor and his incarnadined torso he must have lost a couple of pints. He stretched his legs out, let his head hang over the back of the chair. Gently, he touched his nose. It had sounded as if every bone and cartilage had been pulverized. He sat up and put on his shoes, his old black oxfords, with shiny toe caps. He looked around the room. There was nothing he could use to cover his nudity. It was completely empty. He crossed his legs. His hands were covered in blood and left palm prints all over his body. The blood on his chest and belly was beginning to dry, matting the hairs. He wondered what he looked like: some pallid aborigine involved in an unspeakable rite or ritual? Except the black shoes rather spoiled the image.

He thought about Freeborn, his newfound friend. The man had even called him Henderson. As he had suspected, Gage's paintings had been mortgaged to provide his son with funds and favors. And Sereno and Gint were the brokers finally coming to collect, pick up the markers. Duane's obedient act of destruction was likely to have further fatal side effects. He wondered what Freeborn would do. Stall them? Go back to Luxora, "check out" the garage, find it empty and return to New York to extract the truth from an anipplate Henderson . . . ? The more he thought, the more perilous his position seemed, the more temporary his release. The time bought by his complicity allowed Freeborn the chance to extricate himself in some way or other—and he wouldn't be overconcerned about Henderson's fate.

He prowled around the room. Its sole window was a small casement, with four lights, about three feet by two. There was no catch. It appeared to be nailed shut. From it he could look down into a sodden litter-strewn alleyway that ran between his building and the blank brick rear of the one opposite. Craning his neck he could see gray mat clouds above but nothing else. The rain came down remorselessly. He still had his watch on, he realized. It was four o'clock, and prematurely dark. He felt hungry and thirsty, and his bladder was achingly distended. He had to escape, that was all there was to it.

Five hours later one of his problems had been steamily resolved in a dark corner, and he had narrowed down his escape options to one: the casement window. The door, the walls, the interior window had not yielded to the battering he had visited on them. He had grazed his knuckles vainly plucking at the wire grille over the window and had bruised his shoulder and hip hurling himself at the door. In films these things gave way with laughable ease, but he felt he had been charging at a concrete wall. This necessary reduction in escape routes was further disheartening: not only did safety lie beyond the door but so did his clothes. If he was somehow going to effect an exit via the casement window he was going to have to do it buck naked. . . . Maybe he should just wait it out—tell Sereno and Gint the truth. But he had a suspicion that might not save his life, let alone his nipples. No, he concluded, it had to be escape, naked or not.

By now it was completely dark in his cell. His captors had left no lights on and he was reliant on the window for such faint illumination as it provided. Peering out he could see nothing but darkness.

He picked up the chair and used its legs to smash through the glass panes in the window. The shards tinkled faintly in the alley below. A gust of cool air blew in, bringing with it the din of rainfall and overflowing gutters. He looked out. Nothing had changed; no one had heard. The night was cool but not unbearably so.

For two or three minutes he bellowed *"Help!"* out of the window but there was no response. He smashed the chair against the wall and with a fragment of wood knocked out the remaining slivers of glass from the window surround. That achieved it was an easy matter to batter away the cruciform muntin. As he did this the rain dampened the dried blood on his chest and it began to run again.

He thrust his head and shoulders out of the window. He was about twenty feet up from the ground, he calculated. Some way to his left was a fire escape. To his right was a thick drainpipe, just within reach.

Diligently, he searched the frame edges for any stray glass fragments that might prove an unpleasant snag during his exit. Then he took off his shoes and tied the laces together, slinging them around his neck, before easing himself backward out of the window, face toward the sky.

With great caution and some ricked muscles he managed to buttock-shuffle, haul and claw himself into a shaky position whereby he was standing outside on the window ledge, his upper body pressed flat against the uneven wall, his fingers jammed in the courses between the bricks.

Slowly he edged in the direction of the drainpipe, an old, strong-looking cast-iron thing, as thick as a thigh. He reached out and grasped it with his left hand, and, searching blindly with his left foot, found a collar or molding that gave him a toehold. There he stood: one foot on the window ledge the other on the drainpipe; one hand circling the pipe, the other wedged in a corner of the window embrasure. The rain pattered heavily on his back shoulders; a breeze gusted between his spread legs cooling his dangling genitals.

He gripped and swung, hugging the drainpipe passionately to him and gasping a little at the shock of the cold cast iron on his chest and the inside of his clinging thighs. Tentatively, limpetlike, he began to inch his way down, helped by the numerous bifurcations, knobs and beadings on the pipe. Then his probing foot touched the ground and he sank with a sob of relief.

He put on his shoes and cautiously explored the alley. He felt wholly odd and alien in his nakedness, a soft vulnerable creature entirely unsuited for this world of hard objects. The alley, he found, was no more than five feet wide and no kind of thoroughfare, judging from the amount of rubbish and litter it contained. He discovered an upended wooden crate that provided some sort of shelter, and slipped inside out of the rain. He sat down cautiously, feeling for nails, the coarse wood prickling his buttocks. It was all very well being free, but freedom was drastically confined if you were naked. He looked at his watch. Eleven o'clock. He could wait a while before he went in search of help.

He sat in his box and watched the rivulets of water on the alley floor turn into gushing rills as the rain lanced down. As he sat there he felt at once incredulous and full of self-pity. Here he was, Ph.D., author, "Impressionist man," reduced to the status of latter-day troglodyte, sheltering in abandoned boxes, nude, smeared with his own blood, in the middle of New York City . . . He looked at his bare knees, bald shins and damp black shoes. He held out his hands, as if offering his nails for inspection, and watched the raindrops bounce off them. It was true; it was real.

He got up and ventured palely out into the alleyway again to search for some sort of garb. There were plenty of scraps of paper, tins and plastic containers, polystyrene packing and cardboard boxes, but nearly everything was soaked and useless from the rain. Eventually he found a cardboard box beneath a pile of damp wood shavings. On the side it said in large black letters:

2,000 MARYMOUNT NO-SLAK SANITARY NAPKINS
Complete protection and comfort
Superthin! Superabsorbent!

He nodded. Yes, this was what he was coming to expect. But in his present state he couldn't afford to be choosy. A little further down the alley he found great tangles of discarded plastic belting of the sort used to secure parcels. He tore his Marymount box into a long thin rectangle and wrapped it around his middle. He then wound yards of plastic belting around the box, knotting it as tightly and as best he could. He ended up with a very short cardboard miniskirt that preserved his modesty—just—but had an annoying tendency to slip down when he walked. With more plastic belting he constructed crude braces that held the box in approximate place, even though they chafed somewhat on his shoulders.

It was amazing the difference it made to his confidence

to be clothed at last, even if only a Marymount No-Slak box. He felt profound understanding of Adam and Eve's urge to make themselves aprons of fig leaves after the Fall. Postlapsarian man lived on in him too.

Hesitantly, he advanced to the mouth of the alley. It was nearly midnight. He peered around the corner of the wall. The street was badly lit, deserted and under two inches of water. A car went by throwing up wings of spray from its front wheels. Automatically, he ducked back into the darkness of the alleyway. Why hadn't he stepped out and flagged it down? he asked himself. Remember where you are, was his reply. No one is going to come to the aid of a half-naked, bloodstained, cardboard-box-wearing man after midnight in this city. . . . He saw that the torrential rain was going to be as much his ally as his enemy—driving everyone off the streets, forcing everyone and everything into dry corners, leaving the empty rain-lashed avenues to him.

He worked out a plan. It was too risky, he thought, to head for his own apartment. He had a feeling that Freeborn and the others would be paying it a visit at some juncture. Freeborn might go looking for Shanda; or Gint might be there, with his pliers. He needed friends. He would head north up Manhattan to his only friend: Irene. Go to Irene.

chapter three

AT half past two in the morning, Henderson set out. Se-reno had said his "gallery" was on the Lower East Side, "in back of Canal." Henderson paused at the alley's entrance. This must be Canal Street. The rain still fell; everything was quiet. He slipped out of the alley and loped in a half crouch along the street, hugging the walls.

At Canal and Forsyth he paused and took shelter in a doorway. He was out of breath, not from exertion but from excitement. Across Forsyth was a thin tree-lined park. He scampered over to it. SARA D. ROOSEVELT PARK a sign read. He climbed over the railings and hid behind a tree. A couple beneath an umbrella hurried past, heads down. He followed the park north, sprinting across the streets that bisected it—Grand and Delancey—until he reached East Houston Street.

Hiding behind a bush he looked at the Second Avenue subway station. Wraiths of steam drifted from manhole covers. Two cars went by and a yellow cab. Should he seek help in the subway? It looked like a gate to hell. He climbed over the park railings and walked over to the en-trance. He had no money, he realized, and no identifica-tion. He stood on the sidewalk, indecisive, his chest heaving. A man came out of the subway, glanced angrily at him and went on his way, muttering and shaking his head. Of course, Henderson suddenly realized with tender elation, they think I'm *mad*. Just another fucking weirdo. It was a moment of true liberation. A revelation. He felt all the restraints of his culture and upbringing fall from him like a cloak slid from shoulders. He felt, in the Eugene Teagarden sense, spontaneously, unusually pure.

He saw a yellow cab drive by, its "for hire" light on. Emboldened, indifferent, careless, he stepped out into the street and hailed it. The taxi driver looked disgustedly at him, swore and drove on. Henderson shrugged, smiled, turned and jogged up Second Avenue. He still kept close to the walls and paused in dark doorways from time to time, but he was beginning to reassess and revalue his presence in the city. . . . Even given the lateness of the hour New York was astonishingly quiet. He had the rain to thank for that; judging from the amount of water flowing through the streets New Yorkers would probably wake up tomorrow to find their city declared a disaster zone. Only an occasional car or empty bus interrupted the solitude. Henderson ran steadily on, his Marymount box surprisingly unimpeding and comfortable. He ran past St. Mark's Church, and paused in a doorway at Fourteenth Street. Over to his left was Union Square, but he didn't have the nerve to go anywhere near it, even in tonight's exceptionally inclement weather. The serious people in Union Square wouldn't be deterred by a little rain. He would go north a few blocks and then cut over to Park Avenue South, which, he knew, had a central island running the length of it, planted with bushes and shrubs and up which he could make his way, undisturbed by the rare pedestrian and with plenty of cover should the police come by.

He had thought about telephoning the police, asking

them for help, but had eventually dismissed the idea. There was a good chance—given his state of dress—that they might not believe him, and he was doubtful if he could cope with the exposure of a precinct police station and all the attendant embarrassments of proving his identity. Better to forge ahead on his own, lonely and free, he calculated, and in any event he was making reasonable progress.

He moved off again, skirting Stuyvesant Square, cutting down Nineteenth Street to Park Avenue South. Gradually, confidently, he became less furtive. He realized now that he was effectively invisible in this city. With its madmen, its joggers and its twenty-four-hour existence— finally, at last—he fitted in perfectly: perfectly consonant with its unique logic. Why, he was simply another mad jogger, happily patroling the streets in the taxi-torn, rain-tormented small hours. There were, he was convinced, far stranger things going on around him. And, if he moved fast, his Marymount box, now dark brown from the rain, must look like some bizarre new athletic rig-out, setting new trends in absorbent disposable running wear. . . .

He reached Park Avenue, ran to the central island and crouched down, getting his breath back. A patrol car motored past and he drew himself behind a small bush. He let it go. Above him the stacked lights in the tall buildings quickly grew fuzzy before being enveloped by dark clouds. A few cars hissed by on either side of him but the pavements were deserted. He set off up the central reservation. He wondered what New Yorkers—casually watching the rain fall from their apartment windows—would think if they saw him, a pale ghostly figure slipping from shrub to shrub, darting across streets, incongruous in his heavy black walking shoes. . . . This was surely, he thought as he ran, the apotheosis of his shame and embarrassment.

No basically shy person could experience any ordeal so hellishly demanding and harrowing, so testing as this. After his naked run through Manhattan he could hardly complain about other travails: nothing could be as uncompromisingly *harsh* as what he was currently undergoing.

And yet, he felt surprisingly good. Untroubled, oddly calm. He ran on—not strongly, but steadily—stumbling occasionally, his feet catching in the ivy that grew along the flower beds of the Park Avenue central reservation, the heavy raindrops striking his face and chest.

He made good progress up Park Avenue until his way was blocked by Grand Central Station and the Pan Am Building. At Forty-second Street he paused by a traffic light, halted by a sudden atypical flow of cars. A wet man stood waiting for the WALK sign. Henderson jogged on the spot beside him, intoxicated with his new freedom.

The man looked around, swaying slightly.

"Y'all right, man?"

"Me?" Henderson panted. "Couldn't be better."

"Keepin' fit, huh?"

"That's it."

"Some sorta—what—athlete, huh? Athletics, huh?"

"Yeah."

"Marymount No-Slak," he read slowly.

"My sponsors."

"Hey, congratulations."

The light changed, Henderson jogged on. He had been accepted; the moment had come and gone, but he had joined America at last. He cut up Vanderbilt Avenue on to Forty-fifth and then up Madison. He ran slowly, easily, not exhausting himself, pausing for breath when he got a stitch, enjoying the unfettered luxury of his temporary status as madman, American and jogger. He cut across at Fifty-ninth and loped casually by the Plaza, Central

322

Park's dark-green mass on his right. Irene was now only a few blocks away. He looked at his watch: half past four.

Outside Irene's block he paused. He stood in a doorway and checked himself over. The Marymount box was showing signs of wear and tear; bits were disintegrating from the wet and his flanks showed through gaps where the friction of his running had caused the damp cardboard to wear through. His shoulders were red and a little sore from the rubbing of the plastic braces. Making his fingers stiff claws he tried, incongruously, to put a parting in his hair.

He crept up to the apartment door. The lobby was lit, but no one sat at the lectern. He pressed the buzzer and waited. Nothing happened. He was beginning to feel nervous and ordinary again, now that his heroic, epic run was over. It was beginning to disappear, wear off. He was being normal once more, ringing doorbells, visiting, asking favors. He pressed the buzzer again.

A door opened in the rear wall of the lobby and a small man came out, shrugging on a jacket. Henderson, suddenly wary—like an Amazonian native suspicious of his first encounter with strangers—shrank back against the wall out of sight.

"Yeah?" came a metallic voice from the loudspeaker.

"I want to see Ms. Stein," Henderson whispered loudly in its direction.

"What?"

"Come to the door."

The man advanced cautiously. With dismay Henderson saw that it was Bra.

"Who is it?" Bra asked, peering into the shadows.

"Bra," Henderson whispered from his hiding place, "it's me, Mr. Dores."

"Who are you? Where are you?"

"Here. To the side. Your right." Henderson waved.

"Come out of there, ya fuckin' freak!"

Henderson stood up and stepped into view. Bra backed off in patent shock.

"Hello, Bra. It's me, Mr. Dores. I need to see Ms. Stein. I'm in terrible trouble."

"What? . . . Get outa here! What are you?"

"Look, Bra. It's . . . it's a matter of life and death."

"Get your ass outa here, ya fuckin' geek! I warn you, I got a gun in here!"

"Bra, it's *me*. Mr. Dores. You know me. I was here the other day."

"I count to ten. I call the cops."

He saw Bra lift the phone. With bitter, disgusted tears in his eyes he ran off into the dark. That little bastard *knew* it was me, he swore. He had done that deliberately. He ran full tilt down the road toward Central Park. A significant portion of his box came away, revealing a section of pallid haunch. The rain still fell with healthy force; it showed no sign of relenting. At this rate he'd be naked again in half an hour—swaddled only in a plastic belting. But now he didn't feel so wonderful—so transformed at the prospect. He had no money; he couldn't even phone anyone. . . . What he needed were clothes. They had never struck him as the key prerequisite for survival in the West. If you're half naked you are a nonperson, a subversive, a deviant. You can do nothing unless you are properly dressed. Shoes, trousers, a shirt—the *sine qua non* of social action.

He needed clothes. . . . Perhaps he could mug somebody? Dare he return to his apartment? But what if Freeborn and Sereno were there? What if they had discovered his escape by now? And then, suddenly, he remembered where he kept a second suit of clothes. The Queensboro

324

Health Club. His fencing gear. He looked at his watch. Five o'clock. Only a matter of hours until it opened. He looked up at the sky. Keep raining, he implored. He set off. Straight down Fifty-ninth Street, all the way.

Henderson found a place to hide in a basement well opposite the gym. To his alarm it was beginning to get light with inconsiderate speed. Soon the first keen commuters would be arriving. Like witches and hobgoblins, people like him should be off the streets by the time the first cock crowed, he thought. He felt, lurking close behind him, rank breath stirring the hairs on his nape, a vast implacable exhaustion waiting to pounce. He confirmed the time: half five. The gym opened at seven. He was suddenly gripped by a fierce hunger and realized he hadn't eaten for twenty-four hours.

He looked at the gray empty streets, still hosed by curtains of rain. A puddle the size of a football pitch swamped the intersection of York and Fifty-eighth. A car had been abandoned in the middle, the water lapping at the radiator. Around its perimeter stepped a neat, water-proofed, track-suited figure, carrying small dumbbells in each hand. See, Henderson told himself, there are madder people than me out on the streets. . . .

"Teagarden! Eugene, over here! Over here!"

Teagarden trotted over and looked down at him.

"Well, Mr. Dores. What a surprise."

Henderson clambered out of his basement well. His Marymount No-Slak box was now the consistency of porridge. With every step part of it fell away.

Teagarden looked at him.

"Yeah . . ." He nodded. "Pretty good."

Henderson shrugged. "Well . . ."

"Told you you shouldn't ought to have gone down there. What happened?"

"Long story, Eugene."

"I'm sure."

"Going to the gym?"

"Yes."

"Saved my life, Eugene."

They strolled across the street to the gym. Teagarden unlocked the door and switched on the lights. Henderson sat down opposite his locker with a squelch. He suddenly felt like crying. He also felt like telling Teagarden that he loved him, so abject was his gratefulness, but he refrained.

"Whew," Henderson said. "Quite a night, one way and another." Now that it was over all the emotions he had pent up overwhelmed him, like a football crowd invading the pitch. For a few moments his brain succumbed to the mindless violence.

"Like a coffee?" Teagarden said.

"Please."

The gym was quiet and cool; it seemed like a sanctuary, a holy place. Teagarden went off to boil a kettle. Henderson stood up. With both hands he ripped away chunks of his Marymount box. A shower. A meal. A change of clothes . . ."

"Well, hello there, Mr. Dores."

He looked up. Freeborn, Sereno and Gint stood at the end of his file of lockers. Gint was pointing his gun at him. "Quite a dance you've led us, Mr. Dores," Sereno said. "Luxora and back in twelve hours. Quite a dance."

"Shoot the fucker," Freeborn implored. "Off him, Peter."

"First he has to tell us where the paintings are."

"How did you . . .? I mean . . ."

Sereno waved his address book. "Not many New York

addresses, Mr. Dores. Peter spent the night in your apartment. We've just been there. Missed you by minutes at Ms. Stein's."

"Blow him away, Peter! Waste the bastard!"

Sereno glanced suspiciously at Freeborn.

"Where are the paintings, Mr. Dores?"

"They're burned, destroyed. Duane burned them on Loomis Gage's instructions. Ask Freeborn."

"Give me the fuckin' gun!" Freeborn leaped for Gint's hand but was elbowed easily away. Then Gint went very still.

"Don't move," Teagarden said. "Or else this thing's gonna be stickin' out your mouth."

Teagarden held a saber to the back of Gint's neck, the point on his hairline. Gint stood like a man who has just had an ice cube dropped down his shirt, back arched, chest out.

"Drop the piece and kick it over to Mr. Dores."

Gint did this. Henderson picked the gun up. It was somehow much heavier than he had imagined. He pointed it vaguely at Freeborn.

Teagarden walked around Gint, keeping the point of his saber at his neck.

"OK, shitbrains, beat it."

Freeborn turned and ran. Sereno watched him go.

"So the paintings are burned," Sereno said. "Making sense, at last." He and Gint backed off.

"Duane burned them. Look at the bottom of the garden behind the Gage Mansion."

"Shame," Sereno said. "I never really wanted the house. But beggers can't be choosers."

He and Gint turned and left.

"Very impressive, Eugene," Henderson said weakly. "Thanks a lot. Here, you can keep the gun."

chapter four

WHEN Henderson next appeared on the streets of Manhattan he was slightly better dressed. He wore his whites —polo neck, knickerbockers, socks and gym shoes. Teagarden had lent him a green windcheater and ten dollars for a taxi. In gratitude, Henderson had signed up for a two-week crash course in épée.

He hailed a taxi and it drove him to his apartment. On the way he wondered what Sereno and Gint would do to Freeborn when they caught him.

At his apartment he picked up his mail. The doorman handed him a parcel.

"Special delivery," he said. "Just arrived from the airport. Your friend was here earlier, but he said he couldn't wait."

Henderson ascended in the elevator. The whole ghastly adventure was now, he hoped, over. He pressed the buzzer on his door. Sereno and Gint had his clothes, wallet, address book, keys. Minor inconveniences.

Bryant opened the door.

"Hi," she said. "*God.* What are you wearing?"

"What are you doing here?"

"I can't take it anymore at home, Henderson. Mom, those fucking dogs—"

328

"Bryant—"

"Sorry." She paused. "Henderson, can I stay here? I don't want to go back. Please?"

"Yes, by all means, of course." He went in. She seemed to have forgotten Duane.

Shanda sat on the sofa.

"My God, what are you wearing?" She got up and waddled over. "Hi." She pecked him on the cheek. "That Peter Gint was here all night. Boy, is he off the wall. . . . Then Freeborn and Ben came by real early. Freeborn messed the place up a bit. I was cleaning up when Bryant arrived. You know what?"

"What?"

"Freeborn took his denim jacket back. Can you believe that?"

Henderson sat down heavily in his ransacked sitting room, dumping the parcel on the coffee table. He shuffled his mail: catalog, bill, bill, catalog, letter. He ripped it open.

Dear Henderson,

   Enclosed is a bill for cleaning: $23.50 for removing oil stains from my jacket sleeve. Unfortunately it hasn't worked. The suit cost $275.00. We can settle up when you get back. Too bad about the Gage pix. But it's an ill wind . . . Remember the man in Boston with the Winslow Homers? Ian Toothe went up there last week. It seems he also had two Pissarros and a Renoir and Ian persuaded him to sell them all. Good old Ian—saved our bacon.

Yours,

Pruitt

"You want some breakfast?" Bryant asked.

"Some, uh . . . coffee, please."

Bryant went into the kitchen. Shanda came and sat on the arm of his chair, her belly at eye level, her musky farinaceous smell filling his nostrils.

"Freeborn's throwed me out. He says you can keep me."

"Oh, really? Very big of him."

"Could we get married, Henderson? I'd kinda like for the baby to have a daddy."

"Yes. Yes, of course."

He got up, went into the bathroom and ran a bath. He locked the door, stripped off and soaked for twenty minutes or so. He thought distractedly of the last few days. He got out, shaved and went through to his bedroom. He fell asleep almost instantly. When he woke it was midday. He changed into clean clothes.

Back in the sitting room the air was blurry with cigarette smoke. Shanda scrambled some eggs and brewed some coffee. As he was eating, the telephone rang. Shanda answered.

"No," she said. "My name is Shanda McNab."

Pause.

"Yes, I am staying here. Who is this, please?"

Pause.

"No, I'm Henderson's fiancée. Oh." She looked around. "She hung up."

"Who was it?" Henderson asked with sudden alarm.

"Bryant's mommy. She says you're a cheap bastard and she never wants to see you again."

"Typical," Bryant said. "Hey, are you guys getting married? Congratulations."

Henderson opened another letter. It was from his car rental firm. The letter informed him that the car he had hired in New York had been written off during a car chase after a bank robbery in Biloxi, Mississippi. Could he throw any light on the matter? The cost of the car was $18,750.00.

He asked Bryant to make him some more coffee. Shanda sat opposite him smoking a cigarette. He wondered what he was going to do. He leafed through his mail. Circular, bill, bill, airmail.

Airmail. His own handwriting. Postmark GALASHIELS. Inside, scored sheets of Campbell Drew's strong uncompromising hand.

Dear Mr. Dores,

Thank you for your letter. As you know your father was in six column of Wingate's first expedition across the Chindwin. On the twenty-first of March, 1943, we had made camp just prior to attacking a Japanese base at Pinbon. Before we were to attack we were notified of an airdrop for new supplies.

It had been decided that, due to our being behind enemy lines, it was not safe for airdrops to be made by parachute. The procedure was for the supply plane to fly low over the jungle and the provisions and ammunition were simply thrown out of the hatch. Of course many stores went missing, but, for security reasons, it was far safer than parachutes.

Captain Dores ordered the company to spread out along the area marked for the drop. We had been on the march for weeks and were short of all supplies. This drop was crucial for us.

The plane, a Dakota, as I remember, came over fast and low, the crates tumbling out of the hatchway. We gathered up what we could and reported to company HQ. We assembled there with our collection of supplies. Then it was noticed that Captain Dores was missing. I and three other men went in search of him.

I am very sorry to say, sir, that your father was killed by a tin of pineapple chunks. A crate of supplies had broken up in midair, scattering the tins haphazardly. Your father was hit full on the head. I know he died instantly.

I am very sorry to bring you these unfortunate details. I had been with your father since Imphal. He was a very brave man.

Yours faithfully,

Campbell Drew

Henderson carefully folded up the letter. A tin of pineapple chunks. Embedded in his skull.

"Are you OK, Henderson?"

"Yes, yes."

"Bad news?"

"No, no. Entirely expected."

"What's in your parcel?"

He breathed in deeply. Ach well, he thought, where's the sense? He tore open the parcel. *Demeter and Baubo*, frameless, and a letter from Cora.

Dear Henderson,

Duane couldn't bring himself to burn this one. I found it in his room and he told me everything. I guess Sereno and Gint will be down for the house next week. I thought you should have this, as it's your favorite. Think about it.

Cora

Bryant and Shanda looked over his shoulder. Henderson knew he couldn't keep it. Cora might be able to buy off Sereno.

"I've seen that before," Shanda said, frowning. "Somewhere."

"I don't like it much," Bryant offered.

Henderson held Drew's letter in one hand and *Demeter and Baubo* in the other. What was it old man Gage had said? . . . He knew now what he was going to do. He folded up his letter. Collision of soft gray brain with hard tin of pineapple chunks. A good way to go.

"Make yourself at home," he said to Bryant and Shanda. "I'll be back later."

Henderson Dores walks briskly down Park Avenue toward the Forties. It looks quite different now that the rain has stopped, and the warm midday sun makes everything steam and exhale. He finds it hard to believe that a few hours ago he was creeping through the neat shrubs of the central reservation, clad only in a cardboard box. It might have happened to a different person. . . .

He cuts over on Fifty-seventh and then down Fifth. Huge puddles still prove obstacles to traffic and there is much irate hooting of horns, and colorful oaths fill the air. He turns onto Forty-seventh and walks along it until he sees the delicatessen where Irene goes for lunch. He walks with measured purposeful tread.

If everyone wants to be happy, and everyone is going to die, then there's really no option, he tells himself, suddenly seeing everything with a new clarity. The whole can of worms takes on some sort of focus; the immense hill of beans arranges itself in some sort of order. Teagarden and his zencing, his own shyness, Beckman's blinks, Melissa and her dogs, Bryant's breasts, Gage's boxing, Shanda's baby, Cora's sadness, the general's WAC, Demeter and Baubo and, finally, his own father's fatal encounter with a flying tin of pineapple chunks one hot day in the Burmese jungle in 1943.

He pushes open the door. Irene sits with a pleasant young man, not unlike Pruitt Halfacre. Henderson approaches.

"Irene," he says, "I'm back. It's all over."

Irene swings around, an ambiguous expression on her face.

"*Dores, you bastard!*"

People scream, plates drop with a crash. Henderson crouches instinctively and the first shot smashes into the plasti-pine veneer above Irene's booth.

Duane stands in the doorway, his fat face shiny with hot tears, shaking gun in both hands.

"*You stole her, you bastard!*"

Henderson, bent double, plunges through the bright plastic strips that hang from the lintel of the kitchen door. Various Oriental chefs in damp singlets are surprised to see him scramble through the cookers and kitchen units toward the rear exit. From behind him come more screams and crashing furniture as Duane pursues.

Henderson explodes into the mean alleyway between Forty-seventh and Forty-sixth, barging heavily into a tramp picking through the trash cans.

"Sorry," Henderson gasps, regaining his balance.

The tramp's face is familiar. The shades, the trilby, the raincoat . . .

"The furrier at midnight—"

"I *know*," Henderson yells. "I know all about that now!"

He turns and runs up the alleyway, running as though his life depended on it (and it does), his legs pounding, his hands clawing air, striving with all his might and all his effort to reach the distant, sunlit vision of the teeming streets ahead.

ARMADILLO

The life of Lorimer Black, insurance adjustor, is about to be turned upside down. The elements at play are a beautiful actress with whom he is falling in love; an odd associate whose hiring, firing, and rehiring make little sense; and a rock musician whose loss—in this case of his mind—may be "adjusted" by the insurance company.

Fiction/Literature/0-375-70216-4

THE BLUE AFTERNOON

Sprawling across three continents and two eras, this atmospheric novel opens in Los Angeles in 1936, when architect Kay Fischer is approached by an elderly man named Salvador Carriscant, who claims to be her father—and who insists she accompany him to Lisbon in search of the great lost love of his life.

Fiction/Literature/0-679-77260-X

AN ICE-CREAM WAR

William Boyd brilliantly evokes the private dramas of a generation swept up by the winds of war. As the sons of the world match wits and weapons, desperation makes bedfellows of enemies—and traitors of friends and family. *An Ice-Cream War* deftly renders lives capsized by violence, chance, and the irrepressible human capacity for love.

Fiction/Literature/0-375-70502-3

THE NEW CONFESSIONS

John James Todd is one of the most unappreciated geniuses of the twentieth century. Plagued by bad luck and blind ambition, Todd becomes a celebrated London upstart, a Weimar luminary, and finally a disgruntled director of cowboy movies and the eleventh member of the Hollywood Ten.

Fiction/Literature/0-375-70503-1

ALSO AVAILABLE:

The Destiny of Nathalie X, 0-679-76784-3
On the Yankee Station, 0-375-70511-2

VINTAGE INTERNATIONAL
Available at your local bookstore, or call toll-free to order:
1-800-793-2665 (credit cards only).